A SNOWKISSED WINTER

SCARLETT CLARKE

RHODA BAXTER

MILLS & BOON

First published in Great Britain 2025
by Mills & Boon, an imprint of HarperCollins*Publishers* Ltd,
1 London Bridge Street, London, SE1 9GF

www.harpercollins.co.uk

HarperCollins*Publishers*, Macken House, 39/40 Mayor Street Upper, Dublin 1, D01 C9W8, Ireland

A Snowkissed Winter © 2025 Harlequin Enterprises ULC

Snowbound Nights with Her Best Friend © 2025 Scarlett Clarke

Christmas with the Secret Tycoon © 2025 Rhoda Baxter

ISBN: 978-0-263-41761-6

11/25

MIX
Paper | Supporting responsible forestry
FSC
www.fsc.org
FSC™ C007454

This book contains FSC™ certified paper and other controlled sources to ensure responsible forest management.

For more information visit www.harpercollins.co.uk/green.

Printed and Bound in the UK using 100% Renewable Electricity at CPI Group (UK) Ltd, Croydon, CR0 4YY

Scarlett Clarke's interest in romance can be traced back to her love of Nancy Drew books, when she tried to solve the mysteries of her favourite detective while rereading the romantic chapters with Ned Nickerson. She's thrilled now to be writing romances of her own. Scarlett lives in, and loves, her hometown of Kansas City. By day she works in public relations and wrangles two toddlers, two cats and a dog. By night she writes romance and tries to steal a few moments with her firefighter hubby.

Rhoda Baxter writes award-nominated romcoms with a hint of British cynicism. She also writes multicultural women's fiction as Jeevani Charika. A former microbiologist, she is a bit of a science geek (if her pen name sounds vaguely bacterial, guess why!). She might be a tiny bit addicted to cake and Lego. She lives in Yorkshire, England, with her young family. She can't believe she gets to tell stories for a living. You can find out more about her on her website rhodabaxter.com.

SNOWBOUND NIGHTS WITH HER BEST FRIEND

SCARLETT CLARKE

MILLS & BOON

CHAPTER ONE

Arlowe

THE WHITE WALLS of the castle glittered against the backdrop of a forest awash in late autumn hues. Radiant yellows and glistening coppers offset by fading reds and oranges, the dazzling colors interspersed with soaring evergreens. In the valley beyond the castle, the wood and stone buildings of Lärchenthal hugged the shores of a small lake.

Arlowe Banks blinked back tears.

I'm really here.

A week ago she'd been shoveling dirt and covering plants against the threat of a late spring frost. The bills from her stepfather Robert's last surgery had been glaring at her from the heap of mail on the kitchen table. Each one meant another semester pushed back, classes untaken, her dream degree unfulfilled.

Not, she reminded herself, that Robert didn't deserve her all. Aside from a face and a vague memory of a harsh voice shouting at her mother, Arlowe didn't remember her birth father. Robert, however, had treated her like she was his own, even going so far as to adopt her when she was ten. He'd been there for her and Mom. It was her turn to be there for him.

But, Arlowe thought as she released a harsh breath, there were days when the world pressed in too tightly. When the endless cycle of rushing home from the greenhouse to get dinner ready, shower and then head to Kansas City for her bartending shift weighed so heavily she could barely catch her breath.

Today, though, she was in Austria. Her smile returned, grew. She was in Austria standing on a bridge gazing at a castle where, in less than an hour, she'd attend a will reading for her long-lost grandmother.

When she'd picked up the heavy cream envelope from the pile of mail, she'd anticipated a wedding invitation. But then she'd noted the address in the corner; a law firm in Salzburg. She'd nearly dropped the letter when she'd read that her paternal grandmother, a woman she'd never even met, had passed away and named Arlowe in her will.

A cool wind blew down the gorge, carrying the scent of crisp mountain air and fallen leaves. The letter inviting her to her grandmother's will reading had included a first-class ticket from Kansas City to Salzburg, along with instructions on where to meet the private car that would take Arlowe to a boutique hotel in Lärchenthal. The will reading would take place at her grandmother's "favorite residence on the last Friday of the month."

And now she was here, just half a mile's walk from the castle Desdemona Gruber had called home.

Like a fairy tale.

God knows she could use one. The last two years had been hard. Brutal, really, she acknowledged as she continued to stare at the castle. First Robert losing his job. Dropping out of college to work full-time to help Mom and Robert stay afloat. And then the accident…

Heat pricked her eyes. It had been fourteen months, but there were still moments where it felt just as raw and painful as the day her life had changed. The call from the unknown number that she'd ignored the first two times but finally picked up on the third ring. The frantic rush to the hospital.

The brief flare of hope when Mom had squeezed her hand just before they'd whisked her through the doors. The relief when her stepfather, Robert, had made it out of surgery and she'd sat in his hospital room waiting for an update.

And then tears. Hours, days, weeks of tears as she and her stepfather, Robert, had adjusted to life without Mom. Once she would have tried to push away the pain. Bury it. But now she let herself feel the grief, the bittersweetness of remembering one of the best people she'd ever known.

Swallowing past the lump in her throat, she dug her phone out of her pocket and snapped a photo of the castle. She sent the photo to Robert and got a reply less than a minute later.

Beautiful. Let me know when you get there.

She smiled. Leaving Robert for the first time since the accident had caused her more anxiety than it had him. Perhaps this was what parents felt, leaving their children home for that first overnight trip or vacation, the lingering worry that something would go catastrophically wrong and they would be too far away to do anything about it.

Arlowe's hands tightened around the railing. She didn't resent having to care for Robert. Her stepfather had been a fixture in her life ever since she was six years old. He'd been the one to teach her how to drive and change her own tires, to give her advice about boys in high school, to move her into the college dorms her freshman year when life had been bright and happy.

Most importantly, he'd made Arlowe's mother smile again.

But that didn't stop the exhaustion, the questioning when things would finally start to get better. The car accident had left Robert with numerous broken bones, a herniated disc, surgeries and, starting next month, physical therapy. On the days she wasn't working twelve to sixteen hours, she was taking Robert to appointments, running errands, and getting caught up on the housework. He did what he could from his wheelchair, but his movements were still limited. More than once Arlowe had caught him swallowing hard as he tried to dust, gritting his teeth as he unloaded the dishwasher. To tell him to rest would only erode what little self-confidence he had left.

Most days they made it through. But the nights… Arlowe swallowed past the tightness in her throat. The nights were hard. Sometimes she swore she could hear the faint rumble of the television from the late-night talk shows her mom and Robert always listened to. Other nights she could hear deep, chest-rattling sobs as Robert, a burly man with a thick beard and a huge smile, cried himself to sleep.

Three years ago, she would have called her best friend, Hart, and asked him to come over or meet her at the fence between their two properties and walk the fields at night. Hart would grumble about needing his sleep, but he'd always show up.

But that was three years ago. Now Hart was the millionaire CEO of his family's pharmaceutical manufacturing empire. Successful, ambitious, lauded for rescuing the company his grandfather and uncle had nearly driven into the ground. Dating an international opera star and currently in Lyon, France, for a contract that could elevate BioInnovations into the billion-dollar territory.

Most days she could be happy for him. Her best friend was thriving. And he'd shown up just hours after the accident. He'd stayed for nearly a month, helping Arlowe and Robert adjust to their new normal. He'd even arranged and paid for the funeral, a gesture Arlowe and Robert had accepted with grateful hearts.

Except it had opened the door to a new and unwelcome dynamic in their relationship. More than once Hart had asked if he could help financially with anything else, even going so far as to send her five thousand dollars around Christmas last year. Money she'd reluctantly used to pay for a new pain medication Robert had desperately needed following one of his surgeries. But that had been the second and last time, despite at least four other offers over the last eleven months. Hart seemed to care more about offering her money than investing in their friendship. A twenty-minute phone call would have meant so much more than a check. But aside from texting and an occasional chat that lasted around five minutes before Hart retreated into a meeting or a factory tour or some corporate function, their friendship had boiled down to Hart offering the only thing he seemed to be capable of anymore.

Grief surged, hollowed out her chest as it stole her breath. The last time Hart had called—nearly three months ago—he'd brought up money. When she'd tried to change the subject, to ask about work or his new girlfriend or his travels, he'd told her to stop deflecting. To let go of her pride and just accept help. There'd been no quiet humor in his words, no caring concern. Just frustration with someone less successful. Someone who had gone from friend to burden.

So Arlowe had done something she'd never done with Hart—she'd lied. She'd told him a doctor was calling and she'd reach out later.

Ten weeks. It had been ten weeks since they'd talked. They'd exchanged a few texts about Robert's appointments, but that had been it. And when Arlowe had gotten the largest bill to date from one of the specialists Robert had been seeing, she'd steeled herself and made the hardest decision she'd made to date—selling twenty acres of the farm.

Not just any twenty acres. *The* twenty acres, with the pond and the small hill at the back that overlooked the river valley. The place where she had promised herself she would one day build her dream home.

Another dream gone up in smoke.

But as people had told her over and over since she could remember, real life wasn't a fairy tale. Hard decisions had to be made. Dreams went unfulfilled. God knows she'd had plenty of lessons in reality the past two years.

Thankfully Francine, Hart's mom, had kept her promise to keep the sale a secret. Given the way Hart had talked to her last time, Arlowe wouldn't be surprised if Hart would have flown down and tried to either force money into her hands or buy the property himself.

She didn't want his money. She wanted Hart. The Hart who would walk the fields with her at night and listen to her, who would give her blunt feedback when she asked for it. The Hart who would ask for her help understanding someone's viewpoint when he couldn't see past facts and data.

But he wasn't the Hart she once knew. Just like she was no longer the dreamer with stars in her eyes. Another deep sigh escaped. She'd never anticipated growing up would mean growing apart.

Her phone buzzed in her pocket, jerking her out of her melancholy reverie. She pulled it out and glanced down. Her heart surged into her throat when she saw Hart's name on the screen. Was this sudden phone call after weeks of not talking just coincidental timing? Or had someone told him where she was?

She hesitated before hitting Answer.

"Hey, Hart."

"Hello, Arlowe."

Hart's deep familiar voice rumbled through the speaker. Warmth bloomed in her chest.

"How's France?"

"Good." He paused. "How's Austria?"

Her fingers curled around the phone as the warmth evaporated. He wasn't calling to say hi or chat. He was calling to check up on her.

"Who told you?"

"My mother."

Arlowe rolled her eyes. Francine had been like a constant presence in Arlowe's life ever since they'd moved to the farm next door. She'd been a godsend the past couple years. She'd also been suspicious of the mysterious invitation, the will reading, everything. Francine was normally like her son; quiet and prone to long periods of silence. But on the subject of Arlowe traveling to Austria, she'd been surprisingly loud and belligerent.

Hart's long, drawn-out sigh had same force as a punch to the chest.

"Arlowe, what were you thinking?"

Beneath the surface of his words lay the real question: why was she being so stupid?

Arlowe inhaled deeply. Focused on the fresh scent of pine and the coolness of the autumn wind threading its way through the trees instead of the anger pulsing bright and hot in her gut.

"Right now, I'm thinking the castle looks beautiful this time of year."

"So you received some invitation in the mail to a will reading in Austria and a plane ticket out of the blue and just went? Did you verify any of the information before you left? What about Robert?"

Her spine straightened. Surely Hart wasn't suggesting she'd just up and leave her stepfather for a whirlwind trip to Europe? This was the first thing she had done for herself in over a year. He was not going to ruin this for her.

"What about him?"

She kept her voice pleasant, her tone bright even as she had to mentally resist the urge to chuck her phone over the bridge into the gorge.

"Who's taking care of him?"

Apparently that's exactly what he was suggesting. She pushed away the tendrils of guilt that still lingered at leaving Robert alone. He'd encouraged her to go, wanted her to. She hadn't done anything wrong.

"A couple friends from the nursery and your mother are checking in on him throughout the day. I hired a nurse for overnights."

"And you can afford that?"

For the first time in her life, she wanted to punch Hart. Not a playful slap, but a real, honest-to-God punch in the nose.

"I sold my virginity in an online auction."

Silence reigned. Then came the soft hush of an exhale.

"Look, I'm not—"

"Not what?" The brightness disappeared from her voice as she stared at the castle, used it as an anchor for the chaotic mix of emotions swirling inside her chest. "Not questioning my overall intelligence? Not considering the possibility that I just might have asked a lawyer to verify the firm and ensure the will was legitimate? That I might have called ahead to the inn the firm booked for me here in Austria? Then *verified* it by checking online reviews?" She smacked her palm to her forehead. "No. No, of course not, because Arlowe doesn't do things like that."

This is what she'd been afraid of after accepting his help, that he would start to see her as less than, inferior. He no longer saw her as capable. She already felt as though she was losing, had lost, part of herself since the accident. If he even knew half of what she'd done to keep her head above water the past two years, he'd…

She closed her eyes. Would he be proud? Angry? She no longer knew.

Another long beat of silence. Then another quiet sigh that had her eyes flying open, steeling herself for whatever he was about to say.

"I've hurt you."

Hart's quiet words cut deep.

"Yes. You did." She sighed. "I appreciate you wanting to make sure I'm safe, Hart, and looking after Robert. But I'm twenty-five years old. Robert and I have been doing just fine on our own without you."

"Have you?"

Guilt trickled in. She hadn't told him about selling the acreage. When they were kids still playing make-believe, she'd named the tract of land bordering Hart's family's property the Eastern Woods. Maple trees interspersed with pine and a random grove of persimmon trees with smooth, glossy fruit they'd pick in the fall just before the first snow. The pond had been an ocean, full of mermaids or sea serpents or whatever magic Arlowe concocted and Hart went along with.

It had been magical. It had also been adjacent to the paved road with utilities and that perfect hill at the back just begging for a farmhouse with a wraparound porch and a balcony.

She'd cried in the car after she'd signed the paperwork. But the sale had netted her over four hundred thousand dollars, enough to pay off Mom's hospital bills and make a significant dent in Robert's. And it wasn't like she and Hart had spent any time in those woods together. It had been years. The last time they'd walked it together had been just after his father's funeral. It wasn't like he'd miss it.

"Yes," she answered firmly.

"I'm just worried about you, Arlowe." His voice dipped, roughened as he said her name. "I haven't been around much. I'm sorry."

Just like that, her anger dissipated, leaving regret to fill the space inside her chest. Yes, her life and Hart's were very different. But that didn't mean he didn't have his own struggles. He might have inherited an international company, but it had come with outdated facilities, unpaid bills, and questions about the quality of the pharmaceuticals being produced. That it had rebounded in just three years was a testament to all the hard work Hart had poured into it.

Not just to make a profit, she reminded herself. To honor his father and the legacy that should have been his.

Thoroughly chastened and feeling selfish, Arlow cleared her throat.

"Thank you. I do miss you. But I know you've got a lot going on."

She switched the call over to video. A moment later Hart's handsome, grumpy face filled the screen. The man could have been a cover model; chiseled jaw, sharp cheekbones, and a narrow nose that added a touch of elegance to his strong face. More than one woman had asked Arlowe how she managed to keep her hands off Hart.

Simple. He was her best friend, the older brother she'd never had. Sure, he was attractive. Okay, really handsome. But they'd known each other since elementary school. Their friendship had survived braces, first heartbreaks, and going to separate colleges before they'd both found their way back to Kansas City. That kind of bond went far deeper than any romantic relationship she'd ever had.

Her nose wrinkled. Not that there had been many the last two years.

Shaking off the cobwebs of the past, she tapped her screen to turn the camera around. "Look at this." She panned the camera over the tree-covered hills, the castle in the distance, the plank bridge and the creek below.

"How old is that bridge?"

"Ancient." She stomped on one of the boards, biting back a smile at his muffled groan. "Decrepit." Another stomp. "It's going to break at any second."

"For God's sake, Arlowe—"

She pointed the phone back at herself and gave Hart a

teasing, albeit tight, smile. "The bridge was renovated in the spring. I told the receptionist at the hotel where I was going and had the limo my grandmother's estate provided for me drop me off at a designated trailhead two miles from the castle. Then I texted Robert my coordinates. If I don't check in within an hour, he calls and if I don't answer—"

"Okay." Hart held up a hand. "I concede." He shook his head slightly. "I'm used to you being a five-minute drive away."

A retort rose to her lips, then died. Now was not the time to air her grievances.

"And normally you'd be thousands of miles away," she replied brightly. "How is France, by the way?"

God willing, he'd take the bait and drop the subject of her traveling alone.

"From what little I've seen of it, it's nice."

Hart's dry reply had Arlowe rolling her eyes.

"Come on, Hart. You're in Lyon. You should be exploring ancient Roman ruins or walking through the Old City."

She swallowed past the sudden thickness in her throat as she thought about Hart doing just that with Lucy. Which made her feel even more ugly. On the two occasions she'd met Lucy, the singer had been surprisingly down-to-earth and very kind, despite the aura of glamour and wealth that practically shimmered around her.

"I bet Lucy would like the Opéra National de Lyon. If she hasn't performed there already, of course. I know she's been everywhere."

Okay, time to shut up. Why was she rambling?

A shutter dropped over Hart's eyes. "Lucy isn't here."

Arlowe frowned. "Oh."

"We broke up."

"Oh." She battled back the ugly feeling of relief, focused on the thread of emotion in her friend's voice. "I'm really sorry, Hart."

She meant it. No, she wasn't hurt to hear that Hart and Lucy weren't together anymore, for reasons she'd have to examine later. But she was sad for Hart. Lucy had been his first girlfriend since he'd taken over the company. Six months was not an insignificant amount of time.

"It's all right."

Something in his voice caught her attention. "What's wrong?"

His jaw tensed. "It's fine, Arlowe."

A barrier slammed down between them. A vice clamped down on Arlowe's chest as she stared out over the gorge. She and Hart were less than four hundred miles apart, but there might as well have been an ocean separating them. Unlike three years ago, Hart had no intention of sharing with her.

Just like you haven't been sharing with him.

"Well…maybe we can catch up sometime." She tried for brightness, struggled for a sliver of sunshine. "As you saw, I still have a hike ahead of me."

He sighed again, a deep, heavy one that sank into her bones. She could feel his frustration, his worry, even a flicker of sadness, as if it were her own. It had always been that way, ever since they were kids. They'd balanced each other through the ups and downs of growing up.

But now, despite that tenuous connection still shimmering between them, there was a heavy tautness, as if that connection could snap at any moment.

"Arlowe—"

"It's fine, Hart." She shot him another big smile. "I'll text you when I reach the castle. Talk to you soon."

She ended the call before he could say anything else.

Coward.

She pushed her phone back in her pocket and squared her backpack on her shoulders. She'd known she and Hart were drifting apart. But she'd chalked it up to the growing demands on his time and her increased commitment to Mom and Robert.

But what if it was deeper than that? What if she and Hart were simply no longer who they used to be? What if their friendship had eroded so much it couldn't be repaired?

Enough of that, she ordered herself. *Austria. Castle. Secret inheritance.*

Just repeating the words buoyed her mood. Her friendship with Hart would have to be examined at another date. Right now, she was going to enjoy her walk through the autumn woods of Austria and savor the buildup to arriving at her long-lost grandmother's castle.

She pushed away her last stubborn thoughts of Hart and continued down the trail.

CHAPTER TWO

HART'S HAND TIGHTENED on the balcony railing as he gazed out over Lyon. The red rooftops of Europe's so-called "capital of silk" glowed under the afternoon autumn sun. His hotel was perched on the edge of Vieux Lyon, a Renaissance district with colorful buildings stacked next to each other like painted wooden blocks and winding cobblestone streets.

Arlowe would love it.

Hart leaned against the window frame and stared down at the street below him. A couple walked hand in hand toward a café. When he'd decided to attend this conference, it had seemed like the perfect solution to the rut he and Lucy had found themselves in just a couple months after officially announcing they were dating. A chance to get away to a new destination, let Lucy enjoy some downtime during the day while he attended meetings and conference sessions, and explore the city together at night.

Except Lucy had gently reminded him she'd already been to Lyon when she sang in *Rigoletto* at the Opéra National de Lyon. She'd suggested meeting him at the end of the conference and touring Provence, but his calendar had already been booked solid for the next four weeks.

He'd never given much thought to the phrase "ships passing in the night" before. But it was an apt description of his and Lucy's relationship. Two very successful people who liked each other well enough, but neither wanted to prioritize their relationship over their prospective careers.

A waiter seated the couple at a table. The man pulled out the woman's chair. She tilted her head back to smile at him, and he leaned down to place a kiss on her forehead. The woman's smile reminded him of another brief, beautiful smile he'd seen just a few minutes ago before his and Arlowe's conversation had once again turned sour.

He turned away from the window and walked over to the desk where his leather portfolio sat, carefully organized with notes from all of his sessions so far. It should bother him that his relationship with Lucy dissolved so quickly. But there had been no grief, no anger, not even a sliver of pain. Just a brief flare of nostalgia for the pleasant times they'd spent together.

What bothered him was what Lucy had said during their last phone conversation.

"I just wish you had looked at me once like you looked at Arlowe."

The silence that followed her shocking statement had only reinforced Lucy's ridiculous idea that Hart felt anything for Arlowe other than the kind of love a brother had for a kid sister. He'd pointed out that one, the notion was ridiculous and two, Lucy had only met Arlowe twice. Lucy had quietly laughed and said if anything good came out of their brief time together, she hoped it would be that Hart would finally wake up and see what he had before it was too late.

Her words had lingered at the back of his mind when he and Arlowe had gotten into their argument over money this past summer. He'd been rude. Condescending. When she'd hung up on him, he'd told himself they just needed some time.

Except days had stretched into weeks. Then two months, now nearly three. With Thanksgiving just a few weeks away, he'd decided to go home for the holiday and try to make amends with Arlowe in person.

Until his mother had called. He didn't panic. He barely felt anything since his father had passed. But when Mom had told him Arlowe had gone to Austria for a supposed reading of a will for a woman she'd never met, fear had surged. He'd pushed back a meeting, something he never did, and ordered his secretary to get every bit of information she could on the supposed law firm in Austria handling this woman's estate.

He'd been out on the balcony of his suite when Arlowe had answered. The warm richness of her voice had slid inside him, releasing tension in his shoulders he hadn't even realized he'd been carrying. The beginning of the conversation had been rough, but by some miracle they had reached a temporary truce. She'd let him into her world for a few precious minutes. When her face had filled the screen, amber eyes sparkling as she'd shared the view and teased him, the world below had become brighter, from the rich blue of the sky to those red rooftops gleaming in the afternoon sun. He'd enjoyed her excitement, savored the sight of her happiness.

And then he'd ruined it all by slamming the door between them. Instead of pushing back, demanding to know what was wrong, she'd withdrawn, leaving him standing on the balcony with his phone in his hand and an ache in his chest.

Not that he blamed her. He'd barely been there for her the last three years. His father's unexpected death had ripped Hart's world in two. Arlowe's bubbly personality had always offset his quieter, brooding tendencies. But the rage that had simmered inside him, the sheer fury at the incompetent manager who had failed to keep his father safe on a jobsite, had been like nothing he'd ever experienced. Just thinking about how he'd never hear his father's quiet laughter tied his chest into a knot so tight it almost hurt to breathe.

He'd withdrawn after his father's death, shielded Arlowe from the war inside him. It had been the best thing he could have done for her, even if pulling away from the one person he'd wanted to be with had taken what was left of his heart and ground it into dust.

The couple at the restaurant leaned in and kissed, the man's hand coming up to tangle in the woman's hair. Hart looked away and out over the winding blue ribbon of the Saône River. Inheriting the tainted legacy of BioInnovations just three months later had left him little time to process the monumental changes happening in his life. But it had given him an outlet for the emotions swirling inside him, a place to channel his grief and rage and pain into something productive. The company that should have belonged to his father, and rescuing it from the brink of ruin had taken every bit of focus he had.

Arlowe had given him space in the months after his father's death. She'd known he needed time. But when she'd started to push at the end, right before Hart had learned his grandfather had passed away, he'd resisted.

Where would he and Arlowe have been now if he had shared? If he had let her in the way she had accepted his offers of help and comfort after her mother's death?

He scrubbed a hand over his face. There was plenty Arlowe wasn't sharing with him now. From what little his mother had said, Arlowe spent hours at the greenhouse she worked at, only to come home at night and care for Robert. God knows she needed a getaway. He just didn't like that getaway being in a new country she'd never set foot in before.

You could have invited her to Lyon.

If she were here, she wouldn't have let him set foot inside his hotel room. She'd have been somewhere in the maze of shops and cafés, texting him an address and telling him to come meet her for a glass of wine or dessert.

His chest tightened. He could have done so many things differently this past year. He could have gone home more. Called or texted more. Paid for her to go on a trip. But given how she'd reacted to his last few offers to help with medical bills or any other expenses, that wouldn't have gone over well.

He looked out one last time over the Old City, then retreated back inside. He crossed through the massive bedroom into the living room of his suite. Fame and fortune were still concepts he wasn't entirely comfortable with. But as his secretary had adroitly pointed out, having a suite where he could conduct his own meetings was beneficial. It also added a certain air of wealth and prestige to the BioInnovations name. Something that had been sorely lacking in the years before Hart had taken over.

Yet there had been one grace in the ruins. Rescuing Bio-Innovations had given him an outlet for his suppressed pain and grief. It had taken three years and several million dollars to raise BioInnovations from the hole Hart's grandfather had run it into with reckless spending and lack of attention. But he'd done it, and in the last eighteen months had turned record-breaking profits. He'd created a legacy his father would have been proud of, one that required constant care and attention. He would not let it fail.

He moved to the table and picked up the paperwork from the fax machine. One of his largest purchases to date since becoming an official millionaire. The contract was the last thing he needed to sign before he officially owned the twenty acres between his farm and Arlowe's.

The paper crinkled as his grip tightened. It hurt. It hurt deeply that Arlowe had rejected his offers of help while selling away a piece of her childhood home. Not just any piece, but *her* piece. The land she had dreamed of one day building her own home on. It had taken some prying from his mother after he'd discovered the listing online, but she had finally admitted that not only was Arlowe struggling financially, but she'd specifically asked Hart's mom to not say anything.

He set the paper down and picked up a pen. One day they'd

have to talk about it. About why she rejected his offers, why she listed the land, and above all, why she didn't talk to him about it. She was an adult, and it was her land. But damn it, he knew how much that acreage meant to her. He could see the house she planned to build in every detail because she'd talked about it so much over the years—the white porch with the gingerbread woodwork, the shingled roof, the bay windows along the back to overlook the river.

Once upon a time, she would have come to him. They would have talked things through.

He placed the pen on the paper. A drop of ink bled out and spread across the white. He shouldn't feel guilty. He was helping Arlowe, even if she didn't realize it yet. Helping her the only way he was capable of anymore.

A knock sounded on his door as he finished signing. He glanced at his watch and grimaced. Five minutes to two. His prospective client was early.

Hart opened the door. Blaine Jones, CEO of Nessa Pharmaceuticals, smiled and held out his hand.

"Mr. Sinclair."

Hart accepted the hand, noted the firm grip. "Please, call me Hart."

"As long as you call me Blaine."

Hart shut the door behind Blaine and moved to the kitchen. "Water, tea, coffee?"

"Coffee, black. Thank you."

Blaine eased his big frame into a chair. With light brown hair, a tanned broad face, and a lightning grin, Blaine looked everyone's idea of a former high school football star turned business mogul. He'd started off his career cleaning research labs in college and worked his way up through the ranks of project manager, director of business, chief operating officer, and finally CEO of Nessa Pharmaceuticals.

The proposal from Nessa Pharmaceuticals had everything,

from the perfectly worded executive summary down to the detailed manufacturing requirements. It could have been framed as an example of the perfect proposition.

None of it erased the persistent itch between Hart's shoulder blades. The faint, haunting whisper that something wasn't quite right about Nessa.

He shoved the thought aside as he handed Blaine his coffee. From what Hart's father had said, his grandfather had been prone to following his own whims and beliefs, ignoring details like research documents and safety reports in favor of errant emotion.

It had been data that had helped Hart steer BioInnovations in the right direction. Data that had kept him from slipping deeper into the dark.

And now, as he took the seat opposite Blaine, he needed to focus on the data and not this vague sensation. Ensuring BioInnovations thrived was his responsibility, one that honored not only his father but the people who had poured their heart and soul into rebuilding it.

He accepted the leather portfolio Blaine handed him and opened it to the first page. He'd read the write-up on Nessa's recent successes half a dozen times already. As he skimmed the words, his mind drifted, circled back to Arlowe's falsely cheerful voice and strained smile just before she'd ended the call.

Come on, Sinclair. Concentrate!

"As you can see, our applications for regulatory approval are underway in the US, United Kingdom, and European Union." Blaine oozed confidence as he sipped his coffee. "Once those are approved, we'll submit applications to Japan, China, and Australia before continuing on to South America."

Hart turned the page until he found the clinical trials. "Impressive testing. Over ten thousand participants monitored for six years."

"Yes. We're very proud of our results."

Something in Blaine's tone had Hart's eyes flicking up. But Blaine simply sat, one hand resting casually on the arm of the chair and the other holding his cup.

Why was he doing this? Creating obstacles where there were none? Cementing this deal with Nessa Pharmaceuticals would propel BioInnovations to the top. Investors had cautiously begun paying attention to BioInnovations. A new contract like this was the kind that would attract even more positive attention.

Not signing, however, would introduce concerns. Doubts. And he wouldn't blame anyone for questioning. He had been questioning himself daily since his first meeting with Blaine. There was no basis for his concerns, nothing he could prove. This contract represented everything he'd been working toward with his team ever since he inherited. Stability, credibility, recognition. They had reached this point because of their commitment to logic over emotion.

Yet even as Hart flipped through the slick booklet with its well-crafted charts and professional photos, he couldn't dismiss his instinct that something was wrong.

There had been a time when he would have called Arlowe. His friend thrived on instinct and emotion, but her decisions weren't reckless. She had a knack for people, for knowing what they wanted, needed. When something didn't work out, she gave herself space to grieve and then moved on.

But he didn't want to place this burden on her. It wasn't hers to bear, especially after he'd barely been present in her life these last few years.

"So tell me, Hart," Blaine said with another megawatt smile, "what'll it take for Nessa and BioInnovations to deal?"

Hart's phone vibrated in his pocket. His fingers tightened on the booklet. Probably Arlowe checking in to let him know she was safe at the castle.

Or injured and needs your help.

Before he could give any attention to his intrusive thoughts, Blaine's phone rang.

"Sorry." Blaine glanced at the screen. His face tightened a fraction before he gave Hart a chagrined smile. "Excuse me for a moment."

Hart's phone buzzed again as Blaine walked out. He counted to five before slowly pulling it out. Two texts from Arlowe.

Fought off a dragon and an evil witch, safe at the castle.

His lips twitched. The accompanying selfie showed Arlowe in front of a massive wooden door. Her dark brown hair was caught up into a loose bun on top of her head. Stray curls had slipped out to frame her oval-shaped face. Hart wasn't prone to hyperbole, but her amber eyes were sparkling with excitement. The huge grin on her face catapulted him back twenty years to the day a little girl had bounced up to his fence, clambered to the top, and announced that her name was Arlowe Banks, she was five years old, and he was her new best friend.

His lips curved. Even at twenty-five she still had the same infectious energy, the same kindness.

His smile disappeared as he noticed the dark circles beneath her eyes and the faded coloring of her jacket. Guilt slipped beneath his skin and slithered into his chest. How had he missed the signs?

Because you've barely seen her.

He knew why she hadn't confided in him, let him see the reality of her struggles. But it still hurt. The double standard of wanting her to share even as he held himself back drove the guilt deeper into his gut.

"Sorry about that," Blaine said as he walked back into the room.

Hart took one last look at Arlowe's photo before sliding his phone back into his pocket and turning his attention back to Blaine.

"No problem."

Blaine sat, his smile back in place. "So, as I was saying, what do we need to do to finalize the contract?"

The rest of the meeting moved swiftly. Blaine answered every question Hart posed with detailed responses. Everything aligned with what BioInnovations could offer.

"I'd like to have the contract signed before the end of the conference."

Hart nodded. "I need to complete a final review with my team. But I don't anticipate that being a problem."

"Anything I should be concerned about?"

Hart leaned back in his chair. "Is there anything you're concerned I might find?"

Blaine's brows drew together. "I don't like your insinuation, Sinclair."

"I'm not insinuating anything," Hart shot back coolly. "You came to us because BioInnovations has established itself as a leading pharmaceutical manufacturer. In the past three years we've maintained a spotless regulatory track record, invested in advanced quality control analytics, and achieved faster release times with zero production failures in that time frame."

"I'm aware."

"Then you're aware those records came with the price of making sure we cross-check everything, including our clients." His phone buzzed in his pocket once. His concentration flickered, deviated. He wrenched it back. "This isn't personal, Blaine. It's business. You've submitted everything we need. Barring any unforeseen obstacles, we'd like to work with Nessa."

Hart could see the tension bleed out of Blaine as the other man's shoulders dropped down.

"I apologize." Blaine ran a hand through his hair. "This is the first medication I've overseen from start to finish. It feels like my legacy to the industry."

"I can understand that."

And he could. Whatever misgivings Hart had about Nessa, he understood what it meant to have everything riding on one chance. He'd invested every singe dime his grandfather had left him into rebuilding BioInnovations. He'd spent the last three years in New York, away from his mom, Robert, and Arlowe. If BioInnovations failed, he wouldn't get that time back.

"Thank you." Blaine stood. "I'll look forward to speaking with you and your team later this week."

After Blaine left, Hart wandered back out onto the balcony. Clouds had moved across the sun, stealing some of the late autumn warmth. The couple he'd seen earlier had long since gone. A brisk wind blew through the café, rattling the red-and white striped umbrellas shading each table.

The meeting had gone well overall. Hart would type up a report and share it with his team. As soon as they arrived in two days, they'd sit down for an in-depth meeting and review everything before making a final decision.

They would approve the contract. He couldn't picture an alternative scenario, not with the quality of information Blaine had provided. This was why he had shifted from his grandfather's mindset of making unilateral decisions to approving contracts with a trusted team, including his vice president of manufacturing operations, his head of supply chain management, and his head of business development. They would look at the data with him, provide perspective he hadn't considered.

He sat down in one of the deck chairs. His vice president of quality assurance, Anne Flory, had survived five years under his grandfather before Hart had taken over. He had quickly come to respect her knowledge of the industry and her professional but blunt communication. He wasn't comfortable sharing his concerns with the rest of the team, not when he had zero data to back up any of his doubts. But he could, and would, talk about it with Anne before they met as a group.

He pulled out his phone and read Arlowe's final text.

Heading in. Wish me luck.

He reread her last two texts, his eyes lingering on her picture. What would Arlowe say about all this? Would she understand his reticence? Encourage him to push past it? Or would she tell him to dig deeper, to listen to his instincts for once?

Probably the latter. Which would mean delaying the contract, which would mean upping the likelihood of Blaine walking away from the biggest deal BioInnovations had seen in the entire history of the company.

As he stared at her photo, at the familiar golden-brown eyes and carefree smile, he knew Arlowe wouldn't just listen to his doubts. No, she'd go straight to the heart of the matter and ask him why it was eating at him. She'd press, push until he finally admitted what he was most afraid of.

Failure. If he listened to his instincts and turned down the deal with no foundation for the rejection, the ripple effects of rejecting a client could affect BioInnovations for years. If he didn't listen to his instincts and something went wrong, it could torpedo the monumental progress they'd made in just a few years. The company was the one thing Hart had left, the piece that still tied him to his father. Without it, he was just an empty shell, hollowed out by grief.

A headache started to pound in his temples. He quickly typed up a nonsensical reply to Arlowe and pressed Send before turning his phone on Silent. After he got through this, he'd go back to Missouri for an extended stay. He and Arlowe could reconnect, get back to where they had been before life had intruded. He'd prove to himself that Lucy was wrong about his feelings for Arlowe as he reestablished their friendship.

The clouds darkened as the wind picked up speed, whipping up over the balcony railing with a cold ferocity that had Hart raising his eyebrows at the sky. Lyon was in its rainy season, but the chill lingering in the air hinted at more than just a few raindrops on the way.

He stayed out on the balcony, his mind a whirl of clinical trial statistics and profit margins, as the storm closed in on the Old City. As the first tiny snowflakes fell, he thought of Arlowe in her castle in the Austrian mountains. Thought of the pleasure in her voice when she'd first answered the phone, how *right* it had felt to talk to her.

Thought of those long, drawn-out seconds after she'd hung up when longing had penetrated the void inside and nearly made him call her back.

But Arlowe didn't want him involved in her life. And even if he was concerned about her being alone in a foreign country for the first time in her life with no one there to support her, his focus needed to be here in Lyon. He had no right to interfere in Arlowe's life.

He stood and turned his back on the encroaching storm. He walked into his suite and closed the door behind him with a definitive click.

CHAPTER THREE

Arlowe

ARLOWE SMILED AS she read Hart's reply.

Glad you're safe. Keep an eye out for fairies. They're tricky.
Good luck.

She stared down at the words for a long moment before finally tucking the phone in her pocket. Maybe she was over-
thinking things. Relationships ebbed and flowed. Just because
she and Hart were in a rut now didn't mean their friendship
was over. He had a lot on his mind, as did she.

An idea struck. Maybe after the will reading she could surprise him in Paris. Use up the last couple days of her leave to explore the city while he attended his conference sessions and then
bribe him into joining her for dinner or a walk in the evenings.

A long, mournful howl sounded behind her. Startled, she
turned as a gust of wind tore through the trees just behind
her. Leaves flew off the branches and scattered, turning into
whirling splashes of color as they spun frantically in the air
before drifting down. She turned and stared out over the valley. Beyond the lake the horizon was dark, just a thin strip
of steel gray offset by the brilliant blue of the sky. But it still
made her skin prick as she turned back to the wooden doors
guarding the castle.

She raised her hand. But before she could knock, the massive wooden doors slid open silently to reveal a stunning courtyard. The same cobblestone drive she was standing on continued forward before splitting into two and wrapping around a three-tiered fountain. Water bubbled from the top and down a series of carved stone flowers into the round basin. Beyond the fountain lay the castle. That same gleaming stone, with huge arched windows running the length of the front. Two stone staircases curved up to a mezzanine that featured another set of large doors, one that was opening even as Arlowe walked into the courtyard.

"Fräulein Banks?"

A tall man in a gray suit walked out. With his sharp, angular features and prominent nose, it wasn't hard to picture him as the descendant of some long-forgotten king.

"Yes."

The man smiled, a surprisingly friendly smile that softened his aristocratic presence.

"I'm Franz Blukker, your late grandmother's estate attorney."

Arlowe's smile dimmed as she walked across the courtyard. She'd never met the woman, had never even really contemplated her existence until a few weeks ago. But it still hurt to think of yet another family member being gone.

"It's nice to meet you," Arlowe said as she climbed the stairs.

"And you." He gestured to the open door behind him. "You are twenty minutes early, but the others have already arrived if you're ready to start."

"Others?"

"This way, *bitte*."

Arlowe's mouth dropped open as they walked into a cavernous hall. The huge windows let in sunlight that lit up the room. Elegant woven tapestries hung on the stone walls, depicting colorful scenes of hunters, knights, and royals navigating fields, forests, and castles. A large chandelier glittered overhead as her feet sank into a plush carpet.

"This looks like a museum."

"Your grandmother adored art," Herr Blukker said over his shoulder. "Several of the rooms have been decorated to resemble how they would looked in the early 1900s when this castle was last occupied by royalty."

He led her through a large doorway and into a room that resembled a parlor. Red velvet furniture was arranged around the room, with dark end tables playing host to small sculptures fashioned out of marble. Two women about her age were already in the room. One stood near the massive stone fireplace. Dressed in flowing emerald green pants and a matching blazer, her black hair pulled back into a French braid, she glanced up at Arlowe when she entered the room, then resumed scrolling through her phone.

"*Damen*, may I introduce—" The shrill ring of his phone cut off his next words. He pulled it out and glanced down at the screen with a frown. "*Entschuldigen Sie*. I must take this."

He stepped out, leaving the three of them alone. The woman by the fireplace didn't even look up as he left. Arlowe turned her attention to the other woman seated on a sofa, a sweet-faced red-haired woman with a pert nose, who was rubbing a gentle hand on her rounded belly.

"Hello." She moved over to the sofa and held out her hand. "I'm Arlowe."

"And I'm Mina."

The soft melody of Mina's accent put Arlowe at ease even as she kept an eye on the woman by the fireplace.

"Nice to meet you." Arlowe gestured toward Mina's rounded belly. "And congratulations."

"Thank you. Just a little over three months now."

"Boy or girl?" Arlowe asked as she took a seat in the chair next to Mina.

"I want to be surprised," Mina said shyly. "My mom thinks it's a boy, and she's usually right."

Grief was an emotion Arlowe had rarely experienced until this last year. But now she could feel the familiar pressure building in her chest, the sinking of her heart as her whole body grew heavy. She wanted someone there with her, someone who could squeeze her hand or give her a hug and tell her eventually it wouldn't hurt as much. Robert. Francine. Hart.

She smiled slightly. He'd love it here. The architecture, the history, the legacy of family. Given that Francine's parents had passed away when she was in college and Hart's grandfather had disowned the family before Hart was even born, Hart's familial world had been very small. He'd told her more than once he'd wished for a big family, that having her next door had been like having the younger sibling he'd always wanted.

A sentiment that usually made her smile. But now it made her chest tighten.

Shoving the uncomfortable feeling away, Arlowe refocused on Mina.

"Sorry. A lot on my mind."

Mina nodded knowingly. "Same. It's crazy, isn't it? I didn't know my father, so I didn't even know my grandmother was still living."

Arlowe stared at Mina. Hope flared in her chest.

"I… I was told the woman who passed away was my grandmother, too."

Mina's eyes widened. "Then that means we're cousins!"

Arlowe struggled to hold back tears as her lips stretched into a grin so wide it hurt. "Nice to meet you, cousin."

"Same." Mina clasped her hands together. "It's always just been my mom and me, so this is…oh, this is wonderful!" She winced and placed a hand to her stomach. "Apparently your second cousin agrees, because she just gave me quite the kick."

Months of tension slipped away as Arlowe sat processing the sudden revelation. It didn't solve all of her problems. Not by a long shot. But it was so good to have a piece of happy news, to know she had another family member in the world.

The woman in green sighed as she tapped the screen of her phone with a manicured nail.

"Everything okay?" Arlowe asked, trying to keep her tone as friendly as possible even though her initial reaction was not a positive one.

"No." The woman shoved her phone in her pocket and crossed the room with casual yet elegant confidence, sitting opposite Mina and Arlowe. "I have to get back to London as soon as possible."

"I loved living in London." Mina's cheeks turned pink as the woman's cool green eyes settled on her. "I'm back in Dublin now. But I miss it."

The woman's face softened a fraction, taking the edge off her model-like sculptured features.

"What part of London?"

"The Wick." Mina's hands tightened on her belly. "Maybe someday I'll go back." She cleared throat. "I'm sorry, I didn't catch your name?"

"Ivy Larken." Ivy's gaze flickered to Arlowe. "You said your name was Arlowe. Where are you from? American, I'm guessing."

"Yes. I live just outside Kansas City."

Ivy's dark eyebrows rose. "You came quite aways. Missouri, right?"

"Yes. And I did." Arlowe smiled. "My first time out of the country."

Instead of scoffing or rolling her eyes, Ivy's lips curved up slightly. "Exhilarating, isn't it?"

"It really was."

Ivy paused. "I was also raised by my mother. My invitation said the will reading was for my late grandmother, too."

All three of them stared at each other.

"So…we're all cousins," Arlowe finally breathed.

"Oh wow." Mina's smile lit up her face. "I'm…this is… oh, I'm just so happy."

Ivy's reaction was more muted, but she still smiled. "It is nice."

Arlowe couldn't help but laugh. "Very nice."

Herr Blukker walked back in. "My apologies. Reception up here is not always the best, so I wanted to take that call while I had service. There's a snowstorm on the way."

Arlowe glanced out the window, but the windows faced the mountainside to the south, showing only trees glowing in the afternoon sun.

"A snowstorm?" she repeated.

"Yes. The cold front will hit in a few hours, but the snow should hold off until tomorrow morning." He grabbed a leather portfolio off the table. "So, *damen*, let's begin."

Arlowe took a deep breath. This was it.

"I apologize for not introducing the three of you earlier. Arlowe Banks, Sabrina Callahan, and Ivette Larken," he said with nods to each of them. "I will be reading the last will and testament of Desdemona Gruber. I will be reading the contents of the will as it was written and signed by her in accordance with her wishes. If you have any questions, we can address them after the reading."

He pulled a piece of parchment paper out of the folder.

"Frau Gruber requested I begin with the reading of a letter she addressed to the three of you, her granddaughters."

Granddaughter. Logically Arlowe knew she was someone's granddaughter. But with her mom's father disowning her after she became pregnant and never knowing her father or his side of the family, it was validating to hear the term now. To know that even though she and Desdemona had never met, her grand-mother had been aware enough of her existence to include her. Whether she walked away with a cherished family memento or a little bit of money, being included meant so much.

Herr Blukker cleared his throat. "'To my granddaughters, I'm sorry I learned of your existence when I have so little time left. My relationships with my sons, your fathers, were not positive. Once we parted ways, I cut myself off from them entirely. Unfortunately, that means I missed out on knowing you.'"

Mina sniffed. Arlowe reached over and squeezed her new-found cousin's hand even as she blinked back her own tears. What was done was done. But it was hard not to wonder "what if?"

"'I can only hope that my last will and testament provides some comfort in the years ahead. While my stipulations may seem odd, I believe they will ensure not only your success but the continuation of our family line.'"

Arlowe frowned.

"Stipulations?" she repeated.

"*Geduld*. Patience," Herr Blukker said with a slight smile. "'May the three of you be happy and healthy. With great love, your grandmother.'"

He slid the letter back in and pulled out several more sheets of paper.

"Why didn't she reach out?" Ivy asked quietly.

Herr Blukker stood silently for a long moment. "Her diagnosis occurred only a few weeks before her passing. Her condition deteriorated rapidly. She was bedridden when she dictated this letter to me. While she never said it out loud, I believe she didn't want to be remembered that way."

"Was she alone?"

Herr Blukker smiled gently at Arlowe. "No. I was with her, as were several close friends. Your grandmother was much beloved."

Silence reigned. Mina sniffed again. Ivy stood and moved to the couch, grabbing Mina's other hand and squeezing.

"Regarding her estate, Frau Gruber has bequeathed to each of you the sum of twenty-five thousand euros, to be deposited immediately into an account of your choosing."

Arlowe's mouth dropped open. That was nearly eight months' of salary from the greenhouse. She could get ahead of some bills, make a payment on Robert's last surgery, maybe even take a class or two next semester—

Not yet. As much as she wanted to move forward with her life, it wouldn't do to get too far ahead of herself. She needed to be rational, practical.

"The twenty-five thousand is yours to keep and do with as you wish." Herr Blukker paused, then blew out a harsh breath. "However, each granddaughter is eligible to receive fifteen million euros each, provided they marry within one year of this will reading and stay married for a minimum of three years."

Arlowe's mouth dropped open as Mina gasped. Ivy surged to her feet.

"That's ludicrous."

Herr Blukker's face remained passive. "Shall I continue or not, Fräulein Larken?"

Ivy's hands fisted at her sides. "There's nothing you can possibly say that will make me contemplate marriage for an inheritance. It's ridiculous."

While Arlowe was more shocked than angry, she understood Ivy's feelings. Twenty-five thousand was a godsend. But fifteen million? That kind of money would solve almost everything.

But only if she got married. Within a year. She hadn't even dated since Mom had passed.

"It sounds like she cares more about us having a ring on our finger than who we marry," Arlowe said quietly.

"I encouraged your grandmother to consider alternative options, but she was insistent on this." Herr Blukker shrugged. "There was nothing I could do to dissuade her. Her marriage to your grandfather was a very happy one and provided an escape from an unhappy home. Your fathers' lavish and indulgent lifestyles were a source of pain for her."

"But we're not like them," Mina protested. "She's judging us by our fathers' actions. How is that fair?"

"I can only share what her will includes, Fräulein Callahan. She did include that any granddaughter who is married by the anniversary of the will reading will also have a share in this castle and that it will be up to you to decide what to do with it. Any child born as a result of the marriage will have the sum of one million euros placed into trust and accessible after their twenty-first birthday."

"Do they have to get married, too?" Ivy snapped.

"Ivy." Arlowe waited until her cousin looked at her. "I don't like this either. I know we just met, but we're in this together, okay? All three of us."

Ivy's lips parted. Then, slowly, she took a deep breath and sat back down next to Mina. She gave Arlowe a brief nod before turning her attention back to Herr Blukker.

The rest of the reading was brief. Bequests would be sent to friends and people in the village.

"So what happens next?" Arlowe asked.

"You have up through the first week of November of next year to marry. If you choose to marry, you will receive a share of the castle and fifteen million euros, which is subject to forfeiture if the marriage ends in divorce before the three-year mark."

Anger crept in, pushing out the longing Arlowe had experienced earlier for her grandmother. How could Desdemona have done this to them? Did she care whether or not her granddaughters were happy in their marriages? On the surface, it appeared that Desdemona was using her grand-daughters to right the wrongs of her own sons. A possibility that had Arlowe standing and moving toward the window, arms crossed over her chest as she gazed out over the forest.

Whenever Arlowe had pictured her wedding day, it had always been with the ceremony in the woods between hers and Hart's farms with someone she loved, someone she would spend the rest of her life and raise a family with.

But the woods belonged to someone else now. Meeting someone new and marrying them within a year to inherit money was the opposite of falling in love with someone who would love her for her. Had Desdemona thought about the ramifications of tying such an astoundingly large inheritance to marriage? What if word leaked out? How would she know if someone was marrying her for her?

Because they wouldn't be.

She swallowed past the lump in her throat. Maybe she should just take the twenty-five thousand and forget the rest. The initial money was still far more than she had expected.

Except could she really turn her back on fifteen million? On what it would mean for her and Robert?

Her phone buzzed in her pocket. She pulled it out, her fingers tightening around her phone when she saw the text message from Hart.

How's it going?

What would Hart say if he were here? He'd make a list, that she knew for certain. Pros on one side, cons on the other. He'd logic his way to a solution.

Her breath rushed out as she started to type. Framed logically, there was only one answer.

Looks like I'm getting married.

CHAPTER FOUR

Arlowe

ARLOWE STARED OUT the window of the parlor. The clouds she'd glimpsed earlier had moved in, coloring the trees in dark gray shadows.

She glanced at her phone again. She knew Hart was busy, but she'd expected…well, something in response to her statement. But her phone had been silent for the past hour.

Too busy, like usual.

No, that wasn't fair. Hart may have been distant with her, but she hadn't reached out much either. Every time she thought about the land sale, and specifically asking Francine to keep it a secret, she couldn't dismiss the heat rising to her cheeks or the shame rolling in the pit of her stomach.

Hart may have been the one to pull away first, but she hadn't done much to close the gap between them. Every time she'd thought about calling, fear had stopped her. She didn't know which scenario was worse; Hart not coming because he was too busy for her, or Hart having to choose her over the company that had obviously come to mean so much to him.

A bird flitted past the window. She'd never admit it to anyone, but every now and then resentment crept in. The late nights when she was mopping up spilled beer and peanuts in the bar. The long drive from the farm into Kansas City. Every time she referred a customer from the greenhouse to one of the local landscaping firms for a consultation.

Guilt always followed. Guilt and bone-deep shame that she would ever resent her mom and Robert after everything they'd done for her. Logically, she understood why she felt that way. But emotionally it felt like a betrayal of two of the best people she knew.

She would never place Hart in a position to ever feel that way.

The barrister had spent the past hour with them, answering questions and sharing the documents that made up Desdemona's will. Ivy had finally left the room, color high in her cheeks and eyes blazing. Mina had followed a few minutes later, saying she needed to call her mother. Herr Blukker had excused himself to check on the cars that had brought Ivy and Mina up to the castle.

Leaving Arlowe alone in the parlor with her chaotic thoughts.

Could she do it? Marry someone for money instead of love? She hadn't thought about marriage or even dating in a long time. Hard to think about something like that when her days were jam-packed with work and appointments and her nights were weighted down by exhaustion and grief. But on the rare occasions she had, love had always been prominent. Mutual respect, interests, a desire for family. She wanted a marriage like Mom and Robert's, one rooted in a commitment that transcended the good times and the bad.

Not one that came with a three-year expiration date.

She leaned her head against the window, the cool glass a balm on her skin.

"Fräulein Banks?" Herr Blukker stepped up next to her. "Are you all right?"

"Yes." She paused, shaking her head as she brought her

focus back to the present moment. "Actually, no. The marriage stipulation…"

"I know." Herr Blukker brushed a speck of lint off his lapel. "I tried to discourage your grandmother from including that, but she insisted."

"Why?"

Herr Blukker hesitated. "Your grandmother faced many obstacles early on in life. Life was much harder for women in her time. As I mentioned earlier, marrying your grandfather was one of the few things that brought her happiness and stability."

"But…" Arlowe shook her head. "I'm sorry. I'm frustrated and confused. I need the money, so there's nothing else really to do but follow the instructions in the will."

"You do have a year," Herr Blukker reminded her gently. "And the initial twenty-five thousand."

Which would pay off some of the medical bills. But it wouldn't cover Robert's continuing surgeries and physical therapy. Wouldn't be nearly enough for her to drop down to part-time at the greenhouse and go back to college.

But for fifteen million…she and Robert could have everything. The best possible care for Robert. Fixing up the farm. She might even be able to buy back the acreage she sold and finally get her degree.

Which brought her mind right back to Hart. It appeared Francine had kept her word not to say anything. But Hart would find out one day. If he was mad now, he'd be furious then.

Part of her wanted to call him. Wanted to hear his voice, pour out her troubles and get his guidance the way she had for so many years. He'd always grounded her, helped her take a step back from her emotions and evaluate situations logically.

But after the way their phone conversation had ended, and with his continued silence now, she couldn't call. Hart wasn't a crutch she could lean on when the going got tough. Besides, his solutions usually revolved around money. While he would be leery of marrying so quickly, he'd agree this was the best course of action, given the obstacles she and Robert were facing.

She scrubbed a hand over her face. She needed time to think, to breathe. A place where she could just be alone for a bit while she processed the magnitude of what had happened today. She could extend her stay in the village for a few days, perhaps, or maybe book a hotel in Kansas City. But that would be wasting more money and wouldn't give her the solitude she craved.

An idea dawned on her. She glanced around the cozy room. Her night at the inn and her walk here were the most peaceful moments she'd experienced in months.

"You said the castle was being shut up for the winter?"

Herr Blukker nodded. "Once we reach the one-year anniversary, then you and your cousins can decide what to do with it."

"Would I be able to stay here the rest of the week?"

Herr Blukker's eyebrows rose. "Here? By yourself?"

"Yes."

Excitement chased away her melancholy as she glanced around the parlor. No hotel guests next door. No car horns blaring in the street. No customers asking questions about plants or patrons ordering complicated drinks. No tensing at every creak and thump in the house and rushing out of her room to see if Robert had fallen again.

"You said it's just this main section that's open now anyway," she continued. "I wouldn't go anywhere I wasn't supposed to, and I'd make sure to leave it exactly as it is."

"I don't see any harm," Herr Blukker finally said slowly, "especially since the castle is currently held by the estate. I'll put in an order with a couple stores in the village for groceries, soap, and other incidentals."

"Oh, I can go into town for all of that."

Herr Blukker gave her another fatherly smile. "Allow me to do this for you, Fräulein Banks. You've been through a great shock today. Your grandmother left a generous gift for expenses like yours and your cousins' airline tickets and lodging. I don't think she'd object to this."

Arlowe grasped his hand. "Thank you."

Mina walked into the room, one hand on her lower back and one on her belly.

"My car's here."

Arlowe crossed the room to her. "I'm actually going to stay on for a few days."

Mina's eyes widened. "Here? At the castle?"

"Yes." Arlowe smiled. "You could stay, too. Herr Blukker's kindly offered to order some groceries and things. It could be a great chance for us to get to know each other."

Mina gave her a sad smile. "That sounds nice. But I need to get home. I have an ultrasound in a few days, and I don't want to risk getting stuck here."

"I understand." Arlowe reached into her pocket and pulled out her phone. "Would you mind if we still stayed in touch?"

"Oh, I'd love that!"

Ivy walked into the room as Arlowe typed Mina's number into her phone.

"My car's here, too. Nice to meet you both."

"Mina and I are exchanging numbers," Arlowe called out as Ivy turned to leave. "Would you mind if I got yours?"

"Look, I appreciate how nice you two have been, but I'm not really a family kind of girl." Something flashed in her eyes. "The opposite, actually."

The hint of pain in her voice quelled Arlowe's initial frustration.

"Okay. If you change your mind, Herr Blukker has our numbers."

Ivy paused in the doorway, one hand on the doorframe. Then, with a toss of her long braid, she walked out. A few moments later they heard the front door to the castle open and close.

"She seems sad," Mina commented quietly.

"I agree. But," Arlowe said brightly, "we have each other's numbers. And maybe she'll change her mind."

"True." Mina hugged her pregnant belly. "It's really nice knowing I have another family member out there." She hesitated. "Maybe when the baby's born we could set up a visit?"

Arlowe bit down on the inside of her cheek so she didn't smile like a loon. "I'd really like that."

She walked with Mina down the hall toward the front door.

"So you're going to do it then?" Arlowe asked.

"Get married?" Mina nodded. "It's not my first choice. The father…" Her voice trailed off. She shook her head. "That's not a possibility. But I have a couple friends who would probably be willing, especially if I share some of the money. I can't say no to fifteen million dollars when I'm barely scraping by. The baby deserves better."

"So do you," Arlowe said quietly. "I'm sorry the father couldn't see that."

A fierce light shone in Mina's eyes. "It's better this way. Trust me."

They hugged at the door and said goodbye. Arlowe wrapped her arms around her waist as she watched the car drive off. Today had been full of surprises, good and bad. But she had two new family members, one of whom she could easily see becoming a friend, too. Ivy might be withdrawn now, but her other cousin had surprised her several times over the afternoon. Arlowe chose to hope that maybe Ivy would reach out, too.

Feeling just a little less lonely, Arlowe went back inside. The chandelier gleamed in the dim lighting. The hall was massive, but between the rich tapestries, warm-colored wood floors, and thick, plush rugs, its cozy elegance had Arlowe sighing with contentment.

Five days. Five whole days to herself in an actual castle. Reality and her impending marriage to a faceless suitor still loomed. But for this week, she would enjoy the unexpected rest.

She walked back into the parlor where Herr Blukker was just hanging up his phone.

"Deliveries will be made by six this evening." He glanced at the window and frowned. "The forecast has changed to a few feet of snow."

Arlowe's eyebrows shot up. "Wow. I don't think I've ever seen that much snow at once."

"Unusual, but not unheard of in this region. If it's bad, you could be stranded here for several days."

She grinned. "Stranded in a castle doesn't sound too bad."

"As long as the power holds, no. There is a generator, although your grandmother had planned on replacing it this year."

Arlowe nodded toward the fireplace. "If there's firewood, I'll be all right. We had plenty of snowstorms growing up back in Missouri, some that kept us home for days."

"If you're sure."

She glanced around the room again. "I am."

The grocer arrived an hour after Herr Blukker left. Arlowe won the argument of helping the grocer unload the boxes of groceries, hygiene products, and household items Herr Blukker had ordered. Batteries, shampoo, and spare lightbulbs were unpacked, along with smoked salmon, luxurious cheeses, and caviar. Arlowe's excitement climbed as she slid bottles of Riesling and ice wine into the wine rack inside the massive kitchen pantry.

After the grocer left, she made herself a sandwich, scarfed it down, and then set out to explore. The first level of the castle contained a music room, a massive dining room, a smaller and more intimate living room with a TV, and an actual ballroom, complete with mirrors on three of the walls and windows on the other that overlooked a stunning garden. Whoever had designed it had included seasonal plants that even now peeked through the falling snow with bright bits of autumn color.

An ache settled in her chest. How many nights had she and Mom spent on the porch, dreaming up names for Arlowe's architectural landscaping firm? She'd written up her business plan in high school, a plan she'd tweaked throughout those first few years of college as she'd balanced a part-time job with going to school half-time so she could pay as she went instead of taking on mountains of debt.

It had seemed like such a solid plan. But when life had delivered one hit after another, she'd learned the hard way that having a bunch of classes in agriculture didn't open up many job opportunities. Had she done what her high school counselor had recommended and gone into agriculture education or pursued a degree in nutrition, something related to her passion but with far more job prospects, she and Robert would probably be in a far better place.

The snow fell harder, slowly eclipsing the plants from view. With fifteen million in the bank, it would be easy to go back to school and finish her degree, invest in her own business.

But what if the worst happened again? What if another emergency happened or some other catastrophe befell them? Doing what she should have done in the first place and getting a degree in something sensible would be the right route to go.

She turned away from the garden. Something to contemplate later. For now, she wanted to finish exploring.

The next room, and her favorite by far, was the library. A full two stories tall, it boasted floor-to-ceiling shelves painted white with intricate gold overlay. Herr Blukker must have had the castle cleaned in the last few days because each shelf gleamed. A massive stone fireplace stood nearly eight feet tall, with dark blue wingback chairs and a thick, plush rug in front of it. She plucked a book off the shelf and settled into one of the chairs with a happy sigh.

This had definitely been the right choice.

Something caught her eye. A small wooden horse high up one shelf next to the fireplace. She chewed on her lip for a moment before tossing back the blanket and moving to the bookshelf. She stretched up on her toes and just barely managed to close her fingers around the toy.

The wood was dusty but smooth. She ran a delicate finger across the ridges of the mane, the tiny ears. Whoever had carved it had been exceptionally talented.

Had this belonged to her father? Or perhaps one of the uncles Herr Blukker had mentioned? It sounded like Ivy and Mina had had identical experiences growing up. What must have that been like for Desdemona, to have such a happy marriage and be surrounded by such wealth only to have all three of her sons choose paths so horrendous she banished them from her life?

She cradled the horse in her hand. It was easy to picture Desdemona keeping the toy because she felt like she had to. A woman who held to honor and legacy above her own emotions. Yet as Arlowe rubbed her thumb over a rounded hoof, she suspected it had been more than that. Desdemona had kept this because, despite what her sons had done, she loved them.

Why had her father made the choices he had? If he had grown up like this with two parents who loved each other, why had he moved to the United States? Mom had said they'd met in college, that she thought it had been love at first sight when they'd bumped into each other at the university's art museum. Six months of being wined and dined by one of the handsomest men on campus until she'd found out she was pregnant.

The pregnancy had changed everything.

Arlowe set the horse back up on the shelf. Mom had said her father had withdrawn overnight, disappeared until just before Arlowe was born. When he'd shown up in the last month of the pregnancy, Mom thought maybe he'd changed. But he hadn't. He flitted in and out of their lives until just before Arlowe's third birthday when Mom kicked him out after finding out he'd been having an affair with another woman.

Arlowe sat back down and pulled the blanket around her like a shield. Whenever she thought of her father, she could smell his aftershave, vanilla and leather, could feel his deep laugh rumbling in his chest.

But she also remembered the shouts, that same deep voice raised in anger against her mother. The fear as she cowered in the dark.

And then the warmth of her mother holding her, cradling her in a hug that smelled like flour and soap, whispering that he would never be back as she kissed Arlowe on the forehead and rocked her on the living room floor.

Sadness rose up. For Desdemona, for her mother, even for her father and what he could have been versus what he had chosen.

But if he hadn't made the choices he had, she would have never known Robert. Most likely would have never moved out to the farm and met Hart and his parents. She couldn't imagine her life without them.

She glanced over at the other chair. For a moment she could picture Hart sitting across from her, a book in his hand and a slight smile on his face. It had been too long since she'd seen him just take a moment to relax, to enjoy himself.

Then she shook off her musings, opened her book, and began to read.

* * *

By the time Arlowe emerged from the library, night had settled in, leaving the mountains cloaked in darkness. She made herself a cup of hot cocoa in the kitchen downstairs and added a splash of Austrian apple brandy before venturing back upstairs. She made a quick to-do list that included stocking up on firewood, checking the generator, and making sure all the windows and doors were closed.

The snowflakes started to fall as she finished with the last window in the bedroom she'd claimed as hers. She moved to the window and gazed out over the valley. Snowflakes fell, creating a dusting of white over the trees, a sharp contrast to the darkness overhead.

A soft sigh escaped. Normally she loved being around people. It was one of the things she liked about working at the greenhouse; all the customers who came in and asked questions about plants, soils, fertilizers. Having a customer come back with photos of their yards was usually a highlight of her day. Even working at the bar had its perks, with the repeat travelers who would come through.

But right now, she loved the solitude. The quiet contentment of being safe, warm, and not having anything pressing on her to-do list.

Other than finding a husband, of course.

Regret coiled around her heart and squeezed. She'd imagined her wedding day plenty of times over the years. None of her daydreams had included marrying a husband she barely knew for a fortune.

No. She wasn't going to think about that today. Maybe in a day or two, after she'd had some time to do nothing more than keep herself warm and fed. This was her time to rest, to recuperate from nearly two years of rushing from one thing to the next while she tried to deal with her grief in a way that didn't break her.

Suddenly feeling restless, she drifted across the hall. On impulse, she opened the front doors and stared out over the front courtyard draped in snow. She grabbed the boots she'd left just inside after seeing Mina off and pulled them on. She wouldn't be out long enough to need a coat.

She stepped back out onto the mezzanine and rested her hands on the cold stone of the balustrade. The snow swirled around her, stirring her hair and kissing her cheeks with snowflakes. She smiled as she tilted her head back and stared up at the dark sky.

"I hope you can see me, Mom. I'm having an adventure."

The back of her neck prickled. She lowered her chin, her eyes sweeping across the courtyard.

Then froze as someone walked into the courtyard. Her shoulders tensed, her body poised for flight.

"Arlowe?"

Arlowe's jaw dropped. She must be hallucinating. Or perhaps she was still in the library and had fallen asleep in the chair. Yes, that must be it.

"Earth to Arlowe."

Slowly, her lips curved up into a smile.

"Hart?" A laugh bubbled up and escaped. "Oh my God, Hart, you're here!"

CHAPTER FIVE

Hart

SHE LOOKED LIKE a snow fairy brought to life. Dark curls dusted with snow, a blanket wrapped around her shoulders like a cloak, and a smile that shot through him with a power that left him speechless.

"Hart?" Her laughter filled the air, a perfect complement to the snow dancing in the air. "Oh my God, Hart, you're here!"

She hurried down the stairs, keeping a firm grip on the railing until she reached the cobblestones. Then she raced across the ground and threw her arms around his neck. His arms came around her without a moment's hesitation. He crushed her to him, buried his face in her curls, and breathed in her scent: sweet peaches with an undercurrent of jasmine.

God, he'd missed her. How had he stayed away? How had he convinced himself that a few phone conversations and texts here and there made up for being with her?

"You're here!" She pulled back and laughed. "You're actually here!"

Snowflakes kissed her lashes and rested on her cheeks. He nearly leaned down to kiss one off her skin.

"I just wish you had looked at me once like you looked at Arlowe."

The realization and near intimacy shook him, made him pull further away. Irritated with himself, he glanced down at her and frowned when he realized she had no coat on under the blanket.

"Damn it, Arlowe, it's freezing out here."

Arlowe's face fell at Hart's gruff tone.

"Yeah, I noticed."

He wanted to kick himself. Why was he talking to her like this? Arlowe had proven herself more than capable of taking care of herself, not to mention Robert. Yet here he was, talking to her like a child. He just wanted to make sure she was looking after herself, that he had her back. She deserved that. Not having to go through everything alone.

Before either one of them could say another word, Hart slid one arm around her back and leaned down. She let out a small squeal as he lifted her into his arms. She grabbed onto the lapels of his parka as he stomped forward.

"Hart!"

"We'll talk inside."

She shivered in his arms. He quickened his pace and fairly lunged up the stairs.

"You're not married, are you?"

For a solid four heart-pounding seconds, there was no answer.

"No."

The befuddled amusement in her tone nearly had him growling. He shouldered his way into the grand hall and used his back to push the door shut.

"You can let me down now."

His arms tightened around her at the husky breathlessness in her voice. Was he imagining things? Allowing Lucy's words to affect him?

Thankfully Arlowe didn't seem to notice, because when he set her down on her feet, she stepped back as if his carrying her hadn't affect him in the slightest. He shrugged his backpack off, followed by his parka and gloves. When he looked up, she was still smiling. The sight tugged at him.

"What?"

"I just can't believe you're here." Her smile disappeared. "Why are you here?"

Hart picked up his parka and gloves.

"I was worried about you."

Worried was an understatement. When he'd received her text—Looks like I'm getting married—he'd thought it was a joke. But when his texts had gone unanswered, unease had settled in. Unease that had burst into full-blown panic when he'd called no less than seven times and every single call had gone to voicemail.

Every unanswered call had sent his blood pressure skyrocketing. He'd envisioned Arlowe meeting a tourist on her hike, or a charming stranger at the will reading, of said stranger going down on bended knee and proposing some crazy scheme. The thought of Arlowe getting engaged to another man, let alone marrying him, had taken his usual logic and ground it into dust.

He focused on breathing out, slow, measured breaths. "So you're not married?"

She bit down on her lower lip, a gesture he knew meant she was trying to hold back laughter.

"No."

Relief swamped him. When Arlowe's text had come through, he'd shaken his head and sent a brief reply asking who the lucky groom was. But as the minutes had stretched into half an hour, then an hour, concern had taken hold. His later texts asking if she was okay, followed by his unanswered phone calls, had turned his discomfort into concern. Calling Robert and his mother, finding out neither of them were able to get a hold of her either, had spiraled his concerns into bone-chilling fear.

After his last unanswered call, he'd done the unthinkable; he'd gone with his gut and asked his secretary to book him a private flight to Salzburg ahead of the encroaching winter storm. His team wouldn't be in until Thursday, which had given him two days to track Arlowe down and make sure she was okay.

By the time his plane had landed in Salzburg, a private car had been arranged to take him from the airport to the Gruber estate, a castle tucked into the foothills of the Austrian Alps. The chauffeur hadn't been comfortable risking the trek up the steep drive leading to the castle. So Hart had hiked nearly a quarter of a mile up a snowy road.

All to get to his best friend. The one he had let down far too many times in recent memory.

"So what did your text mean?"

Weariness crossed her face. "My grandmother left me twenty-five thousand euros."

"Okay. That's good, right?"

"It is, but if I get married within a year, it jumps up to fifteen million."

Hart stared at her for a long moment as his brain tried to process both the staggering figure and the ridiculous stipulation.

"Fifteen million?" he finally repeated.

"Yes." She crossed her arms over her chest. "I'm not going to jump into anything, Hart, but I can't turn down that kind of money."

You've turned down my money plenty of times.

He bit back his own frustration. Now was not the time to dig into that sore point.

"So you're going to marry some random man to inherit? Then what? You're stuck with them for life?"

"No. Just three years."

His anger ratcheted up. He didn't like having ill feelings

toward the departed, but his fury with Arlowe's late grand-mother ranked up there with how he'd felt toward his grand-father upon learning the true extent of BioInnovations's troubles. Two selfish people who left behind messes for their heirs without bothering to think about the long-term impli-cations.

"Only three years. Well, that's not so bad."

He rarely indulged in sarcasm, but the situation more than warranted it.

"I won't even be thirty by the time the third anniversary rolls around," Arlowe retorted.

"And just where are you going to get a husband?"

Just saying the words out loud had Hart's entire body tens-ing. Arlowe hadn't talked about her dating life in a long time. Years, really, before he left for New York. Was there some-one he didn't know about?

The possibility had him grinding his teeth.

"Well, I could always run down to the village." Arlowe arched a brow. "Or take out an ad. 'Wanted, one husband for the sum of one million euros—'"

"There is no way in hell you're giving some random per-son a share of your inheritance."

Arlowe glared at him. "People aren't exactly lining up to date me, let alone marry me. I think one million is more than fair for three years, especially since I'd still walk away with fourteen million."

"Is the money the only reason you're contemplating this?"

A shadow passed over her face. It killed him to see her withdraw.

"Don't."

The sadness in her voice stabbed into his chest.

"What?"

"I've already told you I don't want your money, Hart. I'm doing this my way and I can make this decision on my own."

Her arms tightened around her waist as she looked away. "You didn't have to come."

His sadness evaporated. "The hell I didn't."

Arlowe faced him again and raised her chin. A battle was brewing behind her beauty. Beauty he had never been distracted by before. But now, as storm clouds gathered in her amber eyes, he couldn't help but notice the defiance in the tilt of her chin, the graceful yet strong cut of her cheekbones, the riotous curls that seemed to vibrate with an energy all their own.

Except he had no right to be thinking about her like this. To be feeling angry, possessive…jealous.

Arlowe spun away from Hart and crossed over to one of the tapestries. He felt her dismissal down to his bones. He drew in a deep breath, steadied himself. Whatever internal demons he was battling were his and his alone. He had no right to take them out on Arlowe.

"I was worried about you."

Slowly, Arlowe turned around. The sight of her hit him anew. How had he lasted nearly a year without seeing her?

"I know. I just…"

He saw the indecision, the struggle in her eyes. Curled his hands into fists at his sides as he watched the war play out across her face. She'd never been able to conceal much from anyone. On the rare attempts she tried to conceal her feelings, he'd always been able to see her, to know exactly what she'd been thinking. Tonight was no different.

"I didn't mean to scare you." She ran a hand through her curls. "How about I take you to a room upstairs where you can change into something dry. Then we'll talk. Are you hungry?"

Hart stared at her for a long moment. He wanted to push, wanted to resolve this now and secure her promise that she wouldn't do anything rash. Even though he wanted to shake some sense into her, make her see reason and just accept his offer of help, he couldn't help but admire her commitment to Robert and trying to take care of things herself. Her dedication and strength made him want to help all the more, to take some of the burden off her shoulders and give her back some of the support she extended to everyone else.

But he needed a little more time. Patience. He and Arlowe had been in a different place for the last three years. He only had a day before he needed to get back to France, but a lot could happen in twenty-four hours.

He breathed in, then out, steadying himself and pulling away from the emotional ledge he'd somehow ended up on. First his concerns about Nessa Pharmaceuticals and now this. He loved Arlowe—as a friend—but he needed to focus on the logic of the situation, the quantitative details that could be rationalized. Not let himself get caught up in these confusing feelings that were most likely just a by-product of having spent so little time with Arlowe.

Recentered, he gave her a small smile. "Food would be great. Thank you."

She smiled back, her eyes crinkling at the corners. Something twisted inside his chest as warmth penetrated his body.

So much for staying emotionally neutral.

CHAPTER SIX

Arlowe

WITH HIS DARK hair askew and his pants damp with melted snow, Hart looked the exact opposite of his usual well-composed self. Certainly not the suit-wearing millionaire Arlowe saw splashed across social media these days.

A tremor flickered through her. He looked wild. Untamed. He'd tossed logic out the window to fly across four countries just to reach her because he hadn't been able to contact her.

And then he'd stood in the courtyard, snow swirling around him like the storm itself had summoned him, looking so handsome and determined her heart had shot into her throat. She'd thrown herself at him.

But, she remembered with vivid clarity, he hadn't pushed her away. No, he'd grabbed her and held her so tightly it had thrilled her straight to her toes.

Get a grip.

He'd been worried about her. Relieved that she was in one piece and, at least for now, unmarried. There hadn't been anything romantic in what he'd done.

Swallowing past the sudden dryness in her mouth, Arlowe clasped her hands in front of her.

"I am sorry I worried you. When you didn't text back, I just assumed you were busy."

"I tried calling. So did Robert and Francine."

She winced. "Herr Blukker mentioned reception up here wasn't always the best. I'm sure the storm's not helping."

"No." Hart scowled toward the door. "Hopefully I can get out of here tomorrow."

Disappointment shot through her. "Tomorrow?"

"Yes. I have an important meeting on Friday I can't miss."

"Oh."

Hart ran a hand through his hair, the snowflakes melting into the dark strands. "I just wanted to make sure you were okay and hadn't done anything rash."

Hurt cut through her. When had Hart started seeing her like this? Some damsel in distress who couldn't take care of herself? True, she hadn't exactly shared with him everything she'd done to keep her and Robert's heads above water. But even in high school when she'd gotten involved in one too many activities, and college when she'd announced her choice of degree as landscape architecture, Hart had never once condemned her. He'd talked through how to narrow down the activities she was participating in. He'd helped her research internships and job opportunities that would serve as stepping stones toward her ultimate goal of owning her own business.

Now, as he glanced around with cool, appraising eyes, she finally accepted what she'd been trying to resist for so long. The man who had been her best friend for over twenty years had now turned into a stranger.

A stranger her traitorous body apparently found very attractive.

"Well, we'd better get you upstairs to a bedroom so you can rest and get back on the road tomorrow." She smiled thinly. "Follow me."

He grabbed his backpack off the floor as she turned her back on him and led the way up the curving stone staircase. More tapestries hung from the walls, interspersed with candelabras. Electric, as Herr Blukker had shown her just before he left, but no less impressive with the intricate silverwork and the faux melting wax dripping down the candles.

They reached the top of the stairs. Arlowe was just about to walk down toward one of the bedrooms when Hart stopped her with a gentle hand on her shoulder. She sucked in a breath at the warmth of his hand seeping through her shirt.

"Are you doing all right?"

Grief shoved away the warmth, leaving her with a hollow ache and eyes stinging with unshed tears.

"I'm okay."

"Hey."

Hart gently turned her around and slid a finger under her chin, tilting her head back until she was looking into deep green eyes. So familiar with the rings of gold around his irises, the flecks of brown she'd always referred to as "freckles" just to make him blush.

"It's okay to not be okay."

The tears swelled, threatening to spill over as she swallowed hard.

"I know. It's just…" One tear broke free. "I'm tired of the loss. There's…" She sucked in a shuddering breath. "There's just been so much."

Hart pulled her into a hug. She let go of her anger and buried her face in his shirt, breathing in the familiar scents of wood and earth with undertones of spice and a hint of orange. A scent she would always associate with Hart.

"I never knew any of them," Arlowe murmured against his chest. "My grandparents. I only have a couple memories of my dad, and they weren't pleasant."

"But they're gone."

And just like that, Hart understood. Arlowe breathed in, then out. The tears receded, as did the burning in her eyes. But as the ache eased, the awareness returned. Awareness of Hart's arms wrapped around her, the warmth of his body surrounding her, the rise and fall of his chest and the steady thumping of his heartbeat beneath her ear.

She could stay like this forever.

She stepped back, her heart pounding once more. Hart's arms tightened for a fraction of a second before he released her.

Or maybe, Arlowe told herself as she resumed her walk down the hall, *you're imagining things because you've gone crazy!*

"I'll try to keep the bouts of melancholy to a minimum while you're here." She tried to force a cheerful tone as she turned left down another hallway.

"Bouts of melancholy," Hart repeated. "Sounds like you've been reading Austen again."

This time Arlowe's grin was completely genuine. She stopped in the middle of a doorway and arched a brow.

"This place has a library straight out of 'Beauty and the Beast,' including a huge fireplace and the entire Jane Austen collection. Not to mention both Brontë sisters, Nicholas Sparks, Beverly Jenkins, Agatha Christie, Cervantes—"

"I get it." Hart smiled down at her. "Any books on executive negotiations or pharmaceutical production?"

Arlowe tilted her head to one side. "Come on, Hart, you're in an Austrian castle. Surely business can rest for one night."

The teasing light in his eyes died.

"I wish it could. But I'm in the middle of a big deal right now."

Arlowe frowned. "Then why did you come here?"

"Like I said, I was worried about you." He took a step forward. "You're important, too, Arlowe. I haven't done the best job showing it these last few months."

No, he hadn't. But she didn't want to rub that in. Besides, Hart and she were both adults. Yes, she missed him. Missed their friendship. But Hart wasn't responsible for her.

"I've missed you, but I get it. Your business demands a lot, and Lucy…" She winced. "Sorry. Still not used to that."

Hart shrugged. "It's okay. It wasn't a big loss for either of us."

Arlowe frowned. "But you two were together for…what, four months?"

"I promise, I'm fine."

But there was something in his tone, a tightness to his voice, that told her there was more to his and Lucy's breakup than a simple parting of ways.

Whatever that *more* was, Hart had no intention of sharing. "All right."

She opened the door and stepped into the chamber she'd selected for Hart before he could see her hurt.

"Wow."

She smiled slightly as Hart walked in, his eyes wide. The walls soared nearly twenty feet high before arching in to form a dome. The walls had been painted snow-white, while the ceiling was the same deep blue as the thick, silk bedspread spread across the massive bed that dominated the far end of the chamber. Matching curtains were partially pulled open to reveal the snow-covered grounds outside. One single windowpane at the very top had been painted with a single blue wave crashing down onto the sea.

Arlowe moved over to the fireplace.

"I can take care of that—"

Arlowe flipped a switch next to the mantel. The fireplace roared to life.

"Pretty easy." She smoothed her palms over her jeans. "I'll work on dinner while you get dressed. The kitchen is in the basement if you don't mind eating there."

"That's fine."

Hart laid his backpack down and glanced around the room

once more. With his sharp features and quiet yet command-ing presence, he fit in seamlessly with the austere setting.

Sadness crept in. He and Lucy had always looked so… right. Perfect. Both of them with their lives in order, achiev-ing huge successes as they navigated adulthood. Whereas Arlowe worked full-time at a gardening center and spent her nights making drinks at a hotel bar in Kansas City. She was still three semesters away from getting her bachelor's degree, not to mention the graduate degree, internships, and licensure she'd need to be successful as a landscape architect. The first weekend of every month was an exercise in stress manage-ment as she balanced the budget with her two incomes against Robert's medical and physical therapy bills and the leftover bills from when Mom had been in the hospital.

No small wonder she and Hart had grown apart. He was thriving. She was barely scraping by. All her dreams had net-ted her nothing but bills.

"See you in a few minutes."

She started to close the door. Hart's hand reached out and grabbed onto the door, stopping her so quickly she nearly re-bounded back into the door.

"We need to talk more. About the will."

She raised her chin. If he thought he was going to inter-fere with her decision, then he could just go back to France as soon as the storm cleared. No, it wasn't her first choice. But she had a chance to finally put all of her poor choices and bad luck behind her. A chance to provide for herself and Robert in a way that would have taken her years of working two jobs. Hart might think her silly and fanciful, incapable of making hard choices. But this one was cut-and-dried.

"Of course."

Hart started to say something, but his phone rang. Sur-prised, he glanced back toward the room, then back to her.

He'd only arrived ten minutes ago, but already his mind

was back in Lyon. He might be here physically. But his time in the castle wouldn't be like it would have been three years ago, with them exploring every nook and cranny. Chances were, if he wasn't trying to talk her out of her decision to marry, he'd be on the phone or on his computer.

"You should get that. Who knows when you'll have reception again."

She turned and walked down the hall before Hart could say anything else.

CHAPTER SEVEN

Hart

HART CURSED UNDER his breath as he opened yet another door. The castle was full of doors leading into sumptuous, luxurious rooms, including a ballroom, a grand dining room, three parlors, and a music room. He had found the library, too, tucked toward the back and next to another courtyard. It hadn't been hard to picture Arlowe curled up in one of the massive chairs by the fireplace reading a book. Her hair would be caught up in a messy bun and her face scrunched up into either a delighted smile or a furious frown depending on what the characters were doing.

He'd stood in the doorway longer than he'd intended. When was the last time he and Arlowe had simply coexisted in a room together? The last time they'd had a conversation that hadn't included asking after each other's family and the latest at work. Although lately Arlowe had become cagey about work, too. She'd talk a little about the greenhouse. But mostly she'd steered the conversation back to his job. His friend, the one his mother had once described as "liquid sunshine," was pulling away, and he didn't know how to get her back. Worse, he couldn't blame her.

He'd closed the door and resumed his search for the stairs to the basement.

Hart stood in the middle of the grand hall, hands on his

hips as his eyes traveled over the doors he'd already opened. If someone had told him yesterday that twenty-four hours from then he'd be searching through an Austrian castle for his childhood best friend, he'd have laughed. He spied a rounded door in the far wall. He opened it and breathed a sigh of relief at the sight of the stone stairs circling downward. The walls were cool, the air chilly as he moved further down. Light flickered from the electric candles fastened into the walls, creating a spooky, medieval-inspired atmosphere.

Strains of music drifted up the stairs. He smiled slightly. Jazz. Even as a kid when he'd go traipsing across the fields to the Banks' home, he could almost always count on jazz pouring out the open windows as Lynn canned vegetables or Arlowe helped out with cleaning.

He paused on the steps. This jazz, however, was different. Dark, moody, almost haunting. The trumpet would let out one long, melancholy tone before slipping into a muted breathiness. A sound that tugged on his memory…

Arlowe. The soft gasps when her tears had receded but she'd still sat in his arms, her body shuddering with grief over her mother's death.

He resumed his trek down the stairs. The arched doorway at the bottom opened up onto a nineteenth-century kitchen with modern touches. The walls, fashioned of rough stone, rose up to a smooth, rounded ceiling. Windows near the top let in muted light. On a clear day, the kitchen would probably glow, from the polished cutting board tables to the copper pots dangling from up above.

Arlowe stood by one of the tables, her hips swaying gently back and forth as she laid out food. Her hair was caught up in a ponytail. She'd changed into a sleeveless, teal-colored dress that fell all the way down to her ankles. A soft, fluffy white sweater was draped over one chair.

He froze. Awareness wound through him, set his entire

body on edge. His eyes drifted down the length of her neck, over her back, and down. His body tightened. The material clung perfectly to Arlowe's curves, highlighting the flare of her hips, the rounded—

What are you doing?

It had been months since he'd been with anyone. After that first month of dating, he and Lucy had barely seen each other. Their schedules had never aligned, so they'd settled for a quick dinner in whatever city they happened to be closest to, and on one occasion a coffee at the airport. Their relationship had consisted mostly of hurried video calls and texting. Even when they had seen more of each other, the physical side of things had been pleasant.

But he had never responded to Lucy like this. Had never felt a craving to cup her face, lower his lips to hers and—

Shaken at the direction of his thoughts, he cleared his throat. Arlowe glanced over her shoulder. Her smile was small and quick.

"You found it."

"It took a few attempts," Hart admitted as he walked further into the kitchen.

"Yeah, but exploring's half the fun."

He smiled slightly. "I did find the library."

This time when Arlowe turned to him her smile was dialed up to megawatt.

"Isn't it incredible? I could live in that room."

"Can I help with anything?"

Arlowe nodded toward a pitcher and two glasses on the countertop. "Ice water and glasses would be great."

She picked up the plates and walked over toward a long, oval-shaped table with half a dozen chairs arranged around it. Hart followed and sat down, his eyebrows rising at the elaborately arranged plate in front of him.

"This looks like something from a five-star restaurant."

Arlowe chuckled as she sat. "I wish I could say I made this, but that would be a lie. Herr Blukker had a catering company come in and set me up with meals for the next week." She picked up her fork and started pointing out the various foods. "Salad with strips of smoked salmon and horseradish cream, *tafelspitz*, and root vegetables with butter sauce. The *tafelspitz* is a traditional Austrian dish with beef, horseradish, apple sauce, and creamy spinach."

Odd for a family lawyer to buy such expensive food for a woman he'd never met. Hart speared a piece of salmon.

"How old is Herr Blukker?"

"Old enough to be my father," Arlowe replied bluntly. "He was just trying to be nice. He's not trying to seduce me into marriage with good food."

Hart held up a hand. "It's just strange, Arlowe, that's all."

"And I think it's nice." She grabbed a napkin and spread it across her lap, taking extra care not to make eye contact with him. "Sometimes people do nice things simply to do nice things."

"I know, I just "

Hart's voice trailed off as Arlowe picked up her fork and started eating. Was he even capable of saying the right thing?

"I'm just worried about you."

Arlowe sighed and laid down her fork.

"I know, Hart. So you've said. Multiple times. But I am capable of thinking for myself."

Hart frowned. "When was that ever a question?"

Hart gave in to the urge to reach over and grasp her hand in his. "I'm concerned you'll do this for Robert and not think about yourself or what you really want."

Arlowe stared down at the table. The trumpet let out another mournful wail, a sound that mirrored the sadness etched onto Arlowe's face.

"I appreciate that, Hart," she finally murmured. She gave

his hand a squeeze and then slowly pulled away. "But unfortunately that's the way life is right now. I can't just think about myself anymore. Sometimes hard decisions have to be made."

Hart's mind instantly went to the land, to the contract sitting in his bag two floors above. Would she ever tell him? Or would he have to be the one to confront her?

Arlowe nodded toward the snow building up against the windowpanes. "You barely made it in time."

"My secretary was very efficient."

He didn't tell Arlowe about the panic that had bolted through him when she'd hung up. With the storm barreling across western France, it had been a race to the airport to take off before the worst of the snow had hit. He'd spent most of the drive and the first half of the flight on the phone with his team coming in from New York, delegating tasks and making arrangements in case he was out of reach for more than a day. His team, to their credit, hadn't pushed back too hard on him ducking out right as negotiations were about to ramp up.

Light snow had started to fall in Salzburg by the time his plane touched down. The private car he'd hired had taken double the amount of time to reach Lärchenthal as the storm had worsened. By the time they'd started up the drive toward the castle, the snow had been inches thick. So he'd grabbed the hastily purchased parka and gloves from the airport, grabbed his bag, and trudged up the winding drive to the castle.

Arlowe's lips twitched. "You looked like a snowman coming into the courtyard."

He couldn't help his chuckle. "And you looked like…"

His words faded. She'd looked beautiful, standing there in a bright red dress with the snow swirling around her. The smile on her face when she'd seen him had made him feel like he'd just conquered a mountain instead of a slight hill. His name on her lips had banished his worry. Even though they were thousands of miles away, the carefree abandon she'd exhibited as she'd hurried down the stairs and thrown herself into his arms had felt like coming home.

"Probably a wild woman," Arlowe said with a laugh, breaking him out of his musings.

"A princess," he countered. "Commanding the winter to her bidding."

Arlowe's eyes widened even as she grinned. "I like the sound of that."

He breathed in deeply. This was what he needed to focus on. The slight teasing, the normalcy of their conversation. They could talk about farm management and business one minute, then delve into utter ridiculousness the next. The foundation was still there, just buried under months of not being around each other.

Even if he could only stay for a couple days, he could make sure Arlowe was okay, talk through the situation with her and maybe finally get her to see reason.

"How's the conference?"

He yanked his attention back to Arlowe.

"Good. Some good presentations." He grimaced. "A couple not so good."

"Your mom mentioned some big pharmaceutical company is courting you?"

He nodded. The last thing he wanted to talk about right now was Nessa Pharmaceuticals. Especially because Arlowe would probably tell him to trust his instinct. He envied her sometimes, the carefree abandon that carried her through life. Even when she'd been knocked down, she always got back up with stars still in her eyes.

"We'll see. I still need more information before I say yes." He gestured to the surrounding kitchen. "Your grandmother certainly had a good eye when it came to decorating this place."

Arlowe's arched brow told him she saw through his obvious attempt to change the subject, but she let it go.

"She did. Based on her taste in locales and decorations, I think I would have liked her, if not for the will." Arlowe scrunched up her nose. "But Herr Blukker suggested she had her reasons. Maybe I'll learn more after the year's up."

Irritation crept in.

"You mean the anniversary of when you need to be married by? You're going to go through with it?"

"The marriage?" Arlowe shrugged. "I don't really have another option. I know," she said hurriedly as Hart set his fork down, "you've offered me money before. And I appreciate it, Hart, I really do. But I want to do this on my own."

"By selling yourself to someone you don't even know?" Hart snapped.

It didn't just hurt that Arlowe wouldn't accept his help. He'd always known when the time came for Arlowe to marry, he'd struggle. It would take a strong, kind man to be good enough for Arlowe. But for her to sacrifice herself for money to some nameless, faceless person who would marry her for her fortune? That just made him angry. She deserved so much more. Why was she doing this to herself?

"I'll come up with a list of candidates," Arlowe replied.

That she was calmer than Hart was just made him even angrier. He was the calm one, the rational one. He was the one who made decisions based on facts and numbers, not emotions and instincts. He was the one who was steady, dependable.

"Someone from the greenhouse? Or a new neighbor maybe?"

A pale pink stole into Arlowe's cheeks, but she didn't take the bait.

"Or someone from the bar."

"The bar?"

The pink deepened into bright red. "Just…a bar. I go to a bar sometimes."

Hart leaned in. "You're as bad of a liar as you were when we stole into Mrs. Long's blueberry patch and ate all the berries off her bushes."

"One, you ate more than I did. And two…" Arlowe sighed. "Look, I got a second job at a bar, okay?"

Hart stared at her. "You what?"

"I got a job at a bar in Kansas City," she repeated. "When Mom died and I—"

"When your mom died?" Hart leaned back and scrubbed a hand over his face. "For God's sake, Arlowe, I offered you money. You can't be working two jobs and taking care of Robert. When are you going to have time to go back to school?"

"I'm not going back. At least, not for agricultural landscaping. And," she added, nearly biting the words off, "I told you I don't want your money. How many times do I have to say it before you'll hear me, Hart?"

He gritted his teeth and shoved that argument to the back burner. They weren't done. Not by a long shot. But this new piece of information…

"When were you going to tell me?"

Arlowe put her elbows on the table and scrubbed her hands over her face.

"I don't know. You were so busy with work, and at first it was just one shift a week."

"And now?"

When she finally raised her head to look at him, it took everything he had to keep his mouth shut. She was tired, more tired than he had ever seen her. The shadows he had glimpsed in the picture were more vivid in the murky winter light. There was a listlessness he hadn't seen at first.

He gazed back at her, trying to keep his anger in check

even as he wanted to do something, fix the horrible thing that had happened to his best friend.

"Five to six nights a week."

He rubbed at his temple. "Arlowe—"

"It's hard, but I'm providing for my family."

The hint of pride beneath the exhaustion in her voice made him pause. He knew what it was like to take pride in his work. Those first two years at BioInnovations, days punctuated by meetings with creditors, loan officers, and inspectors, nights bleeding into a series of emails with investors and financiers as he sold off bits of his grandfather's lavish lifestyle to pay the massive list of overdue bills.

"And I understand that, Arlowe. I just think you're pouring yourself into caring for Robert and not taking enough time for yourself. Just like you're thinking about debts and Robert's care ahead of your own wants and happiness."

"How would you even know what I want, Hart?" she asked wearily. "You haven't been around for a long time."

Her words sucked the air out of his lungs. He stared at her, guilt pounding through his veins.

"No," he finally said. "No, I haven't."

Her throat bobbed as she swallowed hard. "Why?"

His jaw hardened. How could he possibly tell her everything now when she was under so much stress? How could he expect her to shoulder the burden of trying to shape BioInnovations into a company Dad would have been proud of? Sharing his own insidious grief over the loss of his father when she'd lost both her mother and grandmother far more recently would just be selfish.

"BioInnovations has demanded more than I expected."

She regarded him for a long moment, then sighed again. "You want me to let you in, but you won't even tell me what's been going on with your company. Just vague, noncommittal answers while you demand everything from me and think you can keep our friendship going with offers of money. Money can't fix everything, Hart."

Her words were a straight shot to his chest. Was that what she thought of him now? That money was all he cared about? That he had made his offers out of ease instead of putting in the hard work to maintain their friendship?

"Yet you're planning to marry for money?" he snapped back.

She blinked. When she smiled, it was a sad twist of her lips. One that made him feel like an absolute bastard.

"Yeah. I guess so."

She pushed back from the table and picked up her plate. He sat, not sure what to say to fix the last five minutes, as she put the plate and the other food lying out in the fridge. She stopped by the table, one hand drifting across the wooden surface. He watched her fingers trace the grain of the wood, a dark, circular knot in one of the boards. Soft, gentle caresses he could easily imagine on his skin.

Damn it.

"Text if you need anything."

She started to turn away. He stood and reached out, grabbed her hand.

"Arlowe…"

His voice trailed off as her head snapped around, amber eyes wide as she looked first at his face and then down to where his fingers were wrapped around hers. The sensation of her bare skin against his sank into his skin and ignited little fires beneath the surface. Fires that blazed into searing heat as she looked back up at him with the same want in her eyes.

She feels it, too.

Her sharp inhale broke the spell. Arlowe yanked her hand out of his.

"Good night, Hart."

She grabbed her phone and then she was gone. The somber

cry of the trumpet faded as she climbed the stairs, leaving him alone in the kitchen with shock reverberating through him.

What the hell had just happened? Never in the history of their friendship had either of them reacted to the other like that. But it had most definitely been awareness in Arlowe's eyes. Desire in the way her lips had parted as her fingers had tensed in his.

He glanced down at his plate, then looked away. Any appetite he'd had was gone, smothered by confusion and longing.

Except his longing had no place here. Whether or not they both felt this random physical attraction between the two of them was beside the point. They were both under an enormous amount of pressure. They'd barely seen each other for years. It only made sense for their feelings to be magnified by stress.

Frustrated, he paced to the window. Over half of it was obscured by snow, but just over the line of fluffy white he could see the courtyard beyond. He needed to focus on repairing their friendship, on supporting Arlowe as she dealt with this.

Arlowe had told him more than once she wanted to marry for love the way her mother and Robert had. The way his parents had. She'd lost so much these past eighteen months. From what little he'd gathered, her struggles had started long before Lynn's passing.

At what point had she stopped confiding in him? Why was she rejecting his offers to help? Most importantly, why was she so determined to give up everything she wanted?

The questions swirled in his mind as the storm raged outside.

CHAPTER EIGHT

Arlowe

A LOUD BANG jerked Arlowe out of a shallow sleep. She sat up, heart pounding, as the thunder receded with a slow, grumbling murmur. She blinked against the darkness, confused by the unfamiliar shapes in the room.

Austria. Your grandmother's castle.

Slowly, her heartbeat adjusted to normal. She brushed her hair out of her face as she tossed back the thick silk comforter. The fire still flickered in the grate, the warmth filling her chamber.

She grabbed her robe off of a high-backed chair and moved to the window. The snow was falling so hard she couldn't see anything but twirling white.

Thundersnow.

She'd only seen it twice before, once as a child when she'd been curled up in Mom's lap in the living room during a particularly cold and brutal January. The thunder had clapped and Arlowe had buried her face in her mother's chest. Her mom had gently stroked her back, shushing against Arlowe's hair as she'd whispered fairy tales and myths in her ear.

Arlowe's hand flew to her throat as she fought back tears. She'd been doing so much better lately keeping the grief at bay. Focusing on the benchmarks she'd set as she worked her way toward the ultimate goal of paying off Mom's and Robert's medical debts and earning enough to go back to school.

But one of the downsides of having time to herself was all the time she had to think. To think about Mom and how she was no longer here. To think about her father, grandfather, and grandmother, all gone. To think about the vows she would have to say to ensure her and Robert's financial future.

She turned back to the fire and held out her hands to the flames. She'd been dreaming before the thundersnow woke her. Bits and pieces came back to her in small flashes; her and Hart running across the field as kids. Ambling through the persimmon grove near the lake and popping the juicy fruit into their mouths.

Hart holding her hand as they walked under the stars. Hart hugging her at the base of the trellis before she climbed back into her room. Hart cradling the back of her head as he lowered his lips—

Arlowe snatched her hands away from the fire. What the heck? She had never imagined herself with Hart in all the years they'd been friends. Sure, he was handsome. But he'd always been Hart, her best friend, the big brother she'd never had. Never a romantic interest.

It was that damned moment in the kitchen, she thought irritably. When Hart had grabbed her hand and she'd physically felt little bolts of electricity race up her arm. There had been nothing different than any other time he'd held her hand over the years. But tonight, for whatever reason, it had been different. She'd been all too conscious of the roughness of his palm against her skin, the slight tightening of his fingers around hers when she'd looked at him. The flare of heat in his eyes had both thrilled and frightened her.

A log shifted in the grate, sending up a shower of sparks. Arlowe stepped back, glancing down to make sure none of the embers had fallen onto her robe. Whatever had happened between her and Hart in the kitchen had been an anomaly. A moment of madness in the midst of one of their few and only fights.

Besides, she thought as she grabbed a pair of fuzzy slippers from beside the bed and sat down on a large wooden trunk at the base of her bed to shove her feet into them, she and Hart were friends at the best of times. Right now, though, she wasn't sure what they were. She certainly wasn't going to risk the future of their friendship on one random moment of attraction.

She sneaked out of her room and into the hallway. The candle lights flickered on the walls, creating pockets of golden light on the plush rug. Arlowe slipped out of her room and walked down the hall toward the stairs.

The door to Hart's room was closed. She'd spent the rest of the evening in the library. Just before bed, she'd glanced through a couple rooms and found Hart in the same parlor where Herr Blukker had conducted the will reading. He'd been on his computer, a pair of glasses resting on his nose as he'd frowned at something on his screen. He'd looked...sexy.

She'd almost invited him to join her for a cup of tea. But as she'd watched his fingers fly across the keyboard, the narrowing of his eyes as he'd read something he hadn't liked, that same thrilling fear had intruded again. She wasn't ready to be around him. A good night's sleep would help her reset and face him tomorrow without these ridiculous flashes of attraction.

Arlowe gripped the banister of the staircase as she descended to the first floor. With her robe flaring out behind her and the chandelier glittering in the dim light above, she felt like a heroine straight out of a vintage noir film. It gave her a much-needed spark of pleasure as she made her way to the library.

The library fireplace was one of the few in the castle that

generated heat the old-fashioned way. Arlowe stacked several smaller sticks and lit them with a match. A few minutes later she added a thick log. The flames crawled over the log until a good-sized fire crackled in the hearth. She moved through the shelves, plucking books off that looked good until she had a nice-sized stack in her arms. Not that she'd make it through more than a few chapters of the first. But it was better to be prepared.

Arlowe set the stack down by the huge chair she'd taken up residence in last night. A thick wool blanket lay draped over one arm. Now all she needed was a drink.

She turned around and ran smack into a solid chest. Warm hands closed over her upper arms as she let out a startled yelp.

"Arlowe! It's just me."

Arlowe looked up at Hart, her heart still pounding.

"Why did you sneak up on me like that?"

Hart released her. She shivered, missing the warmth of his touch.

Oh my God, Arlowe, get a grip.

"I'm sorry. I heard you in here and thought…"

He ran a hand through his hair again. With just a T-shirt on, it was all too easy to actually see the muscles in his arm. The firelight played over his skin, creating mesmerizing shadows and hollows.

"Arlowe?"

Arlowe started. Okay, this was bad. Very, very, very bad. She hadn't been on a date since before Mom had passed. And it had been…

She winced. Literally years since she'd been with anyone.

You're tired. You just received multiple bombshells in a short amount of time. And Hart's hot. Of course you're responding to him. Just don't do anything stupid.

Relieved by her internal pep talk, Arlowe focused on Hart.

"Sorry." She gestured to the window. The snow had started

to taper off, but still fell in huge, thick flakes. "The thunder woke me up."

Hart's smile flashed white and bright in the dim lighting.

"Remember the stories your mom used to tell?" His smile faded. "I'm sorry. I didn't mean—"

"No." Arlowe swallowed hard. "That's been one of the hardest parts of the last year and a half. It hurts to think about her, but not thinking about her is worse." She smiled slightly. "I thought about her stories, too." She glanced at her chair, at the cozy little setting she'd arranged for herself, then turned back to Hart. "I was just going to get a drink before I settled in for some reading. Would you like to join me?"

Hart's face softened. "Yeah. I would."

They walked down the stairs into the kitchen. Hart pulled two wineglasses down from a top shelf, while Arlowe pulled one of the bottles of ice wine out of the refrigerator.

"You always helped me live a little outside my comfort zone."

Arlowe smiled as she poured. Golden wine splashed into the crystal glasses.

"I'm glad I'm good for something."

Silence fell for a moment. Then Hart circled around the table, plucked the wine bottle out of Arlowe's hand, and grasped her hands in his.

"You're good for a lot of things, Arlowe."

The dream flashed in her mind once more. The moment when Hart had reached out and grasped her hand in his, threading his fingers through hers with a casual intimacy that had made her feel cared for and cherished, mirrored the last time they'd walked across the field exactly.

But the near-kiss that had followed…that was a figment of her overactive imagination. One she needed to squelch before she did something that would permanently ruin their friendship.

"Thanks."

He reached up and cupped her face with one hand. Startled, she drew in a sharp gasp as her eyes flew up to meet his.

"That doesn't sound like you believe me."

She swallowed hard. "I…it's hard to believe when I feel like I'm failing."

The admission slipped off her tongue. Embarrassed, she tried to pull away, but Hart tightened his grip on her hand.

"You've been through a lot, Arlowe." His thumb stroked her cheek in a gentle caress that made her want to weep with the sweetness of it. "Why can't you give yourself the same grace you give everyone else?"

"It's just…" She let out a frustrated sigh. "Remember how our school counselor thought I'd be really good at nutrition? Or how Mom suggested a teaching degree because I liked teaching people about plants?"

"Yes."

"My life would be different if I'd done something practical. I could help a lot more than I am right now. I'm honestly not sure if I should even finish my agricultural landscaping degree."

"What would you do instead?"

"Education, maybe. Or nursing."

Hart frowned. "But those aren't your passions."

She shrugged. "No. But they'd certainly pay off far quicker than landscaping."

Hart's eyes darkened. "Arlowe, you're working two jobs to pay for your stepfather's surgeries and physical therapy. You're helping far more than most people would, given the circumstances."

Sensing another offer of financial aid was on the tip of his tongue, Arlowe leaned up and kissed his cheek. Her lips brushed his stubbled jaw. An unexpected thread of heat wound through her. She pulled her hand out of his grasp and picked up the wineglasses with an overly bright smile on her face.

"Shall we?"

She didn't wait for a reply but started up the stairs. A moment later Hart's footsteps sounded behind her. She didn't look back until they reached the library and she handed Hart his wine.

"To unexpected adventures." Arlowe avoided his eyes as she clinked her glass to his. "And to good friends."

"To friends."

The conviction in Hart's voice soothed some of Arlowe's tension. If he had given even more than a passing thought to their odd moment in the kitchen, he seemed more than willing to move beyond it.

Thank God.

No, their friendship wasn't what it used to be. But it was still there. Hart had flown hundreds of miles and trekked through the snow because he was worried about her. That kind of relationship wasn't worth risking over some random moment of attraction.

She took a sip of the wine, savoring the rich sweetness of apricot blended with something light and floral.

"Well this is just about perfect." She sank into her chair and pulled the blanket over her lap. "Book?"

One corner of Hart's mouth tilted up as he took in the stack of books.

"Sure you can spare one?"

Arlowe grabbed a Jane Austen off the top. Hart came over and shuffled through the books, opening a couple to read a few pages. Despite her best intentions, Arlowe's eyes drifted from a contentious argument between Elizabeth Bennet and Mr. Darcy to Hart's hands. He cradled a book in one hand, delicately handling the pages as he read. His eyes were fixed on the page, a slight smile on his face.

Her heart swelled. No matter the past eighteen months and the distance between them, Hart had come for her because he was worried about her. He'd left his conference and walked through a snowstorm to get to her. Yes, she was dealing with some pesky hormones. But she'd get over it. She was in a stunning library, reading a book in the middle of a snowstorm with her best friend.

A contented sigh escaped as she refocused on her book. Right now, in this moment, life was good.

Hart

Hart was in hell.

He reread the first page for what had to be the fifth time. But the words were a jumbled mess on the page as his eyes flicked over and over to Arlowe.

She was snuggled deep in the plush embrace of her chair, a blanket tucked around her legs. Her hair fell in a waterfall of dark brown curls over the arm of chair. A small smile played about her lips as she read. Every now and then she'd grope for her wineglass. Her lips closing about the rim of the glass had Hart wanting to climb the walls.

Once he'd hit puberty, he'd become more aware of Arlowe's looks. With her delicate features yet strong, elegant jawline and pointed chin, she had grown into a classic beauty. Yet she'd never lost the hint of mischief in her amber eyes, the spark of happiness that drew so many people into her orbit.

Hart glanced back down at his book. In the first two years he'd taken over BioInnovations, he'd flown back from the main manufacturing facility in New York to Kansas City every other weekend. He and Arlowe had spoken on the phone almost every day. Whenever he'd go home for visits, they'd slipped back into their friendship like he'd never been gone.

But once BioInnovations had started to turn a profit, those

visits had stretched out. Once a month, then once every couple months. That was when the phone calls had started to drop off, too. They'd briefly reconnected over Lynn's passing. But even that had faded as the months had passed.

Was he experiencing this odd and sudden attraction because he was just missing Arlowe? Was this actual attraction or just loneliness rearing its head? A desire to have his best friend back?

That had to be it. While he didn't miss Lucy as a romantic partner, it had been the first serious relationship he'd attempted since taking over BioInnovations. His first try at something personal. Much as he didn't like to admit it, running the company was lonely. He was away from home, from his family and friends. He was under an incredible amount of stress. Reconnecting with his best friend was just magnifying his emotions, making them seem more than they actually were.

Yes. That had to be it.

"You okay?"

His head snapped up. Arlowe was watching him, concern evident in her eyes.

"Yeah." He glanced at his watch. "I should probably get to bed. Early conference call."

"The deal with the pharmaceutical company?" At his nod, her eyes softened. "I'm sorry this is weighing on you."

Hart cocked his head to one side. "What do you mean?"

"You just look like you did during those first couple of years. Tired, stressed."

"Gee, thanks."

Arlowe rolled her eyes and threw back her blanket as he stood. "I'm not trying to insult you. Just…" Her voice faded as she gazed up at him. "I'm worried about you, Hart."

She parroted his earlier words back at him.

"Maybe…"

She cleared her throat. She was nervous, Hart realized with a jolt. Arlowe was never nervous.

"Maybe we could have breakfast in the morning. Say eight o'clock? Talk about…about the will and your company stuff."

An olive branch. One he reached and grabbed with both hands.

"I'd like that."

He wasn't keen on sharing his struggles with the Nessa Pharmaceuticals deal. But if that's what it took for Arlowe to finally open up, so be it.

He forced himself to walk over and kiss her lightly on the forehead. Just like he always had.

Except Arlowe smiled up at him as he pulled back. And when he looked down, he was suddenly close.

Too close.

She let loose a harsh exhale the same moment he drew in a shuddering breath, one full of want and need. Want for the woman in front of him. Need for the connection that had waned between them.

Arlowe lifted her chin. Her eyes focused on his lips. She breathed in deeply, her chest rising and falling as she drifted closer.

He'd never wondered what it would be like to kiss Arlowe. But now, as he gazed at her full lips, the dark sweep of lashes on porcelain skin as her eyes fluttered shut, he desperately wanted to find out.

A piece of firewood broke apart in the grate. The sound of wood on metal echoed through the cavernous library. Arlowe's eyes flew open and she stepped back with a gasp.

"God, Hart…" She ran both hands through her curls as she whirled away from him. "I'm so sorry. I didn't mean—"

"It's okay."

The words came out on a low growl. Arlowe's shoulders curved into a hunch as she winced at his harsh tone.

"Arlowe…"

But what else was there to say? They'd nearly kissed, and for what? To assuage loneliness? A knee-jerk response to the incredible stress they were both under?

"I'll see you at breakfast."

Arlowe nodded but still kept her back to him. The desire to go to her, to spin her around, bury his hands in that wild mane of curls and kiss her until they were both senseless, nearly overpowered him. It was only through sheer will that he forced himself to turn his back on Arlowe and walk out of the library.

Tomorrow, he swore to himself as he stalked up the stairs. Tomorrow they would talk over breakfast. He would find a way to persuade Arlowe to abandon fulfilling the terms of her grandmother's will, or at least take time to think about it.

And then, come hell or high water, he'd find his way out of this castle as quickly as possible.

CHAPTER NINE

Arlowe

THE SOFT CHIMING of a bell woke Arlowe from her sleep. Her fingers groped for her phone, but instead she knocked it on the floor. Groaning, she sat up and pushed her hair out of her face.

The room glowed with a foggy morning light. She'd kept the curtains open when she'd come back upstairs around two o'clock this morning so she could see the snow falling as she'd drifted off to sleep.

Except sleep had not offered her the reprieve she so desperately needed. No, sleep had been fitful bouts of rest, interrupted with lurid dreams of Hart kissing her by the fireplace, Hart sliding the robe off her shoulders, Hart scooping her up into his arms—

With a low moan she flung herself back onto the mound of pillows. What on earth was she going to do?

Her phone let out another soft yet persistent chime. Apparently phone reception was better on the upper floors. She sat up, leaned over the edge, and scooped her phone up off the floor. Frowning at the text from an unknown number, she clicked on the message.

Making sure you didn't turn into a frozen popsicle. This is Ivy, by the way.

Arlowe reread the message as her smile grew. Of all the people who could have reached out, Ivy was the last person she expected.

Still alive. The castle is actually cozy. Still snowing. How's NYC?

Bubbles popped up showing Ivy was replying. But then they faded and the phone went silent. Inspired by Ivy's outreach, Arlowe started up a new message to Mina.

Hey. Ivy texted to check on me, so I thought I'd do the same for you. How are you? How's baby?

She was in the middle of getting dressed when her phone dinged twice. The first was from Ivy.

Other than my arch-nemesis ruining my life, it's great.

Arlowe smiled. It was easy to picture Ivy, elegant and fierce in another vivid suit, going toe-to-toe with some corporate crook.

Knock 'em dead, Arlowe typed back.

Ivy's reply was short and confident: Always do. Stay safe.

Buoyed by the unexpected and pleasant interaction with her cousin, Arlowe opened the second message from Mina. Her face fell.

I'm okay. Ultrasound went great. But I think the baby's father is coming to see me. He wants to talk.

Arlowe quickly typed back: Do I need to come to you?

Mina didn't respond until Arlowe had washed her face and was about to open the door.

No. But thank you. That means a lot. Never fall for the wrong guy, Arlowe. It's hell.

Arlowe read and reread Mina's message.

Never fall for the wrong guy.

Hart's face appeared in her mind, shadows flickering over his face as he'd stared down at her mouth with hunger in his eyes.

Except, she reminded herself as she tossed her phone on the bed and starting pulling clothes out of her suitcase, she wasn't falling for Hart. The moment in the library had meant nothing, just like the moment in the kitchen. They'd both walked away, an unspoken agreement that they didn't want their odd attraction to go any further. This was just hormones, months of being apart, and a huge amount of stress creating an unnecessary and frustrating distraction.

Besides, she and Hart would never work as a couple. He was the definition of "wrong guy." He was serious and occasionally grumpy, focused and successful. She was impulsive and carefree, traits she'd liked in herself before.

But now those traits had backed her into a corner. If she had thought things through, she could be working in a hospital or classroom right now, earning a steady paycheck with health insurance that would have paid for so many of Robert's bills. She didn't have time to be impulsive. Instead, she was working two jobs and barely keeping up with the farm while Hart flew around the world to international conferences and dated opera stars.

Even if they were to talk about the attraction between them, he would never be interested in her romantically. Not when he had the kind of wealth at his fingertips most people could only dream of and could have his pick of successful women. He was stressed, but he had also created something incredible. She could never leave Kansas City. She'd never ask him to leave New York, wouldn't risk the ugliness of resentment developing later on and driving a wedge so deeply between them they'd never recover.

Which meant any exploration of this sudden attraction between them was unnecessary.

The thought should have made her feel relieved. Instead, it just further soured her mood as she sent one last reassuring text to Mina before heading downstairs.

The kitchen was empty. A quick glance at the clock revealed it was just before eight. Arlowe started water brewing for coffee and took stock of what was in the fridge. As the minutes ticked by, her chest tightened. Had Hart overslept? Or maybe he'd just forgotten?

It was nearly eight-twenty before she finally heard his footsteps on the stairs.

"Good morning," she said over her shoulder.

Hart grunted. Her lips quirked. At least some things hadn't changed. Hart had never been much of a morning person.

She glanced over her shoulder, then did a double take. Dressed in black slacks and a navy pullover with the sleeves rolled up to his elbows, he could have easily been a model in an ad for men's fashion. His hair was slightly mussed, his eyes still heavy with sleep.

"Sorry," he grumbled, thankfully missing her wide-eyed gaze. "Conference call ran over."

Of course. Work.

"No problem. Coffee?"

Hart nodded but moved in front of her as she started for the stove. "I can get it, Arlowe. You don't need to wait on me like I'm a guest."

"But you are." Arlowe stifled the fluttering in her veins and shouldered past him. "Besides, it gives me something to do."

"You never were one to sit still."

"Too much to do to sit still."

Arlowe poured him coffee before pulling several plates out of the refrigerator. A few minutes later she had set out a bowl of sweet, fluffy buns filled with raspberry jam, a plate of artfully arranged meats and cheeses, and shredded pancakes dusted with powdered sugar.

"I could get used to eating like this," Hart said as he sat down. "Thank you."

"You're welcome." Arlowe smiled slightly. "I remember your dad always used to make those huge pancakes."

"And cook them using an entire stick of butter."

Grinning at the shared memory, they dug into their breakfast.

"What do you eat for breakfast nowadays?" Arlowe asked between bites of a sweet roll.

"Protein bars. That's if I have time for breakfast."

Arlowe frowned. "If you have time?"

"I usually walk through the factory floor at seven. Shift changes are at seven, three, and eleven. If I get there at seven, I can say goodbye to the crew going off shift and the day crew coming on. And then three o'clock I see the evening crew."

"Your dad would be proud of you."

Hart's fork stopped midair. Suddenly conscious of what she'd just said, Arlowe ducked her head.

"I'm sorry—"

"No." Hart set his fork down and picked up his coffee. "Like you said, not thinking of him is doing his memory a disservice. He started this legacy when he stood up to my grandfather and told him he wasn't going to cut corners on the manufacturing equipment."

Arlowe smiled. "Easy to picture him doing that."

"Everything I learned about honor and integrity, I learned from him. He loved Missouri. But I know a part of him always missed New York. Missed not being a part of the family legacy."

"And now you've rewritten that."

Hart's dark brows drew together in a frown. "I'm trying."

"But something's wrong." Arlowe tilted her head to one side when Hart shot her a mock glare. "You said we could talk about both my problem and yours this morning."

"I did." He sat back in his chair. "There's a deal on the table with a company called Nessa Pharmaceuticals. They've supposedly developed a nonaddictive, highly effective pain medicine. Their clinical trials were almost perfect. The proposal is excellent. They've even offered BioInnovations' employees a chance for profit sharing down the road."

"Sounds good."

"Yes." Hart hesitated. "Too good. I've never had a pharmaceutical company come to me with such stellar data. Profit sharing is almost unheard of."

"Could they have falsified their data?"

"No, I followed up with the centers they worked with. People I've worked with ever since I took over. The preclinical research phase started seven years ago. They've gone through three phases of clinical testing with thousands of patients. The drug just went through the review and approval process." Hart shook his head. "I'm concerned that my personal feelings toward Nessa's CEO, Blaine Jones, are inhibiting my ability to look at this situation accurately."

"There's a history there?"

"No." Hart frowned. "But when I met him, he just seemed to be in a rush. A little too much salesman for my personal tastes." He shook his head. "But I would be pushing, too, if I had just gone through seven years of clinical testing and was trying to get my product on the market. Their trial results are exceptional, and the drug itself could be revolutionary in terms of managing pain without the potential for addiction. It's the kind of deal that could take BioInnovations to the top."

"And that's what you want?"

The determination in his eyes was not unexpected. But the pain lingering beneath the surface shocked her.

"It's what I have to do."

For his father. The word went unspoken, but she felt his resolve, the weight of a grief she had certainly witnessed in that first year after his father's passing but hadn't realized still haunted him.

Hurt lanced through her, followed quickly by guilt. They'd both done their share of concealing. It didn't matter who had first hidden the truth, not when they'd both kept things from each other.

"I admire everything you've done, Hart, and I understand wanting a deal like this. But don't you think you should dig a little more? I know you, and you wouldn't be feeling this if there weren't something to be concerned about."

A veil dropped over Hart's eyes. "The client has given us until Friday."

Arlowe glanced out the window. "But that's in two days. How are you going to get out of here?"

"I have a helicopter on standby to pick me up as soon as the wind is favorable and take me to the airport in Salzburg." He glared at the window. "Hopefully the storm will clear up soon."

Arlowe sat back in her chair. What had she expected? That Hart would spend a few days here and just shirk his duties? He literally ran a multimillion-dollar manufacturing empire. He could barely afford a few hours, let alone days. Just another difference between the two of them.

She forced a smile onto her face. "I understand."

Silence fell between them for a few moments.

"Have you decided how you're going to propose to your unknown Prince Charming?"

It took Arlowe a moment to realize Hart was teasing her. Relief flooded her. He'd just needed time to adjust to the idea of her entering into a temporary marriage.

"Not yet. I need to figure out the details first."

"Such as?"

This was good. Hart had always been her go-to when she'd needed to talk through ideas. He never discouraged her—at least, not until her trip to Austria and the marriage. But, she conceded, those were pretty big leaps from getting his advice on how to deal with a high school bully and if getting a degree in landscape architecture was a good plan.

Still, with his business knowledge, he was the perfect person to talk with about how she could keep this marriage strictly to a business arrangement.

"I need to come up with a list first."

Hart nodded, his eyes on his coffee. "Lists are good."

"No one comes to mind immediately."

No one she could stand being married to for a year, at least. But then again, she didn't need to live with the man. Just say the words, sign the papers, and divorce after whatever period of time she could get away with.

"There are some customers at the bar that aren't bad."

Hart's hand tensed on his coffee cup.

"A barfly?"

Arlowe rolled her eyes. "It's a hotel bar. Most of them are businessmen coming in for conferences or meetings."

"Uh-huh."

Hart's tone had decidedly cooled. But Arlowe ignored it. He didn't have to like who she picked.

"I'm pretty comfortable with offering one million."

Hart's eyes narrowed. "Seven percent? To marry you?"

"Should I offer more?"

"No. For God's sake, no."

Hart stood up and stalked over to the window, his body coiled tight like a spring. Arlowe waited a full minute before she stood and approached him slowly.

"Hart? I'm sorry. I thought…the way you teased me, I thought you were okay with this now."

Hart turned to face her. The kitchen shrank as his eyes pierced hers, her lungs constricting as he closed the distance between them.

"You thought I would be okay with you marrying some random man to inherit what should rightfully belong to you without any stipulations?"

Touched, she reached out and grabbed his hand, ignoring the now-familiar sparks that danced up her arm.

"Hart, it's sweet of you to be upset on my behalf, but I've accepted it." *Mostly.* "It's not ideal, but it's not like it'll be a real marriage. We won't even live together. It'll just be in name only, and then after the third anniversary, I'll get divorced and move on with my life."

If she said it with enough conviction, she could almost believe it was all okay. Almost ignore that a part of her heart ached at her wedding being rooted in necessity instead of love.

Hart squeezed her hand, then released it. Before Arlowe could say or do anything else, he leaned down, placing one hand on either side of her chair and caging her between his arms. Her breath caught in her chest as she slowly looked up to meet his gaze.

"I have a different idea."

"Oh?" she managed to squeak out.

"Yes. Marry me instead."

CHAPTER TEN

Hart

ARLOWE'S EYES WIDENED. "What?"

His eyes dropped to her mouth, then back up to her eyes. He stood, putting needed distance between them as he moved back over to his chair and sat.

"If you insist on following through on getting married, then marry me."

Arlowe shook her head. "No, Hart, I can't ask you—"

"You didn't. I'm offering."

The idea had come to him shortly after he'd left the library last night. If Arlowe was hell-bent on doing things her own way, at least he could ensure she ended up with someone who wouldn't try to steal her fortune. It wasn't his first choice either, especially given the internal battle he was now fighting over his feelings. But at least this way he could help Arlowe and keep her safe.

Stop lying to yourself. Not his first choice? Compared to Arlowe exchanging vows with a complete stranger, marrying her himself was the only choice. The image of her signing her last name as "Sinclair" sent a primal thrill through him.

Except Arlowe wasn't jumping at the idea like he thought she would. No, instead she was watching him with what almost looked like fear.

"I just… I don't think that's a good idea."

"A good idea?" Hart repeated. Anger slipped in, molten hot, and filled his chest. "You'd rather marry a random businessman and risk him coming after the rest of your fortune than marry me?"

"It's not that." Arlowe sucked in a deep breath. "Look, you and I haven't spent a lot of time together recently. We both know things are strained between us."

He watched her, but she wasn't showing any of her usual tells that she was hiding something: the slight wrinkling of her nose, the almost imperceptible blink.

"I noticed it, too."

"And it's understandable. You've been gone and I've been under a lot of stress. Neither of us have been great about reaching out."

He thought back to what she had let slip yesterday. A quick text to Robert the night before had confirmed Arlowe wasn't just working eight hours a day at the greenhouse but another six to eight at the bar. No wonder she looked exhausted.

His hours, however, were self-induced. He had a great executive team he could fall back on. But he didn't want to follow in his grandfather's footsteps and hand them the duties he should be performing. He wasn't going to ask anything of his team that he wouldn't do himself.

Still, as Arlowe bit down on her lower lip, he realized he had carried his obsession too far. What else had he missed out on the last few years? Worse, was it too late to fix things?

"I don't want to lose you, Hart."

Arlowe's quiet words pulled him back into the present. The fear in her voice put a stop to his anger.

"You're not going to."

"Our friendship is already complicated." Arlowe reached out and grabbed his hand. "I don't want to make things worse by adding a marriage of convenience to the mix."

He understood her concerns…to a point. The possibility of

Arlowe's and his friendship ceasing to exist had never been a concern. She had been a part of his life for twenty years. There was life before Arlowe, which was pleasant. And then there was life after Arlowe, which had been like waking up one day and realizing the world wasn't full of muted colors but bright, vivid hues. Yes, he was going to have to come to terms with his errant emotions and reconcile them with Lucy's seemingly accurate observation. But he would resist whatever he had to if it meant keeping Arlowe in his life. He could deal with feelings and still offer her marriage to secure her inheritance.

Their friendship had survived a lot. Why couldn't it survive this, too?

He opened his mouth to ask that very question when his phone buzzed in his pocket. A five-minute warning alarm before his nine o'clock call with his chief finance officer.

"I have another call coming up. Let's take a break, talk again this afternoon."

For a moment, Arlowe looked unbearably sad. But then her expression smoothed out as she raised her chin and nodded.

"I understand."

She understood, but that didn't mean he hadn't hurt her. Every step up the stairs, every step away from her, felt like a chasm widening between them. One he had started years ago when he'd withdrawn from her and thrown himself into work. He'd told himself it had been to keep her safe.

But how much of it had been for himself? How much of his reluctance to share had been more in the interest of self-preservation and not being comfortable with his own emotions?

He paused in the grand hall and glanced back at the door leading downstairs. There had been plenty of tense moments. But sharing meals with Arlowe, relaxing with her in the library sipping on wine, seeing her smile as she tried on those outlandish dresses…he missed the simplicity of what life used to be. He missed not having a schedule written down to the minute of every day.

Most of all, he missed Arlowe. In the one day he had spent there, he already felt more himself than he had in months. Even though they had their share of tense moments, he had forgotten how much he enjoyed just being around her, how much her presence made him...happy.

Among other things.

Heat crept down his spine as he relived the moments of holding her in his arms outside the castle, of nearly kissing her in the library. Aside from a casual flicker of response in high school, which he had chalked up to being a teenage boy, he had never paid attention to Arlowe's body.

He was paying attention now.

He closed his eyes. What was wrong with him? He had never once harbored any romantic or physical thoughts about Arlowe. Yet he could barely be around her now without noticing the traces of gold in her curls, the underlying huskiness of her laugh, the faint dimple in her cheek.

His breath rushed out. Maybe it was better that Arlowe hadn't immediately accepted his proposal. Focusing his attention on work was an opportunity for him to reset, get his body under control, and finish things with Nessa Pharmaceuticals one way or another. God willing, the winds would die down enough later today or tomorrow for him to get back to Lyon in time for the meeting.

He'd take care of Nessa first. Then he'd deal with his feelings for Arlowe. Get them under control so he could be in a better place to argue for her marrying him if that's truly the route she was set on.

He'd fix this. One way or another, he'd fix it.

Six hours later, Hart sat back and let his head drop back. He'd spent almost the entire time in meetings, phone calls, and reviewing even more documentation. His team had done an incredible job, as usual, analyzing the aspects of the contract that pertained to their various divisions. Everyone was on board with moving forward with the contract.

He closed his laptop and stood. He had kept his concerns quiet, waiting to see if anyone else would say something. But everyone had only positive things to say. He hadn't been able to bring himself to throw a wrench into the team's plans this late in the game, all because of an illogical whim.

On the positive side, the series of work calls and meetings had kept his attention off Arlowe. But now, with at least an hour before his next video conference with his vice president, everything came pouring back in. Her refusal to marry him. Her refusal to accept his money. Her refusal to let him into her life, even as she contemplated marrying a complete stranger.

Was that alternative truly better than marrying Hart? Had he screwed things up so badly by his withdrawal that a stranger offered more comfort and security than he did?

With resignation hanging over him like a dark cloud, he walked downstairs. Arlowe was standing by the door, dressed in a parka, gloves, and snow boots.

He frowned. "What are you doing?"

"Going out for a walk."

He gritted his teeth. Arlowe walking through the wilds of Austria was tough enough. The thought of her hiking back up to the castle by herself had his protective instincts kicking into high gear.

"No."

Her hands dropped down to her hips as her eyes narrowed.

"Excuse me, Hart David Sinclair. You don't tell me what to do."

"What happens if you fall in the snow?"

"What would have happened if you did, trekking up here?" she shot back.

"Well, I'm…"

His voice trailed off. She smiled sweetly.

"A man? Yes, Hart, I'm fully aware."

Her words set off a spark beneath his skin. His gaze swept her up and down before he was even aware of what he was doing.

"Oh?"

That same attractive blush stole into her cheeks again.

"Not like that!" she practically hissed. "I just meant…" She rolled her eyes and yanked her zipper up. "I've been stuck inside all morning, and the snow has finally died down. Unless you're going to tie me up and leave me here, I'm going. And," she added with a sudden gleam in her golden-brown eyes, "I'll remind you when we played pirates, I was ten times better at knots than you were."

"Maybe I got better." He stepped back as she walked over to one of the drapes and tugged on the curtain cord. "Don't even think about it."

She shot him a grin. "Glad we're on the same page."

And she walked out the door with her curls bouncing and her head held high. He waited for one moment, tamped down the dueling curls of pleasure and regret, and jogged to the closet to grab his own coat.

Arlowe

It was like walking through a winter wonderland. Snow clung to the thick evergreen branches. Every now and then a stray gust of wind stirred the needles and a shimmer of white sparkles fell to the ground. The mountains were draped in snow. If she looked just right, she could make out the rooftops of Lärchenthal.

She smiled and twirled in a circle.

"It barely snowed last year. I feel like this is my reward for being patient."

Hart snorted behind her. "I don't recall patience ever being one of your virtues."

She turned around and stuck her tongue out. "I was actually very patient. I even ate ice cream the night before."

The pause in their conversation was filled by the soft crunch of their footsteps.

"Ice cream?"

"Yes. Eat ice cream the night before you want it to snow." She scoffed. "Everyone knows that."

A solid thirty seconds passed before Hart asked, "Did it work?"

She huffed. "I didn't eat enough."

Another snort. "One scoop vanilla, one scoop cookies and cream, chocolate syrup?"

Nostalgia warmed her chest. He remembered. It shouldn't have mattered. But it did.

"Clearly I should have two scoops of each."

"Clearly."

The tension knotted around her heart slowly eased with every step they took. This was more like the old them. No odd moments of awareness, of eyes meeting and drifting to places they shouldn't.

No proposals.

The tension was back in the blink of an eye. What on earth had Hart been thinking? It was sweet of him. And not a bad idea. If he'd asked her a few years ago, she would have taken him up on it in a heartbeat.

But this wasn't two years ago. This was now, after months of not seeing each other, after barely even texting. She was worried about whether or not she and Hart could maintain their friendship now that their lives had changed so drastically. Getting married, even just for the sake of a will, would only complicate things further.

That her heart beat a little fast when Hart proposed was

another consideration. She wasn't saying yes to anything as long as she was responding to him like this. That was just setting herself up to say or do the wrong thing in the heat of the moment and completely ruin their friendship forever.

She had lost Mom. She had barely known her father and never met her grandmother, but losing two more members of her family so close to Mom cut deep. She had Robert, Hart's mom, Francine, and Hart.

She wasn't doing anything that could risk her losing him.

Her good mood evaporated as she walked down the drive. She tried to talk herself out of her guilt, but it was hard. If she'd gotten her nursing degree, or teaching, or almost any other degree her counselor had suggested, she'd be further along in life. She could have provided more for her mom and Robert. She couldn't say whether or not the car accident would have happened. But she could have at least made Mom's last couple of years more comfortable.

And therein, she realized, lay another fear. She and Hart had barely seen each other the past few years. He wasn't fully aware of how far behind she'd fallen, how little she'd accomplished while he'd continued to climb. How much confidence she'd lost in herself. If she told him everything—the medical bills, selling the land—would he see her differently? Less than?

Okay, I'm spiraling.

She breathed in deeply. Crisp snow and the woodsy richness of pine trees filled her lungs. It was a hard conversation she needed to have with Hart, and the sooner the better. Her fears were widening the gap between them.

She would invite him to come stay with Robert and her, she decided as her hiking boots sank into the fluffy snow. A long weekend after he wrapped up this business with Nessa. He and Robert had become closer after Hart's father passed, and she knew Hart still called him every few weeks.

She glanced over at Hart. In his navy blue parka and black pants, the wind ruffling his dark hair, he looked ridiculously handsome.

And also ridiculously stressed. Lines of tension were etched into his skin on either side of his mouth. His eyes were distant, focused not on the stunning snowy landscape but probably on this contract that was bothering him so much.

She frowned. Why was he so hell-bent on ignoring his emotions? On not at least sharing his concerns with his team?

They reached the bridge. Arlowe stood for a long moment, breathing in the crisp air as she savored the view. How long had it been since she'd simply had time to stand and take everything in? Appreciate little details like the shushing of the wind through the trees, the little mounds of snow clinging to the evergreen branches?

Out of the corner of her eye, she saw Hart pull out his phone and glance at the screen. She blew out a breath. It was easy to be frustrated with him. But really, hadn't she been doing something similar? Based on what little he had said, his dedication to his company was rooted in more than just personal choice. Grief was driving him, just as it was driving her.

Inspiration struck. She took a few steps back and reached up, grabbing a clump of snow off a nearby branch. She slowly packed it into a ball, waiting until Hart slipped his phone back in his pocket before letting it fly.

The snowball broke against Hart's back. He whirled around, eyes wide.

"What was that?"

She leaned down and started scooping snow.

"Snowball, Sinclair."

She faked throwing the next snowball, waited until Hart darted to the right before launching it right into his chest.

"Bull's-eye!"

Hart stared at her for a long moment. She froze. Had she miscalculated?

And then he leaned down, scooping a large pile of snow into his arms and tossing it toward her. The snow showered down, eclipsing her view for a moment as she threw up her arms.

"Hart!"

A snowball hit her shoulder. She darted off to the side and hid behind a tree.

"I owe you, Banks."

"Bring it on, Sinclair," she goaded, her heart pounding.

She crouched down and made another snowball before standing and peeking around the tree. Hart was stalking toward her, three snowballs cradled in one arm and another in his opposite hand. She eyed a snow-laden branch, waited until Hart was just beneath it before throwing her snowball. It hit, sending a shower of snow cascading down onto Hart's head.

"Ha!"

Her victory was short-lived. He charged toward her. She screeched and tried to run, but Hart was faster. He grabbed her around the waist with one arm and shoved a snowball down the back of her parka.

"Hart!"

Her shriek of indignation was ruined by her giggling. It started as a bubble in her throat until it was bursting out of her. Pure, uninhibited laughter. She twisted in Hart's grip. He stumbled and they both tumbled into the snow. She was still laughing as she rolled off him.

"You're ridiculous," she wheezed between laughs.

Hart rose up on one arm next to her and smiled slightly. "I haven't heard you laugh like that in a long time."

"Yeah, it's been a while." She pushed up on her elbows. "Thank you."

"I should be the one thanking you." He glanced around. "It's been a long time since I just had fun."

"Me, too." She hesitated, then decided to take a leap. "I think we've both been avoiding a lot of things. Easy to do when you're sad."

Hart stiffened. Then, slowly, he nodded.

"It is."

He looked back at her. His smile dimmed as his eyes dropped down to her lips. The air went from freezing to sizzling in a split second as her gaze dipped to his mouth, then back up to his eyes. It wasn't just her.

Oh God, it wasn't just her.

This was crazy. But the thought didn't stop her from swaying forward, from sucking in a shuddering breath in a desperate effort to get some air into her lungs.

Hart—her best friend, her confidant, her rock—leaned down and kissed her.

His lips pressing against Arlowe's made her feel like she was shooting out of a cannon—an exhilarating rush with an underlying current of fear pulsing beneath the surface. But the fear was quickly buried beneath sensation. Pure, wonderful sensation coursed through her body as she slowly leaned into him.

A low growl vibrated against her lips. Thrilled, she sighed just as Hart's mouth parted. The sheer intimacy of the moment seared itself into her brain. One hand shyly crept up before resting on Hart's chest. His heart beat fast beneath her palm.

"Hart," she murmured.

He went still. Then he stood up so quickly she barely had time to catch her breath.

CHAPTER ELEVEN

Arlowe

"ARLOWE..."

This time, the guttural edge to his voice wasn't desire. It was regret—shame, sliced so sharp it pierced right through her ribs.

"I'm fine, Hart." She ignored the offered hand and pushed herself to her feet. "Really."

"That should have never happened."

The pain stabbed deeper, landing somewhere in the vicinity of her heart. Would they be able to move past this? This was why she hadn't wanted to dig any deeper into their sudden attraction. Why the thought of marrying Hart, especially with things so mixed-up between them, sent fear spiraling through her. What if it ruined what little bit of friendship they had left?

She forced out a quiet laugh.

"I agree. That was weird."

His eyes narrowed. "Weird?"

"Yeah. Like kissing my best friend."

Her joke fell flat. His lips turned down.

"Hart." It felt like her lips were about to crack, she was smiling so hard. "A simple kiss isn't the end of the world."

"Simple."

His voice was flat, his face devoid of expression. A string of curse words ran through her mind as she'd scrambled to say something that wouldn't permanently fracture their relationship.

"Yes." She had shoved her hands into the pockets of her parka, trying to portray a confident casualness she'd been nowhere close to feeling. "Come on, Hart. You said it yourself, that was a mistake. Let's just forget it, okay?"

Finally, he nodded. Just once—an efficient movement that made it possible for her to release the breath she hadn't even realized she'd been holding.

"All right."

"Great." She nodded toward the castle. "Hot chocolate sounds good right now."

Before he could say anything else, she started walking. She didn't look back to see if he was following, didn't pause to gaze at the trees or the mountains or the lake shimmering in the distance. She just needed to get inside the castle—and away from Hart.

They made it inside. Hart barely closed the door before she'd shucked off her gloves, hat, and parka. She quickly walked into the mudroom off to the side, yanked off her boots, and laid everything out to dry. She walked back out, eyes focused on the stairs, the chandelier—anything but Hart—as she'd sailed past him.

"I'll get to work on the hot chocolate."

She was halfway up the stairs when Hart called her name. She froze, her hand clenching on the railing. She just wanted to get to her room. Wanted to catch her breath, dissect what just happened between them.

Wanted to nurse her wounds in private.

But she couldn't let Hart see how much that kiss had affected her. So she slowly turned and looked down. Hart stood in the middle of the hall beneath the chandelier. His hair was ruffled, his elegant cheekbones a touch red from the cold. Dressed in all black, he suddenly looked dangerous. Forbidden. Sexy.

Stop, stop, stop!

"You sure you're okay?"

The low rumble of his voice filled the room and echoed off the walls. Who knew an echo could make one's heart beat faster?

"I am."

He stared at her from across the room. She tensed. Hart had always had an inner lie detector that made it impossible for her to get anything by him. He might not have been as in tune with her emotions as he once had been, but if she disappeared down the stairs to the kitchen, he would know something was wrong. So she stood and waited, her head cocked to one side, a smile frozen on her face.

Then, thankfully, Hart looked away.

"I'll pass on the hot chocolate. I have another meeting."

His rejection cut like a knife. Not just rejecting her but choosing his career over everything else.

Hart didn't say another word as he stalked across the hall in the direction of the stone staircase. She waited until she couldn't hear his footsteps anymore before she practically ran down to the kitchen. She forced herself to pour milk into the kettle and set it on the stove before sinking into a chair.

What am I going to do?

The kiss played on a loop in her head. That flare of want in Hart's eyes, blood pounding through her veins so hard she thought she might faint, and then that wonderful moment when their lips had finally met.

It had been exhilarating. Incredible. Yet there had also been one second when a different feeling had rushed through her. One that worried her far more than her physical response to Hart.

Kissing him had felt right. Like coming home after being gone for too long.

Arlowe stood and paced the kitchen, across to the window then back to the door. Over and over again as she bit down on her lip.

Turning down Hart had clearly been the right thing to do.

If she had said yes and married him before dealing with this, it would have been a disaster. Not just for their friendship, but for her. Right now her emotions were manageable. Irritating and ill-timed, but not beyond her power to control.

Marriage would change that. A couple years ago, that wouldn't have been true. But if she were to say yes now, feeling like this… It was easy to imagine saying goodbye to her faceless husband when he was nothing more than a stranger she was marrying for money. The thought of saying goodbye to Hart, though, releasing him to fall in love and marry someone else, tied her chest into tight knots.

Her breath rushed out. If she married Hart, she wouldn't be able to hold back her feelings. She'd fall way too deep.

The kettle let out a shrill whistle that jolted her from her revelation. She finished the hot chocolate and walked back up to the main level. She walked over to one of the long windows next to the massive doors and stared out over the valley. It offered a stunning view of the lake, the town, the mountains. But now, as she gazed at the horizon, she saw a hint of dark building. The trees just beyond the window moved, stirred by an unseen wind.

Arlowe's heart sank. Another storm was coming.

She needed to figure herself out, and quick. If she was right, and the storm was even close to the one they'd just experienced, she and Hart were going to be stuck together for quite some time.

Hart

Hart frowned as wind lashed at the windows of the parlor. Mother Nature had decided to work herself up into another frenzy. The snow had dropped off an hour ago, but the wind hadn't stopped. It wasn't the pleasant breeze of earlier but a harsh, fierce wind, the kind that howled around the corners of the castle and slammed itself relentlessly against the stone walls.

He'd been on a video conference call with Katherine and his head of development, Jack, when Arlowe had texted him that another storm was on the way. That had been followed by a phone call from the helicopter company he'd reached out to, confirming that an extraction was going to be impossible for at least the next thirty-six hours.

He would not be attending the meeting with Nessa Pharmaceuticals on Friday. Not in-person, at least.

Despite the bad weather, the electricity had held. The electric fireplace in the parlor had kept the room cozy. He'd conducted several meetings with various members of his team and a phone conference with Blaine Jones. A conversation that hours later still had Hart's jaw tightening.

Blaine was up to something. His assurances that he was just trying to keep his company moving forward without dallying too long on one specific contract had been a legitimate reason. But there had still been something in Blaine's tone, an underlying urgency, that had made Hart end the call with no resolutions.

He closed the lid on his laptop and rubbed at the bridge of his nose. He'd been on the phone or his laptop for nine hours nonstop. He'd glanced up from one of his meetings to realize three hours had passed and he was hungry. When he set aside his computer to run down to the kitchen, he'd opened the door to a tray on the floor. The smells had hit him and made his stomach growl: roasted chestnuts, crispy chicken, and the rich scent of butter and underlying herbs.

A small piece of paper with Arlowe's looping cursive had rested next to a covered bowl.

Chestnut soup, chicken Wiener Schnitzel, and bread. Don't forget to eat.

He didn't know how long he'd stared down at the tray. But finally he'd picked it up and brought it in. The soup had been silky smooth with a hint of wine. The breadcrumb coating on the Schnitzel had been baked to golden perfection. Even the bread, a dark rye served with rosemary butter, had been delicious, thick and warm.

Despite the way he'd left her, she'd still thought of him.

He picked up the note from where he'd set it right after lunch. Traced his fingers over the familiar handwriting, the elegantly written initials. He read it again. A simple note. Nothing to indicate Arlowe's frame of mind.

Had she been thinking of the kiss when she'd written it? Because, despite Hart's best intentions to focus exclusively on work, his mind had returned again and again to that kiss. To how Arlowe had sunk into him, how her lips had parted for him. How every last worry had fled his mind and the world had dropped away as her hand had settled over his heart.

And then she'd whispered his name in a voice that was both familiar and foreign. Arlowe's sweet, melodic tone, underlain by a husky desire that had sent a cascade of vivid images through his mind.

Images he had no business entertaining of a woman who had just rejected his marriage proposal.

A thump sounded out in the hall. Hart shoved the note in his pocket and stood.

"Arlowe?" he called as he crossed the room and walked out into the hall.

Arlowe, dressed in a fluffy white robe that covered her from neck to ankle, knelt on the floor with several books stacked in the crook of her arm. She was trying to balance them while she picked another off the floor.

"Let me help."

Arlowe grabbed the book on the floor and started to stand. "It's okay. I—"

The stack started to lean. Hart reached Arlowe's side just in time to put a hand on the books and keep them from falling.

Arlowe blew out a harsh breath as she avoided his eyes. "Thanks."

Frustrated, Hart stared down at her. Why was she so hell-bent on refusing anything from him? She'd never been one to mooch off him in the past, but they'd always been there for each other. Always helped one another whenever they could. Even something as small as helping her with a book was rejected now.

He glanced down at the book he'd picked up. Small and bound in leather, two initials had been carved into the cover.

"*DG*," he murmured. "Desdemona? Your grandmother?"

Arlowe nodded. "I found it tucked on a shelf in the library. I spent most of the day doing a little research, but I'm hoping to read some of it tonight. Maybe get a little more insight into…well, everything."

"Research on what?"

She hesitated a moment. Then, finally, she looked up at him. The exhaustion was more pronounced tonight, her eyes slightly dull and her skin pale.

"Going back to school."

"Oh?"

He smiled slightly. At least there would be one good thing coming out of this whole mess. Arlowe was talented. She'd maintained the gardens at her house ever since she'd been in middle school, always adding this native flower or that rare plant no one else had ever heard of. He'd always admired and envied her creativity, the way she could simply talk to someone and then look at their garden and immediately know what flowers to plant, how to lay out the beds, what kind of lighting accents would highlight the foliage at night. No, it wasn't a common degree. But Arlowe had developed a solid plan for herself. She deserved to have another shot at making her dream come true.

"I'm leaning toward education."

His mind screeched to a halt. "What?"

"If I take just a few more agriculture classes and some education courses, I can graduate sooner and get a teaching job."

If there had been even a shred of excitement in her voice, a trace of happiness, he would have let it lie. But there was nothing except resignation, a weary woman accepting defeat.

"Arlowe—"

"I'm not squandering my second choice." Her arms tightened around the books. "I made a foolish decision before. I'm not going to make one again."

"I thought we talked about this. Why would you pick something that's not your passion? Especially when you're so close?" Hart asked as they reached the top of the stairs.

Arlowe sighed. "It wasn't practical, Hart. I had my head in the clouds. Maybe if I'd gotten a scholarship and been able to go full-time, I could have made it work. But dragging a four-year degree out over seven years—"

"So you could pay out of pocket." Hart slid a hand under her elbow and turned her to face him, waited until she finally lifted her chin and looked him in the eye. "How is being financially responsible being impractical?"

"Because I knew how long it would take for me to become successful in that field. I knew," she repeated, her chin dipping toward her chest, "and I still did it."

"And if Robert hadn't lost his job, you wouldn't have had to pause your degree." Hart held up a hand as her head snapped up, her eyes flashing amber fire. "I'm not blaming Robert. The manufacturing plant shutting down was not his fault. Nor was the fact that everyone from the plant then went out applying for the same jobs. I know Robert tried."

Arlowe's lips curved up into a small, sad smile. "He did. He tried so hard."

"Does he know you're looking at other degrees?"

She shook her head. "And if you tell him, I will never forgive you. He has enough on his mind with his physical therapy."

"I won't. But I think you should."

"One day." She nodded toward the stairs. "How were your meetings today?"

Tension knotted the muscles in his shoulders. "Fine."

Arlowe stared at him for a long moment. Then she broke eye contact as her shoulders dropped.

"I'm glad."

He was, Hart realized, being unfair. At one point in his life, he would have asked Arlowe to come into the parlor and talked through all the conversations he'd had today. The one with Katherine, his vice president, who wasn't as torn as he was but still had reservations. A sharp contrast to his chief financial officer, Salzar, who had practically been salivating ever since Nessa had mentioned profit sharing. He would have laid everything out for Arlowe, asked for her opinion.

But now it was as if there was a barrier preventing the words he wanted to share from leaving his tongue. Ever since Lucy's parting words, the gulf he hadn't even realized existed between him and Arlowe had widened substantially. He had no longer felt comfortable reaching out.

Except that had backfired, too. His distance hadn't done anything but let him put off examining what Lucy had said and if there was any truth to it. It had pushed Arlowe so far away she wasn't willing to accept any help.

And still he held back.

Say something!

He breathed in, readying himself to expand just a little, to share something more.

A crackle sounded overheard, followed by a sharp snap. Hart reached for Arlowe just as the castle plunged into darkness.

CHAPTER TWELVE

Arlowe

ARLOWE FROZE. The dark didn't usually bother her. But the unexpectedness of this, the unfamiliar setting, the wind howling outside, came together to send a shiver down her spine.

Until a warm hand settled on her shoulder.

"Are you all right?"

She hated how much the sound of his voice eased the rapid pace of her heart, how it slowed the blood racing through her veins.

"Yes." Soft, nervous laughter escaped her lips. "Just unexpected, you know?"

"Yeah, I know."

His voice carried an odd edge to it, but she dismissed it. Right now she just wanted to get to her room, crawl under the covers, and fall asleep.

Hart turned on the light on his phone and played it over the floor.

"Down the hall and to the right?"

"Yes."

They walked in silence, their footsteps muffled by the plush carpet and the wind still howling outside.

"The forecast said this latest storm was supposed to last at least another day," Arlowe said softly as she followed Hart down the hall.

"I saw. Nothing to do about it but work with what we have."

Arlowe glanced over her shoulder. In the dim light the statues and paintings were no longer works of art. The shadows created eerie shapes with jagged edges that reminded Arlowe of the monsters she'd feared as a child.

Stop being ridiculous.

But she quickened her pace.

Hart paused in front of her door.

"Is your fireplace electric, too?"

"Yeah." She wrinkled her nose. "I'll probably grab some blankets and sleep in the library."

"Mind if I join you?"

Arlowe's pulse started to thump a little harder beneath her skin.

"Join me? Um, no. No, of course not."

Smooth. Very convincing.

"Are you sure?"

"Yes." Arlowe set the books down and picked up her own phone to switch on the light. "I'll grab what I need and meet you down there, okay?"

Once Hart left, Arlowe grabbed the book she'd planned on reading before bed, a pillow, and one of the thickest blankets she could find. She did a quick check in the mirror. The harsh white light from her phone, combined with her oversize robe, made her look like a ghost. Curls were slipping out of the tie she'd used to pull them back while she'd been exploring the library.

But why did it matter what she looked like? It wasn't like she and Hart were having a romantic night in front of the fire. It was sleeping in the same room so they didn't freeze to death.

Disgusted with herself, she put everything in the middle of the blanket, bundled it up, and headed downstairs.

She'd barely walked into the library when she heard a

scraping noise coming from down the hall. She froze. Her eyes landed on the poker by the fireplace. She laid her bundle down as quietly as she could and grabbed the poker.

"Hart? Is that you?"

"Yup."

The door to the library bumped against the wall as Hart walked backward into the room dragging a huge mattress. Arlowe's mouth dropped open.

"What is this?"

"A bed." Hart pulled it over to the carpet in front of the hearth and dropped it with a heavy sigh. He turned, one eyebrow rising as he caught sight of the poker in her hand. "And what's that?"

"A poker." Arlowe raised her chin in the air as she placed the poker back in its place. "The mattress sounded odd on the floor. Just wanted to be prepared."

Hart's grin was quick and devastating. "In case I was a ghost?"

Arlowe tried and failed to keep the corners of her mouth from sliding up into a smile. "That or a burglar in search of hidden jewels."

Hart's grin grew. "You always had the best imagination."

The way he said it with almost a sense of pride had her blushing.

"Thanks."

His smile dimmed. "It would be a shame to waste it."

Arlowe bit back a sigh. She wasn't excited about teaching or nursing. But at least with teaching agriculture she'd still be in the industry she loved, just in a different role. That's what she told herself over and over again every time she thought about saying goodbye to her dream, of never seeing her own business come to life.

It was tempting to entertain the possibility of going back

to school full-time and finally completing her degree. With fifteen million euros in her bank account, she could do it.

But what if life threw her another curveball? What if something happened and she was left back at square one? The sheer number of possibilities piled on until she felt smothered beneath their weight.

"I haven't made any decisions yet, Hart. I'm just trying to do the right thing."

"I know. And I admire you for that."

Shocked into silence, Arlowe watched as Hart grabbed her pillow and blanket off the floor and started making up the bed. It took her a moment to stop mooning over what he'd just said and realize there was only one pillow on the mattress.

"Wait…where are you sleeping?"

Hart nodded toward one of the oversize chairs. "I'll doze in one of those."

"Absolutely not."

Hart crossed his arms over his chest. "Then where do you suggest I sleep?"

"For crying out loud, Hart, this bed is king-size. We've shared a bed before."

The tightening of Hart's jaw told her exactly what he thought of her idea.

"I don't think that's a good idea."

"So you'll propose marriage to me but aren't comfortable sleeping in the same bed when we'll both be fully clothed and have zero interest in being intimate?"

A vein pulsed in Hart's forehead. "After what happened this afternoon, I don't think it's a good idea."

Arlowe walked over to a stack of logs next to the fireplace and started placing them on the still-glowing embers in the grate, focusing on the flickering flames instead of the nervous jump of her pulse.

"Hart, we're both adults. We're friends. We agreed it was

a mistake and neither of us have any interest in pursuing something romantic with the other."

Even if it was the best kiss of my life.

She tossed one log on before turning to face Hart. "You need rest, too. Didn't you say you have a meeting in the morning?"

"More like four." Hart glanced up toward the dark ceiling. "That's if the power comes back on or I conserve enough energy to use my phone as a hotspot."

"You can use mine, too."

Hart shook his head. "I appreciate the offer, but we have to keep at least one phone with some charge in case we have an emergency."

"But your meetings…"

She stopped herself. He'd obviously not wanted to talk earlier. Just because they were spending the night in the same room didn't mean anything had changed.

"Sorry. Hopefully the power comes back on in the morning."

"We could also step outside and try to fiddle with the generator."

Hart frowned. "Maybe."

"How about if the power's not back on in the morning, we at least go out and look at it? The worst that can happen is it's not repairable."

Finally, he nodded. "It's not a bad idea. I haven't picked up tools in a while, but I can give it a go."

Arlowe gave him a look. "Or I can. I've been tinkering around with Robert's tools since I was four."

Hart's lips twitched. "Right before I met you."

"Yeah. I know Mom and I lived in an apartment before she met Robert, but I just have so few memories of it."

She thought of the fields of corn, the red barn with the peeling paint, the huge maple tree out back with the tire swing. The pond glittering beneath the summer sun and the acres of trees on the land between her farm and Hart's.

Land that now belonged to someone else.

She nearly told him then. But something held her tongue. Admitting to Hart what she had done would no doubt invite his criticism. Worse, he'd be hurt that she didn't come to him for help. That, more than anything, had been the primary reason she hadn't told him in the first place. She knew it bothered him that she didn't seek him out more. But how could she when so many of her problems were financial? She never wanted Hart to feel used or taken advantage of.

And yes, she admitted to herself with no small degree of irritation, she was embarrassed. Ashamed. Her pride had taken a beating, and she didn't want Hart to see her, yet again, in the shining role of the downtrodden friend.

Which meant it was up to her to get herself and Robert back on their feet. Yes, she'd made hard choices. But it was her land. She had done what she needed to for her and Robert to survive. One day, when things were better between them, she'd tell him what she'd done. He'd be upset for a while, which she could accept. But hopefully, in time, he would come to at least understand why she'd done it, maybe even respect her for the hard choice she'd had to make.

"Where'd you go?"

Hart's quiet query made her look up. His eyes were dark and calm, a touch of empathy in his gaze. He didn't know the exact nature of her thoughts, but he'd picked up on her internal struggle, her grief.

She moved back to the makeshift bed and slowly sank down onto the mattress.

"Just…thinking about the past."

A moment later Hart sat down next to her.

"Like what?"

She stared into the fire. "Thinking of home. I remember…"

She smiled slightly even as a pressure built behind her eyes. "I remember the first time we drove down the gravel road. Robert and Mom had just gotten married at the courthouse a couple weeks before that. I was over the moon to have a real dad. And then we turned into the farm and…" She swallowed past the lump in her throat. "It was early. Mist everywhere. And there was the house, sky blue with a bright orange door and white trim. It should have looked ridiculous, but it was so beautiful. Mom whispered 'this is it' and we just knew."

The tears escaped. One after the other, cascading in silent streams down her cheeks. An arm slid around her shoulders. She didn't think about the tension, the distance, the kiss lingering between them. She simply leaned into Hart's embrace and let out a shuddering sigh as the tears continued to fall.

"I'm so tired of loss, Hart. But I also feel so stupid."

"Why stupid?"

Hart's voice was a quiet rumble against her side. Arlowe leaned into it, into him, snuggling without shame.

"I don't know much about my dad. I know he and my mom had a summer fling and she got pregnant. I know he showed up off and on until I was two. I don't even know if I actually remember his face or if it's just the couple of photos my mom had of him. But aside from him finally just walking out on her, nothing bad ever happened to me. Mom and I were happy in Kansas City, and then she met Robert and got married and we moved to the farm." She nudged Hart gently with her shoulder. "I met you. I got good grades in school. Not great, but good. I was happy. Really, really happy," she added on a whisper as her throat tightened to the point she could barely get the words out.

Hart pressed a kiss to her hair. Arlowe couldn't help the soft sight that escaped.

"I'm glad I'm part of your happy memories."

"You are. It's just…" Another deep, shaky breath. "First

the plant closing down and Robert losing his job. I'm glad he and Mom got more time together, and I think he actually started to enjoy working on the farm more. It was tight, but they made it work."

"You helped them make it work, Arlowe." Hart's fingers stroked up and down her back. "I know what you gave up to help them."

"And I appreciate that. I just kept thinking if I'd gotten a degree in something more practical I could have gotten a better scholarship and gone to school full-time—"

"Do you feel like Robert let you down?"

Arlowe frowned. "No. You said it yourself, he tried hard to find another job in his field. He even drove seventy miles once for a job interview." Her smile was quick and sad. "He was devastated when he didn't get it. Mom and I were relieved because we didn't want him driving nearly a hundred and fifty miles every day working ten-hour shifts."

"Did he disappoint you?"

Arlowe tilted her head to one side. "Disappoint me? For what?"

"For not achieving what he was trying for."

"No, I…" Her voice trailed off as her eyes glinted in the dim light. "It's…"

"Easier to extend grace to others than to grant yourself some?" Hart said softly. "You and Robert are two of the most amazing people I know. You've overcome so much, yet you both refuse to look back and see how far you've come." He laid his head against hers. "What are you afraid of, Arlowe?"

"Getting my hopes up again."

The words came out before she could stop them. It hurt to say them. She'd once been filled with hope, with dreams and plans. Hope had been a part of her identity.

Until the phone call. The state trooper telling her that there'd been an accident and she needed to get to the hospital as soon as possible. That call had ripped away all sense of hope and replaced it with a hollow yet relentless determination to be strong, resilient, practical.

But Hart didn't pull away. He just sat there with her, staring into the fire until there were no more tears left.

The tears had barely dried when exhaustion invaded. Arlowe yawned.

"Time for bed," Hart murmured in her ear.

"Mmm-hmm."

Hart gently laid her back on the bed, tucking a pillow under her head and pulling the blanket up to her chin. The last time someone had tucked her in…

The tears returned, this time accompanied by a deep, heart-wrenching sob.

Hart was next to her in an instant.

"Arlowe?"

"I miss her." Arlowe tried to get her breathing under control, tried to stop the tears, but she couldn't. Eighteen months of pent-up grief and tears were bursting through the wall she'd subconsciously built to keep them in. "I miss her so much, Hart."

Hart slid under the blanket and pulled her against him. Her arms flew around his neck and she held on as she cried into his chest.

Finally, as Hart gently rocked her back and forth and made gentle shushing noises into her hair, her sobs quieted as she slipped into a deep sleep.

Hart

A bell chimed. Hart stirred. The fire must be down to embers by now. He should get up and put another log on. But he didn't want to, not with the warm, thick blankets and the arm draped across his waist…

Alertness jerked him out of his drowsy lethargy. There was indeed an arm around his waist and the soft tickle of someone's breath on his neck.

Slowly, he turned his head. And nearly swallowed his tongue.

Arlowe had ended up on his side of the bed, with one arm thrown over his waist and her head tucked into the crook of his shoulder. Several riotous curls fell over her face. He reached out, his fingers pausing in midair. Need overruled and he gently slid her hair out of her face.

God, she was beautiful. He'd looked at her for so many years, yet never really saw her, never noticed the smattering of freckles on her nose or the tiny dent in her chin. Certainly he'd never admired how her dark lashes lay against her skin, the shape of her lips.

His body tightened. Kissing her earlier had been…extraordinary. It had only lasted a few seconds. But it had outshot any kiss he'd ever experienced by miles. It hadn't just been the physical pleasure of lips meeting. No, it had been something far deeper and more meaningful, a sensation he'd felt from where their mouths joined all the way down to his bones.

Kissing Arlowe had felt right. So had slipping under the sheet to comfort her when she cried.

So did this. Lying with her in a library as a winter storm raged on, her body pressed against his.

Her skin was back to its usual fairness. The puffiness around her eyes had abated. The tracks from her tears had dried. But he would remember the moment she broke for the rest of his life. The moment he realized just how much Arlowe had been keeping to herself.

And how much he had failed her these past eighteen months.

He shifted on the bed. Arlowe murmured something in her

sleep and moved closer, her arm tightening across his waist. He bit back a groan as a silky curl grazed his arm.

This was torture.

But, as Arlowe settled back down and huddled against him, it was a torture he would accept again and again if it meant holding her for just a little longer.

He hadn't planned on falling asleep with her. He'd intended to slip away and move to the chair after she'd finished crying. Still within reach if she needed him, but not too close to risk temptation.

Except when he'd looked down, Arlowe had been sleeping, her breathing even, one hand curled into the fabric of his shirt. He'd promised himself he would lie there for another ten minutes, maybe twenty.

A quick glance at his watch confirmed it was after midnight. He'd been sleeping next to Arlowe for over two hours.

God help him, he didn't want to move.

When, he thought as he stared up at the dark ceiling, had this desire started? When had he started thinking of Arlowe as a woman and not just a friend? Even when Lucy had suggested there was something more to his and Arlowe's relationship, there hadn't been a sudden response, an instant feeling of lust. Discomfort, yes, along with confusion as to what Lucy had seen that made her think he felt anything romantic for Arlowe.

But obviously Lucy had seen something he hadn't. If he was being honest with himself, he'd felt something when he'd turned and walked into the courtyard and seen Arlowe standing there on the mezzanine, the wind stirring her curls and a smile blooming across her face. When she'd thrown her arms around him, it had hit; the relief, the yearning, the desire.

He braced himself, mentally dived into the past to the week of Lynn's funeral. Back to his last night in town when he'd held Arlowe at the base of the trellis as she'd cried. Con-

fronted the moment when he'd stared up at the stars and wondered how on earth he was going to leave her. A moment so
deep and powerful it had shaken him to his core.

He'd already withheld so much by that point that it had
made it easier to withdraw in the following weeks. Withdraw
and put distance between the moment when he'd felt something far more than friendship for Arlowe.

Had he really been lying to himself for so long? Had he
punished not only himself but Arlowe, too, because he hadn't
wanted the possibility of romance with the one person he
needed to keep in his life?

The realization left him shaken.

He turned his head to look at Arlowe again. His eyes
drifted down to her lips. It would be so easy to lean forward,
brush his mouth across hers. But would there be longing in
her gaze when her eyes opened? Disgust? Fear? Where would
they find themselves after?

That last thought had him turning back to face the ceiling.
When he'd pulled away from their kiss, seen the way she'd
looked at him, his desire had fled, replaced by ice-cold fear.
He had risked twenty years of friendship for a kiss. His romantic relationships up until now had been steady affairs,
connections built on mutual physical interest and shared
viewpoints. He'd enjoyed the intimate side of his relationships.

He'd never lost control like he had with Arlowe. It un-
nerved him almost as much as realizing just how much he'd
failed her by being absent these past three years. How much
of her life he'd missed out on, and how much of his he'd
given up. He'd been so hell-bent on success he hadn't bothered to look anywhere but forward. Perhaps, if he'd bothered
to glance away even just once, he would have seen Arlowe
struggling. He could have held her up instead of leaving her

to shoulder the burden alone. When she'd rejected his offers of money, he should have flown home.

But he hadn't. He'd shifted his priorities, his loyalties, and left her to fend for herself. Had he trusted himself, and her, and reached out three years ago when he'd first spiraled into grief, things could have been different. Yet just like Arlowe insisted on protecting Robert, Hart had insisted that holding Arlowe at arm's length had kept her safe.

He'd made a choice for her. He'd convinced himself it was to protect her. But as he lay there in the dark, her breathing soft and even beside him, he accepted his decision had also been rooted in a lethal mix of pride and fear. He hadn't wanted to let anyone see his pain, had been afraid it would prove to be too much and drive her away.

Instead, he'd made the choice for both of them and achieved the same result. One he thought he had some control over. But all it had done was drive Arlowe away to the point she couldn't confide in him.

So what now?

The thought circled round and round in his mind. The truth of his situation poked at him, goaded him even as he tried to keep it at bay. He cared for Arlowe. Far more than he had allowed himself to accept.

But he wasn't quite ready to confront the full reality of it. Especially not in the middle of the night when he was weighed down already by exhaustion and confusion.

Arlowe's arm slid up his chest, her hand landing just above his heart. She murmured something in her sleep that sounded like his name.

He closed his eyes. *Just five more minutes.*

His arm tightened around her just before he fell asleep.

CHAPTER THIRTEEN

Arlowe

THE POWER WAS still out.

Arlowe glanced up at the clock. Nearly eleven o'clock in the morning. There was no way Hart's phone was going to last much longer.

She looked over her shoulder toward the library doors. She'd woken up that morning to a fire blazing in the hearth and a tray with mini *Apfelstrudels*, two soft-boiled eggs sprinkled with salt and freshly chopped chives, and a bowl of plump blackberries. There had been a note, too, just like the one she'd left him.

Good morning. Working in my room. Hope you slept well.

Her eyes strayed to the bed for what had to be the dozenth time. She remembered Hart lying with her just before she fell asleep. And she had a vague impression of him holding her in the night when the clock had chimed midnight.

But when she'd awoken that morning, there had been no sign that Hart had slept with her. No extra pillow or blankets. She moved enough that she had no idea if the rumpled sheet next to her was because of Hart or because of her.

She was too chicken to ask.

She blew a stray curl out of her face and tried to refocus on her grandmother's diary. A task that was nearly impossible every time she thought about how she'd broken down last night. Her feelings vacillated between an embarrassment she felt all the way to her toes and sheer relief that she'd finally shared a piece of herself she'd been hiding from everyone ever since Mom died. That Hart had accepted all of it meant the world to her.

And made her internal struggle that much more confusing.

She'd cried in front of Hart before. When her first dog, Bear, had passed away. When her first boyfriend had broken up with her freshman year of high school. God knows she'd cried plenty the week Mom had died.

Those tears, however, had been different. Everyone had understood her need to cry then. The nurses at the hospital, the police officer who stopped by to check on Robert and follow up with Arlowe on the accident. For a solid month, no one questioned her need to cry or suddenly excuse herself.

But last night's tears had felt like a confession, a sharing of one of the deepest parts of her grief. When she thought back over the few relationships she'd had to date, she couldn't think of a single man she would cry like that in front of.

No one except Hart.

She shook her head and refocused on the diary. It appeared her grandmother had started it shortly before finding out she was pregnant with her first child, Ivy's father. A child out of wedlock. The fear of being an unwed mother in the first half of the twentieth-century had come through every written word, fear magnified by the father refusing to help Desdemona and even threatening to say it wasn't his.

Desdemona's spidery handwriting was bold, as if she'd been pressing her pen hard against the paper.

I am a fool. He told me loving me was a mistake he will regret to the end of his life.

Arlowe closed the book with a frustrated huff. Apparently, she and her grandmother at least had that in common. Hart had been the one to classify their kiss as a mistake. Whatever was going on between them, he didn't want it going any further than it already had. She wasn't even sure of her own feeling. She needed to stop reading too much into things like her best friend holding her while she cried and do something productive.

Her eyes landed on the dwindling stack of wood next to the fireplace. There was more firewood just outside in the courtyard. She could restock the wood and then work on lunch.

Five minutes later, dressed in her parka, gloves, and boots, Arlowe ventured into the courtyard. The snow had dwindled back down to tiny flakes. But the wind was still relentless. The courtyard provided some protection, but sharp gusts still tore through the bare trees and ripped at her clothes as she grabbed wood from a pile on the far side of the courtyard.

After two trips, she trudged back out to the pile. One more would keep the fire going through the early hours of the night. Hopefully, after Hart was done with his meetings, he would go out with her to take a look at the generator. The wind had been too fierce yesterday, whipping the snow into a frenzy and reducing the visibility to near zero.

A crack rent the air. Arlow whirled around just in time to see a spruce tree start to fall. She dropped the wood and sprinted toward the back of the courtyard, her heart pounding. She hit the back wall and whirled around. The top of the tree had landed against one wall of the castle. Then, slowly, it slid down the side before landing with a thud softened by the snow.

Blocking the door into the library.

Her hand flew to her pocket, only for her to remember her phone was still sitting on the end table next to the chair.

Great.

A quick circle around the courtyard confirmed that the other doors were locked. The parlor was on the opposite side of the castle and faced south. No chance of tossing a stone against a window or getting Hart's attention.

She mentally summoned a map of the castle. She could circle around the north side. There were some steep spots, but it didn't have the literal cliff the south side did. It would take a little bit of hiking, but she could make it.

She trudged out of the courtyard and turned left. A small row of buildings lay behind the castle, one of them a private residence for a lower-level royal. The far buildings included a stable and a barn.

And, she thought with a small spurt of optimism, the generator was just outside the barn.

The wind had blown the lid open, leaving the generator itself exposed to the elements. It took a few minutes to clear the snow from the air intake and break ice off the vents. A quick check showed the fuel tank was thankfully intact and at a reasonable level. The spark plugs could use a cleaning, but no corrosion or oil fouling. It took a few tugs on the starter. But at last the generator started to hum.

"Yes!"

Arlowe grinned. Robert would be thrilled to hear she'd retained all of the tricks he'd taught her over the years tinkering on the farm's generator and other machinery. Hopefully this would help ease some of Hart's tension, too, having the generator back up and running so he could take care of business.

Envy tugged at her. When Hart had told her he had inherited BioInnovations and was moving to New York for a year to try and turn the company around, she'd been devastated.

But she'd kept the true depths of her sadness hidden. The first time, she realized as she trudged through the snow, that she'd concealed something from Hart.

She'd wanted him to go. His management job for an engineering firm had been fine, but it had never challenged him, never sparked any of the passion Arlowe had felt toward landscaping. Hart had assured her over the years that he didn't need passion in his career. He just needed a job that wouldn't bore him and paid well.

Hart may have told himself that over the years. But when she'd gone to New York with Francine to visit him two months after he left, she'd seen it. That spark Hart had always claimed he never felt.

She knew then he wouldn't be coming back to Missouri anytime soon.

She stopped at the edge of the castle wall and stared out over the mountains. Trees appeared, then disappeared just as quickly in the whirling snow. Off to the west, she caught the faintest glimpse of the lake through the shifting snow and clouds.

It was odd to suddenly recognize the moment when their friendship had started to pull apart. Even though they'd called and texted plenty, the physical distance and Hart's devotion to reviving his family's company had taken its toll.

Arlowe blew out a harsh breath, watched the cloud she'd created hang in the air for a second before the wind whisked it away. Had she tried hard enough that first year? Or had she been unintentionally pulling away from him all this time? Building distance one day at a time to prepare herself for the worst, only to create the very thing that would drive them apart?

She shivered. The possibility made her sick to her stomach.

She resumed her trek and turned left, staying close to the castle wall and keeping a cautious eye on the sloping hill to her right. She focused on the crunch of snow underfoot, the whistle of the wind, the cold drops of snow that landed and melted on her cheeks.

Hart

Hart pulled his earbuds out and set them carefully on the table. He closed the lid of his laptop before standing and stretching. Half past noon. The generator had thankfully kicked on an hour ago just as his phone was about to die. He'd been able to jump into a meeting with Nessa Pharmaceuticals' accounting team, and then a follow-up with his own.

Still so many unanswered questions. Three members of his executive team thought he was insane for delaying. But Katherine and his secretary, Linda, had both agreed with him.

He scrubbed a hand across his face. The deadline was tomorrow. Nessa had provided him with everything he needed to make an informed decision. On paper, the decision should have been an easy one.

But the thorn still lingered in his side. The one that said entering into a contract with Nessa was a bad idea.

He needed a break. Lunch for sure, and to check on Arlowe.

His gut tightened. He'd managed to avoid thinking about her for most of the morning, focusing instead on reports, testimonies, sheets upon sheets of data, and a particularly contentious meeting with his head of development. Exactly where his mind should be to keep his company moving forward.

But as soon as he thought of Arlowe curled against his side, the pale morning light falling across her skin as she slept, the contract with Nessa Pharmaceuticals disappeared to the back of his mind. All he could think of was Arlowe.

It should scare him, how quickly she rose above everything else. BioInnovations had become the focus of his life the past three years. It hadn't just been the challenge of resuscitating a company on the verge of collapse. It had been a way to honor his father, to right the wrongs his grandfather had done and create the kind of organization Dad would have been proud of.

Hart walked out into the hall. Dad had loved Arlowe, and Robert and Lynn. Lynn had shown Dad how to put seed out in the fields their first year farming. Robert had come over more times than Hart could count to help out with the numerous pieces of machinery that were always breaking down. They both had drawn Mom and Dad out of their shells, coaxing them into going to the farmers market, the county fair, even trips into the city for dinner at a nice restaurant. It had been a pleasant, bucolic life.

But every now and then Hart had seen the way his dad would gaze out the window. He'd known his dad had been thinking of his life in New York, the company he always thought he'd inherit one day, only to be cut out for questioning Hart's grandfather one too many times.

Taking the reins of BioInnovations had given Hart a purpose. It had also been an outlet he hadn't even known he'd needed, an outlet for his own grief. A grief he'd concealed from his mother so as not to add to the burden she already carried from losing her husband too soon.

A grief he'd hidden from Arlowe, too, because he hadn't wanted to hurt her. Hadn't wanted her to lose that sparkle in her eyes, to see the grim side of life.

He stopped outside the library doors. Is that when things had started to shift between them? Could the distance between them have started so long ago? Had his protective streak actually pushed her away?

And if it had, was it too late to reach her?

Shaken by that possibility, he knocked on one of the library doors.

"Arlowe?"

When she didn't answer, he slowly opened the door and stepped inside. Unease shot through him as he eyed the ashes in the grate, the book left open on the huge chair Arlowe had claimed as hers the first night he'd been there.

"Arlowe!" he called back into the recesses of the library.

No one answered.

He pulled out his phone and dialed her. A moment later a muted jazz tune sounded from beneath the blanket on the chair.

Unease escalated into fear. Where was she?

He was about to head for the stairs when he glanced out toward the courtyard. The sight of the massive spruce tree lying just outside the door sucked the air from his lungs.

"Arlowe…"

He ran across the library. He could open the door inward, but there was no way to get out around the massive branches.

"Arlowe!"

His shout was tossed back by the wind. He couldn't see any sign of her beneath the tree. But it was a big tree, and if she—

No. He was not going to think like that.

He ran back into the hall and grabbed his winter gear from the rack. Arlowe's was gone. Maybe she'd gone for a quick walk in the courtyard and then been blocked out by the tree. She'd mentioned locking all the doors, so the quickest way would be walking around the castle.

He shoved his arms into his parka and rushed out the front doors. How long had she been gone? Had she gotten lost in the storm?

He reached the bottom of the stairs and sprinted across the front courtyard. A quick glance to the left reminded him that the south side of the castle faced a sheer drop-off of nearly thirty feet. Which left the north side of the castle as the best possible route for Arlowe to get back in if she'd been trapped outside.

He had just started to walk when Arlowe appeared around the corner of the courtyard. Her cheeks were red, her pace steady as she looked up and smiled at him.

"Hey. Is the power still on?"

Hart closed the distance between them in long strides. Arlowe's eyes widened as he reached out and grabbed her, yanking her against his chest.

"Don't ever scare me like that again."

And then he crushed his mouth to hers.

CHAPTER FOURTEEN

Hart

ALIVE. SHE'S ALIVE.

The words pounded through him as one hand slipped into her hair, cradling her head as his lips moved over hers. She stood, frozen in his embrace.

And then she moved, her arms sliding up his chest before winding around his neck. Her mouth firmed under his as a soft moan vibrated against his lips. He deepened the kiss, savored the feel of her in his arms, the life that trembled in his hold.

At last he pulled back, rested his forehead against hers as their breaths mingled in the frigid air.

"I was terrified, Arlowe."

"I'm sorry." She rested one gloved hand against his cheek. "I just meant to grab some firewood, but the tree fell and I—"

"Decided to fix the generator on your own?"

She pulled back a little, her eyes narrowed. "I was right there. What would you have done?"

The same exact thing, but he wasn't about to tell her that. "You could have—"

"Hart, I wanted to do it. It felt…" Her smile hit him with the force of a freight train. "It felt good to do something productive because I wanted to, not because I had to."

He blinked. Her words circled around inside his head.

"Do you feel like you have to do all this? Give up your own dreams and dedicate your life to Robert?"

Her smile disappeared. She started to withdraw, but he held her in his arms.

"No more pulling away, Arlowe. For either of us. Tell me."

A shiver wracked her body.

"On second thought, wait." He scooped her up in his arms, his lips tilting up as she shrieked and grabbed his neck much the way she had when he'd first arrived. "Hot bath first. Then you'll tell me."

She huffed as he walked up the stairs. "You just have it all figured out, don't you?"

His arms tightened around her as he nudged one of the massive doors open. Light spilled out, illuminating the snowflakes dusting her curls, the dark slash of her lashes as she winced against the sudden brightness.

"Not by a long shot," he muttered.

Hart reached her room and walked inside. The bathroom resembled his, with its marble flooring, gleaming copper fixtures, and subtle accent lighting. But it was the freestanding tub he was most grateful for as he gently set Arlowe down on a chair next to the tub. She started pulling off her winter gear as he turned on the water, checking to make sure it was warm but not too hot.

"Bath. Then we'll talk."

Arlowe's hand went to her stomach. "How about bath, then food, then talk?"

He nodded. "Fair. But I'm cooking."

Her eyes widened. "Um, are you sure that's a good idea? The last time you cooked you burned—"

"A grilled cheese," he ground out. "Yes, I remember."

"More like a smoked cheese." She grinned at him. "I've never seen cheese that color."

He leaned in, satisfied at the flare of emotion in her eyes, the way her breath caught as her gaze dropped down to his mouth.

"Then I guess you'll just have to trust me."

She swallowed hard. "Hart…"

"Let me do this for you. Please." He reached up and brushed a strand of hair out of her face. "I've done so little for you over the last few years."

"I didn't exactly ask." Her whisper was barely audible over the water gushing out of the faucet.

"And why is that?"

She stared at him for a long, drawn-out moment. Then, finally, she whispered, "I was afraid."

He started to push. But then she shivered again. He forced himself to bite back his questions. They had all night. No more video conferences or phone calls. Even if he had appointments, he would cancel them. Yes, Arlowe, was all right, but God, what if she had slipped? What if it had been even colder outside?

He wasn't wasting another second he could be spending with her.

He leaned in and laid a quick kiss on her forehead.

"Warm up. Take your time. I'll have dinner ready when you're done."

He gathered up her coat, gloves, and hat before stepping out of the bathroom and closing the door behind him. As he moved over to her fireplace and turned on the switch, he heard the telltale signs of the rest of her clothes being discarded. He gritted his teeth as he laid her winter gear in front of the hearth, trying and failing to ignore the gentle sound of water lapping as she eased herself into the bath, followed by a long, satisfying sigh.

He stood, stared at the door to the bathroom. What would happen if he knocked on the door? Would she tell him to go to hell? Or would she invite him in?

He stalked across the room and out into the hallway before he could give in to temptation. They had too much to talk about, too many things to figure out.

One thing was certain, he thought grumpily as he hurried down the stairs. He could no longer blame his attraction to Arlowe on stress or exhaustion or being away for too long. No, his desire for her was a living, breathing thing that had rooted itself so deeply he wasn't sure he'd ever be able to get rid of it.

Arlowe

Arlowe pulled the belt of the robe tighter as she sat on the wooden chest in front of the fire. It had been too easy to stay in the tub, to focus on the way the bubbles drifted across the surface or the steam wafting up every time she added a little more hot water.

Easy to stay hidden. To put off what she suspected was going to be a hard conversation. One made all the more challenging because she'd be trying to focus on what they were actually talking about and not just indulging in the memory of how Hart had kissed her senseless in the snow.

She touched her fingers to her lips. There had been no subtlety, no tenderness when he'd first kissed her. No—just a relentless desperation, as though kissing her had been the only way he could reassure himself she was alive.

She might have been able to chalk it up as heat of the moment. But the heat had lingered in the way he'd brushed her hair out of her face, the closeness with which he'd held her all the way up to her room. The intimacy of that last kiss on her forehead before he'd left.

A shiver crept down her spine, one that had nothing to do with the temperature in the room.

What am I going to do?

Before the kiss, she'd been able to push romantic thoughts of Hart out of her head. But when he kissed her like that, when he held her as if he never wanted to let her go, he took her control and smashed it to smithereens.

It was terrifying how much she wanted him.

She stood with a huff and started to pull away. Something tugged at her robe. Frowning, she glanced back and saw that the hem had gotten caught on the lock of the trunk. She crouched down and braced her hand on the lid as she gently tugged on the robe. The lid bobbed a fraction as the material came loose. Curious, Arlowe lifted the lid.

And gasped.

Inside lay a treasure trove of colors. Silks and chiffons in ruby red, emerald green, and elegant violet. Jewels winked in the faint light.

Arlowe trailed a finger over the green silk. Giving in to curiosity, she grabbed the material and held the dress up. Sleek with a cowl neckline and an open back threaded with strings of what were probably real diamonds, it was sensual elegance personified.

Suddenly, she remembered. Her grandmother had written about this dress in her diary. She'd been wearing it when she had met Auguste Gruber, the man she would eventually marry. A man she had initially had no interest in because she had been involved with her lover, an American soldier stationed in Austria.

She walked over to the mirror and held up the dress in front of her. It fell in long silken folds. Desdemona had written about how Auguste had danced with her, taking great care not to step on her dress as he'd whisked her around the floor.

One corner of Arlowe's mouth tilted up. No, she didn't like Desdemona's marriage stipulation. But she understood it a little better now. How terrified she must have been to fall pregnant, to be rejected by a man she thought she'd loved. To enter into a marriage with a man she'd never imagined herself with to save her reputation and her child's future.

Arlowe's hand brushed against cool metal. She glanced down and saw a pin attached to the waistline with a crinkled piece of paper attached. A paper with Desdemona's elegant handwriting.

First dance with Auguste.

She read, then reread the words. Her grandmother had fallen for someone completely unexpected.

Was it possible she could, too?

CHAPTER FIFTEEN

Hart

CANDLES FLICKERED. The strains of a piano filled the air from a vintage record player. Pumpkin seed crackers with whipped butter and drizzled with olive oil and a plate of pickled forest mushrooms sat in the middle of the table. Bowls of salad sat at two place settings toward the head of the table, both dressed with freshly chopped beets and crumbled walnuts. The main course was kept warm beneath a silver dome. Water glasses, wineglasses, silverware, and linen napkins were all laid out.

Hart glanced toward the door again. Had he gone overboard? Yes. But the urge to do something for Arlowe, to finally take care of her, had overridden his usual good sense.

Every time he thought of her trekking around the castle in the snow, with no access to a phone, his chest tightened to the point it nearly hurt to breathe.

"Wow."

Hart turned. His jaw nearly hit the floor.

"Arlowe."

Stunning. Beautiful. Her long, slender form was clad in an emerald gown that clung to every curve before falling into a pool of silk that brushed the ground. She'd left her hair down, her curls falling past her shoulders. Her smile lit up her face as she looked around the dining room.

"Hart, this looks wonderful."

"Thanks." He crossed to her and took her hands in his. "You look incredible."

Pink bloomed in her cheeks. She smiled up at him with a sweet shyness that touched him even as her eyes dropped down to his mouth. When she looked back up at him, the shyness was gone, replaced by an awareness that had his hands tightening around hers. Kissing her had been impulsive, instinctive. There were plenty of reasons why he shouldn't have. Given the chance, he would do it all over again.

"Thank you. It belonged to my grandmother. She wore it when she danced with my grandfather for the first time."

"How did you find that out?" Hart asked as he escorted her over to the table and pulled out her chair.

"There was a note pinned to her dress. And I found her diary in the library."

Over appetizers and salad, Arlowe brought him up to speed on what she'd read. Her eyes widened as he pulled the lid off the silver serving platter and set a bowl of steaming soup in front of her.

"Pumpkin soup with cream. And there's a beef dish for the main course."

"You're spoiling me," Arlowe said as she picked up her spoon.

"It's about time I did."

Arlowe frowned at him. "What do you mean?"

Hart picked up his wineglass and took a drink as he contemplated how best to phrase his reply. Then he decided to throw caution to the wind and simply speak.

"We both know I haven't been around much since my father died."

"No, you haven't." Arlowe sighed. "But I understood."

"Did you? Then you understood more than I did."

"What do you mean?"

He set down his glass and folded his hands on the table. "When my father died, I…struggled."

Part of him wanted to tell her everything now, confess how low he'd sunk, how dark the world had seemed those first few weeks. How much he'd wanted to call her, lean on her, but how terrified he'd been of dragging her down with him.

Not yet. They had time for that discussion later.

"It's not easy losing a parent, Hart."

"No. But finding out about my grandfather just a few months later, realizing how close my father had come to finally getting back what he wanted…" He smiled slightly as her eyebrows climbed up. "My grandfather didn't come to Dad's funeral. But he did change his will. Before Dad passed, Grandfather's will left everything to him."

Arlowe's lips parted on a gasp. "Oh, Hart."

"BioInnovations was nearly his. I know he was happy in Missouri. But I know a part of him longed to go back to New York. Every time he got a report from one of his old friends at the company, he'd get so quiet. Retreat into himself for a couple days." His father hadn't known how to handle his feelings any better than Hart had. "When I realized I had a chance to turn the company around and reshape it into what my father would have, I couldn't think of anything else."

Including you. He'd needed emptiness, a place devoid of emotion, where he could charge forward without giving his feelings too much thought. Just being around Arlowe made him want to share. If he had, he wasn't sure he'd have been able to hold himself together, to be strong enough to do what he needed to turn BioInnovations around.

"I get that. I felt the same way after Mom…" Arlowe paused, looked down at her soup and swallowed hard. "It's almost like a compulsion, isn't it? The harder you work, the less time you have to remember."

"Yes."

Of course she understood. Arlowe understood him better than anyone else he'd ever met. It was one of the things he appreciated about her as a friend, even sometimes envied. She got people, made them feel welcome and understood.

"I'm sorry, Arlowe."

She looked up at him, a small furrow between her brows. "For what?"

"For leaving."

"You know what would mean more?"

He frowned. "What?"

"If you apologized for withdrawing from me instead of leaving." She reached over and laid her hand on top of his. "I didn't like you leaving, Hart. But that's the selfish part of me talking. You had to leave. You had to do this for yourself and your father. It was the drop-off in communication that hurt the most."

"I'm sorry for that. More than I can express."

Arlowe hesitated, her lips parting several times before she spoke. "I thought, after Mom died, that maybe you were disappointed in me."

His eyes widened. "What?"

"Dropping out of college, working at a greenhouse when you were literally making millions—"

"You thought I was ashamed of you."

Slowly, she nodded. "Yes."

His initial feeling was one of hurt. But he couldn't blame her. He'd given no explanation, no reason for his withdrawal. The first time had been because he hadn't known how to handle his own grief. And the second time, after her mother's funeral…he was coming to accept there had been other factors at play besides his busy schedule.

"Me becoming fixated on work was my problem, Arlowe, not yours. You have nothing to be ashamed of."

"Thank you. And when it comes to your company, you have everything to be proud of. Look what you've built." She squeezed his hand and started to pull away, but he reached out and grabbed hold of her fingers, enjoying the return of her blush as she glanced down at their joined hands. "I hope you know how proud we are of you. Robert, your mom, me. You've created something incredible."

Warmth suffused his chest. He brought her hand up to his lips and grazed a kiss across her knuckles.

"I know the company is doing well when I look at the numbers. But hearing it from someone I trust and respect means more than I can express."

Her lips tilted up into a teasing smile. "Emotions can have their place."

"They can. I'm conflicted over this deal, but I am very proud of BioInnovations and what my team has accomplished."

"You seem happy there."

He paused. He'd never associated happiness with BioInnovations. Determination, yes. Motivation and pride, absolutely.

But happiness? There hadn't been time to be happy. Not when he kept himself going at such a rigorous pace.

"Hart?"

"Hmm?" He shook his head. "Sorry. It's been satisfying to help the company get back on its feet."

Her smile dimmed a fraction. "I'm glad."

He leaned in. "What's wrong?"

"Nothing."

"Arlowe." He waited until she looked at him. "Don't lie. Not now."

She let out a shuddering breath. "I just miss you, Hart."

Her words hit him square in the chest. *Happiness* wasn't a word he'd ascribe to his work. But in the last few days, even with the stress of the manufacturing deal hanging over his head and being trapped in the castle, he'd known more moments of true happiness with Arlowe than he had in the past year alone.

"Dance with me."

"What?"

He stood and gently tugged her to her feet. "Dance with me, Arlowe."

Arlowe

This was a dream. It had to be a dream. Because there was no way Hart Sinclair, her best friend of twenty years, was leading her through a pair of double glass doors into the small ballroom next to the dining room.

"Wait here."

He trailed his fingers up her arm, squeezed her shoulder, and then moved to the far side of the room. With a flick of the switch, the chandelier sparkled to life. A smaller version of the grand one in the main hall, the electric candles created a warm glow that played over the royal blue chairs seated around the perimeter of the room. Mirrors covered one wall, while the rest were painted ivory with gold vines and leaves crisscrossing from one panel to the next.

Arlowe swallowed hard as Hart walked toward her. Dressed in black suit pants that followed the long lines of his legs and a crisp white dress shirt with the top button undone, he looked…rakish. Like a hero from another era.

Her breath caught in her chest as he drew near. When she'd slipped the dress on in her room, she'd felt empowered. Adventurous. Like she'd slid back into the persona of the woman she used to be before life dealt some harsh blows.

Now though, as Hart slid an arm around her waist and pulled her flush against his muscular chest, doubts intruded once more. Right now, in this moment, it felt like they were both caught under a spell. One where she finally saw Hart as she should have seen him without the barriers of fear and ignorance.

But would the spell last once they left the castle? Would whatever was happening between them be strong enough to survive the physical distance that would once again separate them when she returned to Missouri and he to New York?

"Where did you go?"

Arlowe looked up at Hart. His face was so close to hers, their noses nearly touching.

"Into the future." She sighed and leaned her head against his shoulder as they swayed in time to the music playing from the dining room. "It's hard not to think about what will happen next."

"Such as?"

With us. You and me.

But she wasn't ready for that conversation. Not yet.

"The will. Robert's health. My degree."

"Why are you giving up on the landscaping?"

She kept her head down, her cheek resting against the sleek fabric of his shirt. She started to go with the story she'd been repeating to herself ad nauseam. But then she stopped. How could she be frustrated with Hart for cutting her off if she did the same?

"Because I'm scared. And I feel guilty."

His arm tightened around her waist. "What are you scared of?"

"That I try and fail. That I spend money on a degree that could have gone somewhere else, like physical therapy for Robert. Or that, even if things work out with the inheritance, that some emergency will happen later on down the road and investing my education in something more solid will keep us solvent if the worst should happen."

"Because you feel like the worst has already happened enough times that it's become your reality."

"You know, for a guy who says he prefers logic, you just made a very astute observation."

For a moment, Hart said nothing. Just swayed with her as the soft trilling rhythm of a piano played in the background.

"Do you remember the first time we climbed to the top of the maple tree near the pond?"

"I do." She bit down on her lower lip. It belonged to someone else now. "You were scared."

"I was scared you were going to fall. It was disconcerting having a best friend who was four years younger than me."

She smiled. "I'll bet. I was probably pretty annoying."

"No." Arlowe looked up at him in surprise. He was staring down at her with a serious expression on his handsome face. "You pushed me, Arlowe. I did so many things with you I never would have done on my own. Including climbing to the top of that tree."

"We could see everything from there."

"We could." He stopped in the middle of the dance floor but still held her close. "Where did that girl go? Why are you holding yourself back?"

She froze. "I…what do you mean?"

"Why are you convincing yourself to give up on a dream you've wanted for over ten years?"

"Because…" She breathed in, then released it in a rush. "I don't want to get my hopes up, Hart. I don't want to put in all that time and effort and money only to have it all fall apart. I feel like I've failed so much. It's cowardly, but I don't want to fail again."

As she said the words out loud, something shifted in her chest. An uncomfortable realization at just how far she'd actually drifted away from the woman she'd been.

"Arlowe?"

She shook her head. "I… I haven't had this conversation with anyone. And hearing myself… I don't like it. That's not the woman my mother and Robert raised me to be."

"So make a change." Hart leaned down and touched his

forehead to hers. "But give yourself some grace, too. Maybe open yourself to accepting some help."

"Maybe." She gave in to the desire to slide her hands up Hart's chest and circle her arms around his neck. "God, Hart, what's going on between us?"

"I don't know." Hart cupped her face in one hand, the other pressing against her back with a confident, possessive warmth that had her breathing in. "But I don't want it to stop."

"Me, either."

She'd barely finished speaking the words when Hart leaned down and sealed his mouth over hers. When he deepened the kiss, she moaned against his lips and sank deeper into his embrace. She'd never felt so alive, so wonderfully cherished, as she did in this moment with the one man who knew her better than she knew herself. Who now knew about some of those dark bits and pieces she'd concealed and still wanted her.

"Arlowe." Hart pulled back, his eyes dark and his breathing ragged. "I have to stop. Before this goes too far."

She didn't even debate her next move. Just gave in to the need circulating through her, to the spontaneity she used to live her life by, and smiled up at him.

"What if I want it to go further?"

His grip tightened. "You have to be sure—"

"I am." She leaned up and brushed a soft, teasing kiss across his mouth. "I'm sure, Hart."

On a groan he swept her up into his arms. As he carried her up the stairs and down the hall to his room, Arlowe laid her head against his chest and savored the rapid rhythm of his heartbeat.

Tonight, they would just be Hart and Arlowe. No grief, no guilt, no disagreements over money and wills.

Tonight, they only had each other.

CHAPTER SIXTEEN

Arlowe

SUN STREAMED IN through the windows. Arlowe stirred, smiling to herself as she burrowed deeper into the embrace of the arm draped across her chest.

"Good morning."

Her eyes flew open as a voice rumbled against her side. Shock kept her from scrambling out of the bed as she slowly turned her head. She was in Hart's bed. With Hart. After a night of…

Oh God.

"Hi."

Hart leaned down and gently kissed the tip of her nose. The sweet gesture unknotted some of the tension bunching up at the base of her neck.

"Sleep well?"

"The few times I slept, yes." Heat suffused her cheeks as Hart grinned. "I mean—"

"I know what you meant." He brushed his mouth across hers. "I'm glad you said yes."

Before she could reply, his phone rang. He frowned.

"Sorry."

"No, don't be." She reached up and cradled his cheek in one hand. "I get it. Go."

He turned his head and pressed a kiss to her palm before

tossing back the sheets and climbing out of bed. She indulged in a long, lingering look at his muscled body as he yanked on his pants and grabbed his phone.

"Sinclair here." His lips parted as someone spoke on the other end of the phone. "They what?"

She saw the change come over him, could tell the moment his mind switched from what they'd just shared to business. Gone was the teasing warmth, the sweetness. In its place was the cool, decisive CEO who had taken a flailing company and turned it into one of the most reputable manufacturers in North America.

Pride warred with uncertainty. After what they'd shared last night, it hurt to picture him returning to New York and her going back to Missouri. But she couldn't leave the farm, didn't want to say goodbye to one of the last few constants she had. Not that Hart had asked her to, she reminded herself as he listened to whoever had called. Yet even if he did, she'd have to say no. And he couldn't very well give up the life he'd created for himself in New York. Especially after what he'd shared last night, the driving force behind everything he'd achieved.

The truth hit her hard. There wasn't a way for her and Hart to make this work. Not without one or both of them sacrificing something big. Sacrifices that could lead to resentment, to the fracturing of their already fragile relationship.

Even if they could find some way to make it work, what if it failed? Just because they'd been great friends didn't mean they would be great in a romantic relationship. And if they tried and failed, there would be no coming back from that.

What have I done?

She slid out of bed and reached for the emerald dress lying in a crumpled heap on the floor. She ducked into the bathroom and pulled it on, fighting against the panic building in her chest.

Hart had his meeting this afternoon. He'd no doubt want to spend the day preparing for it. That would give her plenty of time to get herself under control and find a way to approach the situation logically with Hart.

A knock on the bathroom door startled her.

"Arlowe?"

She brushed a frantic hand over her hair and steadied herself before opening the door. Hart stood on the other side, bare chested and still gripping his phone. She forced herself to keep her eyes on his face and not on the carved muscles of his stomach.

"Hey," she said brightly.

"Nessa Pharmaceuticals just added a ten-year manufacturing agreement and a capital investment in BioInnovations' facilities to their proposal."

Arlowe's eyes widened. "They want to invest money into your facilities?"

"Yes. And the ten-year guarantee is almost unheard of in the industry."

Arlowe didn't know much about pharmaceutical manufacturing, but she knew enough about business to know this was the kind of deal that could send an already successful company soaring.

But Hart wasn't completely sold on it. She saw it in the firmness of his mouth, the faint line between his brows. No, whatever bothered him about Nessa Pharmaceuticals was still on his mind.

"It seems a little drastic, given that your meeting is scheduled for later this afternoon."

"Blaine said it was a sign of their commitment."

"Blaine?"

"The CEO of Nessa."

"The one who makes you uncomfortable?"

Hart gave her a frustrated glance. "Not liking someone isn't cause for turning down a deal of this magnitude."

"I understand that," she replied as evenly as she could, "but this seems drastic, Hart. Too drastic."

"I appreciate the input, Arlowe," Hart said in a tone that indicated he felt the exact opposite. "But everything else is in order. I can't turn this down."

"Can't or won't?"

Hart's eyes narrowed. "I don't have time to go into this. My secretary found a helicopter company in Salzburg with a Sikorsky in their fleet."

"A Sikorsky?"

"One of the fastest helicopters in existence. It can be here in less than an hour and get me to Lyon before three."

Arlowe's lips parted. Hart was leaving.

"Oh." She forced a smile to her lips. "Well, that's good at least."

"I know it's sudden, especially after last night, but I have to be there, Arlowe."

"I understand." She slipped past him into the room to gather up her shoes and phone. "I appreciate you coming out here, Hart, and—"

"Don't."

Arlowe straightened, her shoes clutched in one hand and her phone in the other. "What?"

"You're pulling back." Hart advanced toward her, a glower darkening his face. "Why?"

"I'm not."

"You are."

She broke eye contact and looked down at the carpet. "Hart, can't we have this conversation later? Maybe after your meeting?"

"It'll take me all of five minutes to pack and the helicopter won't be here for at least forty minutes." He stopped in front of her and slid a finger under her chin, tilting her head up until she could only look at him. "What's going on?"

"It's just…" She let out a shuddering breath. "Last night was incredible."

"But?"

"But it's over." Just saying the words hurt. "We have to get back to real life."

He slid an arm around her waist and pulled her close. She stiffened as she tried, and failed, to fight the attraction rising inside her.

"Why can't this be a part of our reality?"

For one painful, beautiful moment, she let herself envision it. Pictured a life where she and Hart were married, not just for an inheritance but because they wanted to be. Living on the acreage in the house of her dreams, with the river twining through the landscape just beyond the fields as children played outside beneath the trees. Imagined sitting with Hart on the porch, hands entwined, as they savored a rare moment of quiet amidst the chaos of raising a family together.

But Hart wouldn't be sitting with her on the porch. No, Hart would be in New York, where he belonged. Whether or not he had fled to New York to escape his grief, his work with BioInnovations had become a part of him now. A part she couldn't allow him to give up.

"You belong in New York." One hand came up and rested on his chest. "And I belong in Kansas City."

She pushed him back, steeled herself against the flare of hurt in his eyes as he stepped away.

"So that's it? You're not even going to ask me what I want?"

"You told me what you wanted last night, Hart." Heat pricked her eyes. "I can't ask you to give up something you've dedicated so much of yourself to. I know what that's like, to give up a dream."

"Then why not come with me?"

She bit back a sob. "Because I don't want a life in New York. Home for me will always be the river and the farm and the fields."

"Even though you resent it?"

Anger chased away some of her sadness. "You're twisting my words. I don't resent living there, Hart, and you know it."

He held up both hands. "I'm not…you said yourself you feel like you've given up almost every piece of yourself since your mom died, and even some before that."

"I did. And those are choices I will have to reconcile, decisions I will have to talk with Robert about. But once I get my inheritance, I'll have the freedom to help Robert and still go after what I want."

Something dangerous flickered in Hart's eyes.

"How do you intend to get your inheritance, Arlowe?"

She swallowed hard. "I told you, I'll find someone—"

"Someone else. Not me, the man you just spent the night with."

She stared at him, hope draining away as she saw the banked fury in his eyes. How could she possibly explain it to him? She'd already told him how scared she was to lose him. If he didn't understand that, how could he possibly understand her motivations for choosing someone other than him?

"Yes," she finally said. "Someone else."

Hart

Hart stood there, hands fisted at his sides, his heart pounding so hard he wondered if it was going to burst through his chest.

"So you'd rather marry a complete stranger than accept my proposal?"

"Things between us are already messed up, Hart. We…" Pink stole into her cheeks as she gestured at him. "I'm so afraid to lose you."

"What does my proposal have to do with losing me?" How could she do this to them? To herself? "If it's the money, Arlowe, after the deal with Nessa goes through I could give you the money—"

"Because I don't want you to see me as the girl who needs money!" Arlowe started stalking back and forth across the room. "Can't you see? What if you resent me later? As soon as I take that money from you, it'll change everything."

Hart stabbed a finger toward the bed. "More than that?"

"Yes!" she cried. "That was mutual. That was something we both wanted. But you giving me money makes me indebted to you."

Insulted, Hart shook his head. "I would never ask you to pay anything back. I've told you that numerous times."

"Not indebted like I owe you money, Hart, but indebted because you did this massive favor for me that I can never return."

"Because that's what we do for the people we care about!"

They stood there staring at each other. Blood pumped through Hart's veins while frustration pounded away at his temples. Arlowe continued to stare at him with a bleak despair that, had he not been so angry, would have frightened him.

"I care about you, Hart. So much. That's why I can't accept your money or your proposal."

The thought of Arlowe taking another man's last name after what they'd shared last night made Hart want to rip something in two.

"So you don't want to accept my money because you're afraid you'll feel like it will change our dynamic too much. What about the proposal?"

Her gaze dropped down to the floor.

"We already…we already risked our friendship enough. I don't want to risk it any further."

Her words slammed into him. Had she felt any of what he'd experienced last night? Or was this all just a physical attraction, something for her to get out of her system before she slipped back into the role of friend?

"Why," he finally said quietly, "do you keep shutting me out?"

Arlowe stared at him. "What?"

"You didn't tell me about the bills. The second job. The land."

Her face went white. "The land?"

"The twenty acres you sold."

"I…" She scrubbed a hand across her face. "I didn't know how to tell you."

"Why didn't you just come to me, Arlowe?"

"Because I didn't want you to see me as a failure!" Arlowe's entire body trembled, as if she was trying to desperately hold on to the tears glinting in her eyes. "I made so many wrong choices, Hart. If I had made more responsible choices instead of going after my stupid dreams, I would have a career and I could have helped out my mom and Robert so much more. We would have had more money, more stability. And instead…"

He nearly went to her then. Nearly took her in his arms to reassure her that everything would be all right.

But for the first time in a very long time, he realized he was facing down the very real possibility of things not working out.

"I sold the land because I had to make a hard choice, Hart. Just like you had to make a hard choice to move to New York. That's life." Her voice dropped. "I finally learned my lesson."

"And what lesson is that?" Hart walked toward her with slow, measured steps. "That you're not allowed to pursue your dreams? For God's sake, Arlowe, you went to a community college first. You worked to put yourself through school instead of taking out loans. You got the job at the greenhouse to build up your résumé. At what point did you make a mistake?"

"If I had gotten a different degree or a certification—"

"And where's Robert in all this? Your mom?"

Arlowe's spine straightened. "Excuse me?"

"What if Robert hadn't gotten hurt and lost his job in the

first place? What if your mom had gotten a degree in accounting instead of being a stay-at-home mom and working on the farm?" He stopped in front of her, barely resisting the urge to pull her into his arms and kiss some sense into her. "You can 'what if' your life to death, Arlowe. None of it is going to make any of this better."

"Neither will accepting your offer, Hart. You can't fix my problems with money."

"I'm not," he ground out.

"But aren't you?" she pressed. "Do you realize that in the past six months half of the texts you sent me were offers or reminders to help me with bills?"

Hart stilled. That couldn't be true. Yes, he'd lapsed on texting her in the wake of his breakup with Lucy. But he had to have texted more than that.

"It was like the more distant we grew, the more you offered money," Arlowe said quietly. "I didn't want your money, Hart. I just wanted my friend."

Guilt stabbed into him.

"I wasn't trying to buy your friendship. That was never my intention."

"I know it wasn't." Arlowe sighed and sank into a chair by the fire. "But it felt like it at times. I know money's become a bigger part of your life—"

"But it hasn't. I don't live like my grandfather did."

Arlowe held up a hand. "That's not what I'm saying, Hart. You're ten times the man he ever was." She stood and crossed to him, grabbing his hands in hers. "I meant what I said at breakfast the other day. Your father would be so proud of you."

For one moment, their argument fell away. He savored her touch, the strength in her hands, the calluses on the palms of her hands.

He was so damned proud of her. But he also hated this

powerlessness, the inability to do anything to help Arlowe when she repeatedly shut him out.

"Money isn't the most important thing to me, Arlowe."

She shook her head. "I phrased that poorly. Not money, but your company, its success. Understandable after what your grandfather did, all the stress he placed on the people who used to work for him."

Her words revolved around inside his head. BioInnovations had become a huge part of his life, yes. But his mom, Arlowe, they were still the most important people in his life. Robert, too, and the farms.

Arlowe squeezed his hands.

"I'm just worried you're ignoring your instinct on this deal with Nessa because you're worried about listening to your emotions. Worried you'll make the same mistakes your grandfather did."

Hart yanked his hands out of hers, pulled away from the truth of her words.

"That has nothing to do with it. Nessa has everything a prospective client should. Everything they've submitted checks out. There's no logical reason to deny their request."

"But something's bothering you," Arlowe pressed. "Hart, one of the things I appreciate the most about you is how committed you are to logic and numbers. You've always been my rock when it comes to things like that. But you're smarter than you give yourself credit for when it comes to people." Her weak smile nearly undid him. "You always seem to know the right thing to say to cheer me up. I just think you should trust yourself and dig a little deeper—"

"I can't."

He wanted to dig more. Wanted to reassure himself that Nessa was truly who they said they were and their star drug was capable of doing what they claimed. But that wasn't real life.

"They want an answer today by three."

"But doesn't that bother you? That they went from being flexible on the contract to suddenly pushing when they realized you were having second thoughts? That's something I would follow up on."

"The data doesn't lie, Arlowe. I don't just run on emotions and feelings. I'm not you."

The words fell like a death knell. Arlowe stared at him, eyes wide, lips slightly parted. The color drained from her face as Hart inwardly swore.

"Arlowe. I didn't mean—"

"It's okay, Hart." Arlowe's voice was so soft he could barely hear her.

"No, it's not."

Arlowe released his hands and walked back to her side of the bed. She picked her robe up off the floor and slid her arms into the filmy material. Hart stood watching her, knowing that each movement was taking her further and further away from him.

"We approach situations very differently," Arlowe continued as if he hadn't spoken. "You've obviously turned BioInnovations around. I don't know anything about pharmaceuticals."

"That doesn't mean I don't value your opinion."

The words felt empty, hollow. Arlowe apparently took them as such because she just nodded her head as she grabbed the filmy dress she'd worn the night before.

Had it been less than twelve hours ago they'd danced? Since they'd kissed in the mirrored ballroom before he'd carried her up to his room and his bed?

His phone dinged. He opened the text message.

"It's the helicopter company. They'll be here in thirty minutes."

He looked up at Arlowe. She stared at him, then finally nodded.

"I'm glad. You should pack."

She stood and walked toward the door. Hart moved in front of her and grabbed the doorknob.

"What does this mean for us?"

Arlowe slowly looked up at him. "I don't know," she finally said. "I can't imagine my life without your friendship."

Friends. How could she possibly think of them still being friends after what they'd shared last night? Did she really think he would just stand by and let her marry some random man while he stood off to the side as her man of honor?

"And what if I can't go back to being friends?"

Hart's pulse pounded wildly in his throat as Arlowe's eyes widened.

"What?"

"What if, after what we shared last night, I..." He breathed in, then out in a sharp exhale. "What if I want more?"

Arlowe was shaking her head before he even finished speaking.

"But we...we're friends, Hart. I don't want to lose you."

"I don't want to lose you either, Arlowe. But I can't deny what I'm feeling."

"Hart..." A sob underscored his name. "Hart, I don't... I can't..."

Calm stole over him. A peace he desperately needed as Arlowe stared at him with grief-stricken eyes.

"It's okay."

"No." She brushed her hair out of her face. "If I would have known... I would never have..."

She would have never spent the night in his bed. Would have never kissed him. Because Arlowe didn't care for him the way he cared for her. Because she would never ask him to come back home, wouldn't even contemplate exploring a compromise that would give them a way to be together.

One day, he would give himself the time and space to

grieve. But right now he needed to retreat into a space where he could go through the motions, accomplish what he needed to, and get out of the castle.

Before he did something truly stupid like tell Arlowe how deeply he was in love with her.

"It's okay, Arlowe."

He leaned down and pressed a kiss to her forehead. It would be so easy to move his lips down, to capture her mouth in one last kiss. To ask her to take a few days to think about everything that had transpired between them. To ask herself if she could ever feel for him the way he felt for her.

But he couldn't do that to her. Not when she looked so miserable at the barest mention of his feelings. He'd never once pressured her into anything she didn't want to do. He wasn't about to start now.

He stepped back. "I'll call you later."

She stared at him for so long he wondered if she was going to say something. But that hope was dashed when she turned and walked out the door. He moved to the doorway and watched her walk down the hall, the flutter of the dress about her legs, the curls bouncing down her back.

She turned the corner and disappeared. He stood there for several long, torturous seconds. He'd never envisioned he and Arlowe being in reversed roles, she thinking about logical details like choosing where to live and he focusing exclusively on his growing feelings for her. He understood her argument, recognized her fear. But for the first time in his life, he had operated solely on his emotions.

And lost.

This was what came from living off feelings. From making choices rooted in emotion. As he closed the door, he couldn't shake the feeling that their relationship had been completely and irretrievably broken.

CHAPTER SEVENTEEN

Arlowe

SUN GLINTED OFF the lake. The blue of the sky was made even more brilliant by the sea of white beneath. Over two feet of snow had fallen over the past few days, leaving the Austrian countryside blanketed in glittering white.

Arlowe leaned against the balcony railing. It had been five hours since Hart had left. His meeting would be starting at any moment. She wanted to text him, wish him luck even though she didn't think signing was the right thing to do. But since he'd left without even saying goodbye, she didn't think a text would be well received right now.

Was he feeling more confident in his choice? She hoped for his sake, and the company's, that his suspicions were misplaced. She wanted the best for him.

Even if the best meant his living hundreds of miles away.

Her chest tightened. Had she made her decision too hastily? Pushed him away without giving them a proper chance?

No. She knew the truth even if she hated it. She wouldn't be happy in New York. And she definitely wouldn't be happy marrying Hart, especially if they spent their marriage living in separate states.

She'd hurt him. He hadn't understood. She had barely been able to put words to the pain inside her at the thought of signing a marriage license, knowing it was in name only, or the deeper hurt of envisioning writing her name on a divorce decree. But as she gazed out over the valley, reliving the intimate moments of the last few days before reality had come calling, she finally accepted what her heart had been trying to tell her ever since Hart had walked into the courtyard in the middle of a snowstorm.

She was in love with Hart.

A broken laugh escaped. She could lie and tell herself it was a fluke, strong emotions brought on by the incredible events of the last few days. But the truth was she'd compared every man she'd ever dated to Hart. She'd gone out with some nice men, interesting men. None of them had ever gotten her the way Hart did.

Not, she admitted with a sad smile, that she'd ever let them get close enough to try. She'd told herself she was just holding out for her true Prince Charming. He'd been right in front of her all along.

It also explained the tightness in her chest when he'd first told her about Lucy, the ache in her stomach when she'd met the opera star and seen how perfect Lucy had been for the man Hart had become. Symptoms of good old-fashioned jealousy.

A cold breeze stirred her hair. She had plenty of truths to sort through and zero solutions. At the end of the day, it didn't matter how she felt about Hart, or whether he cared for her, too. He'd told her he wanted more. But that was today, fresh after spending an intimate night together and days trapped in a real-life castle in the Austrian countryside.

Would he still feel the same way when they were back in the States? When he was living out his life in New York and balancing his work commitments with a long-distance relationship? They'd barely seen each other the past three years. How could they possibly make a romance work if they hadn't even been able to keep their friendship alive?

Worse, what if they did try? What if, after the glow wore

off, Hart saw her for who she'd become and found her lacking? A college dropout barely scraping by?

The breeze strengthened into a fierce wind that sent her back into the warmth of the small parlor she'd discovered during one of her sojourns. She shut the door behind her and settled into the embrace of a plush velvet chair next to the fireplace before pulling out her phone.

"Hello?"

Arlowe smiled as the comforting familiarity of Robert's raspy voice flowed over her.

"Hi, Papa."

"Arlowe! How's Austria?"

"Good. Beautiful, actually."

A beat of silence. Then, "Uh-huh. What's wrong, kid?"

Her throat tightened as tears welled in her eyes. "Papa... I don't know what to do."

She told him everything. The true extent of how much she and Hart had drifted apart. The will with its binding marriage clause. How Hart had flown hundreds of miles right before a major business deal to check on her, how things had changed between them while he'd been stranded here. The only thing she didn't share was their spending the night together.

"So he's gone to sign this deal that I don't think is a good idea and I... I..." She bit back a shuddering sob. "I love him. I love him and I don't know what to do about it."

"It sounds to me like Hart loves you, too."

She shook her head. "He didn't say that. He just said he wanted more, which, given that we had just..." She stopped and cleared her throat. "It was different here, you know? Like we were different people so far away from home."

"Arlowe, the man flew hundreds of miles to beat out a snowstorm and reach you because he was afraid you were going to get married to some stranger." Amusement laced Robert's voice. "I know you two are friends, but that's the kind of thing a man does to stop the woman he loves from making a mistake."

"But I…we can't…"

"Why not?" Robert's tone hardened with frustration. "For God's sake, Arlowe, why can't you let yourself have this? You've been working yourself to the bone for years now, ever since I lost my job."

"But that's just it!" she cried. "The last few years have been hell. I'm so glad I was able to help you and Mom out, but right before the accident I was so tired and frustrated. I just wanted to go back to school."

Her hand flew to her mouth. Had she really just admitted that out loud?

"I'm sorry. I—"

"Don't you dare apologize, young lady." She could picture Robert right now, sitting bolt upright in his recliner, his square jaw locked tight beneath the curls of his graying beard. "Any young woman who voluntarily gave up her degree to come help out her parents is entitled to feel frustrated. You never once made your mom and I feel like you didn't want to be there."

"I was going to talk to you both. The weekend after…" She stopped, swallowed her tears. "And then it happened and it felt like punishment. I know it wasn't, but I couldn't help but wonder if I had just worked a little harder and been a little more grateful—"

"God, Arlowe." Robert's voice was thick with his own tears. "Why didn't you tell me, baby girl?"

"Because I felt so guilty." The tears were flowing freely now, cascading down her cheeks and leaving hot, wet trails in their wake. "I felt guilty for feeling frustrated, for wanting to get back to my own life. And then I felt guilty because if I had done things differently and gotten a different degree—"

"I would have still lost my job," Robert cut in. "And your

mom…" He paused. "Your mom would still have passed away. None of this is your fault."

"I know that. Logically I know that. But…but I feel…" Her voice trailed off. "Probably too much."

"You're taking on too much responsibility, yes. But I want you to get one thing straight. Your mother lived her life to the fullest. She didn't live by her emotions, but she listened to them and let them lead her when she knew listening to her heart was the right thing to do. It's something I admired about her. Something I loved about her."

"I know." Her hand tightened on the phone. "I wish I could give you a hug right now."

"Same, kiddo." He cleared his throat. "You want my honest opinion?"

"Yes."

"You're backing yourself into a corner when it comes to Hart because you're so scared it's going to fail you can't even begin to entertain the possibility of it going right."

"But how can I ask that of him, Papa? I…"

Shame silenced her.

"You don't want to ask him to give up his life in New York the way you gave up your life at college."

She scrunched her eyes shut. "I offered, and I would do it all over again."

"Which just makes you even more like your mother. That woman was pure sunshine, but she could pull on her big girl boots when she needed to and made some hard choices. Doesn't mean she didn't sometimes wish things could have been different. But I'd say that's what made her, and you, even more honorable. You do the hard things even when you don't want to."

Slowly the tension bled out of her muscles. She sank deeper into the chair.

"Thank you."

"You're welcome." His tone softened. "Life's been hard,

kid. Harder this past year and a half than any of us imagined. But just because some things didn't work doesn't mean this won't. How would you feel if the roles were reversed and Hart didn't at least give you the chance to voice your opinion?"

She bit down on the inside of her cheek. "Fair."

"Said grudgingly, but I'll take it. How do you feel about Hart?"

"I love him." She said it without hesitation. "I'm in love with him. But I'm not Lucy—"

"No, you're not. You're Arlowe Banks, and you've been Hart's best friend since you were five years old. You've stood by him through some of the toughest times in his life, and when he left, because that's what he needed, you wished him the best and meant it even though it killed you inside. Having a woman who will love you through everything means far more than dating a woman with a fancy degree and expensive clothes. Take it from me," he added softly. "I was married before your mother. Money means nothing compared to someone loving you for who you are, faults and all."

"She loved you, too, Papa." She swallowed a shuddering breath and raised her chin. "I'm terrified."

"I know."

"But I'll tell him."

As soon as she got off the phone, she'd call Herr Blukker and figure out the best way to get out of the castle. If she hurried, she might even be able to catch Hart in Lyon. If not, she'd change her ticket to New York. She'd tell him everything, even if the thought of doing it made her heart pound wildly against her ribs.

By the end, she and Hart might be through for good. But at least she would know she had done everything she could. Beneath the fear, excitement flickered. A bit of the adventurous woman she used to be.

"I'm not going to give up just yet."

He might have been thousands of miles away, but she could feel Robert's smile through the phone.

"That's my girl."

Hart

Blaine Jones's face was turning an interesting shade of red. Mottled red, really, Hart thought as he watched Nessa Pharmaceuticals' CEO quiver in his seat.

"What?" Blaine finally choked out.

"My team needs an additional two weeks before we sign."

"You can't be serious. After what we added to the deal, you're going to turn us down?"

"No." Hart forced a pleasant, neutral smile to his face even as he resisted the urge to kick the man out of the conference room. "No, I'm requesting an additional two weeks. My time here in Lyon was interrupted—"

"Yes, I heard." Blaine sneered. "A little sojourn to the Austrian Alps in the middle of the biggest deal of your company's history isn't a good look, Sinclair. Makes investors think you're starting to follow in your grandfather's footsteps."

"That's enough."

Katherine King's voice rang out and silenced the sudden explosion of whispers around the conference room. At sixty she still had the same commanding presence and authority she'd exhibited when the acting CEO of BioInnovations had hired her a year before Hart's grandfather had passed away. She hadn't been able to do much under his grandfather's tight-fisted approach. But she'd still laid the groundwork for Hart to come in and begin righting the wrongs.

"I served for a year under Mr. Sinclair's grandfather. I can assure you that Hart is nothing like him, and any insinuations like that could be taken as slander, Mr. Jones."

Blaine held up his hands. "I'm not—"

"But you were." Katherine's smile was razor-sharp. "Hart is making a reasonable request with a minor adjustment to the time frame. You're the one blowing it out of proportion, Mr. Jones."

"The hell I am." Blaine stood, nearly knocking over his chair as he grabbed his briefcase. "I've made a more than generous offer. Either BioInnovations signs now, or Nessa takes its business elsewhere."

Hart inclined his head. "As you wish, Mr. Jones."

Blaine stared at him before letting out a growl and storming out the door.

Arlowe was right.

As the room erupted around him, Hart sat back in his chair. He still didn't know what exactly Blaine was hiding. But he had no doubt he had made the right choice.

He glanced down at his phone. The screen stayed dark. It had been six hours since he'd left Austria. Three since he'd landed in Lyon.

One since he'd stood inside the conference room waiting for his team and Blaine to join him. Since he'd accepted that Arlowe had been right. He didn't trust himself when it came to his emotions. But in this case, data and reports had meant nothing.

"You were right."

Hart glanced over at Katherine. "I didn't want to be."

"I'll admit I had my concerns about postponing." Katherine shook her head. "But Blaine's hissy fit on his way out… something's not right."

"No, it's not. I want to get to the bottom of it." He paused. "Actually, I have a favor to ask, Katherine."

"Name it."

He smiled slightly. "Just like that?"

"Hart, you don't give yourself enough credit for what you've done for this company." Katherine gestured around the room to the people still sitting at the conference table. "You've proven over and over how much you care." One corner of her mouth tilted up. "You just turned down a potentially multibillion dollar deal because you thought it was the right thing to do, even when some of us in this room didn't agree with it. But you were right." She reached over and patted his arm. "We believe in you. So if there's something we can do for you, we want to do it."

He sat there for a moment, his throat tight. He'd been so fixated on making sure he created the kind of legacy his father would have wanted, on not making his grandfather's mistakes, that he had never once stopped to look at what he and his team had already accomplished. He'd been so focused on himself that he hadn't bothered to look at the people around him who were helping him craft the legacy his father would have been proud of.

"Thank you."

"You're welcome. Now," Katherine said sternly, "what can we do?"

"I'm flying back to Austria in the morning."

"Ah." She leaned in and lowered her voice. "Hopefully for a woman?"

"Hopefully?"

"Please." Katherine rolled her eyes. "I'm sixty years old with three children and two grandchildren. As soon as you went flying out of here on Tuesday, I knew it had to be because of a woman." She arched one brow. "Arlowe?"

He started. "Arlowe?"

"You mention her at least once a week, if not more."

His lips curved up. "Yes, I'm traveling back to Austria to see Arlowe. She's the one who encouraged me to listen to my gut on this."

"Wise woman." Katherine stood. "Don't let her get away, Sinclair."

The conference room emptied out. Hart stayed behind until the last person left, leaving him alone in the elegant space overlooking the Old City.

Had it really been four days since he'd stood on the balcony of his penthouse and watched the couple at the café? Four days since he'd flown to Austria, walked into the courtyard, and laid eyes on the only woman he would ever love?

Hart stood and paced to the windows. He was in love with Arlowe. And she'd turned him away.

No, that wasn't fair. He'd told her he wanted more out of their relationship. But he'd never once told her the depths of his feelings. He'd only acknowledged it to himself in the last hour or so. As the helicopter had taken off from the castle, it had felt like being cleaved in two.

He'd spent the rest of the flight reviewing his relationship with Arlowe. Of reviewing the night he'd held her while she cried, the first time he'd felt that shifting in his chest and the thought of leaving her had nearly made him stay behind. How his feelings, both his grief and his care for Arlowe, had felt like weaknesses that would slow him down, hinder his goal of rebuilding BioInnovations.

Instead, he'd used them as excuses to shut himself off. He'd taken the easy way out.

Arlowe had been through hell. He'd put some of that on her by withdrawing, by not sharing his grief and anger at his father's passing. He'd been the one to first place distance between them, to inflict the first cracks on their relationship. It was no small wonder that she resisted the possibility of more when he'd barely offered her anything but crumbs the past few years. Yes, she was proud of him, understood the need that had driven him.

But that didn't mean he hadn't hurt her. Didn't mean he couldn't have done better and let her in, let her see him at his darkest, just as he wanted her to do with him. He'd made a choice for her without ever consulting her. They'd both suffered for it.

He checked his emails. As the helicopter had landed, he'd messaged his secretary and asked for the first flight back to Salzburg in the morning. Part of him wanted to call Arlowe now, tell her that she had been right and the contract with Nessa Pharmaceuticals was off the table.

But a phone call wasn't enough. He needed to see her in-person, thank her and then tell her everything he'd been holding back.

He glanced back at the conference table, at the brochures and paperwork left behind at his seat. He'd done the right thing today. His team had supported him. Yes, there might be some fallout once the circumstances of what had transpired today became public knowledge. But there was no tightness in Hart's chest, no fear goading him to move on and find the next best thing. No, there was only certainty that the right choice had been made and the company would continue.

A company he no longer needed to obsess over. He had an incredible team manning the helm. He still wanted to be involved. BioInnovations had become a big part of his life.

But Arlowe was more important. He needed to show her that.

He spent the rest of the night packing and pacing restlessly up and down the penthouse balcony. His flight was scheduled for ten in the morning. He needed to sleep. But every time he started to drift off, memories would play in his head, a carousel of images from his last few days with Arlowe. The snowflakes in her hair, that first moment of awareness in the kitchen, the feel of waking up with her in his arms.

She cared for him, too. He just had to show her he could be what she needed. He wouldn't fail her again.

Just after dawn, his phone dinged.

CHAPTER EIGHTEEN

Arlowe

THE SUN ROSE above Lyon's Old City and made the vivid colors of the Escalier Mermet glow. Bright blue, pale yellow, and crisp white colored the staircase that joined the Rue René-Leynaud with the Rue Burdeau. Just beyond the arch behind her she could hear the sounds of one of the district's numerous cafés; the low murmur of conversation, the clink of coffee cups, the quiet scrape of a chair on the cobblestones.

She latched onto the sounds, focused on the mundane as her heart beat wildly in her chest. It had been ten minutes since she'd texted Hart and invited him to join her for an early morning walk. Her phone showed her the text had been read. But there'd been no reply.

Her breath rushed out. Maybe it was too late. Maybe Hart had changed his mind.

She put a mental stop to her runaway thoughts. It had been ten minutes. Perhaps he'd glanced at her text and gone back to sleep. Maybe he had another meeting. There were plenty of reasons as to why he hadn't responded yet.

None of them relieved the stress tying her stomach into knots.

Okay, time to get moving.

She walked up the brightly painted steps, counting each

step as she went. Slowly her breathing evened out and her heartbeat slowed.

No matter what happened today, she was not going to regret coming. She was going to tell Hart how she felt, tell him her fears and hope they could find a way to bridge the gap.

And even if they couldn't compromise, she would be grateful for those few snowbound days.

She reached the top of the stairs, pausing for a moment to catch her breath before she turned to start back down the stairs. Her shoe stuck to something on the top stair and she stumbled, one hand flying up to brace herself on the wall as her bare foot touched the cool stone.

"Oh geez."

"Is that how Cinderella lost her slipper?"

Arlowe froze. Then, slowly, she turned around. Hart crouched down and picked her shoe up off the ground. His eyes were fixed on hers, a small smile playing about his lips as he approached.

"You're here."

"So are you." Hart held up her shoe. "May I?"

At her nod, he knelt and wrapped one hand around her ankle. She shivered as his fingertips pressed against her skin and slipped the shoe back on.

"Thank you," she forced out as he stood.

He towered over her, dressed in black pants, a dark green shirt, and a black peacoat that screamed masculine confidence. For a moment, her own poise wavered. Was she really the best person for Hart? Could they make this work?

She raised her chin. Only one way to find out.

"I realized I let you leave without telling you some things."

He stepped closer, reached up and trailed a finger down her cheek. "That makes two of us." His smile turned quizzical. "Although I am curious as to how you got here so quickly."

"Herr Blukker." She fought the urge to lean into his touch,

to let her eyes drift shut and savor the feel of him. She needed to stay focused, tell him everything before she lost her courage. "Turns out he has a friend in the village who operates a snowplow that clears the train tracks. They plowed the drive up to the castle and got me to the airport for an overnight flight into Lyon."

"And now you're here."

"I am." She sucked in a breath. "I came here to tell you… I wanted you to know…"

Hart placed one hand at her waist. When she didn't pull back, he slid his arm around her and gently pulled her close.

"Tell me what, Arlowe?"

"I love you." Her voice caught. "Not just love you like a friend, Hart, but I'm in love with you. I don't know if we can make it work, but I couldn't let you think—"

Anything else she was going to say was silenced by Hart kissing her. Tears fell down her cheeks as she threw her arms around his neck and hugged him tight.

It would have been so easy to just let Hart continue to kiss her. But finally she summoned enough willpower to plant her hands against his chest and gently push him back.

"I said no to your proposal because I knew it would be too hard to be married to you when I was feeling the way I was." She grabbed his wrists as he reached up and cupped her face in his hands. "Whenever I thought about us divorcing in three years, it nearly broke me."

"As did the thought of you marrying anyone else. Do you know why that is?"

Hope flared in her chest, bright and beautiful. "I know what I'm hoping for."

"I love you, Arlowe." He cupped her face in his hands as fresh tears fell down her cheeks. "I've loved you for so long. I was just too blind to see it."

"We were both blind." She leaned up and grazed her lips

across his. "I'm scared, Hart. Terrified, actually. There have been so many challenges these past few years, and I know it's going to be hard with you being in New York and me being in Missouri, but I want to make this work. Make *us* work."

"What if I could fix that?"

Arlowe's eyes widened. "No. You're not giving up BioInnovations."

"You're right. I'm not. But," he added with a smile as she stared up at him, "I am going to leave the New York plant in the more-than-capable hands of my vice president, assuming she agrees. And then I will oversee the new manufacturing plant that will open just outside Kansas City in eighteen months."

Arlowe blinked, trying to process what Hart had just said. "A new plant?"

"I'll need something to do since we won't be moving forward with Nessa Pharmaceuticals."

Pride filled her. "You said no."

"I did. Because of you." His breath rushed out. "When my father died… I'd never experienced that level of grief before. And you… I was so afraid of hurting you, Arlowe. Of dragging you down with me. I didn't even give you the opportunity to be there for me."

"Just like I didn't tell you how much I was struggling." Arlowe smiled through her tears. "We make quite a pair, don't we?"

"We do." He kissed her forehead. "You make me a better person. As soon as I told Nessa's CEO we needed a little more time, he exploded. I don't know for sure what he's hiding, but I do know that listening to my instincts saved the company from entering into a bad decision. I resisted listening to my emotions because I was afraid of losing control, like I almost did after my father passed, or being too much like my grandfather and making a mistake with no data to back it up."

"You're a good leader, Hart. I'm so proud of you."

"And I'm proud of you." He leaned down and kissed her again. "You are so much more than you give yourself credit for." His arms tightened around her. "We will make this work. Which speaking of…"

He released her. A moment later he fell to one knee. Arlowe's mouth dropped open as he grabbed her left hand in his.

"Arlowe Banks, I can't imagine my life without you, and I don't want to ever again. I don't have a ring yet, but I don't want to go another second without you knowing just how much I want you in my life." His hand tightened on hers. "No expiration date. No divorce. No marriage of convenience. I want you as my wife. I want to build the house you've always dreamed of. I want to create a family of our own."

"And I want you as my husband." She smiled at Hart through her tears. "I can't believe after all this time it's you. It's always been you."

He stood and pulled her into his arms.

"Always."

And he sealed their future with a kiss.

EPILOGUE

Arlowe

ARLOWE'S HEART STARTED beating faster as the music played. Mina and Ivy glanced back at her over their shoulders and smiled.

"See you at the altar," Mina whispered.

"Mind your skirt," Ivy added practically.

Arlowe smiled so hard it was a wonder her face didn't split in two. "Thank you. Both."

They turned and walked through the double wooden doors that had been set up at the top of the bluff between two towering evergreen trees. Arlowe caught a glimpse of Hart standing down on the bluff before the wedding planner closed the doors again.

"Are you ready?"

Arlowe glanced up at Robert. Her stepfather was standing tall and proud with the aid of a walker. His new physical therapist was predicting he'd be walking with a cane by Christmas. He'd never be back to full strength, but the therapist was committed to giving Robert as much physical autonomy as possible.

"I am."

She glanced down at her dress. Ivy and Mina had been

very supportive of her decision to wear one of Desdemona's dresses for her wedding. The cream-colored lace clung to her figure, from the long filmy sleeves to the slender skirt that followed her legs until it flared out at her knees. Her curls had been pulled up into an elaborate updo toward the crown of her head with tiny white flowers woven in the strands. The makeup artist had honored her request for minimal makeup, but had managed to talk Arlowe into a vivid red lipstick that added a hint of sensuality to her look.

Now, as she clutched a bouquet of daisies and roses in her hand, she felt beautiful.

I'm a bride.

Robert's eyes grew misty. "Your mother would be so proud of you."

Arlowe squeezed his arm as she fought back tears. "Thank you. She'd be proud of you, too."

Not only had Robert made significant progress with his physical therapy, but Hart had named him the new plant foreman for BioInnovations' Kansas City location when it opened next year. Less than thirty minutes away, Hart would be spending the majority of his time in Missouri. Business had picked up even more, especially after it came out that Nessa Pharmaceuticals had falsified some of their long-term clinical trial data and failed to report a life-threatening symptom. Word had spread of how Hart had chosen not to do business with Nessa despite the lucrative offer, solidifying BioInnovations' reputation as an international powerhouse, which meant more trips abroad, too.

Trips Arlowe would accompany him on as her schedule allowed. She'd given up her job at the hotel bar and dropped back to part-time at the greenhouse. By the end of the summer, she'd have her degree and would be continuing on to an internship with a landscaping firm in Kansas City.

She glanced over her shoulder at the pond and maple trees

just behind her. The construction workers wouldn't start until next week after she and Hart had left for their honeymoon in the Cayman Islands. If things went well, she and Hart would be moving in to their new home before the winter holidays.

And even if they didn't, she thought to herself with a small smile, it would happen eventually.

The music changed. Arlowe sucked in a deep breath as the doors opened again.

"Ready?" Robert whispered.

"More than I ever thought possible," she whispered back, her eyes already locked on Hart.

They walked slowly down the aisle, the grass covered in red and white petals. Guests on either side wiped away tears or exchanged smiles. People from the greenhouse, from Bio-Innovations, their neighbors and friends.

And there, standing beneath a white arch wrapped in flowers and greenery, was Hart. Dressed in a black tuxedo, his dark hair combed back from his forehead, he looked incredibly handsome as he smiled at her with love shining in his eyes. Francine stood next to him, dotting at her eyes as Arlowe and Robert drew near.

"Hi," he murmured as he walked up to take Arlowe's hand.

"Hi," she whispered back.

"One thing before we say 'I do.'"

He clasped her face between his hands and kissed her. Arlowe smiled against his lips as she leaned into the kiss. A chuckle rolled through the crowd as the pastor cleared his throat behind them.

"We're not quite up to that part."

Hart lifted his head and smiled down at her. "I won't say I'm sorry because I'm not. I just missed you."

She cupped his face in her hand. "I missed you."

As they turned to face the pastor with their family and friends behind them and the river beyond, Arlowe sighed happily. All the twists and turns of the last few years, good and bad, had brought her here to this moment. To Hart.

She glanced up at her soon-to-be husband, her chest swelling when his gaze met hers. She smiled and squeezed his hand.

They were home.

* * * * *

Look out for the next story in the
How to Inherit a Fortune trilogy.
Coming soon!

And if you enjoyed this story, check out these other great
reads from Scarlett Clarke

The Billionaire She Loves to Hate
Royally Forbidden to the Boss
The Prince She Kissed in Paris

Available now!

CHRISTMAS WITH THE SECRET TYCOON

RHODA BAXTER

MILLS & BOON

To my writer friends. You know who you are.

CHAPTER ONE

TRISTAN SOMERSBY STORMED down the plushly carpeted corridor to his office. Members of staff leapt out of his way. They would be whispering about him the minute he went past, because everyone had seen the news. Everyone. When he marched into his office, Walter, his assistant, was already there, carefully stacking a pile of papers.

'What was she thinking?' Tristan threw himself into his chair. 'If she wanted to break up with me, she just had to talk to me. Why would she do this? So publicly as well.'

Walter folded a newspaper over the now-famous photo of Tristan's ex-fiancée, Clementine, in a compromising position with some bitcoin billionaire frat brat. Tristan had seen the image already, but it still unleashed a fresh wave of anger. A throbbing pain started up behind his eyes. His watch vibrated because it mistook the increase in his pulse for exercise. He swatted it off.

'Tristan,' Walter said. 'Are you okay?'

The genuine concern in his voice made Tristan pause. *Was* he okay? He was angry but, curiously, not sad. His engagement to Clemmie had been a practical arrangement, designed to quell rumours that the Somersby Hotels Group was going through a rocky patch because of its unpredictable playboy heir. Her breaking up with him wouldn't have been a big deal if she hadn't done it so publicly. He looked up at Walter's concerned face and shook his head.

'I'm annoyed and embarrassed and, frankly, fed up with all of this political posturing.' He pinched the bridge of his nose to stave off the headache he knew was coming. 'I need a break from all this.'

'You have been working hard.' Walter fetched him a glass of water and painkillers without needing to be asked. 'A break would be a good idea, I think.'

Tristan swallowed the painkillers. For a few minutes, he stared at his plants. In theory, he could have had a corner office with a lot of glass, but ever since he'd watched his mother walk away so many floors below him, he'd hated heights. So he'd chosen a smaller office with one large window. The windowsill held a collection of big, leafy plants in front of it so that he didn't have to look down through it. His home, a penthouse flat at the top of the Somersby Grand, was similarly green and leafy. People thought he liked plants. He didn't really. He just preferred them to looking down.

'Can you get anything of hers that's at my flat sent back to her,' he said.

'The housekeeper is already checking,' said Walter.

When Tristan had become head of diversification performance, Walter had come with the job. The man was only a couple of years older than him, but he was ruthlessly efficient as an assistant. He ran Tristan's schedule with a firm hand. He was also the closest thing Tristan had to a friend in the office. He trod the delicate balance between being extremely professional whilst still show-ing some level of human kindness, which few people around him seemed to manage.

Now that he wasn't quite so furious, the change in adrenaline levels made Tristan feel drained. 'You know what I'd like,' he said, leaning back in his chair. 'I'd like to just…be someone else for a while. Be able to talk to peo-ple as a person, not the heir of the Somersby Hotels chain or the son of Sir Alex Somersby. I'd like to just be…me.'

He couldn't think of a time when people had talked to him without the spectre of his money floating around somewhere in the background.

Walter was already scrolling through his laptop, mak-ing notes. 'Perhaps I can—'

'I don't want to go away to some private resort,' Tristan interrupted. 'I want to go somewhere where I can be the real me.' He leaned forward and rubbed his temples. 'The boutique hotel expansion project is at a delicate stage. I don't want to take time off and leave it…'

'We're still sending secret shoppers to assess the small hotels that we bought.'

'Wait.' An idea coalesced from his anger and weari-ness. 'How about if I went to one of those? I could be a personal shopper. I'd still be accessible for work, but I'd be…undercover.'

Walter nodded thoughtfully. 'In theory that can be arranged.'

Tristan raised an eyebrow. 'In theory?'

'Well, we need to get your father's approval and… he'll never go for that.'

This was true. If he showed any hint of actually want-ing to do it, Sir Alex would nix the idea immediately.

'How about…we frame it as a way to deal with the fallout from Clemmie messing up our engagement?'

Walter's eyes stayed on his iPad. 'The news has affected the share price, which will be bothering him… So your idea might work.'

The phone on his desk rang. 'That'll be him now,' said Tristan. He picked it up. Sure enough, it was his father's assistant, requesting a meeting immediately. 'I'll be right there,' he said, and hung up.

'I've found a few places that would be suitably quiet and away from the tabloid eye,' said Walter.

Tristan stood up, feeling more lively now that he had a plan. 'Let's go and persuade the old goat to have a brilliant idea.'

A few minutes later, Tristan sat in his father's office, trying to avoid looking out of the windows. It was hard, because they stretched from floor to ceiling. The mere thought of the city street with its tiny cars and ant-sized people nine floors down was making him feel lightheaded. He normally had his acrophobia under control, but the stress and drama were making it difficult today.

He angled his chair so that the view over his father's shoulder was of the top of the Somersby Grand Hotel, the flagship property of his father's empire. His empire too, in theory, although sometimes it felt like it owned him rather than the other way around.

'This is unacceptable,' his father said, scrolling through the news articles on the iPad. Sir Alex Somersby wasn't a big man, but he carried himself in such a way that he was often intimidating. Tristan had inherited the fair hair and broad shoulders from him, but not the demeanour. In all other aspects, he resembled his estranged mother. Especially when it came to his height and startling blue eyes.

Sir Alex clicked his tongue. 'This is fuelling speculation about the future of the business again. She obviously thought your fortunes were failing, which is why she went elsewhere.'

Ha. Even the gossip columnists knew what Clementine was really attracted to. The new guy had recently made several billion by selling his tech company, whereas Tristan was yet to inherit. She had left him for a better prospect.

'I don't see why my personal life should affect—' he began.

'This is a delicate time,' his father continued, as though he hadn't spoken. 'We're just rolling out the expansion into boutique hotels. At a time like this, we absolutely cannot deal with scandal affecting our stock price.' He looked up at Tristan, his eyes cold. 'How could you let this happen?'

'*Me?* I didn't do anything. She cheated on me.' She hadn't even returned the ring.

'You should have married her quicker. That would have settled the matter.'

Tristan stared. What kind of logic was that?

'Damage control?' his father asked the PR man, who had been sitting quietly during this exchange.

'There have been a few interview requests,' the PR guy said. 'We have turned them down on account of Mr Tristan being very busy at this time of year, with charities and Christmas events.'

'Can we arrange someone else to accompany him?'

'No,' said Tristan.

Sir Alex turned to face him. 'I beg your pardon?' The tone could have frozen lava.

'No. I have a better idea,' said Tristan.

He hated these corporate events. He was on display and had to be on his guard the whole time. It hadn't been too bad when Clemmie was there to deflect attention away, but by himself, with this scandal around, it would be awful. The gossip press were sharks.

'I suggest we take me out of the picture for a bit. Remove the fuel from the fire altogether. Whatever I do, the press are going to twist it into the playboy rich-kid story they like, so…let's not do anything. That way they have nothing to report. My reputation will recover eventually.'

'Eventually isn't good enough. I need the company's reputation to be intact *now*,' said Sir Alex. 'If you don't see the importance of that, then you're an even bigger fool than I thought you were.'

'Oh yes? And my showing up at these events and fielding questions will help…how exactly?' Tristan adjusted the cuff on his sleeve.

Sir Alex glowered, his face reddening.

'Perhaps,' the PR guy said quickly, 'Mr Tristan might be right. If he disappears for a bit, they'll probably forget about him within a week. We only need him to keep a low profile until after the last of the acquisition agreements is signed.'

Tristan tried not to look smug.

Sir Alex eyed him thoughtfully. 'That would work?'

The PR man cleared his throat. 'It has worked in… the past.' They all knew he was talking about the time when Tristan's mother had left. Sir Alex had disappeared from public life for a year. Tristan had been hidden for much longer.

A muscle twitched in Sir Alex's cheek. 'Hmm.' He turned, making his chair revolve smoothly so that he was facing the decorative spires of the top of the Somersby Grand.

Tristan watched carefully. His father was considering his suggestion. This was a good sign.

'There is an opportunity here to kill two birds with one stone,' Tristan pressed his advantage. 'We haven't evaluated all the new hotels we acquired for the boutique line yet and we've been sending out secret shoppers to stay there. I could go undercover as a hotel guest in one of the more obscure places?'

Sir Alex's chair revolved back to face him. 'How obscure?'

'Heritage property near Manchester?'

'Not obscure enough. They'll track you down.' His dad was watching him now, like he was evaluating a horse before a race.

It was important not to respond to the old man's glare. It only made him worse. Tristan pulled out his phone. Thank goodness Walter had sent him some suggestions.

'Cotswolds,' he said. 'It's a little place called Willerby Dalton. Small boutique hotel. Not very successful. One of the ones we bought for the location.'

Sir Alex continued to glare, but he could sense the wheels turning.

Tristan looked away. Through the window, the Somersby Grand glowed in the late-evening light. He hated chain hotels. They were so…impersonal. He could see how it could be comforting for the busy traveller to find each room exactly the same as the last place you stayed in, but to him they felt like traps designed to keep him in a place where he wasn't really wanted.

He was a numbers guy at heart. The industry was best as columns of numbers to him. Those made sense. Although he had worked in several different departments, he had found his niche in the mergers and acquisitions team. He had enjoyed doing the analysis of which hotels to buy in the latest round of acquisitions, much to the surprise of everyone else in the team, who had expected the son of the boss to accept the post as a nominal title. He just wanted to be left alone to do his job. Or left alone full stop. Remembering he wasn't supposed to look too keen, he scowled some more.

Sir Alex seemed to reach a conclusion. 'Two weeks should be more than enough time. He can come back in January.'

'And Christmas?' Tristan said. The festive events were bad enough; he then had to have that godawful Christmas lunch with his father and stepmother.

Sir Alex shrugged. 'You can see how they handle the strain of the holiday season.'

Which meant he didn't want Tristan around at home this Christmas. Was it his imagination, or did his father sound relieved? He tried not to let that sting. His father not wanting to spend family time with him was not new. Tristan was a constant reminder of the woman who had left him.

'It'll be a chance to see what you've learned from the time you've spent here at the Grand,' Sir Alex told Tristan. 'Use a false name, just in case.'

Tristan nodded curtly, and tamped down the urge to

grin in triumph. 'I trust you can find some appropriate wording to explain,' he said to the PR executive.

'Oh definitely,' the man said.

Sir Alex Somersby moved on to his next piece of work. They were dismissed.

Tristan stood up. 'I'll see you later then, *Dad*.' He saw the flinch. Sir Alex hated being called *Dad*, especially in front of people. *Father* he just about tolerated. He preferred *sir*. Tristan shook his head and left the room. As he put his hand on the door to close it behind him, his father said, 'Tristan.'

Surprised, he turned back. 'Yes?'

'Don't screw this up. Two weeks of total media silence. Once the stock price recovers, you can come back. Understood?'

'Yes.' He closed the door behind him. Walter was waiting for him outside.

'Okay,' Tristan said as they walked back to his office. 'Tell me about this Willerby Dalton place.'

Maddie dragged her suitcase out of the train station. It was good to be home. All she wanted was to sink into the sofa in her parents' house and let the familiar surroundings soothe her.

Willerby Dalton station wasn't the busiest of places, and the car park wasn't full, so it was easy to spot her friend Laura waving to her from a blue car. Maddie grinned, just like she'd done when her mum had texted her to say Laura would come to pick her up.

'Maddie!' Laura sprang out to give her a hug. 'Omigod, it's lovely to see you.' She squeezed. 'It's been ages!'

Maddie hugged her back. She and Laura had been

friends since primary school. Her mum had photos of the two of them on the fridge right from when they had matching plaits—Laura pale, blue eyed and blonde, and Maddie with brown skin, brown eyes and jet-black hair—to more current ones where Maddie's hair was a sleek shoulder-length bob. When Maddie had gone off to London for university and work, Laura had stayed behind to marry her high school sweetheart, Tim. Maddie had been the chief bridesmaid at their wedding.

'It's good to be back,' said Maddie. She meant it. Ever since Alan, her con-man ex, had stolen all her money and disappeared, she had been struggling to keep her life running. Even though her parents had lent her money for bills, there were still calls to the police and the banks and, underscoring everything, the terrible knowledge of how vulnerable she was. She had stuck it out in London, staying strong, but it had taken its toll. For the last few weeks, the idea of being back home with her friends and family had felt like the only thing that had kept her going. She had a warm welcome and safety waiting for her. It was exactly the balm she needed.

'Your mum said you'd want to go straight to the hotel rather than the house. Is that right?' Laura opened the boot.

Maddie threw her bag in. 'Yes. Dad and I are meeting there to get the stuff for the Christmas display out of the basement.'

They got in and Laura started the car. 'So how are things?' she asked Maddie as they pulled out of the car park. 'How's work?'

She chose to answer the question about work. 'Work is good. I... I've just been offered a promotion.'

'Oh, fabulous. Get you! High-flyer!'

Maddie smiled, but said nothing. The promotion scared her. She knew she was able to do the job, but new was scary. Ever since falling prey to Alan, she found everything unfamiliar terrifying. She hated that. She looked out of the window at the familiar roads. Hopefully, a few days at home, working alongside Dad on the display, would help her work some of that fear out of her system. It was good to be here. She glanced across at Laura. With people she knew she could trust.

Laura caught her glance. 'You okay? Anything I can help with?'

Maddie shook her head and smiled. 'Just glad to be back.'

'I'm so happy to see you. Tim will be too.' Laura grinned. 'You know, it's great that you're still doing the Christmas display. We thought that you might not want to. Without your grandad...'

The Christmas display at the Cygnet Hotel was Maddie's grandad's creation. He had been building a model village diorama, with a little train running through it, for the Cygnet for the past twenty-eight years. Maddie had helped him for as long as she remembered. Even after Grandad fell ill, he'd turned up to sit and supervise while Maddie and her dad put it together.

'It won't be the same without him there,' she said. 'Dad and I can do our best, but...it was Grandad's baby, really.' She looked at her right hand, where she wore her grandfather's ring on her thumb. 'I just hope we can do it justice.'

'Might be the last time ever anyway,' said Laura.

Maddie frowned. 'Why?' She and her dad had both

agreed to keep doing the display for as long as the hotel wanted it.

'Oh. You don't know?' Laura shook her head. 'The hotel got sold. This big fancy hotel chain bought it. The deal only went through a couple of weeks ago. They haven't changed anything yet, but everyone is bracing themselves for all kinds of change in the new year.' Laura was one of two assistant managers at the hotel.

How had Maddie not known about that? 'I can't believe Mum and Dad didn't mention it,' she said. Or perhaps they had and she just didn't register. She had been busy getting everything cleared off her desk so that she could have these two weeks off at home. She sighed. She was so tired.

They came into the village. Maddie sat up. 'So what else has changed?'

'Let's see…' Laura rattled off a list of things that had happened in the last year or so. Maddie was relieved to find that she had known about most of them.

CHAPTER TWO

TRISTAN PULLED INTO the small car park behind the hotel. Through the windscreen, he scrutinised the facade with a practised eye. The main building was a grand old Georgian manor house, but the wing that stretched to the side looked newer. Next to the gravelled car park, a walkway covered by leafy arches meant that people could access the gardens behind without looking at the cars.

It was clean and well kept. The window frames were peeling a little and could do with a bit of attention. Aside from that, it looked pretty good. He called Walter.

'I'm here,' he said, by way of introduction.

'Great. You're booked in under the name Christian Samuels. I thought it was best to keep your first name something similar to your real name.'

Tristan snorted. 'So I don't get my poor little head in a muddle?'

'To make your life easier,' said Walter mildly. 'You have a standard room, but I did not specify a ground-floor room for you, so if you've been offered one on the fourth floor, you'll have to request a change.'

He glanced upwards. The windows on the first few floors had window boxes which trailed greenery. The rooms at the top had smaller windows, so those were probably originally meant for staff. 'Okay. It'll be a good test of customer service,' he said. 'I'll ask. Anything else?'

'I've booked you in for two weeks, like you requested.'

'Have the hotel staff been given the standard training to bring them in line with the rest of the chain?'

'They have.'

Excellent, so he knew the standard he should be judging them against. 'So, I have to gauge the general vibe of the place. Do they feel like a Somersby hotel? If not, why not? Are safety standards up to scratch? How can it be improved? That sort of thing. Did I miss anything?'

'No. I think you've covered it.'

'It's an old building, and we'll have to refit it. I'll add any notes in that direction.' He took another glance at the building. 'I'll also make sure to note if there's anything they do particularly well that we could adopt for the other boutique hotels.'

He could almost hear Walter rolling his eyes. Tristan had insisted that all secret shoppers were sent a memo asking them to look for anything that made the smaller hotels special. The way he saw it, emphasising the unique was the way forward with the boutique hotels. Sir Alex had worked so hard standardising the chain that people tended to default to that.

'This one was failing in quite a bad way when you looked at their finances before the buyout,' Walter said. 'We bought it for the building and the location, rather than the existing hotel.'

'Nevertheless, I'll keep an eye out.'

'Yes, sir,' said Walter, which Tristan knew meant *I don't agree with you but I value my job.*

He grinned. 'Is there anything else?'

'Not really. I've packed a few things for you that won't look quite as conspicuously tailor-made.'

'Okay. Great.' He gathered his coat and made to leave the car. The only things he'd packed for himself were his tablet and notes, which were in his shoulder bag. Everything else was his standard travel bag, which Walter sorted out for him with clothes appropriate for wherever he was heading. Admittedly, that was usually abroad, not the Cotswolds.

'Tristan.'

'Yes?'

'I hope you get to find yourself.'

This sent a jolt of excitement through Tristan. The people at the hotel didn't know him. He had a different name, different clothes. He might finally get the chance to be himself without the money being in evidence. 'I just hope no one recognises me.'

'You could do something with your hair,' Walter suggested. 'So that you look different.'

'I have already thought of that.'

'Of course you have.'

He picked the phone out of its holder. 'I'll speak to you later, Walter.'

'Have a good time.'

Since he didn't say 'sir', Tristan knew he really meant it.

He was entering through the back of the hotel. The way to the reception desk was clearly signposted. Tristan wandered through the faded rooms. It was a world away from the gleaming public areas of the Somersby Grand. That was the whole point of the boutique hotels though.

They were all meant to be different from the big London hotel experience.

This building had once been a house for a very rich family. The rooms had huge sash windows and high ceilings. Everything had a feeling of old-world grandeur, but there was also a cosiness to it, which he liked. There had to be a way to modernise and upgrade without losing that warmth. He eyed the carpet, which looked modern. From the edges of the room, he could see that the original wooden flooring remained. What a shame to bury it like that. He added it to his mental list of things to put in his report.

The route wound through a couple of rooms, one of which had a pool table in it and another a cosy lounge bar, before leading him up a set of steps and into the main foyer. There were very few people around. This wasn't a good sign.

Compared to the subtle lighting in the rooms he'd just been in, the foyer was dazzlingly bright. This would have been a grand entrance hall. Light poured in from four wide bay windows. The chandelier in the middle of the room twinkled and scattered the light into rainbows on the walls. The marble-tiled floors gleamed white. A staircase curved gracefully up on one side, rising past the chandelier.

In one corner there was a Christmas tree, big enough to brush the extrahigh ceiling, decorated in Victorian style, complete with lights that looked like candles. There were soft decorations on the walls too, but interestingly, nothing in the windows. He was sure he'd read something about a big Christmas window display.

A woman about his age was at the reception desk. It

took her a moment to notice Tristan. When she did, the smile she gave felt genuine.

'I have a room booked,' Tristan said.

'What's your name, sir?'

'Tr— Chris Samuels.'

She looked it up on the computer. 'Ah yes. Here we are. You're with us for two whole weeks, Mr Samuels. Let me see if your room is ready for you.'

Tristan read the name tag on her lapel. 'Laura. Do you…have a room on the ground floor?'

She hesitated. 'We do, sir. But those are the wheelchair accessible rooms. Do you have an accessibility requirement?'

It was asked with a hint of concern rather than suspicion. He liked that.

'No,' he said. 'I just don't like heights.'

'Ah. Okay. Let me see if we have a room with a view that isn't quite so…expansive.' She frowned at the screen. 'Let's see now. Room twenty-one has a tree outside it and window boxes. You wouldn't actually be able to see the ground unless you really look. Would that help?'

Tristan blinked. That was a level of thought he hadn't expected. The tree probably would help, come to think of it. It wasn't the height that made him feel dizzy and nauseous; it was the thought of the ground being far away. If there was a tree, he wouldn't be able to see the ground. 'Yes,' he said. 'I think that might. Thank you.'

'The room hasn't been cleaned yet, I don't think. Let me just call housekeeping.' She picked up the phone on her desk. Tristan took out his own mobile and pretended not to be listening while Laura spoke to someone and asked for room 21 to be cleaned as soon as possible. The conversation all sounded terribly informal, like she was asking a friend for a favour, rather than a work transaction. It felt unsettling and unprofessional, but he had to admit that the concierge hadn't said anything actually wrong. He had to file that away to think about it.

'Your room will be ready in about half an hour, Mr Samuels. You can wait in the bar, if you like. Or in here. I can order a tea or a coffee for you.'

'I'll wait here, thanks.' He took himself to one of the bay windows at the front. The hotel faced the main square, which was currently full of parked cars. The shops all looked cheerful in their festive finery. It was noticeable that from here, all the shops looked like independent ones rather than the popular chains you saw everywhere else. Interesting. He made a note of that on his phone.

When he looked up again, there was a woman standing on the pavement outside, looking straight at him. She had what looked like a half-eaten baguette in one hand and a backpack slung over her shoulder. She was strikingly pretty. When she didn't move, he realised that although she was looking in his direction, she was lost in thought and not focused on him. Whatever she was thinking about clearly made her sad.

He studied her, fascinated. She had brown skin and black hair that gleamed when the sun caught it. Her eyes were big and the way the light fell on her face made them seem bright. As he watched, her generous mouth curved into a smile tinged with sadness. Beautiful. He could carry on looking at her all day.

He tilted his head and moved closer to the window. The light shifted and suddenly she was looking at him.

It was only a subtle change, but her gaze went from faraway to actually seeing him. It was like she was looking past the surface and seeing right into him. No one had really seen him in the longest time. The thrill of it made him gasp and look away.

Maddie took a bite out of the sandwich she'd just bought, looked up at the Cygnet Hotel and smiled. The white-painted building glowed in the late-afternoon sun. There were four huge bay windows, two either side of the portico that covered the main doors. In the next two weeks, she and her dad would be building a landscape into each window bay, complete with a small train that appeared to chug across from one window to the next. As a child, she remembered running along the front of the hotel from one window to the next to watch the train. She hadn't been the only one either.

A movement in the window brought her out of her reverie to find that she was staring straight into the eyes of a man sitting inside. For a second she felt the thrill of contact. His eyes were blue enough that she could tell the colour even at this distance. He quickly looked away. Awkward.

Maddie finished her sandwich, hitched her backpack more firmly onto her shoulder and marched towards the hotel. Inside, Laura was covering for the concierge at the desk.

'Hello, you.' Laura reached behind her desk and pulled out a lanyard with a visitor badge on it and slid it across. 'Did you get your sandwich?'

'Eventually.' Maddie put the lanyard on. 'I had to give Irene an update about my life first.' The lady who owned the bakery was a friend of her mother's. 'I bet she knows ninety percent of it already.'

She looked around the foyer. The man from before was still at the window, blond head bent over his phone. There were a few other people around, but no sign of her father.

'Has my dad showed up yet?' she asked Laura.

Her friend shook her head. 'I don't think so. He's not logged in as a visitor.'

Someone cleared their throat. They both looked at the desk to find a smartly dressed couple looking unimpressed.

Laura gave Maddie an apologetic smile and returned to her post. 'I'm terribly sorry about the wait, sir and madam. What can I do for you?'

Maddie's phone rang in her pocket, so she sat in a chair by one of the windows to answer it.

'Mum. I'm at the hotel. Is Dad on his way?'

'That's what I'm calling about. You know how he was a bit sniffly yesterday? We just did a COVID test and it's come up positive. He can't come. We're both in quarantine for the next few days.'

She stared straight ahead of her, thunderstruck. 'Is he…very ill?'

'No. Bad cold level, really. He's had his jabs, so it should only be mild. But we don't want to spread it.'

'No. No. Absolutely. You should stay at home.' Oh. This meant she couldn't go home. Her happiness and relief drained away to be replaced by anxiety. What now? Where could she stay?

'Oh darling, he's so upset that he won't be able to come and do the windows with you,' her mum continued.

That was another thing. She looked at the four big

windows. How was she going to do the display? She couldn't possibly manage it by herself.

'I tried calling a few of the people who have helped before, but they're all busy,' said her mum. 'I'm so sorry, darling. I know the contract says winter diorama, but if you talk to the hotel, they might let you do something different this year? Something more run of the mill, maybe?'

Maddie chewed her lip. She could do that, but it would take time to design it and she didn't have that. There were only five days to go before the official switch-on of the decorations. Besides, this was her tribute to Grandad. If what Laura had said was true, it might be the last time she ever did it.

'I'll think of something, Mum,' she said. 'You take care of yourself and don't fall ill, okay?'

'Where will you stay?'

'I'll sort something out.' She thought of her credit card. Could it cope with paying to stay somewhere? Hah. What was she thinking? Of course not.

The big windows of the hotel drew her eyes again. She had to do something, or else Dad would have reneged on his contract. After all the trouble she'd put her parents through in the past year, she couldn't do that to them.

If she worked really long hours…would she be able to do the window display? Sudden tears prickled. She blinked them back. The window displays at the Cygnet had been a part of her life for as long as she could remember. Grandad called her his little elf. She had learned the basics of woodworking and modelling from him before she'd even started school.

Her parents had adopted her when she was very young.

As a brown-skinned child adopted by a white family, in an overwhelmingly white neighbourhood, there had been moments of difficulty, but her family had always been there for her. She often felt that the sight of her, scrambling around helping Dad and Grandad with the display, had probably done more to cement her place in the community than anything else. She was the Christmas diorama kid, not the Asian kid or that poor kid who lost her parents.

No. She *had* to do the display. She just couldn't do it alone.

'Maddie, is everything okay?' Laura's voice was laced with concern.

She shook her head. 'Dad's ill. COVID.'

'Oh no. That's not good. Let me tell some people and we'll make sure they've got food and things delivered.' She made a note. 'Oh. Will you need somewhere to stay?'

'Yes. I was thinking I might find a B&B.'

'Are you kidding? No. Stay with us.'

'You don't have the space,' she said. 'Besides, you and Tim only just moved in there.'

'We have a sofa bed. We can cope with you cramping our style for a week or two. Just stay at ours.'

She gave her a grateful smile. 'Thanks, Laura. I love you.'

Laura grinned at her and waved away the thanks.

One problem solved. The next problem wasn't going to be as easy. She looked at the windows again and bit her lip. 'The next thing is the displays,' she said. 'Dad and I can get it done in a week. I can't do it by myself.'

Laura left her post to come and stand next to her. 'None of the people who help your dad can do it?'

'Apparently not.' She shook her head. 'I'll reuse a lot of the old sets, but they'll need touching up and realigning. I can't have exactly the same display as last year, people will notice. I…don't think I can get all that done.'

'What do you want to do? I can ring round and see if there's anyone halfway competent who can help for a day or two. Maybe I could take a day off to help. I remember stuff your dad taught me.'

'That's kind of you, but you guys are usually busy this time of year. You can't take time off.'

Another sweep of the windows. The idea of not doing the display felt too awful to contemplate. Which left having a go and doing her best. 'All I can do is try, right?' She clapped her hands together and said with a confidence she didn't feel, 'I'll go make a start and see what condition the bases are in. Can I have the keys to the storage room please?'

'Sure.' She went back to her post. 'Wait one second, I'll find them for you.'

CHAPTER THREE

TRISTAN MADE SOME notes on the room. The window did, indeed, look out at a tree and it did make him feel better about being so far off the ground. He should remember that for future reference. He lived in a penthouse apartment and worked in luxury hotels. It was easy to forget that rooms on the first floor existed.

So far this hotel had been…functional. He could already see a lot of things that could be improved. He would have more notes, if he hadn't been distracted by that woman he'd seen through the window.

He paused for a moment to think about her. When she came into the hotel, he had thought she was a guest, but it turned out she was somehow involved with staff. He hadn't been able to stop looking at her, even though she had barely registered him even being there. She looked windblown and cold and yet somehow managed to still be beautiful. He met beautiful women all the time, so why was he so taken with this one?

He shook his head. He had other things to think about. Mainly, Walter had mentioned that he'd got him some new clothes. He found the suitcase rest and opened his case on it. Huh. Walter's selection of clothes was basically some of his own casual wear with a few of the jumpers and jeans replaced with high-street brands. Hmm. Okay. If Walter thought that would help.

He changed into a polo shirt and cashmere jumper and, remembering Walter's suggestion, ran his hand through his hair to make it less groomed. Checking his reflection, he thought he still looked like himself, but less...precise somehow.

After a few minutes' thought, he swapped his contact lenses for the wire frame glasses he used at night. Now he looked even less like his public-facing self. Whenever he went out, like it or not, he was also the face of Somersby Hotels. So he had been trained to always be well groomed in public. He was wearing a suit in most photos. The only people who got to see him when he was his normal, scruffy self were his housekeeper and, until recently, Clemmie.

He mussed up his hair a bit more. He wasn't the boss's son here. Tristan let out a long, slow breath. His shoulders dropped a fraction. He wasn't the boss's son. Or the good-for-nothing rich kid who didn't deserve his position. Or the boy who was so unlovable that his mother had walked away from him. No. He was just some guy called Chris. He rolled his shoulders. It was oddly freeing.

He returned to his suitcase. There was a folder tucked in the side—a reminder that he was here to work as well as play.

He needed to find an excuse to hang around in the main lobby to observe the running of the hotel. It was a shame the bar didn't lead onto it, or he could have sat there and pretended to read or something. Something was bound to show up. He grabbed his iPad and went downstairs to investigate.

* * *

Maddie set up the stepladder by the first window. The job was too big and her brain was screaming at her in panic. She took a deep breath and let out as much air from her lungs as she could. Breathe out the negativity. When she sucked air back in, she felt a little better. The job was big, but she could cope if she took it in small steps.

The first thing to do was to put up the festive banners and decorate the tops of the windows. The banners said Christmas Display Coming Soon. She usually hid the unsightly wires behind green fabric garlands with embedded lights. It also meant that the hotel had something in the windows for the days that it took to get the display ready. They'd packed the fabric garlands that looped at the top carefully last year, so all she had to do was unwrap them and hook them up. This she could do.

She went up the ladder and secured one end, then moved the ladder so that she could safely secure the middle. There were hooks concealed behind the pole for the claret-coloured velvet curtains that covered the windows all the time.

She and Grandad had designed the garlands to complement the dark red. The lights embedded in the fabric, tiny LEDs that she'd punched into place herself, made the whole thing glow with warmth. There were arrangements of tinsel and sparkly baubles to hang on the middle and end pieces to complete the look. These windows were so tall that you had to decorate the top separately, even though very few people looked up. Why would you, when there was so much to see in the display at the base?

She moved the ladder again, and secured the end hook. Next she fished around in the box and retrieved the baubles, tinsel and silver strands that made up the end pieces. Rather than make several trips, she may as well take everything to the top and unravel it there. She gently eased it onto her shoulder and went up the stepladder, using one hand to hold the rungs, while the other kept the decorations from sliding off her shoulder. As she reached the top, her phone rang in her back pocket. She instinctively reached for it with her free hand. The decorations slid off her shoulder.

'Oh no!' She tried to grab everything. Too late. She looked down and to her horror saw that there was someone standing below. The baubles and tinsel streamers landed on him.

'I'm so sorry!' Maddie scrambled down the ladder. Unfortunately, one of the baubles had ended up on the bottom step. She slipped and fell, arms flailing, onto the poor man she'd just covered in tinsel.

She closed her eyes, expecting a crash. Instead she landed against something soft. There was a grunt and a soft 'ow'. She opened her eyes to find that she had been caught by the man who had been standing there.

For a moment all she could do was stare. He had silver streamers hanging over one eyebrow and his glasses were askew, but there was no mistaking those blue eyes. This was the guy who had been looking out of the window. At the time she hadn't been able to make out his features that well, but up close, he was spectacular. Sharp cheekbones, strong jaw. It was the sort of face that wouldn't look out of place on an advertising billboard. She opened her mouth to apologise, but nothing came out.

'Are you okay?' His voice was soft and deep. It seemed to connect to something under her lungs.

His arms, still around her, were solid and warm. It was

amazing, really. She had fallen on him, but he had managed to catch her with only the smallest stagger sideways. He must be strong as well as handsome. Wait. What was she thinking? She had just dropped a whole load of decorations on this poor man and then landed on him. He was looking down at her, with concern in his expression and tinsel sliding off his hair. She swallowed.

He put her feet down and slowly pushed her upright. She put her hand on his arm to steady herself and felt the biceps underneath that very soft jumper. She let go, quickly.

Maddie recovered her balance and her voice at the same time. 'I'm so sorry.' She started removing baubles, silver strands and sparkly red chains from his shoulders.

He glanced up at the stepladder and gave a little shudder. 'I should have checked what I was stopping next to.' He pulled some silver strands out of his hair and handed them to her.

Laura came rushing over. 'Are you okay, Mr Samuels?'

Oh no. He was a hotel guest! Maddie wasn't supposed to annoy the hotel guests.

When the man nodded, Laura turned to help gather up the rest of the decorations.

'I told you to wait until I finished my shift. I'll help you,' she hissed to Maddie as she handed them back.

'I don't have time for that,' she fired back, through her fixed smile.

Mr Samuels glanced from her to Laura and back again. 'I think I'll go sit over there. Out of harm's way.' He gestured with the local magazine he was holding and went over to the other side of the room.

'I'll go get him a drink or something to butter him

up, so that he doesn't give us a bad review,' said Laura in an undertone.

Maddie nodded and returned to work. She went more slowly this time, making sure she didn't drop anything on anyone again. The man, Mr Samuels, had sat at the other side of the foyer, half turned away from her, and ignored her. Thank goodness.

Tristan was trying to focus on what was going on in the lobby, but the woman with the tinsel kept dragging at his attention. He pretended to read his magazine and ignore her, but couldn't help sneaking a few glances at her when she was busy.

She was…magnetic. There was something about the serious expression and the fierce concentration that kept drawing him back. He had a very vivid memory of what she felt like in his arms, all soft and substantial.

He sneaked a glance. The concierge had gone off to talk to a customer and the other woman was up the step-ladder again. He couldn't watch. That ladder should have someone at the bottom of it, holding it. He would have to mention safety in his report.

He wondered what this window display was all about, so he googled it. There were a few YouTube videos and even a couple of local news clips. In one, a model train ran through a ski village. The detail looked amazing. The camera panned up and he saw colourful little skiers going down slopes and, above the mountains, a ski lift disappearing up into the fabric decorations at the top. There was another video of the same scene at night. It looked positively magical.

He knew careful craftsmanship when he saw it. As a

child, Tristan had once been given a set of minifigures to paint by a well-meaning aunt. He had tried it and, much to his own surprise, really loved the all-consuming focus of it. Of course, he couldn't take any of that to boarding school with him—that was asking for a beating—but in the holidays he had painted tiny armies until one year, he'd come back from school to find that his father had had his stash thrown away. Tristan frowned. He hadn't thought about that in years. How old would he have been? Ten? Eleven?

Of course, Tristan Somersby didn't do anything so silly as painting figurines now. These days he did more suitable things like playing golf. Which he didn't actually enjoy.

'Could we…ask one of the schools to come and help?' The concierge suggested, somewhere behind him. Tristan risked another peek.

Tinsel Woman was doing the last window now. She didn't even look down. 'It's not play painting, Laura.'

'Sorry.'

There was a pause and she said, 'I mean, if there's kids who paint models and stuff already, maybe. That's what I need, people who are able to do a little bit of model making and fine brushwork. I can probably manage the big stuff, like setting up the landscape and the trains and the lighting. I need help with the decorating.' She sighed. 'I don't want to have to cancel the display.'

'We can't do that,' Laura sounded genuinely dismayed. 'It's probably the last time we get to have it. The stuff from the new HQ is very prescriptive. Once everything's in place, we're going to have to have the same style of decoration as all the other hotels in the chain.'

This was met with a little tsk of disdain.

'So you can't cancel the display,' Laura finished. 'There's people who come especially to see it.'

Tristan doubted that very much. This place was too small to have that much of a draw. But it did seem a shame to lose something that was a tradition.

Tinsel Woman put her hands to her temples, which made Tristan think of a tragic goddess. 'I just don't have enough hands,' she said.

He needed a reason to be in the foyer. Once upon a time, he liked painting minifigures when he was a kid… It meant spending a bit more time with a woman that he couldn't stop looking at…

'Perhaps I can help?'

What was he saying? What was he *doing*? Tristan had no idea what possessed him to stand up and offer to help like that. But he was on his feet now and Tinsel Woman was looking at him with a puzzled expression so he had to go through with it.

'Pardon?' she said.

'You need someone who can paint models. I've done a bit of that…many years ago, but I'm sure I could remember how to do it.' He wouldn't normally admit to having painted Warhammer figurines, but as Walter said, no one knew him here. It would be fine.

The look she gave him was part confusion, part wariness. 'That's very kind Mr…er…' she said, cautiously.

'Mr Samuels,' Laura supplied.

For a second he was insulted. No one spoke to him like that. Then he remembered. Of course, he wasn't himself right now, was he? 'Christian,' he said, trying out his new name for size. 'Chris.' It was close enough to Tristan. He could live with that.

'I'm Maddie Attwater. Nice to meet you,' she said. 'It's really kind of you to offer to help, Chris, but I don't think that would work.' She smiled gently at him and turned away.

Wait. She was dismissing him, just like that? That would never do. He took a step forward. 'Why not?'

She turned back, slowly. 'I can't pay you.'

Ha! She thought he needed money. That was so sweet. 'You wouldn't have to pay me.'

Her face was a picture. 'Oh no.' She shook her head. 'I can't exploit your good nature.'

The idea that someone *didn't* want to use him to get their own way almost floored him. Was this what it was like to be a normal person? Did people just…interact with you without seeing pound signs floating around your head? He had to think quickly.

'Oh, you'd be doing me a favour,' he said. 'I…' He cast about for a reason for him wanting to mess around painting things. *I need to observe this hotel and this would give me an excuse to be in the foyer for hours* was probably not going to go down well. So, a different truth then. For once, his lonely childhood served him well. 'I used to really enjoy painting miniatures, but I'd forgotten all about that until I heard you talking about it just now. I've been told I need to take time off and relax… and I really think going back to detailed work like that would do the trick much better than sitting around eating and drinking…which, to be honest, was the only thing I could think of that was relaxing. Until now…'

She stared at him, a small crease on her otherwise smooth brow. Her eyes were so beautiful, he had to force himself not to stare into them. He was here under an assumed name and supposed to be keeping a low profile. He couldn't get involved with someone who was connected to the hotel, no matter how attractive he thought she was.

She seemed to reach a conclusion. 'Okay,' she said. 'I need the help. What say we give it a trial of two days? Then if you or I feel it's not working, we go our separate ways?'

'Sounds like a deal.' He walked across the room and held out his hand, partly out of habit.

She shook it. Her hand was small and unexpectedly rough. This was a woman who did things with her hands. That was…kinda hot, if he was being honest. Which was not a helpful thing at all.

The first thing Maddie had to do was get the bases out and set them up. A few years ago, Grandad had put casters on them so that they could work on the display and then push it into place in the bay window when it was done. Once upon a time, they'd done the prep work in the basement, but as the hotel got quieter in later years, the manager had suggested they work in the windows as it brought people up to the hotel to watch. Some of them even came in and used the cafe bar.

She knew how to do this. She really did. Even if she hadn't done it by herself before. Technically, she wasn't by herself anyway. Chris was helping her. Hopefully, he was a useful sort of person, rather than a liability.

He was in front of her at the moment, pushing the trolley that they'd lifted the first base onto. She strode confidently out of the basement storage room of the hotel, with the rest of the props in her arms. He seemed to be quite strong and had nice, wide shoulders that tapered to a slim waist and a very nice bum. She shut that thought down. This was not the time.

They reached the lift. There wasn't enough room for both of them and the trolley, so she offered to run up the stairs.

'No,' he said. 'You go in the lift with the stuff. I'd worry about damaging it by mistake. I'll take the stairs.'

So she ended up by herself, with Grandad's models, in the lift. She let out a long breath. Wow. Chris was… unfairly attractive. She didn't fully trust him, of course, because who volunteered to do work for free? Especially when they were on holiday. But she needed the help and he was all that was available. Having to spend all that time with him could be very distracting.

She patted her cheeks. She was better than this. Just because the guy was hot didn't mean she had to melt into a puddle over him. The last time that happened, it hadn't gone well for her. Focus on the work. Getting this model set up in time for the unveiling was going to be a heck of a task. She should spend less time admiring Chris's shoulders and jawline and more time working out how useful he was going to be.

She glanced down at the base of the diorama, still covered in the cloth it had been stored under. 'I'm going to do my best, Grandad,' she whispered.

It had been less than an hour and Tristan was already enchanted. Maddie was telling him about how working with her grandfather and father had shaped her love for design. She spoke fast, her voice vibrant with enthusiasm. Her eyes sparkled as if she was lit up from within. He had never seen so much emotion play across someone's face before.

He helped to uncover the first diorama. What emerged was a base, built to fit the bay window. A snowy mountain landscape cut out of MDF made the background. The bulk of the model was a town, with a sloping street. A railway track, with a tunnel at either end, ran along the width of the display at the bottom.

'These are where we put the more detailed models.' Maddie knelt on the floor, and carefully unpacked one of the boxes she's brought up from the basement. 'The bigger ones are the buildings for the village scene. They go behind the track, so that the train runs past in front of them. The smaller things are people, benches, a post box, that sort of thing.' She pulled something out and carefully unwrapped it. 'This is the sweet shop.'

He hunkered down next to her to look at it. It was the frontage for a shop, made mostly out of wood. The resin in the windows looked uncannily like the small paned windows of a Victorian shop, right down to the warping in the glass.

'That's incredible,' he said. 'It looks too precious to touch.'

'It's reasonably robust,' said Maddie. 'We've used it for several years in a row. But, as you can see, it needs touching up a bit.'

She pointed to the sign that said Hurley's Sweete Shoppe in swirly writing. The paint had chipped off in several places. The roof looked badly scuffed too.

Tristan tentatively reached out to touch it.

'That's from gluing on the fake snow,' said Maddie. 'We'll have to repaint the tiles before we can put it out again.' She looked up at him, her beautiful brown eyes luminous. 'By *we*, I mean you, of course. Do you think you can do that?'

He examined the roof of the wooden building. It even had tiles carved into it. 'Of course I can,' he said. 'I'll even sort out the lettering on the sign, if you have a brush fine enough.'

She smiled at him then and his heart nearly stopped. 'I have a brush that's fine enough,' she said.

She turned back to her rummaging and Tristan sat there, staring at her. She had the most incredible smile. Right now, she was looking down and he could admire the lines of her neck and the soft fan of her dark lashes.

'Ah,' she said. 'Here's the back of the shop.'

Tristan hastily went back to examining the model in his hands. 'There's a back to the shop?' He had assumed they would just use the front and rely on illusion for the back. After all, the model was going in the window, people wouldn't be getting too close.

'Of course. The shops light up, so people can see inside. We don't need the detail to be as exact inside, obviously, but it should look vaguely convincing.'

She gently removed the packaging to reveal the interior of a shop. Shelves painted onto the back wall held boxes and bottles. The counter was carved and had little jars full of coloured sweets glued to it. There was an old-fashioned cash register and even a stand with some newspapers.

Now that he was looking for it, he could see the hooks on the side of the shopfront, where it attached to the back half. 'That's incredible,' he said. 'Look at the detail.'

'Grandad was an exceptional model maker,' said Maddie, with pride in her voice. 'He used to get commissioned to make doll house furniture for very rich people. They'd send him photos of things and he'd make them.'

She tilted the model this way and that, then took out a soft paint brush and cleaned off a few specks of dirt. 'I think,' she said, 'we can get away with just using the interiors as they are. It's only the outsides that'll need a bit of attention. And the wiring, obviously.'

Still holding the model, she slowly got to her feet. 'Here. Let me show you where it goes.'

They had set the base back from the bay window. Tristan watched as Maddie shuffled around so that she was sitting in the bay window, with her back to the glass. She placed the sweet shop on the flat section, where a faint pencilled rectangle marked the place.

'What goes in the other rectangles?' He pointed to other faint rectangular marks.

'The other shops,' she said, smiling down as though she could see them there already. 'There's a florist, a baker, a toyshop… That one there is the post office, which means this little one here is the post box. Apart from the post office, the rest are the same size, so we can swap them round.'

'That's an interesting set-up for a town,' he said. 'Is there no hotel?'

'That's in a different window.' She grinned. 'We'll put the shops out and then add the people and benches and trees. The idea is that it's slightly different each year.' She smiled, eyes shining. 'One year, Grandad made a dragon to fly over the scene. That was special.'

'We're not doing that this year?' He tried to picture what the scene would look like when it was done. He could just about imagine it.

'No. I think we'll stick to the basics this year,' said

Maddie. 'We're pushed for time.' She frowned at the model sweet shop. 'I need to get you the paints and brushes. Dad was supposed to bring them when he came. I'll have to walk round to my parents' house to get them.' She glanced at her watch and her lips tightened.

'I have a car. I could drive you,' he said.

She looked up warily. 'Are you sure?' she said. 'You're already helping me for free and I don't want to take advantage…'

She looked genuinely worried and something inside Tristan melted. 'You're not. I promised I'd help you, and I can't do that without the right equipment, so it's all part of the same thing.'

For a moment, she just looked at him, as though she was weighing him. It felt like a test. He desperately wanted to pass. He wanted this woman to like him. Not fancy him, exactly, although that would be nice…but to actually *like* him. She didn't know he was rich, so all she had to go on was his actual personality. She didn't seem the sort to suffer fools and he really wanted to have earned her respect.

Maddie nodded slowly. 'That's a good point,' she said. 'Okay.' She smiled at him. 'Let's go.'

Feeling pleased with himself, Tristan led her to the car park at the back. It was only when she saw his car and said 'Nice car. What do you do exactly?' that he wondered if he'd made a mistake.

He had used one of his own cars, turning down Walter's offer of hiring him one. It was a twenty-year-old Porsche 911 and he'd thought it was low-key enough for the Cotswolds. Clearly, he'd underestimated how noticeable it was.

'I…uh… I work in business diversification and expansion,' he said. Not exactly a lie.

'You're a banker?' Now she sounded mistrustful.

'Not exactly, no. I'm more like a…consultant. I advise.'

She got in and put on her seat belt. 'I see.' There was a small tremor in her voice.

'Is something wrong?' he asked.

She looked away from him. 'I'm so embarrassed,' she said. 'I said I couldn't pay you and I was so patronising.'

'You weren't patronising,' he said. 'As you can see, I don't need the money. What I need is something relaxing to do. So you're helping me out, really, rather than the other way around.'

Now she finally turned her head to look at him. 'You know you can walk away whenever you want to. I won't mind. You're supposed to be on holiday.'

'I will bear that in mind,' he said. 'Don't worry. Okay?'

Her gaze met his. 'Okay.' She returned his smile. 'And Chris?'

For a second he didn't respond because he'd forgotten that 'Chris' was him. 'Hmm?' He started the car.

'It's still very kind of you and I'm ever so grateful.'

'My pleasure.' He pulled out of the hotel car park and followed Maddie's directions, but his thoughts were elsewhere for a while. He liked this woman, but he couldn't do anything about it because she didn't know who he really was. She thought he was some sort of management consultant called Chris. He couldn't tell her the truth, because then she would look at him the same way everyone else did and see the wealth first. He sneaked a glance at her. Maddie, unlike Clemmie and all the girls he'd dated before, would probably dislike him for being rich. He could fancy her all he liked, but he could never ask her out, because he had been lying to her from day one.

CHAPTER FOUR

THEY DREW UP next to Maddie's parents' house, set well back in a neatly tended garden. The sight of it sent a pang of longing through her. A few more days, she told herself, and she could be home.

'Stay here,' she said to Chris, before she grabbed a cloth mask from her pocket and stepped out.

The front door opened almost before she'd opened the gate. Her mum, Sarah, appeared, in jeans and a chunky Christmas jumper, and said, 'Stop. Don't come closer.'

Maddie stopped.

'Two metres,' Sarah said. 'I don't want you to catch anything. I'll put the things out for you and come back in. You can pick it up after that.'

'Mum. Is that really necessary?'

'I don't want you to fall ill as well.' There was a set to her mouth that told Maddie that arguing was useless. 'Apart from you not being well, who's going to do the display if you're laid up too?'

Maddie studied her mother's face, trying to gauge the severity of the situation. 'How is he?'

Sarah looked over her shoulder and made a face. 'You know how he gets…'

She did know. Dad was a terrible patient. Grouchy and convinced no one had ever been as ill as he was.

'But he is quite poorly,' her mum continued. 'Nothing too terrible. Just tired and flu-like.'

In the same way that her dad exaggerated his illnesses, her mum tended to minimise them. If she thought he was ill, he must genuinely be in a bad way. 'Is his breathing okay?'

'That's all fine,' she said. 'He's just headachey and miserable. He's well enough to complain about it though, so I suspect he'll recover in a few days.'

'Are *you* okay?'

She smiled. 'Yes. I'm fine so far.' She leaned her head against the door frame and studied Maddie. 'How about you, darling? How are you?'

'I'm good, Mum. Honestly.'

'You're not worrying too much about work and everything?'

'No. I'm—' Suddenly, she was engulfed by another wave of sadness. For the past few months, she'd been running on high alert, waiting for the next thing to go wrong. She wanted, more than anything in the world, to sit in Mum's warm kitchen and let herself be looked after. That was what coming home for Christmas was all about. She had dreamed of days where she could spend time with her dad while she worked and lazy evenings chatting to her mum. But instead, she had an impossible job to do. She cleared her throat. 'I'm okay. I promise.'

'Are you going to be able to do the display by yourself?' There was a familiar crease in Sarah's forehead now. 'It's all right, I have help.' She gestured towards the car.

Sarah's eyebrows shot up. 'Oh.'

Maddie glanced over her shoulder to look at Chris. He was leaning against the car, all golden haired and handsome. He looked like a model, especially with that fancy car. He smiled and waved.

'Oh!' said Sarah.

'That's Chris,' said Maddie quickly. 'He's a guest at the hotel and he's kindly offered to help me with painting the buildings and things like that.' She tried to convey the message that there was nothing more going on, using just her eyes.

'I see…' It was clear from her mum's expression that she didn't see at all. She leaned forward and said in a loud whisper, 'He seems nice.'

Maddie suppressed a groan. She would have to field endless questions about Chris now. She glanced over her shoulder again. Oh dear.

'Anyway,' Maddie said loudly. 'I guess I should get back to the hotel and start work.' She took a step towards the house and her mum retreated inside.

Maddie hunkered down and picked up the toolbox and the bag of paints. 'I'll pop by tomorrow,' she said 'If there's anything you need, give me a call and I'll try and sort things out for you.'

'We'll be fine,' her mum said. 'Don't worry. The neighbours are already getting any shopping that we need and people are offering to drop dinner off for us. We're well looked after.'

'I know, but—'

'You go get on.' Sarah's eyes flicked back to Chris. 'You'll be anxious to get back to…work.'

'I'll call you this evening.' Maddie smiled. 'I love you, Mum.'

Sarah's face softened even more. 'I love you too, darling. Stay safe.'

* * *

On the ride back, Tristan was quiet. Seeing the obvious affection between Maddie and her mum awakened the burning sensation in his chest that he sometimes got when he thought about his own mother. He had noticed the way Maddie and her mother had leaned slightly towards each other when they spoke and the way Maddie's mum's arms had twitched as though longing to hug Maddie. That was how parents were supposed to be.

His father didn't do affection. Tristan had had nannies, some of whom believed in a firm hug, but that was different. Their love was paid for.

He thought of the many girlfriends he'd had. They hadn't cared about him so much as the money.

'Go left here,' said Maddie.

He obediently turned. 'We're not going the way we came in?'

'No. I need to stop by the hardware shop, so we're going in a slightly different way, if that's okay.'

'Sure. No problem.'

After a pause he said, 'Your mum seems nice.'

'She is,' said Maddie, her voice full of warmth. 'She's the best.'

He wanted to comment on how Maddie didn't look in the least like her mum. They were different ethnicities for a start. But he didn't know how to broach the subject without it coming out wrong.

Maddie unexpectedly solved the problem by saying, 'She's my adopted mum.'

'Oh,' he said. 'I wondered. What with your name being Attwater…'

'Yeah. I took their name when they adopted me. My

first name is Madhuri. My biological parents were Sri Lankan.'

That made sense. 'How old were you when you came to live with them?' He imagined a tale of a childless couple adopting internationally.

Maddie shook her head. 'I was born around here. We lived about ten minutes away. My biological parents were really good friends with my mum and dad. So much so that my parents—the Attwaters, I mean—used to babysit me a lot. One night, I was staying over with them while my real parents went out to an event in London and… there was an accident and they never made it home.'

'Oh. I'm so sorry.'

She gave a small shrug. 'I was about four maybe? I don't really remember them. As far as I'm concerned, the Attwaters are my parents.'

'So you just carried on staying with them?'

'Sort of. My grandparents came over from Sri Lanka. I knew who they were, but I didn't *really* know them. So I clung to Mum-Sarah because I knew she was a safe person… The Attwaters had been looking after me until then and begged to be allowed to adopt me. Eventually, everyone agreed that I should stay with Sarah and Pete. So it was quite a civilised adoption process in the end, or so I'm told.'

'Wow.' He felt a bit silly for jumping to conclusions about her life. 'Did you keep in touch with your grandparents?'

'Oh yes. We've been on holiday to Sri Lanka a few times and we WhatsApp each other on a regular basis. I've got a few cousins over there that I don't really know, but maybe one day I'll get to know them.'

He had no cousins. No family his age to spread the weight of being the heir to a hotel empire. He had his father, but Dad barely even looked at him these days.

He couldn't imagine what it was like to have so many people love you. 'Your family sounds so supportive,' he said wistfully. 'You're very lucky.'

She raised her eyebrows at him. 'Aren't yours?'

He gave a little laugh and shook his head. 'My mum… left when I was young.'

Maddie's mouth was a horrified O.

Tristan swallowed. He didn't tell this story often, but in the face of Maddie's incredulity, he felt he should. 'I was about seven. She…er…found it all too much and left us.'

It had been the summer holidays and they were travelling a lot because Sir Alex was expanding the brand globally. They had been somewhere in Asia. Singapore, maybe? His mum had taken young Tristan to his father, planted a kiss on his cheek and just…left. Tristan's abiding memory of that day was his father making him get into the big glass elevator that was in the atrium and him pressing against the glass as the lift rose, watching his mother getting smaller and smaller below him. Just thinking about it now, he could feel the nausea and panic. He forced himself to breathe normally.

Maddie looked horrified. 'That's awful. You poor man.' She reached out and touched his arm.

He glanced down at the warm, brown fingers resting against his sleeve and wished he could ask her for a hug. But Tristan Somersby didn't go around needing to be hugged. So he didn't.

'Did you ever see her again?'

He forced himself to concentrate on the road. 'A few years ago. I tracked her down. She remarried. She has a new family now. She…' He swallowed. 'She doesn't want to see me.' In all honesty, he didn't particularly want to see her either. All he had seen in her face was a strong resemblance to his own features, but no love or sorrow. She didn't care about him. He had made his peace with that.

Maggie sat on the floor and fiddled with the wiring. One of the lights in the sweet shop was off and she had to figure out where the circuit was broken. Sitting not too far from her, with his back to the window, Chris was carefully painting over scratches and scuff marks to the shopfronts. At the moment, he was working on the front of the toyshop. She paused in her work to watch him, his face fierce in concentration as he added a touch of gold to the sign above the door. He had pushed up his sleeves. He had very nice forearms.

He was intriguing. There was an innate confidence in his manner, as though he was used to being listened to, but at the same time, he seemed to be happy to take instructions and go along with whatever she wanted. He clearly had money. In fact, the confidence suggested that maybe he'd been to a fancy school. He had a fairly nondescript accent, but occasionally slipped up and sounded posh. That being the case, why would he give up his holiday to help her? He had no connection to the town or the Christmas display. It seemed very strange.

On the other hand, she was getting help. Competent help, by the looks of things. It would be foolish to look a gift horse in the mouth. Maybe she could find out a bit more by chatting to him.

She watched him tilt his head to examine his handi-work and then lean forward to do some more. There was more to this than met the eye. She was sure of it. She had to keep an eye on him.

A tiny traitorous voice in her head said that watching the nice handsome man wasn't exactly a hardship.

There was an obvious flaw in Tristan's plan to watch the comings and goings in the foyer. He had to actu-ally watch, which he couldn't do if he was focusing on painting tiny letters onto a miniature shop sign. His as-sertion that painting models needed you to concentrate to the point of escaping your troubles was true. It was impossible to do both.

On the other hand, he got to spend more time with Maddie. Right now, she had wriggled underneath the base and was muttering to herself as she did something with the wiring. All he could see of her were her denim-clad legs, bent at the knees, sticking out from under the diorama. She was incredible: pretty, confident and com-petent.

She also wasn't in the least bit interested in him. Her focus was all on the models and how he could help. Was it a bad sign that he found that charming? Was he that badly smitten?

He hoped this was just a passing interest. Maybe the novelty of a woman who didn't know about his money. He couldn't let her know who he really was, so there was no chance of him actually going out with her. It would be painful if he really fell for her.

There was more muttering and then Maddie declared, 'Ha. Gotcha.'

He watched as she shimmied out and stood up, dusting her hands down. 'Let's try this.'

She went over to where the switches were mounted—each one carefully labelled—and flicked one. The lights in the sweet shop came on. Tristan leaned over to have a look. There were tiny lamps inside the shop, which were lit up now. The little shop glowed and you could see the merchandise inside it. Magical.

'That's adorable,' he said.

'Isn't it?' She pushed a stray strand of hair back. 'The toyshop is my favourite though.' She pointed her screwdriver towards the Ye Olde Toy Shoppe front he was holding. 'How's that coming along?'

'Pretty good, I think.' He leaned back to inspect his own handiwork. It was delicate and precise. Just the sort of thing that he was good at. Not that his work with the hotels ever called on these skills.

'Let's see.' She stepped carefully over the set and squeezed in next to him. When she leaned forward to look closely at the shop, her thigh pressed along the side of his. He would have moved, but there was nowhere to move to. So he had to sit still and feel every tiny movement of her next to him.

'Oh wow, you are good,' she said. 'You've even got the little curlicue there. That's brilliant.'

The pure enthusiasm in her voice made his breath hitch. There was no equivocation in her praise. No hidden dig. She meant exactly what she said. She thought his work was good. Something shifted in Tristan's chest and an ember popped into flame.

Maddie stood back up and turned to say more. Her face was inches from him. His heart raced, as though it was trying to escape from his chest. The watch on his wrist vibrated. He swatted it off without looking at it.

Whatever she was going to say faltered. Her eyes widened and she looked away.

She stood up abruptly and then carefully moved over to the other side of the diorama again. 'That's really great, Chris. Keep going.'

He cleared his throat. 'Thanks.'

'So, how come you're so good at painting small details then?' she said, disappearing behind the set again.

Tristan rubbed at a spot of paint on the back of his hand. No one knew him here. May as well confess. 'Uh... Warhammer figurines.'

'Oh, right. I used to make little sets for them. Small ones.' She popped up and made a shape with her hands, roughly the size of a paperback. 'I used to sell them sometimes to people who played.'

The lack of judgement from her was a relief. 'Did you ever play?'

'No.' Her voice echoed slightly, as she did something inside the hollow. 'I just wanted to make the sets and paint them. So, I did that.' She reappeared and fished around in the toolbox. 'I made this big one once, a sort of postapocalyptic industrial building. It was part of an art project. We put all the parts together and it covered the whole tabletop. It was very cool.' She smiled at the distant memory, then disappeared again.

It was strange talking to someone who didn't laugh. He had stopped telling people about his childhood hobbies a long time ago; they either teased him or, in the case of his father, shouted at him and told him to do something 'improving'. The only thing that seemed acceptable was playing video games. Even then, he had to tone down his enthusiasm. Kids were brutal in their judgement.

There was no such judgement here.

He smiled and picked up his brush again. They worked in silence for a few minutes. It was surprisingly relaxing. He didn't have to worry if he was doing a good job. He already knew, because she'd told him so. How nice was that?

Was this what it was like for normal people? Did conversations just exist as conversations, without any political subtext to read?

After a while Maddie stood up and dusted herself off. 'I'm just heading back to the storeroom,' she said. 'I'll fetch the train. Let's see if the track is still okay.'

When she'd hurried away, Tristan put his brushes down and took a break. From where he was sitting, he could see into the bar, where the bartender was making some sort of eggnog type drink for a couple of customers. He should really go and check out the bar one evening, so that he could add that to his report. The report was looking sparse at the moment. He needed to get on that.

He looked down at the paintwork he had just done. He wanted to do this instead.

He had been told he was good at this. Praise, he realised, was something that had been rationed for him all his life. His father never praised him. The best he'd get was a nod and no criticism. Maybe that was why Maddie's enthusiasm for his painting was making him feel so good.

Maddie returned with another box. 'This is the train for this set,' she said and put it down on the floor.

'Can I see?'

'Sure.' She pulled the top of the box open and jumped. 'Oh.'

A small spider scuttled out of the box and ran towards the curtain. Maddie rolled her eyes, went to the reception desk and came back with a glass and a feedback postcard.

Feeling that he ought to help, Tristan said, 'Do you want me to—'

She waved him away and dealt with it herself. 'Got you.' She went outside and released it.

Tristan shook his head. Maddie was so self-sufficient. Given that she seemed to know her way around most minor electrical and woodworking tasks, she was probably a pro at DIY too. It was hard to imagine her needing anything from anyone. It made him feel unmoored and light. If he hadn't already been halfway to being smitten with Maddie, he would have definitely fallen for her now.

Maddie returned. 'Where were we?' she said, kneeling at the box again.

'So, I guess you're not afraid of spiders then,' Tristan said and then suppressed a cringe, because obviously she wasn't. She'd just calmly and humanely got rid of one.

'No. I'm okay with those,' she said. 'Slugs now. Bleaugh. Can't stand slugs.' She pulled a disgusted face. 'I would never help Mum with the garden because of those horrible things.' She looked up suddenly. 'How about you?'

Tristan laughed. 'I am slug ambivalent. Don't love 'em. Don't hate 'em. Wouldn't like to touch one, I don't think.'

She gave a theatrical shudder and went back to uncovering the train in the box.

Should he tell her about his fear of heights? He wasn't

sensitive about it and it might become relevant. He glanced up at the decorations at the top of the window. Clearly this project involved some stepladders.

'I…er… I'm bad with heights,' he said. 'So if you need someone to help with the high-up decorations. That's… not me.'

Maddie looked up, thoughtful. 'Okay,' she said. 'That's useful to know, actually. Because, on the last window, I'll need someone to attach the cable cars to the hook. They go up and down on a loop.' She pointed to the window at the far end. 'I'll know to ask someone else to help me for that bit.'

'Sorry.'

'Nothing to be sorry about. I'm just glad you told me.' The smile she gave him was so warm that he couldn't help smiling back. She bent her head back to her task. 'Ah. Here it is.' She lifted out a lovely blue locomotive. 'Grandad's pride and joy. It's nice to see this again.'

She placed it on the track. Tristan moved around to get a better look, making sure he was out of sight from the window, because Walter's warning not to be photographed was still strong in his mind. The track ran in a big loop—only the front of it was visible to people looking at the display through the window. Maddie was working at the back of it. Maddie carefully added two passenger carriages behind the engine.

'Let's see if the track needs resetting.' She went back to the control panel and flicked a set of switches. She turned the dial and the train moved slowly along the track.

'How does it work?' he asked. It looked complicated.

She pointed to the line of track that ran all the way

along the front of the scene. 'That's the visible bit of the track.' The train came out of one tunnel and ran along the visible section. When it got to the end of the window, it went into another tunnel, where the track curved around and disappeared into the back of the diorama. Maddie slowed the train to a stop in front of her.

'Each of the windows has a track that runs along the front like that,' she continued. 'We time it so that the train from this window disappears into a tunnel at the edge. Then the train at the next window appears. If we get the timing right, it looks like the train runs all the way along the length of the building.'

He leaned back to look at the placement of the windows. 'You'd need four identical trains.'

'We *have* four identical trains.'

He played it out in his mind. 'Wow. That's clever.'

'My grandad was the best.' She practically glowed with pride.

He smiled at her. 'He sounds like an amazing person.'

'He was.' Her smile faded. 'I miss him. This model was his favourite thing though. I want to do it right, for his sake.'

Tristan thought of his own grandfather, the one he knew. He was a stern old man who had given lavish presents that Tristan had politely put away, but rarely anything so human as a hug. He didn't miss his grandfather at all.

Maddie threw a second blanket over the bed Laura had made for her on the sofa. 'Thank you so much for letting me stay with you. I know you guys probably don't need me cramping your style.'

'Pfft. We don't mind,' said Laura. 'Besides, where else were you going to go, with your mum and dad's house in quarantine?'

Maddie straightened out the blankets and draped them so that they covered the whole of the sofa. 'True.'

Laura finished putting a pillowcase on a pillow. 'How are they? Have you spoken to them?'

'I called after I finished at the hotel. Dad's no worse, so that's a relief. Mum's feeling a bit ill, but seems mostly okay. I think they'll be all right.' She sank down onto the sofa, on top of the blankets. Laura sat down beside her.

Maddie twisted out the stiffness in her back. 'Argh. All that leaning over the displays has made me really stiff.' She stretched her arms out and tried to loosen her shoulders.

'Hmm,' said Laura. 'Can't be all bad though. You get to work with Mr Hotness.'

'Hey,' Laura's husband, Tim, called from the kitchen where he was doing the washing-up. 'I'm right here.'

Laura rolled her eyes. 'You're the only hotness for me, obviously. But the lovely Chris seems to have noticed Maddie…'

Maddie shook her head. 'Stop it. I'm really grateful that he's helping me out, but that's all there is to it.'

'I dunno,' said Laura. 'He keeps looking at you, when you're busy concentrating on something else.'

'He does?' Maddie shook her head. 'I mean, he's probably not. Are you sure you're not imagining things?' She picked up her glass. 'Don't you think it's a bit weird that he volunteered to help?'

Laura pulled a face and took a sip of wine. 'It does seem a little strange. The man is on holiday but…maybe he saw you and thought that hanging out with you was better than, I dunno, sightseeing or relaxing or whatever he'd originally planned...'

'He said he likes painting and hasn't had a chance to—' She frowned. 'Which does sound weak now I say it out loud. He is quite good at painting fine detail though and I do need the help.'

'And the fact that he's nice to look at is no bad thing.'

Maddie shook her head. 'I don't know anything about him. I only agreed because I need the help and I'll be in public the whole time.'

Laura leaned forward and put her glass down on the coffee table. 'Maddie. You can't hide away just because Alan lied to you.'

'And stole all my money.'

'That too. But you can't let Alan ruin the rest of your life too. He was a skilled con man. You weren't the only victim. He was really, really persuasive.'

Maddie took a gulp of wine. 'I feel so stupid though.' Alan had suggested moving in together after less than two months. She still hadn't thought anything of it and had just let him walk in and access everything. 'How did I not see it? There must have been clues. I missed them all.'

'Of course you did. You had no reason not to believe him. It wasn't your fault.' She put her hand on Maddie's. 'That's not the point though. The point is that you can't let him stop you from moving on with your life.'

Maddie snorted. 'Sure, I can. I owe my parents so much money now.'

'You can't stop dating entirely because of him. Just...

be more careful about the plans you make for the longer term.'

'I know what you're saying, but no. I'm not ready. I don't think I can trust my instincts anymore.'

Laura sighed. 'Pity, because Chris seems very nice.'

'Or…he could just be charming and handsome. That doesn't mean anything. Alan was too.'

'Aha! So you do think he's attractive.'

Maddie shook her head. 'Shut up.'

Tim finished the washing-up and brought his own glass over. He sat down on the floor next to Laura and leaned his head against her knee. 'Do you want me to see if I can find anything about him? Do a background check of sorts?'

'Sure.' Maddie shrugged.

'How exactly would you do a background check?' said Laura.

'I was just going to google his name and maybe see if there's any other information I can glean from his booking.' Tim worked in the hotel's admin office.

'There are rules about customer confidentiality, you know.'

'I won't be digging around in their bank details,' said Tim. 'I'm looking on Google.' He took a sip of wine. 'I'm just looking out for my friend.'

'Well, I hope you don't find any dirt on him,' said Laura. 'I think he's keen on Maddie and it's about time she had something nice in her life.'

Tim raised his glass. 'I'll drink to that.'

Maddie looked from one to the other and smiled. 'I love you guys.' She joined the toast.

CHAPTER FIVE

IT WAS WEDNESDAY afternoon and Tristan was making snow-covered trees. Part of this diorama had been squashed out of shape when it was in storage, so he and Maddie were rebuilding it. His job was to twist wire shapes into trees. He was getting the hang of it now. It was delicate work and he'd acquired a few scratches from the wire ends, but it was satisfying to see the tree shape emerge. Once he'd wrapped the trunk with tape and given it a coat of paint, it looked pleasingly realistic. This was so much more rewarding than his usual work.

He had turned off his email notifications and taken to not checking his email until the evening, which meant he was up late responding to things and writing his report, but it was worth it to be able to focus on these fun things during the day.

Maddie was fluffing up the flattened pine trees, adding fake snow to them and placing them into a winter woodland. It was magical to see it taking shape.

She had pulled her hair back into a severe ponytail. She had a smudge of white paint on her forehead. He wondered if he should tell her.

He was so busy watching her that he wasn't paying attention to the wire shape in his hand. It slipped. Instinctively he caught it and yelped when the sharp wires cut into his palm.

'What happened?' Maddie was instantly at his side.

He moved his hand quickly out of the way, so that he didn't bleed on the model. When he cautiously opened his hand, he could see that the tree was ruined and his hand had several puncture marks in it.

'Oh no.' Maddie hopped out of the model. 'Let me get the first aid kit.'

'It's nothing—' he began, but she was already rushing across to the front desk. Within minutes, she was back with a first aid kit. She knelt on the floor next to him and held out her hand for his. He offered her his open palm. She wiped it clean and tilted it to check the wounds. 'Nothing too deep,' she said. 'But we should clean it anyway, just in case.'

'Just in case of what? These are new wires, no rust. There's nothing else on them.'

She gave him a stern glare. 'I'm not going to be responsible for you getting something nasty like sepsis.' She got a Steri-Wipe and tore it open. 'This might sting.'

It did sting. When he winced, she said, 'I'm sorry.'

He tried to look like he wasn't bothered. She tore open another wipe and made another pass, cleaning the small wounds thoroughly. The alcohol in the wipe bit and stung. Tristan clenched his jaw to stop from responding. Then, much to Tristan's surprise, Maddie leaned forward and blew gently on his hand.

The pain lessened. The sensation of her warm breath on his palm raised goosebumps on his arms. She was so close to him, her eyes lowered as they focused on what she was doing, her lips pursed, as though waiting for a kiss. Suddenly, his heart was the loudest thing in the room.

She looked up and her eyes locked with his. Time slowed. He could kiss her. He wanted to. He leaned slowly closer. On his wrist, the watch buzzed.

Maddie blinked. She dropped his hand and moved back.

Damned watch. Tristan drew a sharp breath and sat back. Embarrassing.

She cleared her throat. 'It...should be okay now.' She thrust a bandage at him. 'You might want to cover it.'

He looked at the bandage and at his hand. 'I...might need some help getting that on.'

'Um...' She cleared her throat again. 'Right. Yes. Um...let me do that. Then I have to get back to work.'

He held his hand out to her and she slapped a gauze dressing on the palm, working quickly, avoiding eye contact.

Laura came over. 'I heard you needed first aid. Is it okay?' she said. 'Do I need to call an ambulance or find someone to drive you to the minor injuries unit?'

'No,' said Tristan. 'It's fine. Maddie's done a great job with the first aid.'

She taped it up, her mouth set in a grim line and then packed away the kit.

'Are you going to be able to paint with that on?' Laura asked.

Tristan flexed his hand, twisting it this way and that. It was stiff and the punctures stung a bit, but he could hold a brush. 'Yes,' he said, cautiously. 'If I take it slow, I should be okay.'

He looked up to see a glance pass between Laura and Maddie.

Laura put a hand on her friend's upper arm. 'It'll be okay. It doesn't have to be perfect,' she said.

Tristan couldn't see Maddie's face, but he knew what she was thinking. It did have to be perfect. This was a tribute to her grandfather and, potentially, the last time this diorama would be on display before they retired it.

He glanced at the window. Beyond the wooden structure, he could see people in the street. A few of them, mostly people with children, stopped to peer in. There was a sense of anticipation that he could feel even from inside.

If he was being himself, he could have paid for some expert help, but he was merely Chris Samuels right now. All he could offer was his own hands. They would have to be enough.

Someone came in and Laura hurried back to the reception desk, taking the first aid kit with her.

Maddie glanced at Tristan and swallowed. 'Are you sure you're okay to keep going?'

'Yes.' He wasn't going to let a few holes in his hand stop him. 'I'm having fun.'

She avoided his eyes and nodded. 'That's good. You're doing a great job.'

Tristan tried not to think about how good it felt to hear that.

Maddie was struggling to concentrate. She'd nearly burned her fingers on the soldering iron twice now. She was sitting on the floor, fixing a broken connection on the track. Chris was sitting with his back to the window again, carefully fixing the trees they'd made onto the foreground.

This scene had been damaged, so it would take them longer to set up than the others. The hardest part, remaking the models, was done now. The track fixed. The lights wired in. Once Chris finished the trees, all they had to do was add the model people and the base of the fake snow. She checked her phone. They were making good time.

Chris sat back. 'I'm done. What's next?'

Maddie scrambled to her knees. 'Let me just check the track.' She placed the train, without its carriages, carefully onto the track, turned the battery pack on and gently nudged the dial to get the train up to speed. The little engine disappeared under the diorama. She strained upward to see over the set. The train appeared through the tunnel entrance and chugged cheerfully along the front of the display and disappeared into the tunnel at the end. Maddie slowed it down so that it stopped in front of her. 'That works.'

'That's wonderful!'

She looked up to see Chris grinning, his expression pure delight. She couldn't help smiling back. There was something about toy trains that seemed to turn grown adults into children again. She loved that. Grandpa had loved that too. Children were pure and hadn't been hurt by the world yet. What could be a greater gift than to take a person back to that?

'I'm glad you like it,' she said.

He beamed at her. 'Like it? This is the best holiday I've had in years.'

He sounded like he meant it. This made her smile. 'If this is the best, what sort of holidays do you usually go on?'

The smile faded. 'The...uh...usual sort.' His eyes slid down to the scene in front of him. 'Monaco in the summer. Skiing in the winter and such, usually.'

That was an odd response. 'That sounds like it would be fun.'

He rubbed the back of his head with his good hand. 'I'm not a big fan of heights.'

'Oh.' She remembered him mentioning that. 'So…can you ski? How does that work?'

'Oh, I can ski,' he said. 'My parents made sure I got skiing lessons pretty much as soon as I could walk. But I can't do chairlifts now.' He seemed to be focused intently on the trees he'd just stuck down. 'I…fainted on one, once. When I was about eight. I was with my dad. He had to drag me off it when we reached the top. He was so angry.'

Maddie leaned forward to get a better view of his face. His face looked gaunt and serious, his eyes hooded. Whatever he was thinking about, it was hurting him.

'That's horrible,' she said. 'Why on earth was he angry? It wasn't your fault.' She couldn't imagine her parents responding like that to any sort of illness, physical or mental. Parents were meant to be on your side.

'My dad,' said Chris. 'He likes things his way.'

'That's no excuse,' she said. 'You were a child. Parents don't do that to children. Your father sounds horrible.'

He shrugged. 'He's the only parent I've got.'

She remembered then that his mother had left him. Left him. How did a mother leave her child? Her own parents had died—they hadn't left of their own free will—and that had hurt enough. She couldn't imagine the pain of a parent actually abandoning you.

Chris was busying himself and avoiding eye contact. She wished she could kneel next to him and hug him.

Show him that some people cared. She couldn't, so she said, 'You deserve better.'

He glanced up. 'Yeah?'

She nodded solemnly. 'Yes. You deserve good people who love you without being cross when you're not at your strongest.'

He stared at her for a moment, not quite meeting her eyes. She couldn't read his expression. Then he smiled. 'Thanks.'

She smiled back. Unsettled by the conversation, she turned her attention back to her work.

'I have been skiing more recently though,' Chris said. His voice sounded brittle. 'They had cable cars. That was okay, because I could look down at my phone and not see the drop.'

'You and your dad worked out a compromise. That's good.'

'That wasn't with my dad. I went with my fiancée at the time. My…ex-fiancée now.'

Now his expression was familiar. Sadness, but a hint of shame. She busied herself picking up the box of tiny figures. 'What happened?'

He rubbed his hair again and gave a tiny mirthless laugh. 'She…met someone who was a better prospect than me and dropped me like a hot potato.'

She opened the box. 'A better prospect than you? What was he? A movie star?'

The atmosphere changed. Maddie's head snapped up. Oh no. What did she just say? She sneaked a glance at him.

He was smiling again, a little lopsided smile that managed to make him look shy. 'No, just a billionaire.' He rolled his eyes. 'A good-looking one. I didn't stand a chance.'

How did she rescue this? Heat licked up her cheeks. 'Ugh. Such a cliché, am I right?'

Now he laughed properly. A deep, warm laugh. The sound made her stomach tingle.

'Right. Exactly.'

Oh, he was lovely when he laughed. Try as she might, she couldn't stop sneaking glances at him. Earlier that day, she had almost kissed him. Thank goodness his watch had notified him of something or she would have embarrassed herself. She wasn't ready for a relationship. Not after what Alan did to her. It wouldn't be fair to flirt with Chris and let him think that something could come of this. It couldn't. She wasn't ready. She might never be ready again. She turned away and started to unpack the figurines.

He came across and stood next to her. 'So, what are we doing now?'

'We are taking these figures and putting them in the landscape. We'll fix them to the base.' She handed him a little figure of a man in a red Christmas jumper. These figures weren't as tiny as some of the models her grandfather had worked on—after all, they had to be big enough to be discernible to people peering in through the window—which meant that they had to have some detail on them. But they were still in proportion to the model train that ran through the scene.

'Do we need to check these guys for damage?' He turned the figure over and gently swiped some dust away with his fingertips. He had a remarkably delicate touch. Imagine that light touch on her skin…

No. Not thinking about that. She checked the figure she was holding. 'Not unless it's really obvious. They're

small enough that we can get away with minor imper-
fections.'

He held the figure up closer to his face. 'There's quite
a lot of detail for something you can only see at a distance.'

'Grandpa felt it was worth doing it right.'

'He sounds incredible.'

'He was.' She passed him the box. 'Here. You unpack
some too.'

They worked quietly side by side, unwrapping and in-
specting the figures. The ones that could be dusted off
and put back into service went into one stack, while the
ones that needed a little attention went into the other.

'Listen,' he said. 'Thank you. For making me laugh
earlier.'

'It's okay.' Should she tell him about Alan? It was the
first time she'd even wanted to talk to anyone about him.
Her parents knew all about it, of course. So did Laura and
Tim. But other people…no. She had been too ashamed
of having fallen victim to say anything. She glanced
at him. Maybe…maybe she could. She didn't think he
would judge her. 'I sort of understand what it's like. You
know, to be used and dumped like that.'

He didn't look at her. 'You do?'

'I was dating this guy and…' This was harder than
she'd thought. Her throat felt tight.

He lowered the figure he was holding. 'And he left
you for someone else?' He frowned. 'He was obviously
an idiot.'

'Worse. He…er… Turned out he was a con artist. He
stole quite a lot of money from me—' She blinked hard
to keep the tears from coming. 'I—' She had to wipe

her eyes on her sleeve. Talking about it was a bad idea. It was still too soon.

'Oh my god, Maddie, that's awful.' He placed a hand on her shoulder.

She sniffed. Her shoulder was demanding her attention where the warmth of his hand was radiating along it.

'I'm so sorry that happened to you. You don't have to tell me. It's hard for you.'

She shook her head. 'I should talk about it. You know, make it less...less of a big deal.'

He was quiet for a second, then he removed his hand and rubbed the bandage on his injured hand distractedly. 'It sounds like it was a fairly big deal.'

She pinched off a piece of Blu-tack and secured a seated figurine to one of the benches in the scene. 'I haven't talked about it for nearly a year now and that hasn't helped, so maybe talking will work better.'

'Well, I'm happy to listen.' He was looking at her, she could tell. She could feel the weight of gaze. She kept her eyes on the task and nodded.

The next figure she unwrapped was a woman in a lilac swing skirt. 'Oh. I painted this one.' The face on the figure was lumpy, so she'd wrapped a scarf around the neck to hide it. Grandpa had stiffened the fabric of the scarf so that she could make it stream out behind the figure.

'That's cute.' Chris had leaned closer. She was hyper-aware of the warmth of him standing right next to her.

'Thank you.'

'So, how do we know where to put them on the scene?'

She took a small step away from his distracting warmth. 'Well, we used to make up little stories about them. So…' She looked at the figure in her hand. 'This woman has left a bad relationship and she's striding off to the shops to buy herself something nice, because she deserves it.'

'She does. Is she going to meet someone at the shops?' He held out a figure of a man carrying a stack of presents. 'This guy, maybe?'

Maddie made a show of thinking hard. 'No. I think maybe it's still too soon for her. She's still feeling fragile.'

He shrugged. 'Yeah. You're probably right.' He reached past her and placed his figure at the other end of the scene.

'What's his story?' she asked.

'Oh, he's been dumped by the woman he was going to marry. It's left him feeling a bit down about himself. So, he needs to do some work on himself to get his self-esteem back up to scratch.'

Was he talking about himself? She didn't think there was anything lacking in his confidence. 'He seems pretty confident,' she said. 'And successful, judging by that pile of presents he's carrying.'

'Well, maybe people only like him because he buys them fancy presents. They judge him without knowing him. Maybe…he would like to meet someone who doesn't need him to buy them things. He just wants to be seen for who he is. Not the gifts he buys.'

She raised her eyebrows and picked out another figure. An elderly man in a suit. 'Maybe this guy here will give him some magical advice that will give him a whole new outlook in life.'

'Oh yeah. What would he say?' There was a hint of laughter in his voice.

'I don't know. Something like, "If you don't love your-self, how do you expect other people to love you"?'

'Deep.'

'He's very wise, this old man.'

He held out a pair—a woman holding the hand of a little girl. 'What about these two?'

She gave them some consideration. 'They are…going to the sweet shop. The little girl has been very good and done all her chores, so her mother is going to let her buy some pick-and-mix.'

'Nice! Lucky kid.' He put them in front of the right shop. 'Does she have a dad who loves her too?'

'Of course,' said Maddie. 'This is a Christmas di-orama. Everyone has someone who loves them. Or they will have, by Christmas Day.' She stuck down another figure.

'What? Even the girl in the lilac skirt?'

Oh. Was he suggesting something about her? Or ac-tually talking about the figurine? 'She…has lost every-thing.'

'Not everything,' he said. 'I'm sure she has people who love her. People who would understand that she can't buy them presents this year, but she loves them too.'

'Ah. I see. Silly me. It's obvious when you put it like that.'

She glanced at him. His eyes creased lightly at the edges as he smiled. He raised a figure of a carol singer. 'Where do these ones go?'

'Let's have the choir…here.' She pointed to a spot be-neath the clock tower. 'There's a collection of singers. We'll have to put them together.'

'Let me see.' He passed her another.

It took a few minutes to get the carol singers all grouped together in a realistic way.

'You know,' Chris said, 'this is so much fun. I haven't enjoyed decorating for Christmas like this in…well, possibly ever.'

'That's because you haven't met the wonderful world of modelling before.'

'Not this type of modelling, certainly.'

What was that supposed to mean? Was he a model? She let her gaze take in the full form of him—the expensive-looking jumper, the neat collared T-shirt, the jeans. Everything fit perfectly. Take away the glasses and artfully do his hair and he could be a model. He certainly had the physique for it.

He glanced sideways and caught her looking. She looked away, horrified that he'd caught her checking him out. Again. It was so embarrassing.

'I…need to go check something on the other display.' She rushed back to the covered display and pretended to look under the cover at the track at the back of it.

She had to get it together. Sure, the man was attractive, but Alan had been attractive too and look how that had turned out. She had no reason to trust Chris. It would be stupid to fall for the same trick twice.

A quick glance. He had his back to her and was leaning over the display, settling figures into it. Even his back was attractive. Maddie gave herself a little smack on the back of her hand. *Pull yourself together, Attwater. Be an adult.*

By the time she walked back to the piece they were working on, she was firmly in control of her feelings. She hoped.

CHAPTER SIX

THE NEXT MORNING, Tristan went for a run. He had been up early replying to work emails and he needed to get himself into a better headspace. His watch buzzed when his heart rate rose past a certain point. It made him think of Maddie, praising his work painting the front of the toyshop. When he first got his watch, it had already been set to buzz as a little note of congratulation when he got his heart rate up. It had been his father's idea, in order to encourage him to exercise. Tristan had been ten and his love of cake and sedentary activities like painting had added pounds to him. His father, who he'd barely seen since the disastrous first skiing holiday without his mother, had suddenly taken an interest and decided that he needed to be healthier. Young Tristan had taken the buzz from his watch to mean that his father was praising him—something that never happened in any other context.

He picked up his pace. It was quite sad, really, that he still had the thing activated. It was nice to have his efforts acknowledged, but he was a grown man now. He liked running and would do it even without his watch encouraging him. Maybe he should just turn that feature off. Or remove his watch. He had a phone that told the time perfectly well. What did he need a watch for?

Besides, he thought, frowning, the watch had buzzed at the worst possible time yesterday. He'd definitely had a moment there with Maddie...

He came to a crossroads and paused to check his route on the phone. He worked out which direction he had to go in and set off again.

It was probably a good thing he didn't try to kiss Maddie. She had pretty much told him that she wasn't ready for a relationship. The idea that someone would take advantage of Maddie's good nature and steal from her led to a spike of anger. How could anyone do that? To Maddie—who seemed to be genuinely open and caring with everyone. It hadn't escaped his notice that many people dropped by to chat to her. Some of the staff even spent their lunch breaks doing little jobs on the model. They were nice to him, of course, but it was Maddie they wanted to talk to.

In the last couple of days, he had heard so many tiny conversations about what the Christmas model train display and Maddie's grandad had meant to people. Tristan knew all about tradition and legacy. His father talked about it all the time. The first Somersby Hotel, which was not the Somersby Grand, but another, smaller one in Surrey, had been opened by Tristan's great-grandfather and passed down from father to son. Sir Alex had taken the brand and expanded it to the international powerhouse it was today. At some point, it would come to him. So, as far as he knew, legacy was all about buildings and money and keeping up appearances so that you didn't let your forefathers down. But with Maddie, tradition was all about people her grandfather or her father had helped. Carpenters, electricians, artists and teachers who had been inspired by them. To them, legacy was a feeling. An empowerment.

In every conversation, Maddie's grandfather was there, being remembered with love. What would his own father be remembered for? What would *he*? Wouldn't he rather be remembered for more than a bunch of build-ings?

He was running past bigger buildings now. He must be getting closer to the hotel. He picked up the pace.

This two-week hiatus from his real life was turning out to be a more deeply moving experience than he'd anticipated.

He recognised where he was now. He took a corner and turned into the town square. It was still early, but there seemed to be a lot of activity already. A group of men was unloading large pallets, noisily. Across the square, at the hotel, one of the gardeners checked the winter hardy foliage in raised flower beds.

One of the shops he ran past was a bakery. The smell of fresh baking hooked him. He slowed to a halt and, after a brief tussle with his conscience, he went inside. There was a display of pastries. He looked down at them and tried to work out which ones to have. Technically, they had a pretty good breakfast at the hotel, but he re-ally fancied something buttery and flaky and warm.

'Can I help you?' The lady behind the counter had the tongs and a paper bag ready.

'What smells so nice?' he asked her.

'Ah, that'll be the peach pastries. They've just come out of the oven.'

'I'll have two of those, please. No. Make it three. I'll eat one now.'

'A good choice.' She put one on a napkin and passed it over to him and carefully put two more in the bag. 'Are you staying at the Cygnet?' she said as she moved towards the till.

'Yes, I am.' Then some impulse prompted him to add, 'I'm helping Maddie with the window displays.'

'Oh, you're the guest who's helping out for free. Well, I think that's very kind of you,' she said. 'There's not enough people who do a good deed these days.' She handed him the pastries. 'Are you going to share those with Maddie?'

'That is the plan.'

She told him the price and he frowned. That sounded less than it should be.

'I haven't charged you for the one you just ate,' she said. 'Call it a thank-you for helping out.'

Bewildered by this, he paid up. 'That's very kind of you.'

'One good turn deserves another,' she said, beaming at him. 'You have a lovely day now.'

As he came out, he spotted Maddie coming out of another shop.

He called out her name and waved.

She stopped and watched him run towards her. She was wrapped up warm against the cold and her beautiful eyes peered at him past a woolly scarf. 'Morning, Chris.' Her voice was a little muffled, but she sounded pleased to see him.

'Morning,' he said, breathless from the exercise. 'You're having an early start.'

'There's a lot to do.'

He fell into step beside her as they headed towards the hotel. 'What's the plan for today, boss?'

'I'm going to put some finishing touches on diorama two and then we'll make a start on number three.'

'What's in this scene?'

'The one with the big hotel and kids playing in a park. The track runs a bit further back on this one.'

'Oh nice.'

They reached the hotel front. Someone said hello to Maddie and she stopped. Tristan walked ahead a few steps. His shoelace was loose. He crouched down to tie it. As he stood back up again, he spotted something on the pavement ahead of him. Was that…was that a slug? What was it doing here? More to the point, wasn't Maddie scared of them? He glanced back at Maddie, who had finished her conversation and was walking towards him. And towards the slug. He quickly stepped in front of it.

Maddie stopped in front of the entrance to the hotel. 'I guess I'll see you in a bit?' she said.

'Um…yes.' He shuffled awkwardly to the side a bit, so that he was still between her and the slug. 'I had better go and do some stretches and have a shower.'

Maddie gave him a puzzled look. 'Is everything okay?'

'Yes. Of course.' He rubbed his nose. 'Although, you wouldn't have a tissue to hand, would you?'

'Sure.' She pulled a packet of tissues out of her pocket and handed him one. 'I'll see you later.' She headed inside.

He waited until she had gone in and using the tissue, picked up the slug. He carried it at arm's length to the nearest bin and threw it in. Yuck. He definitely felt like he needed a shower now.

As he entered the hotel, he spotted Laura standing by the window.

'Hi Laura.'

'Good morning,' Laura said. 'If you don't mind me asking, what was that all about just now? You picked something up and threw it away. Was there something there that shouldn't have been?'

'Oh. Only a slug. I knew Maddie doesn't like them, so I thought I'd best get rid of it before she saw…' Now he said it out loud, it sounded weird.

'A slug?' Laura shook her head. 'That definitely shouldn't be there. I'll get someone from groundskeeping to go and check the plant beds for any more. Thanks for bringing it to my attention.'

Taken aback, Tristan nodded. 'Great. Sure.'

He headed the stairs to his room. It was odd hearing towards Maddie call him Chris. He felt relaxed and happy with her, because she saw him for who he really was. Except she didn't know him at all.

Going undercover in this quaint hotel had seemed like such a neat way to avoid the press scrutiny and the embarrassment of Clemmie's departure. He had known he'd have to lie, but fooling strangers hadn't felt like such a big deal. But now, he'd met someone he actually liked. He wanted to get to know her better…and she thought his name was Chris.

As he let himself into his bedroom, Tristan wondered if this had been as good an idea as he'd originally thought.

Maddie thought Chris was behaving suspiciously. There was clearly something he hadn't wanted her to see this morning. She couldn't think what it was.

When she got into the hotel, she had rushed to the window to see if she could work out what was going on. She watched him pick something up and put it in the bin. When he started towards the door, Maddie asked Laura to find out for her and then fled down to the storeroom.

When she carried the tools back up to the foyer, she was glad to see that there were no guests at the reception desk. Laura was busy at the computer, but she looked up when Maddie rapped on the desk.

'Hi. Did you find out?' she asked.

Laura grinned. 'Nothing sinister at all,' Laura said. 'Our man was just saving you from a slug.'

'A *slug*?'

'Apparently, there was one just by the entrance and he made sure you didn't see it. I guess you told him about your slug phobia.'

'I mentioned it.' She smiled. The thought that he'd remembered and cared enough to do that gave her a warm glow in her chest. 'Aw. That was really thoughtful of him.'

'It was.' Laura leaned her elbows on the desk and dropped her voice. 'So...what do we reckon? He seems like a nice guy to me. I haven't seen anything to suggest that he's a serial killer or anything.'

She had to agree. The more she got to know him, the more she liked Chris. But she still wasn't sure about letting her guard down. 'I don't know,' she said. 'He's only here for a couple of weeks. Best not to complicate things.' She tapped her hands on the desk. 'Right. To work.'

Picking the tools up again, she went over to the dioramas and tried, not entirely successfully, not to think about Chris and his kind gesture. She had only mentioned about the slugs in passing, but he had remembered. It was such a tiny thing, but it felt important. He had actually listened to her. She *mattered*. There was nothing for him to gain from doing that. The fact that he hadn't told her only made it more kind.

Alan had bought her extravagant gifts. She had thought that meant he loved her, but now she knew he didn't. He had always been good with the big things— the showy things. Like flowers. He'd often bought her flowers, bunches of red roses or big colourful bouquets. He'd made a fuss of the smallest milestones—one month together, one hundred days together, a month since he met her parents—and bought her presents to celebrate. These were always accompanied by praise of how beautiful and special she was. Now she saw it for the love bombing that it was.

Despite the grand gestures, the little things passed him by. Like forgetting to ask her how her day was. Or how she took her tea. The number of times he mistakenly put sugar in her tea! It was such a basic thing and he forgot so often. He always made a joke and got her a fresh one, but…her preference hadn't really mattered to him. It was like he was working to a tick list of what he felt should matter and didn't actually care about her at all. How had she missed those warning signs?

Maddie looked down at her hands. Here she was, thinking about Alan again. She wasn't over his betrayal. It still coloured everything she did. It was too soon for her to be thinking about romance again. Especially with a guy who was, essentially, a stranger. All she knew about him was what he'd told her. There was no reason to think that it wasn't all true, but…there hadn't been with Alan either. Sure, he made her feel like she mattered, but what if that was how he played these games? Besides all of that, he was only here for a short while. So was she. They would have to go their separate ways soon. It was too much of a risk to even think about falling in love again.

She sighed and got to work.

Maddie had just removed the covering from diorama three when some instinct made her look up. Chris was walking towards her carrying a paper bag. His hair looked damp, he was wearing the same jumper and jeans as the day before, judging by the paint splatters on it, and he looked absolutely delicious. He gave her the most delighted smile. A flash of happiness ran through her. She smiled back. Was it suddenly hot in here?

'Morning,' he said. 'Have you had breakfast?'

'I have.' She managed to arrange her features into something resembling nonchalance. 'Why?'

'I popped into the bakery to grab something after my run, and the woman in there practically forced me to take these pastries. She said it was to say thank you for helping with the Christmas display.' He opened the bag and showed them to her. 'I thought we could have them at our tea break.'

'Oh, I love those,' she said. She knew exactly which bakery he meant. 'Irene makes excellent pastries.'

He put them in a corner, out of the way, and pushed up his sleeves. Maddie tried not to look at his forearms, but her eyes were drawn to them anyway. This was ridiculous. She had to focus. Hadn't she decided a minute ago that she had to be strong?

'What are we doing today?'

She nodded towards the display. 'Manor house…or hotel—we were never sure which—and gardens.' This one was relatively easy to manage. Most of the display was taken up by the gardens of the house, which had been stuck down onto pieces that slotted together like a jigsaw. Of all the views, this one required the most dusting and cleaning. It was mostly green, though, so it was easy to touch up any patches.

There was a plan that she'd made for it a few years ago. She showed it to Chris. He stood next to her, looking at it over her shoulder. The proximity of him made her skin tingle. It was an effort to keep her mind on the job. 'Why don't you set out the gardens, while I find the train for this set.'

'Sounds like a plan.' His arm gently bumped her shoulder. 'Let's do this.'

Maddie ended up sitting on the floor, with her back against the wall between the two windows, while she carefully unpacked the parts of the house. There was no train. There was space in the box, so it looked like the train had been removed. She messaged her father, asking if he knew where it might be.

Where on earth had it gone? She should check the boxes for scene four as well. If she didn't find the trains, they were in big trouble.

She checked her phone. Her message had been delivered. If Dad didn't answer within the next half hour, she would call him.

What now? She unpacked the parts of the manor house and started building that. From where she was sitting, she could see Chris and talk to him while he carefully dusted down the various trees. It was surprisingly cosy and comfortable.

Around ten o'clock, Maddie carefully put down her brushes and pliers. It was time to call her father. She needed to know where the train was. She got up and brushed a few bits of foam and dust off herself.

'I've got a call to make,' she said. 'After that. I'll get us tea. Since you brought the snacks.'

When Maddie left, Tristan couldn't help watching her walk away. She had generously proportioned hips that swayed when she walked. Jeans worked for her. They really, really did.

She paused at the far end of the room and he hastily looked out of the window with what he hoped was a thoughtful expression. There was a man with a camera outside. Tristan quickly turned away and jumped when he found Laura standing next to him.

'Uh…hi Laura.'

'Things are going well with the display then, Mr Samuels?' Laura said with a smile.

'Please. Call me Chris.' It was still weird saying it. At least it sounded a little bit like 'Tris'. He hadn't been called that since school. There were very few people now who called him anything other than Tristan.

Laura nodded. 'Okay. If you're sure you don't mind.'

'We're practically colleagues.'

There seemed to be something on Laura's mind. She nodded again, slowly, keeping her eyes on him. Then said, 'About Maddie…'

Here we go. This was clearly what Laura had been wanting to talk about. 'What about her?'

'I…couldn't help noticing the way you look at her.'

Was it that obvious? Every time he saw her, he fell for her a little bit more. It was the strangest sensation. Painful, because he knew he couldn't do anything about it, but still exciting enough that he would rather die than be away from her. He couldn't say any of that, so he said simply, 'Oh?'

Laura moved a fraction closer. 'Listen, Chris. You seem nice, but I don't know anything about you.'

There was a good reason for that. Tristan felt a twinge of guilt. He decided the best form of defence was offence. 'Laura, I don't understand how my interest in Maddie is any of your business.'

Laura's expression hardened. 'I've known Maddie since we were six. She's my best friend. She means a lot to me and I feel I should watch out for her.'

Okay. He already knew that. 'I see.'

'She's had a hell of a time over the last year and she's very fragile,' Laura continued. 'So if you're thinking of having a fun fling with her for two weeks and then leaving, just…at least be upfront about it with her, will you? Don't trick her. She doesn't deserve to be treated badly.'

Tristan stared at her. Part of him was amused at the sheer awkwardness of this conversation. Part of him was a little envious that Maddie had friends who cared. He had friends. He wasn't sure any of them would step in to help him though. When Clemmie ditched him, most people who called were after some juicy gossip.

'I will bear that in mind,' he said. 'I have no intention of hurting her.' Which posed a problem, because if he wanted to see her as anything other than a colleague who worked on the diorama, then he would have to come clean about who he was. That could be a disaster. For one thing, she would be angry with him for deceiving her. For another, he risked other people finding out who he really was and that, he felt, would not be popular.

Laura seemed to take him at his word. She let out a sigh. 'Good,' she said. 'I'm sorry to have raised the awkward conversation, but…well, glad it's all out in the open now.'

Which wasn't strictly true. Tristan nodded, glad for the reprieve.

'Laura!' A man came in, bringing a gust of cold air with him. He was the guy who had been photographing the hotel earlier. Tristan eyed the camera warily.

'Oh, hi Nate,' said Laura.

'Is Maddie around? I wanted to get a few quotes from her about the Christmas display. For the paper,' Nate said. He waved his camera in the general direction of the window.

Tristan tried to make himself inconspicuous.

'Maddie's just gone to get tea,' said Laura. 'But maybe Chris can help you?'

What? No. Tristan looked at her in alarm. 'I don't—'

'This is Chris Samuels,' Laura said. 'He's helping Maddie with the display.'

A Dictaphone appeared out of a coat pocket. 'Are you a friend of Maddie's from London? From the packaging design place?' Nate asked. When Tristan frowned, Nate added, 'I'm a journalist for the local paper and e-zine. I'm covering the lighting of the Christmas display as a local-interest story.'

Journalist! Alarm bells rang. His shoulders tensed.

'I…er…no. I'm just helping out,' he said.

'We were really stuck,' said Laura. 'Pete Attwater is ill and there was no one to help Maddie. We thought we were going to have to cancel everything, but then Chris here volunteered to help. Out of the goodness of his heart.'

'How wonderful! A good Samaritan! What a lovely, heart-warming Christmas story.'

Tristan faked a smile and nodded, afraid to say more.

Nate put his Dictaphone back in his pocket and raised his camera. 'Can I take a photo of you standing by the model?'

Tristan instinctively raised his hand to his face. 'Er… no. I don't like my photo being on social media.'

Nate narrowed his eyes. 'Are you an actor or something?' He studied Tristan. 'Or a model?'

Tristan laughed. 'No. I'm not an actor.'

'He's not,' said Laura. 'Oh! Unless… Do you have a stage name? That would be why I couldn't find anything on the internet.'

Find anything on the internet? What the— Had they been searching for dirt about him?

'I'm not an actor,' he said firmly. He wasn't really a model either, but he was the poster boy for the hotel group, so technically, you could argue he was. 'And I don't have a stage name. I just don't like the idea of my face being out there in front of goodness knows who. People do weird things with photos these days.'

Nate continued to study him for a moment, then said, 'Okay. Fair enough. Can I interview you then? Just verbally?'

It would look suspicious if he refused. 'Of course,' he

said. 'But I really can't be of much help. Maddie tells me what to do and I do it. That's the extent of my expertise.'

'Laura said you volunteered. Why did you end up helping?'

'He's a guest at the hotel, actually,' Laura chipped in. Tristan sent her silent shut-the-hell-up vibes.

'I…er…am supposed to be relaxing and got the opportunity to help with this beautiful diorama,' Tristan said. 'It was the chance to do something different.'

Nate's eyes flicked to Laura, who shrugged and said, 'Maddie needed all the help she could get.'

'Enjoying it?' Nate asked.

'Oh. Here's Maddie now,' said Laura.

When Nate turned, Tristan let himself relax a fraction. No photos had been taken. He had given his name as Chris Samuels. It would be okay.

When Maddie reached them, Nate stepped forward and gave her a quick hug. The familiarity of the gesture sent another jab of unease through Tristan. Maddie, who was still holding a mug in each hand, couldn't hug Nate back, but she gave him a happy smile of recognition.

Nate quickly explained what he was doing. 'Can I take some photos of you?'

'Of course you can.' Maddie handed Tristan his tea. 'Would you like me to uncover window number one for a bit? We completed that one already.'

'Yes please. Would you mind being in the pictures? It makes such a real difference to show the people behind the story, you know.'

'Oh, we should have Chris in the photo too then,' said Maddie. 'He did a lot of the fine painting work.'

Nate shot a glance across to Tristan. 'Oh, I already asked. Chris refused.'

Maddie gave him a puzzled glance.

Tristan smiled and shrugged. The longer he stayed near this journalist, the more difficult this conversation was going to become. 'If you're doing that, would you mind if I nip off and make a call?'

'Oh, sure,' said Maddie.

Leaving her talking to Nate, Tristan went up to his room. He took the bag with the pastries with him. He had been looking forward to this tea break very much, but now it all felt hollow. This was a good reminder of why he couldn't be with Maddie. She thought he was someone else. Now that he knew that someone had lied to her and taken advantage of her in such a terrible way in the past, he definitely couldn't say anything, no matter how much he wanted to. He was already lying to her. She would be so annoyed when she found out. His heart settled somewhere in his trainers. Added to that, it seemed she was friends with a local journalist. So if she did find out who he was, he would have basically handed an angry woman a scoop that would get him into a world of trouble.

As he entered his room, his phone rang. It was one of the managers from work. He had specifically asked not to be disturbed while he was here.

'Tristan, I'm sorry to bother you, but I need last month's data file for—'

'I left a link in my handover email,' Tristan snapped. 'Have you checked it?'

'I… No.'

He had left *specific* instructions. Did people not read

instructions? 'Please talk to Walter. He can send you everything again. Goodbye.'

He hung up and stared in the mirror at the paint-spattered, bespectacled guy in it. This guy in the mirror wasn't who he was. He was the guy who wore a suit. He was the guy who shook hands and greeted VIPs and knew how to make them feel like the centre of the world, so that they would keep coming back to the Somersby Grand.

His world was about as far removed from this one as you could get. He backed away and sat on the bed. Suddenly, he had a craving for this kind of life. To belong somewhere. To have people that loved him enough to go and warn other people not to hurt him. To be greeted every morning with real smiles, rather than polite, duty-induced ones. To have friends. People he could trust.

Maddie had those. He didn't. With the exception of maybe Walter, he was pretty sure that if his money disappeared, his so-called friends would disappear too.

In the last few days, he'd met people who seemed to genuinely like him. They thanked him for volunteering. They pressed baked goods into his hands. They made him mugs of tea. He wanted this life.

A glance at his watch suggested he should go back down. His expensive watch that gave him a little buzz for doing exercise. The closest thing he got to praise.

He thought of Maddie exclaiming over how well he'd painted the signs on the tiny shops. It had made him feel so good. He shook his head. This was ridiculous. She was a friend and, for the time being, a colleague, not his emotional support person. He reminded himself sternly that this was not his real life. This was a holiday. He was here to do a job, which frankly, he should be paying more attention to.

So he liked her. That was fine. He could continue to like her, it wasn't as though he could stop himself. But he wasn't a teenager. He didn't have to let it go beyond attraction. When the display was finished, he and Maddie would part ways. She would go to stay with her parents and enjoy the rest of her Christmas. He could...do some sightseeing or something. And then he would go home and write a report. This time he spent with her would become a treasured memory that he could take out from time to time, when he was sitting alone at home.

Tristan drained his tea and got back to his feet. Enough of this moping around. He had model buildings to paint.

CHAPTER SEVEN

Tristan cast a quick glance at Maddie. It turned out that her father had lent out two of the trains to a local manor house for part of a summer display. Tristan was driving them to Fitling Manor to pick up the two missing trains. She was looking out of the car window, and seemed to be enjoying the view in the afternoon sunshine. She had let her hair out of its ponytail and put lipstick on. This was presumably what the smarter, more professional Maddie looked like. He liked it. In fairness, he liked all the versions of Maddie that he'd seen so far.

They drove through a quaint Cotswold village and Maddie pointed out a brown sign for a well-known gastropub called the Silk Purse.

'That's meant to be a really good place,' she said. 'Laura and Tim got engaged there.'

'Maybe we should stop there on the way back, for dinner.'

She laughed. 'Oh no. You have to make a reservation months in advance.'

'Ah.' This was not a problem that he normally encountered. Most places could conjure up a table for two for the heir of the Somersby chain of hotels. He didn't like doing it, but…the idea that he could give Maddie something she really wanted thrilled him.

When they arrived at Fitling Manor, Maddie's directions took them to a side entrance and into a staff car park, away from the main tourist area. Maddie called her contact.

Tristan got out and looked around. He had been to Fitling Manor before, but had stayed in the main house. These were the offices, so the chances of him meeting someone he knew were slim. All the same, he was glad that he was dressed differently and was wearing glasses.

Maddie's contact came out to meet them. When they had disappeared into the house, Tristan got back into the car and called Walter.

'I need you to do me a favour,' he said. 'Do you know the Silk Purse—the gastropub? Is it still owned by Toby Farrinham?'

He heard a keyboard clicking. 'Yes,' said Walter. 'And yes. Mr Farrinham.'

'Can you get me a table for two tonight? I know it's hard to book, but if you tell Toby it's me…'

'Let me see what I can do. I'll call you back.'

'Don't call me. Message me. I'm out running an errand with Maddie.'

'I see. Will do. Anything else?'

'No. That's it. Thanks, Walter.'

Maddie returned a few minutes later with a box. They put the box in the boot.

'Do you need to head back, or shall we have a little look around?' he asked.

Maddie hesitated. He could see the pull between wanting to get back to work and the temptation of walking around the beautifully landscaped gardens.

'Come on,' he said. 'You've been working all hours,

staring at models. Let's walk to the end of the lawn and back.'

'I guess it would be good to stretch my legs.'

It was a crisp winter afternoon, where the air had a sharp, crystalline quality to it. It was peaceful walking side by side down the paths that wound through the formal gardens. Tristan felt knots in his shoulders unravelling. Maddie being next to him made all the difference.

Chris was looking at his phone. He was wearing jeans and a chunky white jumper that looked so soft that she wanted to bury her face in it. Maddie couldn't stop staring at him. He really was quite nice to look at. There was no harm in looking, she decided. It was only wanting anything more that was risky. Chris had hardly told her anything about himself. She had told him quite a lot of things about growing up in the town. See, this was her problem. She was too open a book. Alan had had no trouble getting hold of her identity because she'd probably told him everything: the name of her first pet, her birth mother's maiden name—which was, frankly, impossible to guess or spell, so he couldn't have worked it out for himself—all those little snippets that went into a person's safety data. The only thing she couldn't have foreseen was him cloning her phone so that he could use her two-factor authentication. That had made everything so much harder when it came to talking to the banks.

Maddie turned and looked back towards the big house.

Chris didn't show up on social media. He didn't talk about himself. Should this be a warning sign?

Maddie herself didn't have any social media accounts

either. But that was because she had deleted everything after Alan.

Her phone rang, shattering the tranquillity of the afternoon and making her jump. She mouthed 'sorry' to a couple of tourists who were walking by and answered it. It was Laura. Why was she calling? Her first thought was that it was about her parents. 'Laura. What's wrong?'

'Nothing's wrong. I just wanted to check how you were getting on your adventure with Mr Hotness.'

She quickly took a few steps away, in case he heard. 'I found the trains,' she said.

'You know that's not what I meant.'

Maddie did. 'I'm not going anywhere with that,' she said firmly.

Laura sighed. 'Do you have any plans for tonight, after you get back?'

Chris gave her a little wave by way of excusing himself and walked off in a different direction, thumbs moving over his screen.

Maddie took her opportunity to talk to Laura properly. She cupped her hand around the phone. 'Look, will you stop hassling me about him?' she said. 'I'm just not ready for another relationship yet.'

'Who said anything about a relationship?' said Laura. 'Don't take things so seriously, Mads. Just bask in the interest of a handsome guy. Maybe flirt a little. He'll be gone in a week and a bit and you'll be back to your old life knowing that there are other men in the world than Alan. Just treat it as a bit of fun.'

Maddie scoffed. 'You make it sound so easy.'

'It is that easy. Just don't think about it too much.'

'How would you know?' said Maddie. 'You've been with Tim since we were seventeen.'

'Fair point,' said Laura. 'I got lucky. You will too. The right guy for you will come along, eventually. You may as well have fun while you wait.'

'I've got to go—'

'Actually, have you got any plans for after you get back?'

'Um. Yes. I don't think so.'

'Tim and I are meeting a few people from school in the pub. Want to come?'

'Oh yes! That would be lovely,' she said. She hadn't seen people in the longest time. It would be good to see them.

She looked up to see Chris walking towards her. The sight of him made her stomach flutter.

'I'll completely understand if you get a better offer, obviously,' said Laura.

Maddie really hoped the suggestive tone in Laura's voice didn't carry. 'Bye Laura.' She hung up.

Chris came back towards her, putting his phone away. 'Shall we continue our walk?' he said. His smile seemed genuine and wonderful. She could watch him all day.

Suddenly *Just flirt with the handsome man and enjoy it* suddenly didn't seem like such terrible advice after all.

Tristan hadn't had such a wonderful day in a long time. He was here, walking around these delightful landscaped gardens with a girl he liked. Walter had just miraculously sorted an early dinner reservation for them at the restaurant that Maddie had mentioned. He could surprise her with something fun. Excitement fizzed in his chest.

They got to the ha-ha, the ditch that marked the end of the garden, and walked back through the rose garden. By now, the sun was lowering in the sky and the house glowed in an orange sunset.

'Did you know,' Maddie said, 'that people actually live in this house?' She looked around. 'Imagine living in a place like this. All this beauty maintained automatically, just for you.'

'Yes. Imagine.' He didn't have to imagine; he knew. He had been at school with Monty, the oldest son of the house, so he'd visited often. Despite rumours they were thinking of selling it, Monty's family still lived there. When Tristan was last here, the house had been closed to tourists and there'd been a summer ball that spread through the gardens. It was a very different experience being there in the winter, with Maddie. He knew which he preferred. 'Would you like to live in a place like this?' he asked her.

She gave it more thought than he'd expected. 'Maybe.' She nodded thoughtfully. 'It's nice inside. Like a family home.'

Now he thought about it, it was. Huge and sprawling, but filled with homeliness in a way that the places he lived weren't. 'What would your ideal home be?'

'Somewhere cosy and safe.'

He laughed. 'It's your dream home. You must have more details than that.'

'Okay,' she said. 'Since you ask, it would have enough bedrooms so that everyone in the family can have their own room and a kitchen big enough that you can have a sofa in it.'

It only took him a moment to work out why she wanted that. She wanted a place where a family could be a family. Where they could be together and Maddie could know every corner of it. He could see it in his head. A place that felt like home.

All of sudden, he longed to have that too. How wonderful it would be to have a home that he had chosen. Where he knew he was loved. Where he could look out of the window and see grass. Where, if he was dreaming of impossible things, Maddie would be too.

She smiled up at him, making his heart stutter. 'How about you? What sort of house would you live in?'

'Somewhere with a garden.' He nearly said *with you*, but caught himself just in time.

'That sounds lovely.'

They exited the rose garden and Maddie gave a little squeak of delight. The top of the manor was still aglow with the sunset, but it was definitely dusk in the lower shadows. The lights had come on and they were standing in an orchard full of fairy lights. Pinpoints of light twinkled on and off, outlining the branches of the trees. The path they were walking along looked like it was framed with stars.

Maggie let out a breathy 'Ooh!' Her eyes were wide and shining. She looked radiant. Tristan realised that if it could make her look that happy, he would buy her an orchard in a heartbeat.

'Isn't it beautiful?' she said, turning around to take in the whole of the twinkly, sparkling wonder.

'Yes,' he said, not taking his eyes off her. 'Beautiful.'

It was dark when they set off to go back, but not particularly late. Maddie would have plenty of time to head to the pub.

'How about we stop for something to eat?' Chris said.

She had thought she could grab something to eat when she got to the pub with her friends. She cast a quick glance at Chris. On the other hand, spending more time with him was so tempting.

'That sounds good.'

The car headlights picked up a brown sign to the Silk Purse pub.

'Let's try here.' He indicated and took the turn-off. 'My treat.'

'Seriously, you have to book months in advance to get in here. Let's try a normal pub in the next village.'

He gave her a quick grin. He looked quite pleased with himself. Maddie frowned. 'What?'

'See…in my line of work, you often have contacts,' he said. 'And I happen to know someone who could book me a table at short notice. It had to be an early table, which is fine, because we're here now. Just in time.'

They pulled into the pub's car park.

Unease stirred in her chest. 'But I'm not dressed appropriately,' said Maddie. She was in jeans and a nice enough jumper, but it wasn't smart.

'There's no dress code. I checked,' he said. 'They often get people on walking and hunting holidays, so they're not bothered, so long as you clean your boots and don't traipse mud into the carpet.'

Posh people lived by completely different rules to everyone else, it seemed. She had been right when she'd thought he'd come from money.

He held his arm out to her. Maddie was charmed. It was almost as intimate as holding hands, but still maintained a good distance. When she placed her hand in the crook of his elbow, he tucked it closer to his body and escorted her into the pub. It made her feel...valued.

The table they were given was tucked away, giving them privacy. Despite the white-tablecloth-draped tables and candlelight that gleamed off the glasses, the pub felt old-fashioned and cosy. A fire crackled in the grate at the end of the room. The walls were garlanded with winter greenery and silver baubles. It was beautiful.

The menu was limited—which she was grateful for, because otherwise she would have been paralysed by choice. She ordered miso-glazed salmon with vegetables dressed with lime, chili and coriander, while Chris confidently ordered the confit of duck with mash and savoy cabbage. The food, when it arrived, was lovely too—all the flavours balanced to perfection. Across the table from her, Chris seemed relaxed and completely at home.

It couldn't have been easy to get this table booking. Why had he done it? Was he hoping to impress her? A chill ran down her spine. Alan had bought her things: love bombing. It was something abusers and con artists did to get their victims to trust them. Was Chris...?

'What's wrong?' His expression was concerned. 'Maddie?'

She shook her head. 'It's nothing. Just...surprised at how you got a table here at such short notice.'

'Like I said, I know people. The guys here owed me a favour and I called it in. It's not... It's nothing dodgy. Don't worry.'

He didn't look pleased now. If anything, he looked worried. Even a bit scared. She didn't know anything about him. Maybe pulling strings and getting tables in expensive restaurants was something that he did in his world. At least she didn't need to worry about him thinking she had anything worth stealing.

The waiter arrived with the pudding menu. She used it as an opportunity to hide her face and think. Today had been wonderful, but it was an afternoon out of real life. She had let her guard down and allowed herself to dream about a world where she went for walks in lovely gardens with a handsome man. This wasn't her life. She had to be careful.

She glanced over her menu at Chris, who was looking really worried now.

'I'm sorry,' he said. 'I didn't mean to make you uncomfortable. I didn't think—'

He seemed genuinely upset. That was a good sign. Alan had never been contrite. Now she felt bad about reacting the way she did.

'It's okay,' she said. It was, wasn't it? Poor Chris was just trying to do something nice. He was rich and used to being able to pull strings. He wasn't trying to dazzle her. She should give him the benefit of the doubt. Besides, she was here now.

She lowered the menu and tried a smile. 'I think I'll have the chocolate mousse.'

He looked at her for a second, his expression still worried, then seemed to come to a conclusion. 'I'll have the same.'

As they drove the rest of the way back, Maddie looked out of the window. Chris was quiet too. She felt bad for bringing down the mood, now. The Silk Purse was a really nice pub that did great food. She'd finally had the opportunity to eat there and she had ruined it with her paranoia.

Alan's gifts had been showy and extravagant. All Chris had done was take her to a meal at a place she'd said she liked. Okay, he had done the seemingly impossible by getting them a table at short notice, but that had to have been a genuinely spontaneous gesture. There was no way he could have cynically planned that.

Which made her really ungrateful, didn't it?

'I'm sorry,' he said, suddenly. 'I didn't mean to put you in an awkward position like that. It's just that you mentioned you wanted to eat there and I knew I could get us in and… I was out of line. I'm so sorry.'

Maddie looked down at her hands. She had to remember that Chris wasn't Alan. What he had done wasn't remotely like Alan cynically love bombing her to keep her off balance.

'No, I'm sorry,' she said. 'You did a nice thing. I just wasn't expecting it, that's all.'

'I thought a surprise would be fun. That was stupid of me.'

'Don't worry about it.'

Another awkward silence filled the car.

'The food was really good,' she said.

'It was, wasn't it?'

'Thank you,' she said. 'For the meal.'

'You're very welcome.'

More silence. They were coming into the town. This was awful. Chris had done a nice thing for her and she had made it weird. There must be something she could do to make it better.

When they pulled into the car park, Maddie said, 'I…

er… I'm going to the pub in the square to meet some friends. Would you like to join us?'

'Yes,' he said, almost before she'd finished speaking. 'I'd love that.'

Okay. Maybe she hadn't ruined everything. 'Great. I'll put the trains in the storeroom and I'll meet you in the foyer.'

When Maddie and Chris walked into the pub a few minutes later, a shout of 'Maddie!' alerted her to where Laura, Tim and Nate were sitting. Unlike the gastropub, this one was brightly lit, crowded and noisy.

She waved. 'Let me get you a pint,' she said. 'It's the least I can do after you paid for that lovely meal.'

When she got to the table, there was a seat waiting for her, next to Chris. Once she was seated, Nate said, 'So, how's life in London?'

'Not bad.'

'Do you like it there?' asked Chris.

He sounded polite and hesitant. She turned to look at him. In the warm light of the pub, set against the white of his jumper, the startling blue of his eyes stood out. For a moment, she forgot about everything. Oh. Yes. He'd asked her a question. She forced herself to answer honestly.

'Yes,' she said. 'But I miss home. London is so big and impersonal and lonely.'

'That's because that awful git Alan scared off all your friends,' Laura said.

Nate said, 'You can't let that guy ruin an entire city for you.'

Laura put down her glass. 'There's lots of nice things about London, right, Chris?'

Chris looked surprised. 'Um…yes. There's lots of things to do.'

Maddie tilted her head. 'Such as?'

'There are some great places to eat. You can get just about any type of cuisine you want.'

'Are you a bit of a foodie then?' Laura asked.

'I suppose, yes. I do like good food,' Chris said, as though surprised at himself.

That would explain why he was so pleased with himself when he'd got a reservation at the foodie pub. She had judged him so harshly. All because of Alan.

'But it's not really about the things you do, is it?' Chris smiled. 'It's about who you do it with.'

His eyes met hers and something fluttered in her stomach.

'Hey, maybe when you get back to London, you and Maddie could hang out,' Laura said.

Chris's eyes widened and he looked down at his pint. He didn't respond to Laura's comment at all.

Did that mean he didn't want to keep in touch with her? She had thought he liked her, but maybe she'd been wrong about that too? Now she felt stupid. She took a sip of wine. This was, after all, just a holiday to him. He had a whole other life that he rarely talked about, waiting for him to come back to it. He lived in a world where eating in swanky restaurants was normal. What would he want with the likes of her?

Nate interrupted her thoughts. 'So, Chris? What do you do?'

Chris tensed. 'I'm a…business consultant.'

'Oh yes? What sort of business consultant?' asked Nate.

Chris's head snapped towards him. For a second, he

frowned, then his expression cleared. 'Depends on what the client wants,' he said. 'But I'm on holiday right now and I'd really rather not talk about my work.'

When Maddie looked at Chris, his expression was neutral, pleasant, even. But it was also very bland. He took a sip of his drink. There was something different about him now. He was sitting more upright, tense. She caught his eye and his expression softened. Oh. He was uncomfortable. She felt an unexpected urge to protect him.

'I don't want to talk about work either,' she said. 'I want to just hang out with you guys. I haven't seen you in so long.' She gestured towards the three friends sitting opposite her. 'It's so nice to be home.' Where she was safe from people who lied to her and stole from her. She didn't have to second-guess everyone's intentions, because these friends had been there for her for years, through thick and thin. Meeting new people was hard. She cast another glance at Chris. Even ones you were attracted to.

Nate raised his glass. 'One last work question then. For Laura. Are the Somersbys going to close the Cygnet?'

Next to Maddie, she felt Chris twitch. She glanced at him and found him looking down, fiddling with his watch.

Laura narrowed her eyes. 'Is this off the record?'

'Fine,' said Nate. 'Off the record.' He leaned even closer. 'So, how do you feel about the takeover? Is this a positive thing for the hotel?'

Laura thought about it, before saying, 'I think it's too early to tell. It depends on how they want to position us. The big hotels are geared towards the corporate and luxury end of things. We're a country hotel. We do old-world luxury, not modern glitz, like the big hotels do. So…if they try to force us into their model, it'll be a disaster. But if they adapt things so that we can lean into our strengths, then that would probably be quite good.'

'Heaven knows, we could do with a bit of an upgrade of the decor,' said Tim.

Maddie watched Nate thinking about this.

'What do you reckon, Maddie?' Nate said.

Maddie held up her hands. 'I have no opinions on this. I don't work there.'

'Chris?'

Chris startled. 'Me? I don't work there either.'

Nate said, 'Hmm.' While he spoke, he was still watching Chris. 'That's not much use for me as an angle.'

'And,' said Laura, 'this conversation is off the record.'

'Oh yeah,' said Nate. 'That too.'

While her friends were bickering, Maddie nudged Chris. 'Are you okay?'

When she looked sideways at him, he had lowered his head to look at her and his face was now closer than she'd expected. She could see the blue of his eyes, the gold sweep of his lashes, the soft gleam of moisture on his lip. Every other thought in her head was crowded out by the thought that his mouth looked soft enough to kiss.

'Yes. Why?'

She drew back, away from the temptation to kiss him. 'That's good.' Her face was aflame. She took a sip of her drink to cover it up.

The conversation moved on. They had more drinks and Maddie relaxed. It occurred to her that Chris didn't know most of the people they were talking about, but he seemed to be taking it all in his stride. A few drinks in, he seemed to unbend a little and go back to his normal self. Thank goodness. She was so glad she'd asked him to come to the pub.

When was the last time she'd had this kind of laid-back evening? Before Alan. He had stolen more than money from her. He had stolen her friendships and her social life too. What if Laura was right and the reason she was so lonely was because Alan had deliberately prised her away from her friends? If that were the case, could she rebuild a social life for herself? Rediscover the joy of living in a thriving city? Maybe even learn to trust a man with her heart again?

Chris made a joke and everyone laughed. He picked up his glass and drank the last of his pint. She watched his throat move as he swallowed.

He lived in London. He'd said so. For a minute, she entertained the fantasy that she could explore the city and discover its gems with him.

Of course, he didn't want to keep in touch. He had made that clear. But a girl could dream. Maddie sighed and took another gulp of wine. A girl could dream.

Laura and Tim claimed they were taking a detour before going home, so Tristan offered to walk Maddie home from the pub. He didn't want this evening to end.

'Your friends are nice,' he said to her as they walked through the quiet streets. They walked a few seconds in silence. The awkwardness that had arisen during dinner had melted now, thank goodness.

He had definitely misjudged something with his surprise dinner reservation. He wasn't sure what, but he was glad they seemed to have moved past it.

'Was it weird for you with us all talking about people you didn't know?' Maddie asked.

'A bit, but that's okay.' He was used to making small talk with people he had nothing in common with. He was used to polite dinners or wildly drunken parties, but nothing like this evening with its warmth and relaxed laughter.

'I haven't sat in a pub and chatted in years.' Not since university. The minute he started working for his father, all the fun had stopped. He remembered his father's lectures on how he must represent the Somersby brand at all times. How drunken antics would not be tolerated. All the training he'd been given on handling the press, decorum, entertaining people from different cultures had kicked in. He had been given a nominal title and pushed into the Somersby marketing machine.

He thought he had done really well following the rules and schmoozing, but the reputation gained in his late teens was hard to shake off. The fact that he hadn't found anyone to date more than once hadn't helped. The newspapers loved to paint him as the playboy heir. That's why he'd ended up with his little arrangement with Clemmie. That had worked wonders until she'd ruined everything.

It amazed him that no one recognised him here. He hoped his luck would continue to hold for a few more days. He had apparently passed Laura's googling attempts, but Nate worried him. If the journalist decided to dig deep into Chris Samuels, it was possible that he might find Tristan Somersby.

He looked across at Maddie. She deserved to know

the truth, but if he told her, everything would change. They had talked about the Somersby chain as though it was soulless. There was no way Maddie would see him as a friend if she knew who he was. Besides, he was supposed to be a secret shopper. No secret shopper worth their salt let slip their identity.

So he remained trapped in this ridiculous situation, where he couldn't ask out the girl he liked because she thought he was someone else.

'I love my friends,' said Maddie. 'They make me feel safe.'

'Maddie, "safe" means a lot to you, doesn't it? Is that because Alan stole from you?'

She didn't respond and continued walking.

'He didn't hurt you physically, did he?' The very thought made him hot and cold with fury and fear.

'Not physically, no,' she said. 'I'm starting to realise exactly how much he took from me though. It wasn't just the money. It was my friendships, my confidence, my peace of mind. I struggle to trust people. I feel so stupid.'

It decimated him that she felt like that. 'Oh Maddie.'

'I want to come home. I want to be who I used to be.' Her voice wobbled. She sniffed. 'Sorry. I've had too much to drink.'

'No, don't worry about it,' he said. 'Can I…can I give you a hug?'

'Yes, please.'

He stopped walking and wrapped his arms around her. She leaned into him, warm and soft. When her arms tightened around him, he cradled her head against his shoulder and fought the urge to kiss the top of her head.

'You're not stupid,' he said. 'Con men are just very

good at kicking away your support structures. It's not your fault.'

'He cloned my phone,' she said, into his chest.

He couldn't even comprehend how invasive that must have felt. 'That's horrible,' he said. 'There was no way you could have defended yourself against that.'

'He used to buy me stuff all the time. It's called love bombing.' Her voice was muffled against him. 'They buy you things. Surprise presents. Unexpected dinner reservations…'

No wonder she had freaked out when he arranged a surprise reservation at a fancy gastropub! 'And I just sprang an expensive dinner on you. I had no idea, Maddie. If I'd known I would never—'

'I know,' she said. 'I'm not good at judging what's right anymore. I overreacted. I'm so sorry.'

He leaned back so that he could see her face. 'Don't be,' he said. 'It's not your fault. I probed something that hurt you.'

She let go and stepped back. It took everything he had not to reach for her again. If he ever met her ex, he would demolish him.

'Sorry,' she said again.

He put his hands on her shoulders. 'Listen to me, Maddie. What that guy did to you was unforgivable. You have to believe that you couldn't have prevented it. It's nothing that you did or didn't do.' He tilted her chin up so that she was looking at him. Tears glistened on her cheeks. He wiped them away. 'Maddie, you're a wonderful person. You're warm and clever and kind. Don't let him ruin that. He's not worth it.'

Her eyes met his. They gazed at each other. The moment stretched between them. She was sad and vulnerable. He was pretending to be someone else. If he kissed her now, it would be a betrayal and she'd had enough of that in her life already. He took a deep breath and stepped back.

Maddie looked confused for a second, then wiped her hand across her cheeks. 'I'm nearly home,' she said, pointing to a building not far away. 'That's where I'm staying.'

They walked the last few yards.

'Thank you for walking me home,' she said.

'Thank you for letting me join you in the pub in the first place.' He took a couple of steps backwards so that he had some space between them. 'I'll see you tomorrow.'

She dug out a key and let herself into the building. He watched her wave and disappear inside before he turned and headed back.

He was going to have to tell her who he really was before he left, because if he didn't, she would feel silly when she found out and he would be no better than that con man who had destroyed her. He just had to work out the best time to tell her…and keep his distance from her until then.

CHAPTER EIGHT

THE LAST DIORAMA was a ski village. The background was higher and it included a ski slope. The buildings in the foreground were ski lodges, which didn't need any repairs. There was a ski lift terminal at the base of the slope and a collection of food carts. Tristan was given the task of making sure the food carts were presentable while Maddie stood on the lower rungs of a stepladder and worked on the skiers going down the ski slope.

It seemed to involve a rotating loops of white rubber with the figures of skiers stuck to it. Maddie frowned as she attached the loop to rollers. He watched her work. She had clever hands, he decided. She moved them, attaching and pinning confidently. When she was concentrating hard, she bit her lower lip, which was the cutest thing ever. Occasionally, she'd get a smudge of paint or oil on her face and she would barely notice it because she was so focused on what she was doing. He loved that.

He looked back at the hot dog stand he was retouching. Had he always found competence attractive? He had, come to think of it. Even Clemmie. She was a social climber, but that meant she had an impressive mental catalogue of who was who and what levers to pull in a conversation. He had seen her outmanoeuvre hard-nosed businessmen and persuade them to donate to charities. The other thing he'd liked about Clemmie was that she didn't expect him to smile all the time.

As a child, Tristan had been told over and over again that he had to smile. *Your dad is coming, be a good boy and smile.* Why? His dad rarely bothered to smile at him. He'd got into trouble for *being bloody miserable* so often that he'd relented and come up with a smile that meant absolutely nothing to him. This was the one he wore when he met important people. The one that made it into press cuttings. A carefully cultivated, smooth smile that he could summon at a moment's notice, regardless of how he was feeling inside.

He had smiled more in the past few days, talking to Maddie, than he had done in months. These were real smiles that rose out of him unforced. For a moment, he indulged in a fantasy where he really was an unremarkable man called Chris, who'd met a woman who liked him back. Did Maddie like him back? He thought she might. But what happened when she found out that he wasn't who he'd said he was? She had already been hurt by the worst kind of liar once. It would crush her.

Above him, Maddie finished one section and moved on to the next and set up the mechanism for the skiers there. He couldn't understand how this was going to join up together, but he was sure Maddie would make it work. She looked up from her work and caught him watching her. She smiled, and Tristan felt something respond in his chest.

'Everything okay?' she said.

'Yes, yes.' He cast around for something to say. The bustle outside the window caught his eye. 'I was just wondering what all the activity was about out in the square, that's all.'

'Oh, that'll be preparations for the Christmas fair. It starts tonight.' She paused and looked past him. 'The official Christmas lights switch-on is tomorrow night.'

'What's at the fair?'

'The usual things,' said Maddie. 'Stalls, food carts, carol singers, that sort of thing.' She turned back to her work and secured the third and last segment of the ski slope. 'They unveil the window display fifteen minutes after the official switch-on, so that it's part of the celebrations.' She raised her hands off the display. 'There. All wired in.'

Tristan carefully nudged the little hot dog cart into its place and put his brush away. 'So how does that work then?' He nodded towards the ski slope she was building.

'Let me show you.' She came down the ladder, moving far too carelessly for Tristan's liking. She reached for the switches hidden around the back. The figures started to move; those at the top part zigged and the next part zagged. 'We'll just put some trees and snow to cover up the place where they join, so it'll look like they just skied underneath the trees and appeared in the section below.'

It was a clever little arrangement. 'That's very neat. Is that your grandpa again?'

Maddie smiled proudly. 'Actually, no. That one was me. He helped me build it, but the idea was mine.'

'Wow.' He peered closer. 'That little guy has a chip of paint missing on his top. I'll touch that up when I'm done here.'

'Thank you.' She moved around and turned the skiers off.

He found the finest of brushes and a pot of the red that the damaged skier was wearing and leaned over the set so that he could very, very carefully cover up the small flash of white that was showing where the paint had chipped off.

When he was finished, he looked out of the window again. The wooden stalls were being decorated. He had a sudden vision of being out there, with Maddie, just wandering around a Christmas market. It sparked off a longing so fierce that it made his breath catch.

Well, why not? It was just a Christmas market. It was right outside where they worked. He just had to make sure he didn't do anything over the top and upset her again.

'Maddie?'

'Hmm?' She was still behind the set, and whatever she was doing was causing rustling noises. All he could see was part of her back.

'Would you like to go round the Christmas fair this evening? With me?'

The rustling stopped. Slowly Maddie crawled backwards and sat up. There were bits of styrofoam in her hair. She frowned. 'I… Sure. I'll show you around the Christmas fair.'

That wasn't what he'd meant. He didn't need a guide. But the result was the same, so he said, 'Great. Meet you in front of the hotel at…seven thirty?'

'Sounds like a plan.' She nodded and disappeared again.

Tristan smiled and went back to what he was doing. There was a curious feeling in his chest that felt a bit like hope.

'You have a date?' Laura said. 'Nice work, Mads.'

'It's not a date.' Maddie dug through her suitcase and

found a clean jumper. She didn't have much stuff with her, because she'd been expecting to be at home, where most of her Christmas clothes were, not sleeping on Laura's sofa. 'I'm just showing him around the Christmas fair.'

'It's a Christmas fair,' said Laura. 'There's nothing to show round. It's a date.' She nudged her. 'I'm so proud of you.'

'Ow.' Maddie scrubbed her arm in mock pain. 'It's not. I'm not ready for that sort of thing yet. I don't know anything about the guy.'

'So…tonight is a good chance to get to know him.'

Maddie sank down onto the sofa bed, next to her suitcase. 'I dunno. Don't you think it's a bit weird though? He's clearly rich. He's supposed to be on holiday, but he's randomly helping me with the display.'

Laura sat on the other side of the suitcase. 'That is a bit strange, I'll admit. But I was watching you guys work this afternoon and it looks like he's really enjoying painting stuff. He seems really focused, not messing around or anything.'

Maddie chewed on the corner of her fingernail. 'Oh, he's not messing. He does a really good job, even with one injured hand.'

'He sometimes stops to look at you. His face goes all soft and wistful…'

When Maddie didn't respond, Laura said, 'I think he fancies you. Just in a normal way. I don't think he's scoping you out to be a target.'

'I've told him I have no money,' Maddie said. She put down the jumper she was holding. 'You have to admit it's weird that we can't find anything about him on the internet. Who has no presence on the internet? He said he was a consultant. Surely he'd have a website or something.'

'Well normally, yes. But from talking to my friends from the hotel management course…there's like a whole other level when you get to the really fancy people. They don't advertise. They just work through contacts.' She waved an arm in a flourish. 'Like those who need to know…just know. It's a different world for posh people.'

Maddie thought about Chris. 'He does sound quite posh, doesn't he?' Not posh, exactly. More…polished. 'His accent changes as well, I've noticed. Like, when he talked to Tim, he got a hint of local Oxfordshire.'

'Oh. Oh. I heard about this on TikTok. Where people pick up the accent of the person they're talking to. Apparently, it's quite common in people who've moved around a lot when they were kids.'

'Hmm.' She went back to chewing on the edge of her nail. She hadn't questioned any of what Alan said. She had just been swept up in this whirlwind romance with a man who seemed to adore her. It had never occurred to her that he might be lying. Being fooled once was allowed, but she wasn't going to be taken in twice. 'I dunno. There's something not right here.'

Chris was almost the opposite of Alan. He didn't buy her things or flatter her excessively. When he'd realised that the dinner reservation bothered her, he had been mortified. She thought about how he'd got rid of a slug before she saw it…and hadn't even mentioned that to her. She only knew because Laura had told her. He was clear that he didn't need money. There were no wild declarations of affection. Nothing apart from this insistent pull from the core of her towards the core of him. Which was simply how you felt when you liked someone.

But she had felt that towards Alan too. She put her head in her hands.

She didn't want to develop feelings for him. What if she really fell for him? What if he turned out to be a liar, the same as Alan?

Laura put her hands on Maddie's knees. 'Maddie? Do you like him?'

Her face felt hot. There was no point lying to Laura. They'd known each other too long. So she nodded.

Laura grinned. 'Then go along with it. Sweetheart, you can't lock yourself away because you're scared of someone hurting you again. You have to let it go and move on.'

Maddie looked at Laura's hands. Maybe she was over-thinking this. Being with Chris felt different to being with Alan. He was helpful and smart and had a smile that made her melt. She deserved to have someone who made her feel like that. 'I… You're right.' She looked at her friend, decision made. 'I should give this a chance. I just won't move in with him and let him near my money until I'm really, really sure.'

'That's my girl.' Laura jumped to her feet. 'Come on then. We need to get you ready for this date.' She looked at the jumper Maddie had picked out. 'Oh, that'll never do. Let's go see what I have that might fit you.'

When they were younger, they had shared clothes all the time, but now they were different shapes. Maddie said, 'It's not a date.'

But she got up anyway and followed Laura into the bedroom.

* * *

Tristan was trying on the clothes that were in his case. He had no idea how to dress for a walk around a Christmas market on a…not-exactly-a-date date. He had spent a good twenty minutes trying to scrub flecks of paint off his face and hands.

He put on a shirt and pulled a new jumper over it. No. Too formal. T-shirt? He checked his reflection. Too casual.

His phone rang. He checked the caller before he answered.

'Walter, hi.' He put it on speakerphone and threw it on the bed.

'Just checking in to see how things are going,' Walter said.

Tristan hesitated. 'Are you asking as my assistant? Or as my friend?'

'Either,' said Walter. 'Do we have to choose one?'

'Yes.'

'Friend then.'

He let out a long breath. 'Okay.'

'What's the matter? Is something wrong?'

Tristan pulled on a rugby shirt with a collar. Okay. That would do. 'No. There's a good thing and a bad thing.'

'Oh. This sounds intriguing.' He heard a click as Walter shut the door.

'Are you still in the office?'

'Maybe.'

'Remember how we talked about work-life balance?'

'Get back to the point, Tristan. What's the good thing?'

'I have a date. Well, sort of.' He outlined how he'd met Maddie and how things were going.

'Oh, I see,' said Walter. 'Is this something serious? Or

are you simply getting out of your funk from the Clemmie debacle?'

He tucked his shirt into his chinos. It was a shirt from the rugby club. He eyed the logo. Did that mark him out as posh? Best to wear a jumper. It was freezing outside anyway.

Was this just him getting over Clemmie? He didn't think so. He'd liked her, but their engagement had been a practical one. There was nothing to get over. 'It's not a rebound thing,' he said carefully. 'I don't *need* a girlfriend. Anyway, Maddie is…nothing like Clemmie.'

'That can only be a good thing,' said Walter solemnly.

'She's brilliant at making things and the people here seem to love her. They keep popping in to talk or to help. She's got this whole community who love her.' He pulled on a jumper. Cashmere, but from John Lewis. Good.

Walter made listening noises.

'She's not fake at all,' Tristan continued. 'In any case, she doesn't know who I am.'

'Sounds like you like her quite a lot.' Walter paused. 'Tristan, do be careful.'

He sat down on the bed. 'That's the problem.'

'I don't follow.'

'She thinks I'm a business consultant called Chris! I'm lying to her. Not just with my name, but about what I'm doing here.' He plucked at the mass-produced cashmere. 'Even my clothes aren't what I'd usually wear.' He flopped backwards onto the bed, so that his head landed next to the phone. 'She's going to hate me when she finds out.' He pressed his fingertips into his temples. 'She's been hurt before. It's going to be awful.'

'I see,' said Walter solemnly.

'What am I going to do, Walter? If I tell her now, she's going to be angry. If I tell her later, she's still going to be angry. If I blow my cover and news gets out that I'm hanging around building a Christmas set for a hotel we just bought, the press will have a field day.'

'I'm thinking,' said Walter. 'I'm thinking.'

'Why did I think this was a good idea?'

'It wouldn't have mattered, if you hadn't got involved,' said Walter. 'If you'd just been a guest, like we'd planned.' There was a hint of admonishment in his voice.

Which was fair, he supposed, but then he wouldn't have met Maddie or got to know her like this. 'I don't regret that,' he said firmly. 'These few days, working with Maddie, have been the most fun I've had in a long time. I didn't have to think about who's who or worry about being papped or have Dad in my ear. I get to make beautiful things with my hands. I'd forgotten how satisfying that could be…and I got to meet Maddie. She makes me feel…' He raised his hands above him, trying to find the word he wanted. 'Liked? No. More than that. Welcomed. Like I'm enough.'

'Oh,' said Walter. He was quiet for a few seconds. 'Tristan? Do you think she might be the real deal for you?'

He considered how the very thought of her made him smile. 'I think she might be.'

'Oh dear.'

Tristan sat up. 'I can't ask her out while I'm lying to her. I have to tell her.'

'That's not a good idea. What if she goes to the press?'

'She wouldn't do that.'

'Even if she was really, really angry about being lied to?'

'N—' He frowned. She wouldn't. Would she? Even if

she didn't mean to, might she let something slip to Nate? 'She'll be so upset!'

'I think we should abort this project,' said Walter, always infernally sensible. 'Given the risk.'

Tristan considered this. 'I can't do that just before the Christmas display is unveiled,' he said. 'I promised I'd help. I'll tell her as soon as the display is finished.'

'When is that?'

'Tomorrow night. They unveil the display just after they light the town's Christmas tree.'

'Sounds like a plan,' said Walter. 'And then, do you plan on staying until your fortnight is over?'

'No. I'd have to leave. This is her hometown. I can go stay somewhere else. I'll submit a report of what I have so far and you can send a different secret shopper after Christmas.'

He could hear Walter drumming his fingers on the desk. 'There are no photos of you while you were there?'

'No. Not that I know of.'

'My instinct is to get you out of there now,' said Walter.

'One more day won't make much difference,' Tristan countered. 'I will tell her by 8:00 p.m. tomorrow,' he said. 'And if it looks bad, I'll leave the same night. Does that sound good?'

'*Good* is not the word I'd use, but okay. I'll cover for you about your early departure.'

'If anything comes up before then,' said Tristan, 'then I'll tell her sooner. Otherwise, I'd just like to enjoy another day before she hates me.' He peered in the mirror and combed his hair. 'I'm going to hang up now, Walter. I have a date to prepare for.'

'Wait. I need an update on your review.'

Tristan lowered his comb. He had been sending reports back each night. He had been so wrapped up in working on the display today that he hadn't had a chance to write up his observations. That was probably why Walter called. He pressed his fingers to his forehead and forced his mind to change gears. 'Can you make some notes, please?'

'Of course.'

He dictated his observations.

The sound of typing. 'Sounds positively idyllic.' There was a hint of laughter in Walter's voice. 'There's nothing that you think should change?'

'There is, but...' Tristan said thoughtfully. 'I think we need to be careful that when we put our standard processes in place...we don't iron out the things that make this hotel friendly. There are people here who come every Christmas. There's a great sense of loyalty. It would be a shame to lose that.'

He listened to Walter's keyboard clicking away. 'We don't want these hotels to be smaller versions of the Somersby luxury hotels,' he added. He had to keep reminding his father of this. 'We bought them so that we could diversify our offering. So we should do that properly. So we can do...erm...' He frowned and raked his mind for a phrase that described what he meant. 'So that we can have Somersby quality mixed with each hotel's unique charm.'

'I like that,' said Walter.

'Me too. Make a note. I'll have to use that in the final report.' He glanced at his watch.

'Anything else?'

'Yes, actually. Can you chase procurement for the figures I asked for two days ago?' He rattled off a few more instructions. 'Got all that?'

'Yes. That should reassure everyone that you're working and not living it up in sleepy Oxfordshire.'

Tristan rolled his eyes. 'I'm glad I got out of London. It's so much nicer here. Is keeping a low profile working with the press?'

'Actually,' said Walter, his voice suddenly serious again. 'There's been some speculation in the press about where you are. Rumour is that you had an alcohol problem and you've booked yourself into rehab.'

'What!' Okay, he had been a drinker when he was younger, but not anymore. 'These people! Honestly.' He thought of Nate. Should he mention him to Walter? No. Probably no need. Nate hadn't shown any signs of recognising him.

'It's only a few gossip journos trying to provoke a response,' Walter said. 'There's no actual substance, just speculation. I don't think it's anything to worry about. Keep away from journalists anyway.'

'No one knows me here,' he pointed out.

'Keep out of photos. Like, if this woman wants to give you credit for all the help you've been giving her, just… don't make it into the local paper.'

He wasn't a complete fool. 'Obviously. Already avoided that. They have me down as Chris Samuels. No photo.' He checked his watch again. Nearly time to meet Maddie. 'I have to go, Walter. Was there anything else?'

'Nothing that can't wait,' said Walter. 'Go enjoy your date. Be careful.'

Tristan grinned and grabbed his coat.

He was a few minutes late, so he practically ran down the stairs and across the lobby, which set his watch buzzing.

Maddie was standing outside the hotel, looking at something on her phone. She was wearing well-fitting trousers, high-heeled boots, a fluffy red jumper and a warm-looking coat. Her hair was loose and lay thick and glossy on her shoulders. It made him wonder what it would feel like flowing through his fingers.

He said, 'Hi.' He had intended it to sound calm and sophisticated, but it came out breathless.

She looked up from her phone and smiled. Tristan's world stuttered. He always thought she was pretty, but tonight, she was positively enchanting.

'Ready?' she said.

He tried to get his brain back into gear.

'For the market,' she said.

'Yes. Let's go. Show me the joys.'

The market space in the centre of the village was just outside the hotel. All they had to do was cross the road and they were surrounded by noise and bustle. The huts that were being set up earlier in the day were now cheerfully decorated and formed successive islands of light. Tristan inhaled the smell of hot waffles and doughnuts and his mouth watered.

'Have you eaten?' he asked her. 'Let me buy you dinner.' He gestured towards the many stalls. 'Anything you like.'

Maddie laughed, her beautiful eyes sparkling. 'Tonight, I am in the mood for mulled wine and a sugar overload.'

'Well then.' He offered her his elbow and slipped her

hand through. They headed to the waffle stand and stood in the queue.

Maddie bobbed up onto her toes to read the list of toppings. Tristan took the chance to look at her again.

He had been attracted to women before. Wanted them, even. But this was different. He was attracted to Maddie on so many different levels. She made him feel liked. He had never been himself with any of the women he'd been with before. People didn't want him, not even his parents. They wanted the heir to the Somersby empire. So he gave them what they wanted. But here, with Maddie, he was relaxed in a way he'd never been before. Being with her didn't take effort. There was no performance. The days he spent with her felt simultaneously longer and shorter than any other days in his life. The idea that he would have to walk away from her in a few days was too terrible to contemplate.

Maddie turned to him. 'I'm having chocolate, bananas and cream in mine,' she said.

He jolted out of staring at her. 'I'll…have a savoury one, I think.'

'You can't!' she said, with mock horror. 'It's Christmas.'

'I can, just watch me,' he said. 'I don't need to be any sweeter than I already am.'

She rolled her eyes and he laughed.

When it came to their turn, he watched her order. He had to tell her the truth, but it would ruin everything. All the money in the world couldn't buy him a solution.

He would tell her tomorrow. Tonight, he would just lean into the fantasy that he could have this amount of joy in his life and not have it snatched away.

CHAPTER NINE

MADDIE LICKED THE last of the chocolate off her fingertips. So good. She glanced sideways at Chris, who was busy examining an intricately carved wooden puzzle box at one of the stalls. The lights on the kiosk picked out the gold in his hair and made his eyes look particularly striking. He smiled at something the artist said and the corners of his eyes crinkled into smile lines. He had a nice smile. Nice lips too. She looked away before he caught her staring.

Given the chance, she would have looked at him all night. She was having the best time. It had been so long since she'd been able to forget about all the things that had happened and just have fun. Laura was right. Why should Alan ruin her present as well as her past? She deserved fun.

Chris paid for the puzzle box and the artist gift-wrapped it for him. As they left to go look at the chilli jams in the stall next door, he handed her the package. 'Here,' he said. 'Merry Christmas.'

'You didn't have to—'

'I know. And you definitely don't need to get me anything,' he said. 'I spent so long chatting to her about it, I felt bad not buying it.'

She nodded. 'In that case, thank you. I've got one of her jewellery boxes already.' She'd thought it was her meagre jewellery collection that needed protecting. She'd known to keep that safe, but she should have been watching the plastic and the information instead. Alan had basically stolen her identity to the point that he could syphon her money away from her. He had even taken a loan out in her name. She had found all this out far too late. It had taken her ages to clear her name. Her credit score was still a mess. She didn't know what she'd have done if her parents hadn't been able to help her out.

She tucked the little box into her bag.

Chris looked around as he walked slowly next to her. They paused to admire the assortment of artisan work on display—the hand-blown glass baubles, the paper-cut sculptures and all the food stalls. 'I am having such a great time,' he said suddenly. 'It's so nice to be out without having to watch—' He stopped. A small frown flitted across his face. 'It's just so nice being here.'

'It's a very cool Christmas market. Not as exciting as the ones in London, obviously,' she said, acutely aware that he was probably used to bigger things.

He gave her a small grin. 'The company's better.' He looked around. 'What's next? What's traditional?'

She blamed her earlier daydreaming for what happened next. 'There's mistletoe over there,' she said. 'Maybe we should go stand under it.'

'I'm game.' He took her hand.

Her brain caught up with her mouth. 'Oh. Oh. I was joking,' she said.

He turned so that he was facing her, her hand still in his. His eyes met hers. 'That's a shame,' he said quietly.

Heat raced up her body. Her surroundings melted away. All she could see were his eyes, and then, his mouth. She wanted to kiss him. So why fight it? She took a small step closer. His very inviting lips curved into a slight smile. He moved closer too.

'Maddie!' A familiar voice made her jump.

She turned, guiltily, to see Nate, a few feet away. He raised a camera and took a photo. Chris lifted his free hand and turned away.

'Hi Nate,' Maddie said.

'Nate,' Chris said dryly. He dropped Maddie's hand. His expression had faded to something polite and bland, just like it had done in the pub. He smiled, but it wasn't his usual smile. There was no warmth in it.

'I'm just showing Chris around the Christmas fair,' Maddie said.

Nate looked from one of them to the other. 'Remind me, were you guys friends before this week?' he said.

He never did have any tact. She supposed it was useful in his line of work to keep digging when it would have been far more polite to leave.

'No,' she said. 'But we're friends now.'

Nate's gaze dropped to her hand, now dangling empty by her side. 'I see.'

'We'd best get on,' Maddie said.

Chris said, 'Nice to see you, Nate.'

'I'll see you tomorrow,' said Nate. 'I'm covering the lights switch-on. I'll cover the "possibly the last time we have a Christmas display because the big corporation will shut it down" thing too.' He was still looking at Chris. 'It would be a shame to lose it. It's been a part of Christmas here for so long.'

'Yes,' said Maddie. 'But big hotels do what they do, I guess.'

Nate nodded slowly. 'Yes.'

Chris took a couple of steps away. Maddie gave Nate a wave and followed Chris. They paused at the next stall, which was selling cards. Something had fractured the atmosphere. Chris seemed tense and closed off compared to before. He had ducked his head down and kept glancing around.

A cute print of a robin on a log caught Maddie's eye. 'I think Mum would like that,' she said. She flicked through and found another nice thank-you card for Laura and Tim. A sideways glance at Chris showed that he was still looking tense. 'Is everything okay? Sorry about Nate. He never did know when to stop asking questions.'

Chris's eyes focused on her again and she felt a little flash of heat at the thought of what Nate had interrupted. 'It's fine.' He looked over his shoulder. 'I forgot that you know just about everyone here.'

Maddie shrugged. 'Small town. Grandad was a personality, Mum teaches in the local primary school...so, yes. It's a small world here.'

He gave her a thoughtful look. 'Is that a bit oppressive? Like being watched all the time?'

She hadn't thought of it like that. 'No,' she said carefully. 'It's comforting. If...' She swallowed. Moving on from Alan involved being able to talk about it. 'If I'd been here when I was with Alan, I don't think he would have been able to steal from me without someone spotting something and warning me.'

Chris didn't say anything for a second, then said, 'All these people, they don't just know you, they love you. I imagine they'd come down hard on anyone who hurt you.'

Maddie laughed. 'I wouldn't go that far. But yes, when

it comes to the big things, I'd have thought they would all be on my side.'

He shook his head. 'Wow. That's…really great, actually. You're very lucky.'

She paid for her cards and slipped those into the bag too. 'You must have people like that. Everyone does.'

He looked down. 'Not really. I mean, I always had people around me. Heaven knows, there are enough people watching me at every moment.' He rolled his eyes. 'But not in a good way.'

She tried to understand. 'But how can that be? You're nice, you're bound to have people who care about you.'

His expression was suddenly sad. 'I can think of only one person. And he's a work friend, so he doesn't really know me that well. Not really.'

She couldn't imagine how lonely that must be. She remembered the image he'd painted of his mum leaving. That poor lost little boy was still very much a part of him. She put a hand on his arm.

He looked at it and put his bigger hand over hers. 'It's fine,' he said. 'Because I'm here now and I'm learning that my life could do with some changes.' He gave her hand a squeeze and moved it so that it was tucked into the crook of his arm. 'The first of which is that I'd love one of those hot chocolates. Can you believe that I've never had one?'

'Never had a hot chocolate? I don't believe that for a minute.'

'Plain hot chocolate, yes. But not one like that, with marshmallows and all the cream and…' He frowned. 'A gingerbread man drowning in it?'

'You're supposed to dip it and eat it,' she said, laughing.

He grinned. 'Okay. Fine. Let's do that.'

* * *

By the time Chris walked her home, Maddie's feet hurt from wearing Laura's boots. She didn't want to complain though, because she was still having the most incredible time. Being back home for Christmas was wonderful, but being able to sneak glances at this handsome man, who had her hand in his, was…slightly dizzying. She hadn't felt this head rush of attraction in the longest time.

As they approached the building where Laura and Tim lived, she had to remind herself that she needed to be careful. She still didn't really know much about Chris. She had only known him for four days. But it felt like so much longer. She liked him. She thought he liked her too. If only there was a way of knowing for sure that he was genuine and not playing her like Alan had. But there wasn't and the uncertainty was just part of life.

'This is me,' she said, gesturing up towards the second floor.

He glanced up. 'Right.' He turned towards her. During the course of the evening, he had ended up carrying her bag. He handed it back to her.

'Thanks.' She didn't want the evening to end. It felt like she'd stepped outside of her real life for one night. She got to be the girl that the handsome man wanted to be with. Where there weren't debts and unpaid credit card bills and a Christmas display that wasn't quite finished. 'I… I had a lovely time this evening.'

'Me too.' He took a small step closer. 'Thank you for showing me around.'

She gave a little laugh. 'It's hardly streets and streets. It's just a tiny little market in the town square.'

'But it felt like more because you were there.'

The light from the street lamp cast the planes of his face in light and shadow. His eyes met hers. She could kiss him. She had wanted to kiss him before, but now the feeling was almost overwhelming. Her heart picked up speed. She couldn't stop looking at his mouth.

Chris raised a hand and touched the side of her face. He had removed his gloves and his bare fingertips grazed her jaw. She could barely breathe for wanting him.

He leaned closer and whispered, 'May I?'

She breathed, 'Yes.'

His mouth was warm against hers. The brush of his fingers against her cheek sent an electric shiver down her spine. This kiss made her whole body tingle, as though her nerves were waking up from a long sleep. As though the world had been slightly wrong all this time and now had finally, finally fallen into place. She moved closer and slid her hand up to his shoulder. He leaned in, his hands moving into her hair.

A sudden buzz right in her ear made them both jump apart.

'What was that?' she said, too breathless to speak properly.

'Bloody thing.' Chris did something to his watch. 'I… uh.' Even in the low light, she could see the embarrassment colouring his face. 'It's my stupid watch. It thinks I'm doing some exercise because my heart rate—'

She had asked for proof of his feelings and here it was. He wasn't lying about wanting her. His own heartbeat betrayed him. She went up on her toes, took his face in her hands and kissed him.

He wrapped his arm around her waist and pulled her

against him as he kissed her back. This was a kiss that she never wanted to end.

She lost all sense of time, or of the cold or anything. All she could feel was the sensation of his mouth moving against hers. His hand leaving a trail of heat as it stroked up her back and moved to cradle the back of her head. Of the tingling need that was welling up inside her. Until someone wolf-whistled and shouted, 'Get a room.'

She moved back, her face flaming. It wasn't like her to be caught snogging in the street. But it was worth it. She looked up at Chris, who gently released her. She rested her head on his chest, just briefly. 'I…should go inside,' she said.

'Probably a good idea.' He was smiling—the kind of smile that made his eyes dance and sparkle. 'I guess I'll see you tomorrow morning.'

She bit her lip and nodded. 'Bright and early. Ready for work.'

'Yes.'

Neither of them moved. She gave him a little push. 'Go on. Go. You know your way back to the hotel, right?'

'I do. I do.' He grinned at her, took a few steps backwards and turned to go.

Maddie let out a long shaky breath. A smile tugged at the corners of her mouth. Right now, she felt so happy, she could take on the world.

Chris turned back, strode over and gave her another kiss. 'For luck,' he said. He stroked her cheek, kissed her again and left, leaving her feeling like her knees had melted.

MADDIE PRACTICALLY FLOATED back into the building and up the stairs. At the door, she paused and tried to dampen the grin off her face. When Laura found out, she would never hear the end of it. But try as she might, she could not stop smiling. Ah well. She would just have to put up with Laura's teasing. Right now, she was too happy to care.

The minute she stepped inside, she sensed something was wrong. Laura was standing in the middle of the room, both her hands pushing back her hair. Tim was on the sofa, laptop on his knees.

'It could be anyone,' Laura said.

Tim's eyes flicked across to Maddie.

This didn't look good. That hands-in-her-hair pose was what Laura did when she was stressed. Maddie looked from one to the other. 'What's going on?'

'The hotel…' Laura waved an arm. 'The Somersby HQ is sending out spies to check out the new hotels they've bought.'

Maddie tried to catch up. 'Hang on. Hang on. Spies?'

'Secret shoppers,' said Tim. 'They send people to act as hotel guests, just to see what the service is like.'

Maddie perched on the arm of the sofa. 'Your service is excellent. I don't understand why you're worried.'

Laura started pacing. 'No. No. This is more than that. They've just bought up a whole load of small hotels like our one. They want to make a boutique arm for Somersby Hotels. If they don't like what we've got, they'll just close the Cygnet down, gut it and start again.'

Maddie glanced at Tim, to check if this was true, or was just Laura making too much of something. He nodded, his face serious. Oh no. The Cygnet Hotel was gorgeous, but it was old-world.

'That's…' She sat down. 'Okay. Have you noticed anyone acting weird? Like, being extra nosy or anything?'

Laura shook her head. 'Just about everyone has been before. Or business people who have only been using the conference rooms. The only one who isn't one of those is Chris and he's spent all his time with you.'

Laura frowned. Then she looked at Maddie and shook her head. 'No. Can't be him He's spent the whole time making eyes at you. He hasn't had time to be nosy.' It was a testament to how worried she was that Laura didn't ask Maddie how her date had gone. Laura's phone buzzed and she pounced on it.

Tim glanced at Maddie and shrugged.

'Do you really think there's a secret shopper?' Maddie whispered to him.

'Maybe not yet,' Tim whispered back. 'But I reckon there will be after Christmas.'

'How can you tell?' They were still whispering. Laura was typing with her thumbs.

'I can't,' he said. 'But it makes sense they'd do it after Christmas, right? Because…well…'

'Ha!' said Laura, still looking at her phone. 'Apparently, Tristan Somersby has gone missing. Maybe he's gone out to spy on an unsuspecting hotel.'

'Now you're being ridiculous,' Tim said.

'Am I? Why is that so ridiculous?' Laura's voice had gone up in pitch.

Maddie stood up. This was veering towards a domestic disagreement that she shouldn't be part of. 'I…might go have a shower,' she said.

Neither of the other two acknowledged her.

'Because he's too obvious,' said Tim. 'A posh bloke like that, we'd spot him straight away. I mean…' He typed furiously on his laptop. 'Just look at him. He looks like—' His eyes widened. 'Oh my.'

Maddie paused, half turned to leave. She was curious, despite herself.

Laura leaned so that she could see Tim's laptop. Then they both looked up at Maddie.

Unease prickled between her shoulder blades. 'What? Why are you looking at me?'

Laura shook her head. 'Oh Maddie, I'm so sorry.'

Tim turned the laptop round. It was a shot of a handsome man in a suit. He looked familiar. Maddie leaned closer. He looked like a well-groomed version of Chris.

Maddie stared. The world narrowed until all she could see was the picture on the screen. There were differences—different hair, no glasses, but… He was smiling. She knew that smile. It was the same one that Chris had given Nate a few hours ago.

Laura shook her head. 'Is there any chance that this guy and Chris just look similar?'

Maddie sank back down onto the arm of the sofa and

pulled out her phone. 'Tristan Somersby?' She glanced at Tim to confirm and searched the name.

'There's a Wikipedia entry.' This guy was famous enough that someone had collated information about him to make a wiki page. Another photo. This time, he was looking down, listening to someone. That was even more familiar. It had to be the same man. Nausea clawed at her. She scrolled down, skimming through the page. Details jumped out at her. Mother left when he was seven. Winchester. London. Photo after photo of him with different glamorous girlfriends. Engaged to socialite Lady Clementine Thrupp-Wilmott...who broke their engagement recently... Her throat closed up. Finally: 'Tristan takes his place in his father's empire as the head of diversification performance for the hotel group.'

So many of the details that she knew about him were the same. 'It's the same man,' she said hoarsely. 'He lied. He lied to me.' Other things started to fall into place. The way he didn't want to be photographed. The way he tensed when people were discussing the fate of the hotel. The way he got a dinner reservation at almost no notice! It was so obvious. How had she missed the warning signs?

Laura was immediately beside her, wrapping her in a hug. 'Oh Maddie, I'm so sorry,' she said again.

Maddie sat still, too numb to feel the hug.

Tim growled. 'I'm going to kill him.'

'You can't say anything to him,' Laura said quickly.

'Why not?'

'Because he's Tristan Somersby. You can't let him know we know.' Laura rubbed Maddie's back. 'Oh Maddie.'

She shook her head. No. She *couldn't* have fallen for

a con. Not again. 'I can't believe—' When she looked up, everything blurred through tears. 'He seemed so—'

Laura tightened her hold around her. 'That bastard.'

Tim was beside her on the other side. 'Is there anything we can do to help?' he said. 'What do you need?'

Thoughts were chasing each other around her head. He had lied. He had kissed her. How could this happen? How could she have been so stupid? How could this happen *again*? 'I need… I need to think,' Maddie said. 'Can I have a…few minutes of space?' Her own voice sounded far away.

Laura gave her a gentle squeeze. 'Are you sure you want to be alone?'

Maddie didn't look up. 'Yes.'

'Come on, love, let's go for a little walk. See what the market has to offer, eh?' Tim guided Laura towards the door.

The door clicked shut and the quiet rushed in. Maddie let herself slide onto the sofa. She looked at her phone again, hoping that she was somehow mistaken. Chris's face looked back at her. Oh. There were videos of him shaking hands with people. She watched them. He moved differently, more straight backed and tense. At one point, he ran lightly up some steps, hesitated and looked at his wrist quickly before smiling that plastic smile and shaking hands with someone. His watch must have buzzed.

That very specific action felt like a stake in her heart. His watch, which had buzzed when he kissed her, because his heart was beating too fast. That kiss that had melted her. All the hours spent together, bent over the tiny model buildings. All that was built on a lie. How could she have fallen for a con man for a second time?

How stupid was she? She stared at the phone, unable to stop watching the clip again and again and again. She had lowered her guard and let him in. And he had done this.

Why had he volunteered to help her? She chewed the inside of her lip. Helping her meant that he was always in the reception area. Was he using her display to spy on Laura and her colleagues? Ugh. She had been an accessory to that. Not only had he lied to her, Chris— no, Tristan, she had to get used to the fact that he was someone else—Tristan had used her to compromise her friends' jobs. She felt dirty thinking about it.

She threw the phone away from her and curled up into a ball. Her heart was in shreds again, but she was almost too angry to cry.

CHAPTER ELEVEN

THE NEXT MORNING, Tristan hummed to himself as he got dressed. Last night had been the best, happiest date he'd been on in years. He felt like he could fly. Well, not fly—that would involve being up high—but float a few inches off the ground maybe.

Kissing Maddie had been a bad idea, but he couldn't bring himself to regret it. He had been attracted to people before, but with Maddie it was something different. It was as though his muscles and bones remembered her. Like he had always been meant to be with her. He couldn't be near her without feeling that attraction inexorably making him hers. And she liked him back. Kissing her was bliss. The idea that someone who had so many people who loved her thought *he* was worthy of loving was mind-blowingly wonderful to him.

It all had to end tonight. The thought was like ice down his spine.

There was no point worrying about it yet though. He couldn't tell her until after the display was switched on. He didn't want to ruin that for her.

It was still early when he set off for his run. The hotel staff were setting up for breakfast. The new shift had started, so everyone looked fresh faced. He nodded and smiled at everyone he passed. They usually greeted him warmly—working on the display made him somewhat different to the other guests. This morning though, something felt off. They were still smiling, but the smiles felt different. There was a weird tension in the air. Maybe it was because they were expecting it to be busy today. Tristan put his ear pods in and left by the back way for his customary run.

He was halfway around. His watch had buzzed to tell him heart rate was well raised, which had made him smile. Now the buzzing not only felt like praise, but it also reminded him of kissing Maddie. His phone, strapped to his upper arm, rang. He stopped and pulled it out, thinking it might be Maddie. It was Walter. Disappointed, he answered it anyway, running on the spot to keep his muscles active.

Walter's voice was tight when he said, 'Tristan, where are you right now?'

'I'm out for my run. What's the matter?' He had been hoping to call Walter later and tell him how well his date had gone.

'Have you seen the overnight gossip blogs?'

He stopped jogging. 'What? No.'

'Your cover is blown. I told you not to get photographed. Some local gossip e-newspaper printed a photo of you from last night.' Walter's voice was clipped. 'You have to come back to London. Sir Alex is livid.'

Tristan closed his eyes and cursed.

'Tristan,' Walter said urgently. 'There's a board meeting to discuss damage limitation at ten.'

Tristan's eyes flew open. He had checked his email that morning. 'I didn't have a meeting request.'

Walter said, 'Exactly.'

Tristan scowled. His heart rate picked up again, making his watch buzz. He swiped at it. Not now. What was his father playing at? 'He's having the meeting without me so that he can do his the-boy-is-still-young speech, isn't he?'

Walter said nothing. Tristan growled, fury rising. 'He's doing it again. Trying to keep me in the role of pretty idiot. He doesn't trust me to do anything.' His father liked to keep Tristan in check. If he achieved anything, Sir Alex undermined it. He had done the same to Tristan's mother. No wonder people were surprised when Tristan actually read the reports they sent in.

'No.' He said firmly. 'I'm not doing this anymore.'

'Sir?'

'I am coming to the board meeting. Walter, send me a driver please. I drove myself here, but I have some work to do on the way back. Please can you also find me any interim reports from the secret shoppers that have already come in for the boutique hotels? And the corresponding feasibility reports for each of those hotels from before we bought them?'

'The driver is already on his way, also someone to take your car home,' said Walter. 'You'll have to come straight into a meeting with key members of the board, so I took the liberty of sending a suit. He'll be there in about…half an hour.'

Tristan smiled grimly. Walter was a great assistant. He had anticipated Tristan's reaction and set things in motion already. 'Thanks, Walter. You're a gem.'

There was one more thing he had to know though. 'Is Maddie compromised in any way?'

'Curiously, no. There's mention of a "new girlfriend" and there's someone's shoulder. It says the photo was taken last night. I'll email you screenshots.' Walter cleared his throat. 'The dimensions of the photo suggest that she's been cropped out. It's possible they are holding back her identity to sell as a scoop later.'

That was bad. Bloody Nate. It had to be him. 'I need to talk to Maddie. I'll call you when I get back to the hotel.'

'Tristan, don't—'

He hung up on Walter. He didn't have Maddie's number. She had been careful about that. He ran back. No longer jogging, but running full pelt.

By the time he ran in through the main doors of the hotel, he was an out-of-breath, sweaty mess. His watch was going crazy, but he didn't bother turning it off. He put his hand on the reception desk and tried to get his breath back.

Laura looked up from her computer. 'Good morning, Mr... Samuels,' she said. Her smile did not reach her eyes. 'Good run?'

'Is Maddie here yet?'

'Not yet. I expect she'll be in later.' All this was said in a perfectly pleasant voice, but there was no warmth there at all. Until last night, he thought he and Laura had got on well.

'I need to talk to her. Can you give me her number?'

'I'm not at liberty to divulge that, sir. I'm terribly sorry.'

Laura must have seen the news reports. Did that mean that Maddie had too? 'Give her my number, then? I can explain. I need to talk to her.'

'I'm afraid, Mr Samuels, that Maddie asked me not to do that. I can only apologise.'

No no no no no. 'Come on, Laura. I have to talk to her. To explain. It's important.'

Laura gave him an apologetic shrug. Someone came up to check out and Laura said, 'If you'll excuse me, *sir*,' and turned away.

Tristan was too stunned to move. As far as he could tell, Laura had followed the hotel script perfectly. She was, of course, right not to give out people's personal phone numbers. What was he thinking?

Tristan looked down at his running outfit. He would have a shower and try to think of his next move. He had less than half an hour.

He sighed. He needed to get a move on. He moved to the front of the desk, so that he was next in line again, after the people checking out.

Laura looked up, her eyes widened a little, but she smiled the plastic smile again and said, 'Is there something I can help you with, Mr Samuels?'

Tristan drew a deep breath. 'A man is going to arrive bringing a suit bag for me.' All his good humour from that morning had disappeared. He just felt tired and sad now. So he retreated into his professional demeanour. 'Please can you send the suit up right away. I may be in the shower, so ask them to bang on the door loudly.'

Laura made a note. 'Yes, sir. We'll keep an eye out for your delivery.'

He dropped his voice. 'Laura. I can explain. If I write Maddie a note, please can you give it to her? I'm asking you as Chris. As a friend.'

Laura leaned forward. 'I think you've hurt her enough. Leave her alone.'

'I had good reasons. Please. Just give her the note.'

The fury in her eyes was unmistakable. 'You knew you would hurt her,' she said, still very quietly. 'You did it anyway. I don't have to do anything for you.' She straightened up, fake smile in place. 'Will that be all, sir?'

The word *sir* was an extra stab at him. 'I would like some paper and a pen, please.'

'Of course.' A hotel notepad and paper was slid towards him and Laura smoothly moved over to the computer and looked busy.

It took a moment for Tristan to work out what to write.

Maddie. I'm so sorry. By the time I met you, you already thought I was Chris Samuels and I didn't correct you. Later, I wanted to tell you, but I didn't want to ruin the delicate and beautiful thing that we had. You liked Chris more than you could ever have liked Tristan. With you, I was Chris. I may have misled you about my name, but everything else you saw and heard was the absolute truth. I am that guy, not the Tristan Somersby you see in the press.

I meant everything I said last night. Please talk to me. Let me explain why I was here on false pretences in the first place.

I have to go to London now, but I'm leaving you all my contact details.

He wrote down all his phone numbers, the landline, the private mobile, the company mobile and his email addresses. What did he sign as? After a few seconds' thought, he wrote 'Tristan S' and in brackets 'also always Chris'. Folding the paper in half, he wrote 'Maddie Attwater' on it and handed it to Laura, who took it without a word.

Then Tristan went up to his room to change out of being Chris Samuels and go back to being Tristan Somersby again.

Maddie stood in the staff room with Laura. 'What if I see him? I don't want to see him,' she said. She felt raw and in pain, but there was still stuff to do before the display switch-on later that day. 'I don't know if I'll burst into tears or try to stab him with the soldering iron.'

'I know, honey, I know.' Laura patted her arm. 'I saw him earlier. He keeps saying he can explain.'

'I don't think there is much to explain, is there? He lied about who he was. He just wanted a convenient excuse to hang around in the foyer and there I was.' He need not have kissed her though. That was what hurt the most. The kiss had been something special for her and was just part of the subterfuge for him. It was unnecessarily cruel. Oh, what was she thinking? The whole thing was unnecessarily cruel. He could have been a secret shopper by simply being a regular tourist who came to the town. He didn't need to do any of the stuff he'd done.

'Look,' Laura said. 'You're nearly done with the display, right? Just hang in here. I'll call you when Chris— I mean, Somersby—goes out, then you can go and do whatever needs doing before this evening.' She looked at her watch.

Maddie realised that Laura's break was ending. 'You go to work,' she said. 'I don't want you to be late. Especially with a spy in our midst.'

'Will you be okay?'

Life carried on. She could give in and sit around feeling sorry for herself, but the display still had to be finished. She had promised her dad and this was her tribute to Grandad. No stupid playboy liar was going to stop her from doing that. Maddie drew herself up to her full height. 'Yes. I will.' She grabbed her bag. 'Let's go.'

When she got up to the foyer, the first person she spotted was Nate, standing at the reception desk, talking to the other concierge. She had seen the morning's internet gossip. She had been cut out of the picture, but she recognised it as the one Nate had snapped last night. She glared at him, not sure if she was angry with him for outing Chris or grateful for saving her from sinking further into Chris's lies.

'Maddie.' Nate hurried towards her. 'Maddie, I'm sorry. I didn't know that you weren't in on it. I saw you guys together and sort of assumed you knew. I cut you out of the photo, just in case. I'm so sorry.'

'Why are you sorry?' she said. 'You're just doing your job.'

Nate's gaze roamed over her face. She realised what he must see. Red-rimmed, puffy eyes. Hair that had been hastily pulled into a bun. She had the face of someone going through fresh trauma.

'I wish you hadn't,' she admitted. 'But it's not your fault I'm upset.' *You didn't lie to me. He did.* 'Look. I need to get this display sorted for tonight. So I'd best get to work.' She hurried across to the last window and started to remove the sheet they'd used to hide the display overnight.

'Actually, I'm covering that too,' said Nate. 'I was

wondering if I could get some close-ups of the model to use. I'm writing it up as a "the last time the local tradition is observed" type nostalgia piece. I've found a couple of photos of your grandad with the first model in the archives. I'd like one with you now. It's a shame your dad can't come.'

'He's feeling much better,' she informed him. She'd had her morning text from her mum to say so.

'Yeah. I spoke to your mum this morning,' said Nate. 'I've got a time booked to chat with your dad.'

'You won't ask him to comment about this…other thing, right?'

Nate stared at her for a moment. 'Okay,' he said finally. 'I won't. Your dad isn't part of the hotel anyway. I will ask a few members of the hotel staff about what they think though.'

When she glared at him, he said. 'It's my job, Maddie. I'll protect you as much as I can, but this is the biggest scoop I'm ever going to get and I have to.'

She understood that; she really did. Hated it, but understood. 'So. What did you want to photograph?'

Nate was suddenly alert, looking at someone behind her. She turned to look.

Tristan Somersby strode in, wheeling a bag. He looked like Chris, but also nothing like him. No glasses. The contacts made his eyes look even brighter blue. His hair was neatly pushed back in the style she'd seen in the photos online. He was wearing a suit which was cut to fit him magnificently. The way he held himself was different. Stiffer. The smile that she liked so much was nowhere in evidence. Instead, it looked as though his jaw was tense. He looked tall, dangerous and magnificent.

He caught sight of her and his expression changed. He was Chris again. 'Maddie.' He took a step in her direction, but suddenly there were people in between them. The concierge had come out from behind his desk. Laura had rushed in from somewhere. Even Nate had placed himself more squarely in front of her. Her people were protecting her. *Hah. Take that, Tristan Somersby. You thought that poor people were powerless playthings? Think again.*

She lifted her chin and then, very deliberately, looked away.

Did she just blank him? She did. Tristan's throat felt tight and his jaw hurt. The change in the room was subtle, but it seemed that everyone who was local was willing to get in there and stop him talking to Maddie. This was her world. He had intruded and lied to her. He deserved this.

He was still Tristan Somersby though. He switched his attention to the desk. Laura was standing just in front of it. Tristan cleared his throat. 'I'd like to check out early, please.'

Laura was instantly in the concierge's place. 'Did you have a pleasant stay, sir?' She went through what Tristan recognised as the script the staff used at the main chain hotels. He responded politely, agreed that he would rate them on a review site and took the card with the QR code on it. All the while he could feel the draw of Maddie just out of sight behind him.

He had to look at her again. She had her back to him and appeared to be examining a model ski chalet. He had touched up the paint on that one yesterday. The memory gouged another chunk out of his heart. He had been so happy. He'd known it had to end. So why was he feeling this bad?

His driver took his case. Tristan hitched his laptop bag onto his shoulder and left, head held high, as befitted his media training. Stepping out of the building into the car park at the back, it felt like something was being torn out of him. He had only been here for a few days, but in those days he had been allowed to be who he was, which was the quiet, slightly geeky man who loved to paint. No one had criticised him for not being good enough. No one had eyed him up with a view to getting money out of him. People had treated him like a normal human being. And the ones that made friends with him, he knew, liked him for himself. It was an unexpected oasis of warmth in his chilly, corporate life. He should remember that. It wasn't something he was going to get the chance to do again.

And then there was Maddie. Her blanking him hurt more than anything had any right to. He thought of his mother, walking away and never turning back. Of Clemmie not bothering to tell him it was over. He was an easy man to turn away from.

But this was different. He had hurt her badly. The idea that she thought he didn't care buzzed around in his head. He did care. The date last night and the kiss had been the most perfect experience of his life. He would do anything for Maddie. Anything. He loved her.

The knowledge that he'd fallen in love wasn't a revelation. He had known last night when he went out to meet her that his feelings for her went beyond a little bit of flirtation. The way she made him feel was…amazing. Last night, when she looked at him with her heart in her eyes, he had thought his own stupid heart would explode with happiness.

As the car left the village and made its way to the main roads, Tristan pulled the laptop open. He could think of ways to force Maddie to talk to him, but what would that achieve? It would only cement what she thought of him—that he had power which he used with no care for anyone else. No. The kindest thing he could do for Maddie right now was to leave her be.

He thought of the atmosphere in the hotel foyer. Maddie had people who loved her, which was more than he had. She was safe. Safe was important to her. She would be okay.

He clicked on the first of the emails Walter had sent. It started with the drop in Somersby Group share price that morning, which, on top of the drop the week before, was not good news at all. His boutique hotels project would be the first casualty of this. Between now and arriving in London, he had to arm himself with an argument that would help him keep the Cygnet Hotel from being turned into a soulless identikit hotel.

He also needed an explanation as to why he was at the Cygnet in secret in the first place. Unlike Maddie, he didn't have people who cared around him. Even Walter ultimately worked for Sir Alex. Tristan had to look after himself.

The bellboy came back to the main foyer and said, 'He's gone.'

Everyone let out a breath. Maddie sank down to the floor, hollowed out with emotion.

Laura put a hand on her shoulder. 'Are you okay?'

She nodded. Her throat felt swollen and tight. The pressure behind her eyes was painful.

'Well, good riddance,' said Laura. 'I can't believe he thought he could come here and use people like that.'

Behind Laura, Maddie saw Nate's eyes sharpen. She poked Laura in the leg and shook her head. Nate was still a gossip journalist. Chris… Tristan…had mentioned about being in the public eye. What had he said about everyone recognising him and judging him without knowing him?

'He looked pretty worried when he came in,' Laura said. 'He said he wanted to talk to you and asked for your number. I didn't give it to him.' She looked at Maddie, as though asking if she'd done the right thing.

Maddie didn't know whether she had or not. Everything Chris had said was a lie. But that kiss couldn't have been a lie. No one was that good a liar.

'He…left you a note,' said Laura. 'Would you like to see it? Or I can bin it for you.'

Part of her desperately wanted to hear some sort of explanation. To be told that no, she hadn't just fallen for a con man again. At the same time, she was too angry to give Chris any chance to explain. Tears rose in her eyes.

'I'll leave it here, in this pigeonhole,' Laura said. 'In case you want to read it.'

Maddie wiped the tears out of her eyes. 'Thanks.'

She looked at the last display and wiped her eyes again. 'I'd better get to work. This display isn't going to get itself ready, is it?'

Maddie had hoped that working on the display would help take her mind off things. But as she sat in front of it, carefully sticking figures down onto the landscape, she thought of how, for all the other display windows, she had done this with Chris. There had been warmth and laughter and teasing. How could all of that have been fake?

She finished the corner she was working on and looked up. There was no one at the reception desk. She got up and retrieved the note from the pigeonhole. She couldn't read it here. People kept popping in, checking to see if she was okay or giving up their tea breaks to help her get the display ready in time. She was grateful that they cared, but she needed privacy. So she ended up in the ladies' toilets. She locked herself into a cubicle and read the note. It swam before her eyes. *I meant everything I said last night.*

How could that be true? She would be a fool to believe it. But that kiss. His watch buzzing. How could all of that have been fake? Tears again. She didn't have time for tears. She had work to do. The door to the ladies' opened and someone came in. Maddie quickly wiped her eyes and ran back to her work.

CHAPTER TWELVE

TRISTAN'S HEART WAS racing so much that he had to take his watch off. The buzzing wasn't helping him focus. It had gone from a nice, encouraging thing to a nuisance overnight. He stood in a quiet alcove around the corner from the boardroom, hidden from view, and took a couple of deep breaths. The reading he had done in the car had helped firm up a plan.

His first priority was to try to preserve the Christmas display at the Cygnet. His plan for the boutique hotels would let him do that. The grand buildings and big event spaces, the luxury suites, the high-net-worth clients—these were his father's bread and butter. The boutique hotels were part of a different niche for people wanting a different kind of experience. Their unique quirks were part of the attraction.

His stint being a 'normal' person at the Cygnet had shown him something he had never really experienced before. Community. Maddie's parents were ill, so people took food around for them. The Christmas display needed more helpers, so people dropped in during their lunch breaks to help. Everyone knew everyone. The guests at the hotel too, they came back year after year, because they felt welcomed by the community. For a few days, he had become part of it too. This was something he'd never had before.

Sir Alex didn't believe in community. He didn't believe that people did things out of altruism. It was all about the bottom line. Which was true, to an extent. But there was something to be said for intangible things like friendship.

Tristan thought about the subtle shift in everyone's stance in the hotel foyer that morning, as they prepared to defend Maddie from him. Even Nate the journalist, who was the snake who had told the gossip press who he was, *even Nate* had been prepared to step in.

Oh. It suddenly occurred to him that maybe Nate had cropped the photo to protect his friend. Not to sell it as a secondary scoop. He hoped that was true.

The report he had prepared needed polishing, but it was good enough to share now. If he sent it to his father, Sir Alex would axe it before the board even saw it. But Tristan had done his homework on this and he was sure he had a solid idea here. He needed the other board members to see it. In order to do that, he had to go up against his father.

He checked his phone. Nearly time to go into the meeting room. He straightened his spine and got himself into his working mindset. He was Tristan Somersby. Heir to the Somersby hotel fortune. This was his company too and he was going to bloody well act like it.

Maddie's face flashed into his mind, her little frown of concentration as she worked so hard to honour the things that her grandfather had built. Well, Tristan's grandfather had built this empire. His father has expanded it. Now it was his turn. He pulled his jacket straight, picked up his iPad and strode out to the meeting.

* * *

Maddie checked the wiring on the tiny cable cars. Each of the little carriages had a light in it. Inside, skiers sat on the seats. The cars were rigged up so that when the cables were fitted into the circuit, they ran up to the top corner of the window and back down again. On the wall, behind the curtain, there was a little hook that they always used. The cable cars were always on the last window because of it.

She needed to get the system hooked up. Despite her best efforts, her mind kept wandering back to Chris. Of course, he wouldn't have been much help with attaching the cable ride to the hook, because he was afraid of heights.

You liked Chris more than you could ever have liked Tristan. With you, I was Chris.

All of the things he'd told her about himself had been at least partially true. In fact, from her obsessive reading of everything Tristan Somersby last night, she knew that nearly all of it was. The departure of his mother. The lonely childhood. The father whose approval he could never have. So much so that he still let his watch buzz to tell him he did a good job with his exercise because no one else did that.

He saw himself now as the man carrying the pile of gifts—but people only wanted to talk to him because he had presents for them. Not because they cared about him at all. And she was the woman who tried to buy him lunch because she couldn't pay him minimum wage! She would never have done that if she'd known he was a millionaire.

She looked down at the carriage she was holding in

her hands. The paintwork had a small chip in it. She decided it was small enough to leave it without patching it up. If Chris had been here, she would have asked him to patch it up. He would have, with his face set in fierce concentration. All of the details he had painted onto the buildings...he had put so much into them. She wouldn't have let him help at all if she'd known who he really was. She definitely wouldn't have talked to him, relaxed and open as she had been. So yes. She had liked Chris more than she could ever have liked Tristan.

Did he have the same problem with everyone? He didn't talk about friends. He had mentioned a work friend, who, she now realised, probably worked for him or maybe even his father. There hadn't been any other friends. It must have been really important to him that someone liked him for him and not for the famous name.

She shook her head. That still didn't make it okay. He had still lied to her and she had still fallen for that lie. She was just finding excuses because she missed him so much.

The admission triggered a wave of pain. She felt like a piece of her had been ripped out. He had made her world feel...corrected. Now that he was gone, it felt all out of kilter again. She wiped an incipient tear with the back of her hand. Coming home was meant to make her feel safe again. All that had happened was that she'd lowered her guard only to fall for the same thing again. Not even home was safe. How was that fair?

'Hey.' Laura came up. 'I'm on my tea break. Do you need anything?'

Maddie looked up. 'Actually, yes. Can you hold this?' She handed Laura the mechanism that would attach to the hook at the far corner of the window. 'Now walk back until it's taut. Thanks.'

Peering into the hollow under the landscape, Maddie flicked on the switch. The lights came on in all the little cable cars and the line slowly started moving.

'Oh,' said Laura. 'That's magical. It gets me every time I see it.'

'Yes. I'm glad it works.' She turned the switch back off. 'I'll just run up the ladder and fix it to the hook.'

Leaving Laura holding the loop, Maddie got the stepladder set up as close to the window as she could. She went up carefully. When she'd first met Chris... Tristan...she had been up this ladder. She had literally fallen on him. It wouldn't do to repeat that fall with the display right below, so she forced herself to focus. She held her hand down and Laura passed the cable car wire up to her. She had to stretch a bit to reach and put the loop over the hook. There was a chip in the plaster where the hook met the wall. Maddie gave it a little poke with her finger. It looked wobbly. It would stay in, but she needed to find some plaster and fix that soon. It wouldn't do for the cable cars to crash into the idyllic snow scene below.

She came down the steps, intending to find some plaster. Her phone rang.

'Mum. How's Dad?'

'He's tested negative!' Her mum sounded tired. 'He's still coughing a lot, but we thought, if we're careful and wore masks, we could come and see the display being switched on.'

'Oh Mum. That would be wonderful.' Her dad would get to see Grandad's special gift to the village being used for the last time. This was what was important now. Not her stupid love life.

'We don't think we should come inside...'

'You'll get to see it better from outside anyway. I'm so glad he's feeling better. Are you okay now?'

'I'm fine. Tired, you know, what with looking after your dad and doing everything, but apart from that, I'm fine.' There was a pause, then she added. 'Would you mind staying at Laura's for a couple more days? I'm still worried about you catching something.'

She suddenly wanted, more than anything in the world, to see her parents. 'You said you're both testing negative, right?' Her voice wobbled. She cleared her throat quickly.

'Maddie? Is everything okay?'

She hadn't mentioned Chris to her parents. There was no reason to worry them now. 'I just miss you, that's all. I'll come round tomorrow and I'll help you disinfect the house. How about that?'

'I don't know...'

'I'll wear a mask the whole time.'

Her mother gave a soft laugh. 'Okay. Yes. That would be nice.'

'Great. I'll see you this evening for the switch-on then.'

In the background, her father called out, 'I'm really proud of you, Maddie.'

'He hasn't seen it yet,' she said. 'Tell him to hold his praise until he's seen what I've done with it.'

'We have complete faith in you,' her mother said.

When she hung up, she felt a tiny bit better. Her goal today was to get this display up and running. Thanks to Chris's help, she had done most of what was needed. She could do this. More to the point, she had to. It was important.

She got back to work with renewed vigour.

Tristan waited. The marketing and communications lead was talking about what he termed 'the current situation'. 'Obviously, Mr Somersby's personal life has had a greater impact on the share price than we'd anticipated, so we have come up with some angles with which to address this.'

Tristan raised his hand.

The man stumbled and glanced at Sir Alex. Tristan felt for him. Obviously, the unspoken agreement here was that Tristan was the problem and his view wasn't invited. But Tristan was also Sir Alex's son, so couldn't be ignored.

Without waiting for permission, Tristan spoke into the silence. 'If I may. I absolutely agree that my personal life has had an unexpected impact. The reason for this, I believe, is that people are now seeing me as the future of the business. The expansion project was widely reported to be something I felt strongly about—which is true. So instability in my life at this critical juncture would look bad.' He stood up and leaned forward. 'But. The reports from last night weren't the gotcha the gossip reporters are claiming to be. I was there on company business. We have often sent secret shoppers to check out new ventures to see what needs changing. That is not a departure from normal.'

There were a few nods of agreement. Sir Alex did not move.

Encouraged, Tristan carried on. 'I care deeply about the boutique hotel expansion. For too long, my management colleagues and I have made decisions based on reports alone. I felt it was time to get involved personally. I wanted to see how life was on the ground.'

He didn't dare glance at his father. The other members of the board were listening. One of the women had the ghost of a smile on her face, as though she had guessed exactly what he was doing. He knew her well enough to believe that she really did see through him.

'So, to address the first problem—the one of the gossip blog.' He gestured to the man from PR. 'Please release a statement to the effect that I was supposed to be there. I was there working for the company.' He wasn't asking. He was stepping into his role, so he was telling them to get on with it.

'As regards to the second—the speculation that I have no plan and am just bumbling along. I had been hoping to have more time to prepare this for you, but under the circumstances, I hope you will excuse the slightly rough-and-ready feel of this presentation.'

The secretary glanced first at Sir Alex, who nodded, frowning. She used the remote control to turn on the projector.

The presentation was little more than a few slides of the hotels with a few bullet points. 'As you can see,' Tristan said, his voice steady now that he was in his stride, 'each of these hotels has a unique character. When we sent the briefing note to the secret shoppers I added a request that they gather information on what sets each particular venue apart from the rest—location, tradition, aesthetic, unique quirks of service. For example, the hotel I was assigned has a Christmas window display that is lit every year just after the main Christmas lights in the town are turned on. It has been used for over twenty years and is so well known locally that people make day trips to come and see what's changed each year.' He put up a photo from the year before. A small crowd was gathered outside the windows of the Cygnet. The diorama was clearly visible through the lit window.

He felt a pang at the sight of it. He didn't belong there; he knew that now. But the least he could do was help preserve it. 'These are things that guests will remember. The unique quirks, the atmosphere, the people. What we were looking for with these boutique hotels was individuality. These hotels were never intended to be small clones of the main hotels. They are meant to be something else entirely.

'Each hotel has a unique character and is part of its own community. We hope that visitors will feel welcomed into that community and, with luck, will want to come back time and again. What we are aiming to provide is luxury, comfort and—' he clicked onto the last slide '—a home from home.'

The lights came back up. Tristan risked a glance at his father's face. Sir Alex's expression was completely neutral. This meant that he was furious. This should have made him more anxious than it did. Ah well, in for a penny, in for a pound.

'I would like to put out a statement that encompasses some of that,' said Tristan. This was unprecedented. Normally, this would have gone through at least one lesser committee and across Sir Alex's desk before it reached here.

There was silence. Sir Alex was glaring at him. Tristan sat down before he was asked to.

'The floor is open for comments,' said Sir Alex, his mouth barely moving.

In the end, they decided to go through with his plan. Marketing was to finalise a statement and put together a better version of his hastily made presentation. The meeting ended, not with Tristan being told off for his perceived indiscretion, but with a general agreement to his plans.

Sir Alex paused on his way out. 'Tristan,' he said, without looking at his son. 'My office.'

'Yes, sir.' Tristan gathered up his things. He had got what he wanted out of the meeting. He had taken control of the narrative about his presence at the Cygnet Hotel and he'd preserved the tradition of the Christmas display. Now he had to deal with his father.

One of the other board members paused next to him and said, 'I like the idea, Tristan.'

Tristan murmured his thanks and then hurried, through a few more back slaps and congratulations, to follow his father.

The door to Sir Alex's office had barely shut behind him when his father thundered, 'What the hell was that?' He slammed his hands on the desk.

Tristan had been shouted at in this office many times before. He usually took it because he deferred to his father. Not today.

'Crisis management,' he said simply. 'You needed a plan to make my being seen at a rural hotel, using an assumed name, plausible. I gave you one. It has the added advantage of being the truth.'

'You do not get to make statements and put me on the spot like that.'

'Why not?' He lifted his chin. If his time at the Cygnet had taught him anything, it was that being loved by someone should not be hard work. He had tried all his life to meet his father's expectations, because he'd thought it would make his father love him. Now he knew that was not going to happen. It hurt, but it meant that he could stop trying to please. It was strangely liberating. 'I am the heir to your empire…and you keep telling people the boutique hotel acquisition was my idea. So why the hell not?'

'How dare you—'

'No, Dad. How dare *you*? All my life, you've bullied me and dismissed my competence. All the while telling me that I will be responsible for all of this. You can't keep giving me responsibility with no authority to carry it out. Decide. Either you are going to trust me with this business or you're not.'

'Are you threatening me?' His father's face was going red now.

Tristan considered it. Was he?

'Not really. I've realised that, no matter what I do in this business, you're not going to approve of it—because it's not you doing it. So I've simply stopped trying to please you.' He walked to the desk and leaned forward, resting his hands on it. 'You know this idea that it's dangerous to hand over the business to me? That I will ruin things? Guess where that's come from? You. Your every interaction with me undermines me.'

'You don't understand the business.'

'Don't I? I grew up around here.' He gestured to the

Somersby Grand behind his father. 'I spent my half-term holidays running around behind the scenes in that hotel because you didn't want me underfoot. You keep telling me I'm the heir to your empire. Do you know what your hotels mean to me? Loneliness. Sterility. The worst, most unwelcoming places. Do you think I want to inherit that?'

'I can retract all of the orders from the meeting within the hour,' his father said, eyes cold and furious. 'What then?'

'When I was put in place as the head of diversification performance, you insisted that I had the same sort of contract as all the other managers. You. Insisted.' Tristan glanced quickly at the Somersby Grand again and, just as quickly, looked away. Did he really want to say this? There was a chance his father would call his bluff. He realised in a flash that he didn't care. 'So, if you do embarrass me in this, I will hand in my notice.'

His father went very still.

Tristan held his nerve and stared him down.

'You would lose everything.' Sir Alex said finally. 'I will make sure of it.'

'Yes.' They both knew he wouldn't lose everything. If Sir Alex disinherited him, he'd lose a lot, enough to hurt, but he still had a top-notch education, experience working in the industry, a modest property portfolio and, frankly, quite a lot of money.

'All I wanted from you,' he said quietly, 'was your approval. I did everything you wanted me to do. I tried to twist myself into the shape you wanted me to be, but you were never happy. And I give up. I can't make you care for me. I can't make you respect me. I'm sick of trying.'

He drew a deep breath. 'Now, I know… I *know* I'm not incompetent at this. And I know that my suggestion is a good one. You know that too. But you're not willing to acknowledge it. I think you need to choose—which is more important to you? Keeping me in my place? Or the good of the company?'

Sir Alex's nostrils flared. He looked away. 'If I approve your suggestion, you will never embarrass me like that again.' It wasn't a question.

This was now a negotiation, Tristan realised. Sir Alex wasn't trying to bulldoze past him. This was a better result than he'd expected. 'I can't promise that. I can promise that I won't make a habit of it though.'

His father gave a sharp nod and said, 'Hmm.'

Tristan waited. There seemed to be nothing else. 'Okay, well. Thanks for your time. If you'll excuse me, I have to get going or I'll be late.' He made for the door.

'Wait. Where are you going?'

Tristan grinned. 'I spent the last five days helping set up the decorations in the Cygnet Hotel. I would hate to miss seeing them being switched on.'

CHAPTER THIRTEEN

As DARKNESS FELL OUTSIDE, Maddie felt her stress levels rise. At dusk, she had removed the sheets covering the displays. The lights above the windows were off, so that anyone wanting to catch an early glimpse of the displays would have to press up to the window. Indeed, a few people already were doing exactly that. When the lights went on, they would be able to see the details.

She pushed the displays carefully into place so that they fit snugly into the shallow bay windows. She had already tested and retested the trains to make sure they ran at the right speed.

She did a last check of the models. Chris drifted into her thoughts again, as he had done every few minutes throughout the day.

I was already Chris when I met you.

It had been Laura who had introduced him to her as Mr Samuels. By the time she'd met him he was already someone else.

Thinking about him dug at the pain in her chest. She missed him. He had done so much hard work on this display. She couldn't have got everything done without him. It seemed unfair that he didn't get to see it go live.

But he had lied to her. She had told him about Alan

and he had still lied to her knowing full well how much it would hurt her.

If he had told her the truth, would she still have relaxed around him? After all, it wasn't as though he was going to steal her money. He was a millionaire. One who had dated supermodels and film stars. How would she have reacted if he'd told her? She wasn't sure.

What did he want with her anyway? He could have had anyone he wanted. Why her? Was he just slumming it for a bit, for fun?

All those things he had told her about himself. How much of it was made up?

She grabbed a brush and leaned over to clear a clump of snow off one of the people standing by the food cart that Chris had repainted.

It hadn't sounded like a lie. She could definitely see the boy who lost himself in painting figurines could lead to the man who did the same, given the chance. The satisfaction on his face when he finished each model…you couldn't fake that. Nor could you fake the surprise and delight when she complimented him on a job well done. The first time she'd praised his work, he had stared at her for what felt like ages before he'd accepted it. He was a man who hadn't heard his efforts appreciated before.

Alan had lied about everything. He had showered her with gifts, pretended he cared about her and then taken everything he could.

Chris hadn't been like that. He'd been careful with her and given far more than he had taken. She knew that. She was angry and hurt, but she was also sad. But most of all, she missed him. The display seemed less interesting without him around.

She thought about the figurine carrying the pile of presents. He thought people only wanted him because of what he could give them. His fiancée left him for someone richer. His father sounded awful. And his mother had walked away from him, leaving him with his horrible father, without a second glance. He must be so lonely.

She had blanked him. Oh no. She was supposed to be his friend and she had turned her back on him too. As though all the help he'd given her meant nothing. As though their connection meant nothing.

He had hurt her when he lied to her, but to her shame, she realised that she had hurt him right back, in the worst way possible.

It was nearly 7:00 p.m. Maddie was now a bundle of nerves. It had taken her until about ten minutes ago to get everything ready. She peered around the side of the display to see that the village square was full of people, bundled up against the cold. Most of them were over at the other side of the square, waiting for the Christmas tree lights to be turned on. Then there would be a slow tide of people drifting towards the hotel. When the church clock struck quarter past the hour, they would turn the first window on, then, following the train, they would turn each window on in turn.

There were always little kids who moved along with the train, rushing from window to window. She remembered the joy of it all too well. Looking around, she caught sight of two people standing apart, closer to the hotel than the others. Her parents.

She gave a little squeak and pulled her head back. 'My

mum and dad are here,' she said to Laura. She leaned back out and waved. Laura joined her. Her parents waved back.

'Do your parents know? About Chris?'

Maddie shook her head. 'They know he's helping me, but I didn't mention anything else. I'm glad I didn't tell them now. I can't believe I fell for a con artist, again.'

Laura gave her arm a little squeeze. 'Oh Maddie.' Someone called her from inside the hotel.

'I'm okay. Go,' Maddie said. 'Just be back in time for the switch-on.'

She went about doing her final checks. The last window she looked at was the first one she and Chris had made together. Her eyes fell on the woman in the scarf, striding towards her happy ending. That wasn't her anymore. She was the idiot who got taken in by a liar. Again!

And she really should have seen it coming this time. There had been so many holes in his story. She had noticed, but chosen to ignore them because she was so into him. Not like before, when there had been no signs. Chris wasn't even a good liar. Not like Alan.

Chris's words came back to her. *Con men are just very good at kicking away your support structures. It's not your fault.* She stopped moving and stared at the little figure. What if…what if he had a point?

She had heard it before from a lot of other people— her parents, Laura and Tim, the police—but somehow it hadn't hit home in the same way before.

The clock struck seven and there was an 'ooh' from the crowd as the Christmas lights went on. The windows were next.

Laura ran in. 'I'm here. I'm here.'

Still thinking, Maddie handed her a stopwatch. 'Um…

Laura, at any point, did you guess that Alan was lying about everything?'

Laura stopped. 'This is not really the time to discuss this, but no. I didn't have a clue. Neither did Tim. We've gone back to see what red flags we missed and we just can't spot anything.'

'He was a very good con man,' said Maddie. 'Thanks.' It really wasn't her fault. She was just a normal victim of a con artist.

She went to the first of the windows and knelt down by the controller. The plan was that she turn on the display just as Tim hit the window lights. She then had ten seconds to be at the next window to turn it on so that the train appeared at exactly the right moment. The gap between the next two was longer and then it was ten seconds again. Laura was keeping time and counting down.

'Places!' said Laura, her phone in her hand.

Maddie and Tim, who were already in their places, exchanged a glance. Laura was clearly enjoying this.

They tensed, ready for the chime from the village clock.

CHAPTER FOURTEEN

THE ROAD INTO the centre of the town had been closed when Tristan reached it and it was nearly time for the switch-on. So he'd got out in a side street and run to the hotel. The route brought him in through the car park at the back. He was still in his suit and work shoes, which were not made for running. His feet were going to be agony tomorrow. But it didn't matter. He had to see Maddie.

He walked briskly through the back rooms of the hotel. A few members of staff were around, but almost no guests. They must all be out, enjoying the festive cheer. He had a flashback to him and Maddie walking around the Christmas market together, and he picked up his pace.

When he got into the foyer, no one noticed him. Everyone's attention was focused on the front where Tim was standing by the light switches and Maddie was kneeling on the floor, her eyes trained on Laura, who was staring at a stopwatch.

The entire front of the hotel was dimly lit. The display, the model he'd worked on, was being switched on. He couldn't disturb her now. He walked quietly over to the last window and stood on tiptoes to see past the high mountain backdrop. There was quite a crowd outside.

Laura's voice rang out, counting down. 'Nine…eight…'

The crowd joined in. 'Five…four…three…two…one.'

The first window lit up. The light from above was a spotlight. On the model itself, the street lamps glowed, the shops lit up from inside, illuminating all the painstakingly modelled details inside. The crowd went 'Oooh.'

Laura was counting down again. Maddie darted to the next display and knelt, hand poised on the next switch. Her expression fierce with concentration, face glowing. If there had been any doubt in his mind that he was in love with Maddie, it was now gone. The idea of never seeing that face again was too terrible to contemplate. If his father made him choose between a hotel empire and Maddie, he would choose her in a heartbeat.

Maddie flicked on the second window and leapt forward to the next position. A movement in the last window made her look up.

The hook that was holding up the mechanism for the cable cars slipped slightly forward. It was coming away from the wall!

If it fell, the cable cars would crash into the ski scene below and the miniature joy would turn to miniature carnage.

Oh no! All that work!

'Laura,' she said. 'Take over.' She had maybe thirty seconds to get up a ladder and tape that hook back to the wall. She ran to where she'd left the tools, hooked the duct tape onto her wrist and grabbed the stepladder. Wrenching it open, she positioned it by the wall so that it wasn't visible from the window. She should test the stability of it, but she didn't have time.

The hook slipped again. Maddie ran up the ladder and shoved the hook back into place.

Behind her, Laura was counting down again. She got to 'one' and the display came to life. The train whirred on the track. Through her fingers Maddie felt the vibration of the line of cable cars moving. She heard cheers and applause.

Okay. Now she needed to get the hook taped to the wall. As she removed her hands from the ladder, it wobbled. She pulled out a length of tape and tore it off with her teeth. The ladder tipped. Time slowed. She slapped the tape on as hard as she could. She might fall, but she wasn't going to take her grandad's legacy with her.

Tristan saw Maddie run and grab the ladder. *What was she doing?*

That ladder wasn't stable. Anyone could see that. Everyone else was focused on the display. Laura was counting down. No one else could see the danger Maddie was in. Tristan set off at a run.

The lobby felt endless. He kept his eyes on Maddie. He watched in horror as the ladder tipped over and Maddie fell off. He made it underneath her, just in time to catch her. They landed on the floor together. With his hand protecting her head, he rolled over her so that the ladder landed onto his back.

Maddie had expected more pain. Her ears were ringing from the metallic crash of the ladder falling. It took her a second to realise that someone had broken her fall. She uncurled herself with a groan. The person above her gave a small grunt and lifted his weight off her by bracing one arm. Chris. He was still lying over her, his hand cradling her head.

For a moment they stared at each other. Emotions tumbled inside her. The first was overwhelming relief. And then joy. She should be annoyed or worried or just wary seeing him again, but her body had gone for joy. He was back. He had caught her. Seeing him made her happy.

'Are you okay?' he asked.

She could barely breathe, but she wasn't sure whether that was because she was winded from the fall or because he was so very close to her right now. 'I think so.'

'Are you hurt?' Laura's voice asked, as someone lifted the ladder off them.

They both snapped 'Fine' in unison.

He moved off her and sat on the floor. He rubbed the back of his head. The stepladder might have hit him there when he fell. She knelt beside him. 'Are *you* okay?'

'Yeah. I think.' He looked up. 'Is the display?'

She glanced across. She couldn't see anything wrong. 'Yes. You saved it. You did a great job.'

He smiled briefly, then his expression sobered. He got to his feet and offered her a hand to pull her up. When she was on her feet, he didn't let go of her hand. 'Maddie, I'm so sorry.' His eyes burned into hers. 'I'm sorry I didn't tell you my real name, but I swear to you that everything else was true. Helping you set up the diorama was one of the best things I've ever done. It made me realise so many things.'

She tried to shush him. There would be time to talk about this later. Because, she realised, she did want to talk about this. Even though it had only been a day, she had missed him. What he had just done—those weren't the actions of someone trying to trick her. They were the actions of someone who truly cared.

He carried on, quieter now. 'Chris… I want to be that guy. Not…this.' He gestured to himself, in his dishevelled suit and shiny shoes. 'I know you're upset…and lying to you was the worst possible thing I could have done, but you have to believe me. I never lied to you about what sort of a person I was or how I felt. I have… I have never been more myself than I was in the past few days with you.'

She did believe him. The guy currently clutching her hand was no cold, calculating millionaire. This was the guy who had made her smile, her friend whose kiss made her knees melt, who ran under a ladder to catch her. How could she ever have thought he was anything else?

'Please,' he said. 'Please forgive me.' His grip on her hand tightened. 'When I went back to London, I thought I could handle not being with you, but I don't think I can. Without you, my life is just…lonely and colourless. I don't want to take anything away from you, Maddie. And I wasn't using you as some sort of tourist trip to see how the other half live, I promise.'

'Tristan,' she said slowly.

He winced.

'Well, I can't call you Chris, can I?' she said. Because that seemed wrong now.

He stared at her, breathing normally now. 'Tris?' he said sheepishly. 'A compromise.'

'Tris…' Okay. She could work with that. Tristan sounded all kinds of wrong, but Tris might work. 'Okay. Let's go with Tris.' She cleared her throat. 'First of all, thank you for catching me. If you hadn't been there, I would definitely have got hurt.' She looked down at his hand, holding hers tightly. 'I'm sorry I blanked you this morning. That was unkind of me.'

'That's okay.' He glanced down and loosened his grip. 'Maddie, you…you make me a better person.'

She could see the truth in his gaze. He meant this. All she had to do was believe him. The internal voice that told her to take care protested. But it was weaker now. She understood why he had let her think his name was Chris. She believed absolutely that his pain was real and that she could make things better. She wanted to. Because the idea of him hurting made her hurt too. She cared far more than she'd realised.

'What are you doing here anyway?' she said, trying to slow down the rollercoaster of her emotions. 'I thought you were going back to London.'

'I did. I had to go to a board meeting to discuss this… "PR crisis".' He rolled his eyes.

She sat back on her heels. Her hand was still in his. 'And?'

His voice was low when he answered. 'And I had a bit of a showdown with my father.'

'Your father?' She matched her volume to his. After all, Nate was still about and Tristan probably didn't want any of this in the newspapers. 'The horrible one who finds fault with everything you do?'

'Yes. Him.' There was something different about him when he said it. Something hard and unlike Chris.

'What did he say?'

'He threatened to disinherit me.'

She finally looked into his eyes. 'Oh.' The fact that he'd risked that much for the display…for her…was lovely, but it was also too much. She knew what it was like to lose everything. She didn't want that for him. 'Oh no. What happened?'

He leaned forward. 'I called his bluff. He backed down eventually.'

'Risky.'

'I told you. Being with you makes me happy. I would, really would, give it all up if it meant a chance with you. You have to believe me.'

Right now, with his rich-boy hair all mussed up, he looked more like her Chris than ever and she wanted to kiss away the little frown between his brows. 'I—'

Someone cleared their throat. Maddie pulled her hand away from Tristan's. A glance over her shoulder revealed Nate. She was very glad that they'd been speaking quietly.

In her back pocket, her phone rang. She took it out and saw it was her mum. She glanced at Tris, who sat up straighter and tugged his jacket back into place. She could almost see him putting on his Somersby persona. He gave her a small nod, as though to say it was okay to leave him.

She retreated a small distance and answered her phone. 'Mum.'

'Oh, the display looks wonderful,' said her mother. 'You did a brilliant job, darling. Your grandad would be so proud.'

'I didn't do it alone,' she said. 'Chris helped too. We had a bit of excitement. The hook holding the cable cars nearly fell off and I had to fix it so quickly there was almost an accident. Thank goodness Chris was there to catch me.' She quickly added, 'I'm fine though, so is he.'

'Chris? Nate said he'd gone back to London. He's back?'

Maddie glanced back into the foyer where Tris was standing now, talking to Nate, Laura and Tim. From the way he held himself, she could see that he was tense. That was probably because of Nate's presence.

'He came back,' she said, smiling.

'Oh. I see.' She could hear the suggestive smile in her mother's voice. Then: 'Are you...okay?'

Was she? The way her heart had leapt when she saw him... 'Yes. I think so,' she said.

'What happens now?'

'I don't know yet, Mum.'

There was a pause. 'Maddie,' she said. 'I know you'll be careful, but I hope things will work out. You know we love you, no matter what.'

Suddenly, there was a lump in her throat. 'I know.'

'So if you need to take a risk and see if Chris is right for you, you can. We will always be here to catch you if you fall.'

Tears threatened. She couldn't reply.

'I can tell from the way you've talked about him this week that you like him more than you let on,' her mother said. 'Listen to your heart. Not the part of you that Alan destroyed.'

Once she'd hung up, she turned back to look at Tristan. He was still talking to Nate, standing tall and moving his hands around as he spoke. This was him in his work persona. She could tell simply from the way he stood. The relaxed, open guy was gone. Tristan at work was tense and aware of his surroundings. Aware that he was being watched. What must it have been like to grow up under such scrutiny? Was that what he meant when he said he had never been more himself than with her? Was the man he wanted to be the shy, slightly nerdy guy who painted figurines and loved savoury waffles?

She had liked that guy. A lot. This new version of him… Tristan Somersby looked fine though. Just look at the way he wore that suit! Could she cope with being with both?

Tris looked up and caught her eye. He gave her a crooked little smile that was so familiar that she felt temporarily winded. There he was. Her Chris. Suddenly, it was clear what she had to do. She couldn't tell if she would get hurt in the future but…if she didn't give this a chance, she was definitely going to get hurt now. The world felt like a better place when he was around. The only thing getting in the way of her being happy right now was her. She took a few steps towards him.

'I couldn't help but notice your little intervention there.' Nate had his phone in his hand. 'I don't think it's an exaggeration to say that you stepped in to save the display in a very physical sense.'

Tris gave a little laugh that sounded unlike his real one. 'Well, I helped repair the models, so I had a special interest, in a way,' he said. 'Besides, it's important. It's a local tradition.' He raised his voice, just a little. 'Which is why I've asked the board of Somersby Hotels to keep the tradition alive.'

Heads turned. Everyone dropped all pretence of not listening in. Maddie smiled.

Nate was clearly recording all of this. 'Is that a formal statement from the hotel chain?'

'No. Just an ardent wish from me.' Tristan looked

over at Maddie. 'I was given the rare opportunity to be a part of this very special celebration,' he continued. 'I couldn't not be here to see the tribute to my friend Maddie's grandad being lit up, could I?' He held out an arm, gesturing towards Maddie.

There was a spontaneous round of applause. Maddie blushed and took a small bow.

Nate said, 'That's true. Maddie and her family are all part of the tradition.' He lowered his phone.

'Is that enough for you to be getting on with?' Tristan said.

'Perfect,' said Nate. 'Off the record, how much of that is actually approved?'

Tristan grinned. 'Some of it. I have spoken to the board about it. We'll have to see what happens.'

He shook hands with Nate and strode over to her. In his suit and his rich-boy swagger, it was such a dramatic stride that she nearly forgot to breathe.

'Maddie,' he said. 'Can we talk? Somewhere…' He glanced over his shoulder at the people dotted around the room. 'Somewhere private.'

Maddie made a decision. 'I know just the place. Follow me.'

She took him through the leafy walkway down into the back garden. Everyone was at the lights switch-on, so the garden was deserted. It was always lit so that the paths were dotted with little lights and the trees were uplit to make a dreamy atmosphere. Because it was nearly Christmas, the hedges had been covered in lights so pinpricks of light pulsed lazily on and off. The beginnings of a frost made her glad she'd picked up her coat. She led him to the rose arch, which glowed against the twinkling darkness.

'Maddie,' Tris said, as soon as they got there. 'Please forgive me. I—'

She shook her head. 'I'm sorry I didn't give you a chance to explain.'

They gazed at each other for a moment. His eyes were wide and brimming with emotion. Maddie knew what she had to say.

'I'm sorry I blanked you this morning. I know that hurt you and I'm sorry.'

'I'm sorry I lied to you.'

She put her hands on his lapels. He reached up and rested his hands lightly on her wrists. His thumbs gently stroked circles on her skin, sending tingles up and down her spine.

Leaning into him, she said, 'You promise you won't ever lie to me again?'

'I promise.' His eyes never left her face.

'Good.' She went up on her toes and kissed him.

When she lowered herself back to the floor, he gave her a smile that lit up the whole world. He put one arm around her waist, pulled her snug against him and lowered his lips to hers. This kiss was almost as perfect as the one the night before. She slid her arms inside his jacket and felt the heat radiating through his shirt. When she ran her hands up his back, his breath hitched and he pulled her even closer, his fingers tangling in her hair. He moved, laying butterfly kisses along her jaw and down her neck. She tipped her head back and sank into the sensation. Tristan's mouth found hers again. Maddie felt weightless, boneless with want.

Something cold landed on her forehead. She moved back and looked up. 'Is it…snowing?'

It was. Light, fluffy flakes that fell lazily down around them. They should go inside, but neither of them moved.

Tristan said, 'I think I love you, Maddie Attwater.'

'I think I feel the same, Tristan Somersby.'

He kissed her again and rested his forehead against hers. 'We should go in. I need to book myself into a room again.'

'How is this going to work?' she asked him as they walked, arms around each other's waist. She was still leaning against him. He was so warm that she barely noticed the cold around them.

'We'll manage just like everyone else,' he said. 'I might have to drag you along to some fancy events. Hopefully not too many. Would you mind?'

They walked through the passageway and back into the hotel. 'I… How fancy are we talking? I don't have the wardrobe for black tie.'

Tristan laughed. 'Trust me, that is not going to be a problem. I'm sure my people can get you kitted out.'

'Your people, huh?'

'They're nowhere near as great as your people.'

He cupped the side of her face with his hand. 'You'll be okay, I'm sure of it,' he said. 'We'll be together. So I'll be okay too.'

She smiled and kissed the tip of his nose.

'I hope you don't mind that I have to be Tristan Somersby some of the time.'

They carried on towards the hotel lobby.

'I don't mind,' Maddie said and then, face flaming, she added, 'Besides, you look kinda hot in a suit.'

Tris gave a delighted chuckle. 'You like this?' He gestured to his suit. 'Well, why didn't you say? I have a whole dressing room full of those.'

'A dressing room? I suppose you live in some sort of mansion.'

'Actually, I live in a penthouse at the Somersby Grand.'

'Seriously? That must have an amazing view.'

He shuddered. 'Yeah. I hate it. I have a lot of plants on the windowsills to distract me from the view, and a balcony that I never use. I think I might move.'

She smiled. 'Where to?'

'I'm thinking of buying a house. Something with a kitchen big enough to put a sofa in.'

She laughed. 'That's my dream home.'

He grinned. 'If you're in it, mine too.'

They turned the corner and went up the short flight of steps. When they got to the top, Maddie said, 'That's weird. Your watch hasn't buzzed.'

'I took it off this morning before the board meeting because my heart was racing so much.' He looked at his wrist. 'It'll probably go off all the time now that I'm near you. I think I'll just leave it off.'

Maddie grinned and nudged him. 'I'll make sure to tell you when you're doing a good job.'

Tristan laughed, raised their joined hands to his lips and kissed her knuckles. 'I'm counting on it.'

EPILOGUE

One year later

The Willerby Dalton Examiner

Christmas Sparkle Turns to Diamond Twinkle!

There was an extra surprise in store for everyone who came to see the switch-on of the famous Christmas display at the New Cygnet Hotel. The multiwindow diorama has been put on every year by three generations of the Attwater family. Maddie Attwater, who redesigned the display this year, was in for an unexpected celebration as, soon after the lights were switched on, her boyfriend, the handsome heir to the Somersby fortune, Tristan Somersby, went down on one knee and proposed. Much to everyone's delight, she said yes! What girl wouldn't?

The pair have been dating for a year and many people credit Maddie's steadying influence for turning former playboy Tristan Somersby into a stable and respected leader, tipped to take over the Somersby Hotels empire soon. In an EXCLUSIVE interview for the *Willerby Dalton Examiner*, the couple revealed that they have bought and refurbished Fitling Manor and that the couple will be living there when they are not in London. With that much space in their family home, surely it won't be long before there's the pitter patter of tiny feet?

Turn to: How romance blossomed while working on the Christmas diorama—an interview with Maddie Attwater and her fiancé, Tristan Somersby (written by Nate Bloom).

* * * * *

MILLS & BOON®

Coming next month

HOW TO FAKE DATE HER BILLIONAIRE
Clare Miles

'Ready to practice, Nic?'

'Always,' he said with a bravado he hoped to be true, mentally rolling his shoulders and tightening the reins of his control.

The instant Eleanor placed her palms against his chest, he hissed out a breath and jack-knifed like she'd scorched him.

Finally, she pressed her lips against his, and like a fuse igniting, heat roared between them. It was no polite, pretend kiss. It was hot and demanding. Linking her fingers behind his neck, she gripped his hair. He wrapped his arms around her waist, pulling her fully against him.

Eleanor moaned, then stilled and reared back, pushing against him.

'Stop!'

Disoriented, he opened his eyes, bringing her into focus—her lowered lids, flushed face and puffy lips devoid of gloss. A primal beat of satisfaction curled through his veins that he'd caused that.

'That should convince everyone,' she said flat and firm, her words penetrating the roaring in his head, and—like a bucket of ice had been thrown over him—reality hit. *Hard*.

This was an act.

Continue reading

HOW TO FAKE DATE HER BILLIONAIRE
Clare Miles

Available next month
millsandboon.co.uk

Copyright © 2025 Clare Miles

COMING SOON!

We really hope you enjoyed reading this book.
If you're looking for more romance
be sure to head to the shops when
new books are available on

Thursday 18th December

To see which titles are coming soon, please visit

millsandboon.co.uk/nextmonth

MILLS & BOON

LET'S TALK
Romance

For exclusive extracts, competitions and special offers, find us online:

☐ MillsandBoon

𝕏 @MillsandBoon

☐ @MillsandBoonUK

♪ @MillsandBoonUK

Get in touch on 01413 063 232